코코넛 향기의 기억

코코넛 향기의 기억

1판 1쇄 인쇄_2015년 12월 20일
1판 1쇄 발행_2015년 12월 24일

지은이_김은향
펴낸이_홍정표

펴낸곳_글로벌콘텐츠
등록_제 25100-2008-24호

공급처_(주)글로벌콘텐츠출판그룹
이사_양정섭 디자인_김미미 편집_송은주 기획·마케팅_노경민 경영지원_안선영
주소_서울특별시 강동구 천중로 196 정일빌딩 401호 전화_02-488-3280 팩스_02-488-3281
홈페이지_www.gcbook.co.kr

값 30,000원
ISBN 979-11-5852-075-5 03810

Remember the Coconut Flavor

코코넛 향기의 기억

김은향

글로벌콘텐츠

코코넛 향기의 기억

나는 어린 시절부터 그림그리기와 글읽기 그리고 글쓰기를 무척 좋아했다. 대구국제중학교를 입학한 이후는 미국, 프랑스, 중국을 매년 교류하면서 유학을 다녔기 때문에 일찍 혼자서 결정하고 판단해야 할 일들이 많아서인지 무엇이든지 기록하기를 좋아했다. 그리고 어린 시절, 혼자서 외국 유학을 하는 동안 엄마와 가족에 대한 그리움을 잊기 위해 책을 읽고, 또 골프, 농구, 배구, 육상 등 다양한 스포츠를 좋아했다. 마치 선 남자아이들처럼. 그러나 난 역시 여자아이이다. 감성이 풍부하여 소설이나 영화를 보다가도 잘 울었다고 기억된다. 나는 생각을 많이 하고는 곧 바로 그런 생각을 그림이나 도형에 그려 넣기를 좋아했다. 그래서 화가가 되는 것이 한때 나의 꿈이기도 했다. 지난 어린 시절의 내 그림일기를 뒤져 보면 손을 다쳐서 병원에 입원하여 수술을 한 뒤에는 갑자기 의사 선생이 되고 싶어 하기도 했다. 이처럼 꿈이 많았던 만큼 여행하기를 즐겨하였다.

얼마 전 사랑하는 엄마가 내 어린 시절의 기록물을 한 상자 내 앞에 내놓았다. 그 상자 안에는 일기, 그림일기, 그림 등 온갖 내 유년기를 회상할 수 있는 기록물들과 사진들이었다. 틈틈이 읽어 보니 참 그리웠다. 꽃들의 여행이랄까? 코코넛 향기의 기억이 묻어 있었다. 이제 내가 이 사회와 주위의 많은 사람들과 함께 어떻게 살아가야 할 것인지를 결정해야 하는 시점에, 또 스스로 내 삶의 미래를 예측하고 결정해야 할 순간인 것 같다.

국제 정치학이나 동양철학, 역사, 사회복지 전공 등 여러 가지 미래를 어떻게 선택하고 결정을 지을 수 있는지 지난 시절의 김은향을 한 번 되돌아보라는 엄마의 무언의 지도이고 요청인 것 같았다.

김은향이라는 나는 구조화, 패러다임을 만드는 것을 참 좋아한다. 생각이나 상상의 구조화라고 할까? 이 쓰레기 같은 내 유년기의 기록물을 구조화해 읽으면 좋겠다는 판단을 했다. 코코넛 향기의 기억이 묻어 있는 나의 일기, 그림, 만화, 독후감, 유학기 등을 모아서 한 권의 책으로 꾸며 보았다. 그리고 나의 자라온 일상과 여행기록을 남들과 함께 나누어 읽어 보고 싶어 한 권의 책으로 만들기로 결정했다. 이 결정을 내리는 데에는 내가 평소 존경하는 한국의 국립국어원장을 지낸 이상규 교수님의 조언과 도움에 용기를 얻었다.

어릴 때 쓴 글을 그대로 두었다. 문법에 맞지 않는 것을 고치지 않은 것은 나의 성장 과정을 그대로 보여주고 싶었기 때문이다.

고등 3학년인 내가 그리는 나의 미래는 아마도 내 이웃과 사람들을 위해 일하고 봉사하는 쪽으로 선택할 것 같다. 다국적 시대에 국경을 초월한 따뜻한 인류애를 내 가슴에 안고 미래를 향해 달려 가리라. 주님의 끝없는 가호와 사랑을 우리 모두 함께 하기를 기도하면서 머리말을 거두어 둔다.

사랑하는 가족과 나를 키워준 많은 선생님, 친구들에게 감사드린다.

2015년 12월 20일

김은향

Remember the Coconut Flavor

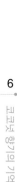

Since I was a child, I have enjoyed drawing, reading and writing.

Because of my studies abroad in America, France and China after attending an international middle school, I learned how to make my own decisions and grew an interest in recording of everything that I do in a young age. I alleviated the loneliness of being marooned in foreign countries, away from my family, by reading and engaging like a boy in such sports as basketball and track and field. After all, I am a girl; I remember myself as a girl who could not contain her overflowing emotions and wept while watching sad movies as if the tragedies on the screen were my own. I am a deep thinker, and I like expressing my thoughts by drawing them out and manifesting them as shapes. So deep was the love of drawing in me, that I once dreamt of becoming a painter. Looking through one of my old visual diary entries, I discovered an old desire to become a doctor after a visit to the hospital for my injured hand. With so many dreams, I enjoyed traveling.

A few days ago, my loving mother placed a box filled with my childhood memories in front of me. In that box were my diaries, visual journals, and drawings, which brought nostalgic childhood memories back to me. Reading and going through them made me miss those days. I would like to call it the journey of flowers; It had a coconut flavor. Now, I am to make decisions of how to navigate my life facing the real world with many people around me.

At a time where I have to sincerely think about my future and decide whether to major in an international politics, Asian history or social welfare, my mother handed me an object to look back on my life.

As I mentioned before, I like making structures and paradigms. I would say they are the structures of my thoughts. I thought it would be nice to make my rubbish records of my childhood in to a book. I created a book by composing my diaries, drawings, cartoons, book reports, and studies abroad that are stained in the remembrance of the coconut flavor. I also wanted to share the journey of the flowers with others. To make this decision, the advice and support of Professor Lee Sang Gyu, the former principal of the National Institute of Korean Language, played a vital role.

I see myself in the future working in the community helping my neighbors and other people. I will live with a warm humanity that crosses borders in a diverse and tolerant era. As I pray for God's unconditional blessing and love to all, I end my preface.

December 12, 2015

Kim, Eun-Hyang

Le souvenir de l'odeur de la noix de coco

Depuis mon enfance, j'aime bien à peindre, lire et écrire. Parce que j'ai dû aller en Chine, en France et aux États-Unis pour mes études à l'étranger après je suis entrée dans un collège étrangère, il y a eu beaucoup de choses que j'ai dû juger et décider tout seul, j'ai alors aimé à tenir registre de toutes les choses.

Pendant mon séjour seul à l'étranger, J'ai fait du basket, du valley-ball et de l'athlétisme comme si j'étais un garçon afin d'oublier la nostalgie de mon pays natal et de ma faimille. Mais j'étais encore une fille à en juger par le sentiment riche. Je me souviens que je pleurais souvent en regardant un film ou en lisant un roman.

J'exprimais ce que j'avais pensé en peinture ou en figure après mûre réflextion. Il semble que J'ai une fois voulu devenir un peintre. D'autre part, il semble que j'ai soudainement voulu devenir un médecin après l'opération sur ma main fini dans un hôpital. Autant qu'il y a eu beaucoup de choses que j'ai voulues faire, j'ai beaucoup navigué dans mon enfance.

Il y a quelques années, Ma maman a donné un boîte à moi. Il y a eu plein de papiers, photos, journaux et journal ilustrés qui me font souvenir de mon enfance dans ce boîte. J'avais bien la nostalgie de mon enfance après les avoir vus dans mes moments libres. C'est le voyage des fleurs? Je pensais que c'était le moment de prendre une décision comment vivre et de prédire mon avenir et de décider quoi faire à l'avenir avec beaucoup de gens autour de moi dans cette société.

Il me paraît que ça serait son conseil implicite de me souvenir de mon passé pour que je puisse faire mon choix sur la specialité à l'avenir comme la politique, l'histoire orientale, le bien-être public, etc.

Encore une fois, j'aime à structurer mes idées et créer un paradigme. C'est une structuration des pensées? J'ai voulu structurer mes sovenirs d'enfance de rebut et ensuite les lire. J'ai enfin mis les journaux, les peintures, les bandes dessinées, les impressions d'un livre et les souvenirs du séjour à l'étranger qui portent l'odeur de la noix de coco en ordre et je les ai ensuite compilés dans un livre. En dernier, j'ai décidé de publier un livre pour avoir l'itinéraire du voyage des fleurs en commun.

J'ai été très encouragée par le conseil et l'aide du professeur Lee Sang-gyu à prendre cette décision, qui était une fois le directeur de l'institut national de la langue coréenne.

Je crois que j'irai peut-être traviller dur pour mes gens et mes voisins. Je souhaite que je puisse avoir de l'amour pour l'humanité qui va au-delà des frontières nationales dans mon cœur à l'époque de la multinationalité.

Finalement, je prie que le Dieu nous donne sa protection et son amour et que nous les ayons en commun.

Le 20 Décembre, 2015

Kim, Eun-hyang

椰子香的记忆

我从小就非常喜欢画画、读书还有写作。

就读于国际中学以后，因为每年都会去美国、法国、中国交流学习，所以喜欢把一些事情都记录下来。我小的时候自己在国外留学，为了不去想妈妈和家人，喜欢读书或者打篮球、排球、田径等，简直像个男孩子。但毕竟我是女孩，更多的还是感性的一面。记忆当中，我经常会因为一些小说或者电影而掉眼泪。我喜欢把我想的一些画下来，也曾想过成为一名画家。小的时候因为翻看画册伤到了手，因为住院做手术，也曾想过成为一名医生。就像这样畅游在梦想的世界里。不久前妈妈把我小时候的一些东西，一整箱的放到我的面前。箱子里有我的日记、图画日记、画的画等，都是可以回忆我孩提时期的东西和照片。有空读一读，满满的都是回忆。花儿们的旅行？现在是我决定和社会以及周围的人们如何一起生活下去、也像是预测我的人生和做决定的时刻了。

成为优秀的国际政治学家、东洋史学家，或者是社会福利方面？我的未来将何去何从呢？就像是妈妈说的，回首看一下以前的日子吧。

总而言之，我很喜欢把东西具体化、条理化。思想的具体化？把这些凌乱的像垃圾一样的、我幼年时期的纪念物品规整后读一下，真的很好。椰子香般的记忆，我决定把我的日记、画作、漫画、读后感、游学笔记等做成一本书出版。在做这个决定的时候，曾担任过国立国语院长的李相揆教授给了我很大的勇气。

我的未来，应该是能够帮助我周围的人样子。我要心怀超越国境的爱长大。感谢主，怀着感恩的心作此序言。

2015年 12月 20日

金恩香

CONTENTS

Mom and Dad,
Merry
Christ
mas

Part 1

항해의 시작

1 탄생·성장

〈나의 출생 이야기〉

1998년 09년 5일 여자 갓난 애기가 태어났다. 이름은 김은향.

은혜로운 향기를 날리면서 살으라고 나의 할아버지께서 붙여주신 이름이다.

나는 2남 1녀 중 3째로 태어났고, 나는 오빠들과 20살 차이 가깝게 나이차가 나는 늦둥이다. 나는 평생 다른 늦둥이들보다 특별할 것이다. 왜냐하면 나는 엄마의 10년의 기도 끝에 태어났기 때문이다. 늦둥이라서 부모님과 오빠의 지극한 사랑을 받았다. 또한 할아비지 할머니로부터 많은 사랑을 받았는데, 한번 뵐려면 서울까지 기차를 타고 올라가야 했다. 대구에서 온 우리를 할아버지, 할머니께서 항상 반갑게 맞아주셨다. 사진첩을 뒤지다보면 할머니댁에서 내가 복숭아를 먹고 있는 사진이 많다. 나는 어렸을 때 엄마보다는 우리 할머니와 외할머니 밑에서 거의 자랐다. 나는 태어나서 한 번도 의사였던 외할아버지 모습을 본 적이 없다. 외할아버지에 대한 이야기도 많이 들어본 적이 없다. 알고 있는 사실이라곤, 엄마가 나를 임신하기 전부터 오래 전에 돌아가셨다는 거다. 외할아버지가 살아계셨다면 역시 나를 많이 사랑해 주셨을 것이다. 나는 늦둥이였던 터라 여러 사람으로부터 많은 사랑을 받으며 태어났고 자랐다. 그 사랑 덕분이었는지 어릴 적 사진 속의 나는 항상 웃고 있다. 많은 분들의 사랑에 보답하기 위해서 나는 앞으로도 열심히 살아나갈 것이다.

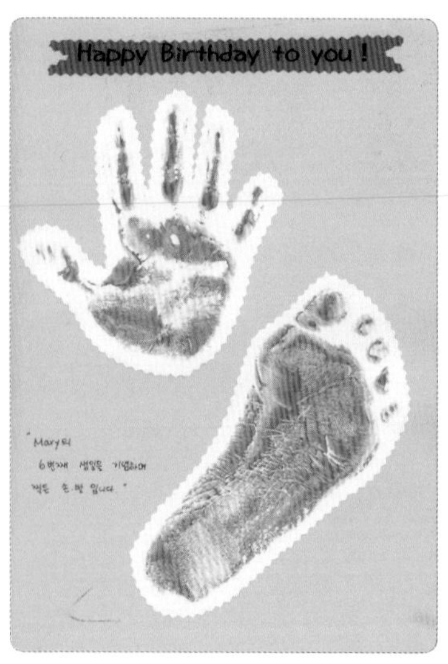

돌잔치날

<L'histoire de ma naissance>

Je suis née le 5 Septembre 1998, et je m'appelle Kim Eun-hyang. Mon grand-père m'a nommée Kim Eun-hyang, afin que je vive avec grâce et parfum.

J'ai deux frères aînés, alors je suis la cadette des trois enfants. Je suis une enfant tardive, donc il y a une grande diffirénce d'âge entre mes frères et moi. Je serai plus spéciale toute ma vie que les autres enfants tardifs, parce que je suis née avec de longues prières de ma mère. J'étais bien auprès de mes parents et mes frères car je suis la dernier-né. J'étais surtout bien auprès de mes grands-parents qui habitent à Séoul. Mes frères et moi, nous avons dû prendre le train pour y aller. Ils ont toujours fait bonne chère à nous. Il y a beaucoup de photos qui sont prises chez mes grands-parents et une petite fille mange de la pêche dans la plupart de ces photos. Dans mon enfance, ce n'était pas ma mère qui m'a élevée, mais ce sont ma grand-mère et ma grand-mère maternelle. Je n'ai jamais rencontré mon grand-père maternel qui avait été médecin, et je n'ai jamais entendu parler de lui. Je ne connais qu'il avait déjà été mort avant que ma mère enfantât une fille. Si mon grand-père avait été en vie, il aurait bien agi envers moi aussi. Ainsi que je viens de dire, du fait de ma naissance tardive, j'ai été bien aimée de beaucoup des gens. Il semble que la petite fille sourit toujours dans les photos qui sont prises dans son enfance, grâce aux soins des gens. Je ferai tout mon possible pour répondre au bienfait des gens.

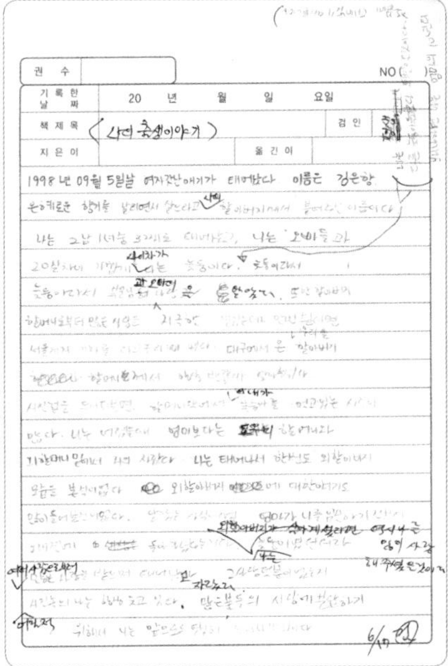
권 수 NO( )
기록한 날짜 20 년 월 일 요일
책제목 <나의 출생이야기> 검인
지은이 옮긴이
1998년 09월 5일날 여자갓난애기가 태어났다 이름은 김은향

〈关于我出生的故事〉

1998年9月5日，一个女婴出生了，名字是金恩香。

爸爸希望我像恩情深厚的香气一样，所以给我取了这个名字。

我是家中2男1女中作为老幺出生的，和哥哥们几乎相差20岁，算是爸妈晚年得女。和其他家庭晚出生的孩子相比，我应该是比较特别的。因为妈妈为了我的出生，祈祷了十年。作为家中的老幺，父母和哥哥们都非常疼爱我。我也很想经常见爷爷奶奶，但是见的话，需要坐火车去首尔才行。爷爷奶奶见到从大邱来的我们，总是很高兴。如果翻看相册，总能看到许多我在爷爷家吃桃子的照片。比起在妈妈身边来，小的时候我更多的是在奶奶和外婆身边长大。我出生以来，从来没有见过当医生的外公，也很少听到关于外公的事情。只是知道在妈妈怀孕前，外公很早就去世了。如果外公也在的话，最疼爱肯定是我了。因为在家中最小，所以从出生到长大，我都是最受宠爱的。因为备受宠爱，小时候照片中我总是笑着的。为了报答所有人对我的爱，我将会努力的生活。

내가 태어나자 할아버지와 할머니가 너무 기뻐하셨다.

〈나의 이력〉

1998 서울 출생

경동초등학교 1~2학년

미국 3~4학년

경동초등학교 4학년 2학기~5학년 1학기

프랑스 5~7학년

국제중학교 8학년

중국인민중학교 10학년

현재 국제중학교 12학년

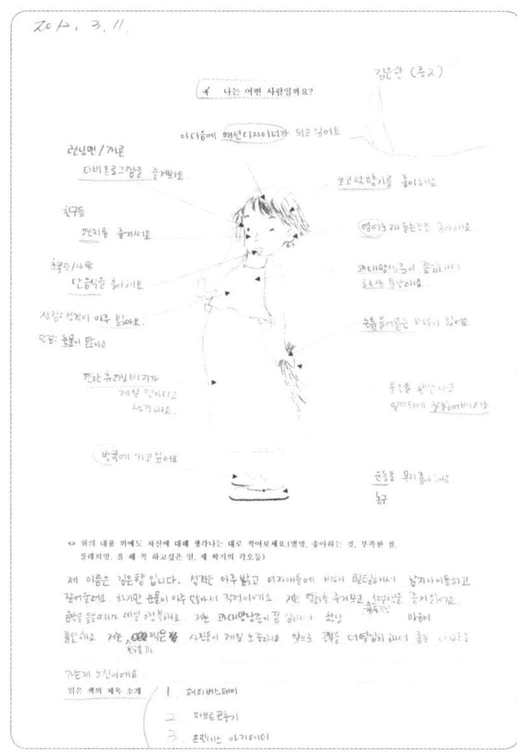

나는 어떤 사람일까?

<My Record>

1998 Born in Seoul

KyungDong Elementary School 1st~ 2nd Grade

United States 3rd~ 4th Grade

KyungDong Elementary School 4th Grade 2nd Quarter~ 5th Grade 1st Quarter

France 5th~7th Grade

International Middle School 8th Grade

China 10th Grade

Currently International School 12th Grade

〈나의 소개〉

나는 2남 1녀 중 막내이다. 내 오빠들은 32, 34살이며 가족들의 사랑을 듬뿍 받으며 자라왔다. 나는 친구들과 시내를 가는 것이 가장 큰 소원이다. 학교에 가면 공부를 해서 싫다고 하지만 나는 친구들과 이야기를 할 수 있어서 좋다.

나는 프랑스어, 영어, 중국어, 한국어를 할 수 있다. 특히 프랑스어를 할 수 있다는 거에 대해 자랑스럽게 여긴다. 나는 운동하는 것을 무지 좋아한다. 골프, 럭비, 농구, 축구, 배구, 하키 등 안 해본 운동이 없을 정도다.

<Introduction>

I am the youngest of two sons and a daughter. My two older brothers are 32 and 34 years old, and I was raised with all the love from my family. My biggest wish is to hangout in downtown with my friends. Although going to school and studying aren't my favorite things to do, I like the fact that I can hang out with my friends.

I can speak French, English, Chinese and Korean, and I take the most pride in speaking French. I have a strong passion for sports. I've played rugby, basketball, soccer, volleyball, hockey – just about any sport you can imagine.

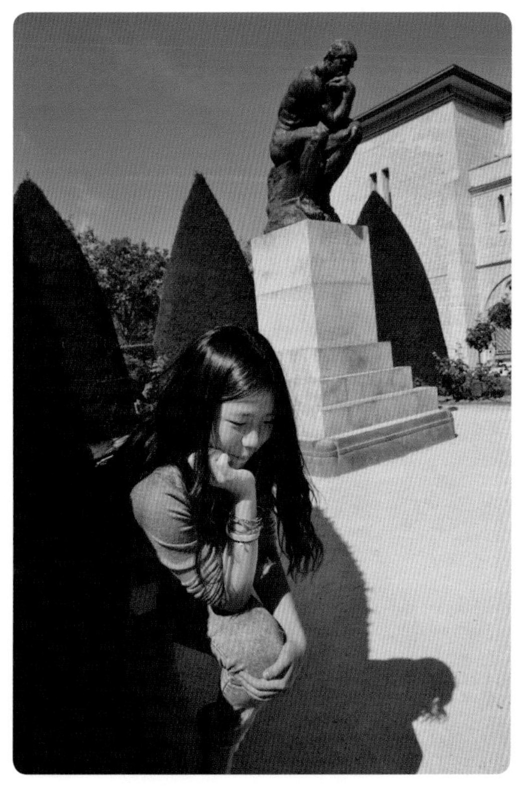

로댕상 앞에서 생각하는 은향

"부모님의 걱정을 지우고 혼자서 일어섰다.
거대한 바다를 향한 항해를 시작할 것이다."

2015. 11. 20.

〈나는 어떤 사람일까요?〉

이 다음에 패션디자이너가 되고 싶어요

런닝맨/개콘 티비프로그램을 즐겨봐요

친구들 편지를 즐겨써요

초콜릿/사탕 단 음식을 좋아해요

장점: 성격이 아주 밝아요.

단점: 눈물이 많아요.

편한 츄리닝 바지가 제일 편하다고 생각해요.

방콕에 가고 싶어요.

운동(농구)를 무지 좋아해요.

물건을 한번 사고 얼마 뒤에 잘 잃어버려요.

손톱 물어 뜯는 버릇이 있어요.

과대망상증이 좀 심해서 항상 불안해요.

영어 노래 듣는 것을 좋아해요.

코코넛 향기를 좋아해요.

<나의 이력>

1998 서울 출생

경동초등학교 / 1~2학년

미국 3~4학년.

경동초 (2학기) 4~5 1학기.

프랑스 5~7 학년

국제중 8학년

<나의 하루>

오전 ; 학교수업.

오후 ; 과외 및 숙제.

밥 먹고 쉬기.

<나의 소개>

나는 2남 1녀 중 막내이다 내 오빠들은 32, 34 살이며 가족들의 사랑을 듬뿍 받으며 자라왔다. 나는 친구들과 시내를 가는 것이 가장 큰 [illegible]이다. 학교에 가면 공부를 해서 싫다고 하지만 나는 친구들과 얘기를 할수있어서 좋다. 나는 프랑스어, 영어, 중국어, 한국어를 할수있다. 특히 프랑스어를 할수있다는거에 대해 자랑스럽게 여긴다. 나는 운동하는것을 무지 좋아한다. 럭비, 농구, 축구, 배구, 하키등 안해본 운동이 없을정도다 -

제 이름은 김은향입니다.

성격은 아주 밝고 여자애들에 비해 털털해서 남자 아이들하고 잘 어울려요.

하지만 눈물이 아주 많아서 걱정이에요. 저는 영화를 즐겨보고 감동적인 소설책을 즐겨 읽어요.

음악을 들을 때가 제일 행복해요. 저는 과대망상증이 쫌 심해서 항상 마음이 불안해요. 저는 친구들과 찍은 사진들이 제일 소중해요.

앞으로 공부를 더 열심히 해서 좋은 대학을 가는 게 소원이에요.

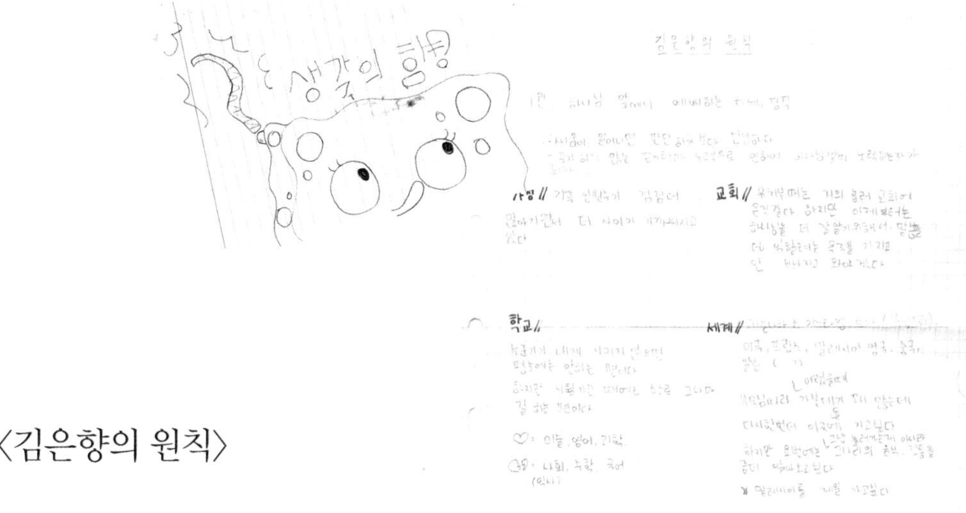

〈김은향의 원칙〉

가치관: 하나님 앞에서 예배하는 자세, 정직

원칙: 싸움이 일어나면 판단하기보다 반성하자.

포기하지 않는 끈기력과 노력으로 인하여 하나님 앞의 노력하는 자가 되자.

가정//가족 인원수가 점점 더 많아지면서 더 사이가 가까워지고 있다.

교회//유치부 때는 거의 놀러 교회에 온 것 같다. 하지만 이제부터는 하나님을 더 잘 알기 위해서 말씀을 더 익힐려는 목적을 가지고 안 빠지고 와야겠다.

학교//누군가가 내게 시키지 않으면 평소에는 안 하는 편이다. 하지만 시험기간 때에는 스스로 그나마 잘 하는 편이다.

♡: 미술, 영어, 과학

♡(X): 사회, 수학, 국어, 역사

세계//가본 나라: 이스라엘, 로마(북성교회), 미국, 프랑스, 말레시아, 영국, 중국, 일본, (?). 부모님따라 어렸을 때 가본 데가 꽤 많은데 다시 한번 더 이곳에 가고 싶다. 하지만 요번에는 그냥 놀러가는 게 아니라 그 나라의 음식, 전통을 좀 더 알아보고 싶다. 말레시아를 제일 가고 싶다.

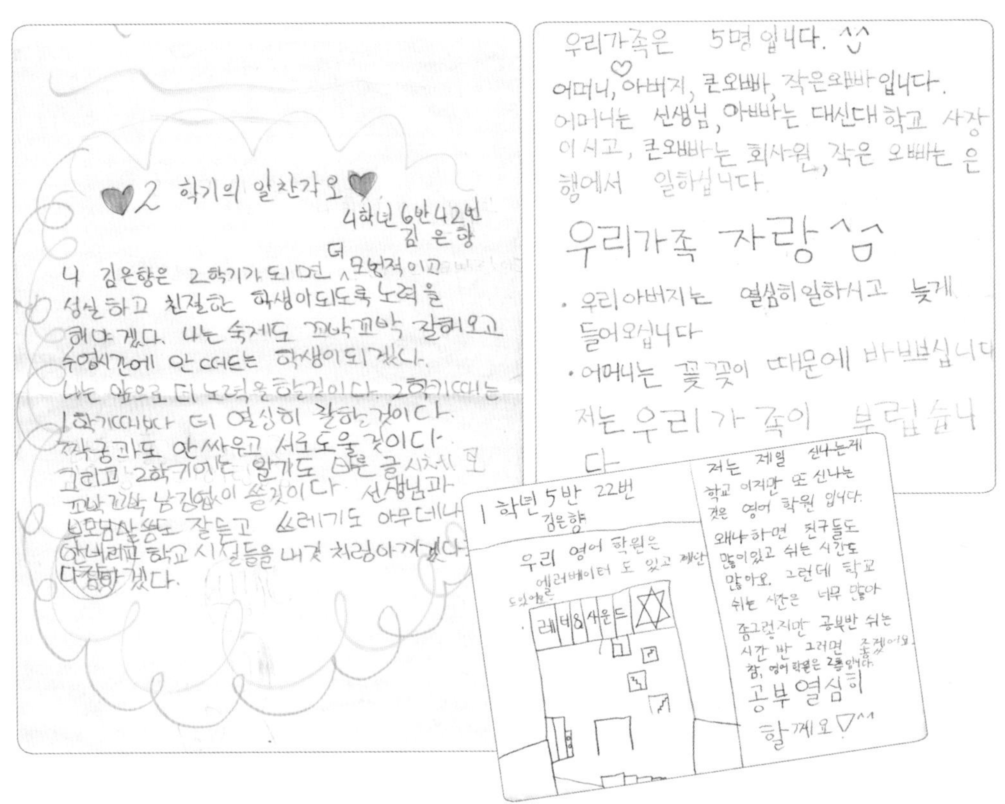

〈2학기 알찬 각오〉

4학년 6반 42번

김은향

나 김은향은 2학기가 되면 더 모범적이고 성실하고 친절한 학생이 되도록 노력을 해야겠다. 나는 숙제도 꼬박꼬박 잘해 오고 수업시간에 안 떠드는 학생이 되겠다.

나는 앞으로 더 노력을 할 것이다. 2학기 때는 1학기 때보다 더 열심히 잘할 것이다.

짝궁과도 안 싸우고 서로 도울 것이다.

그리고 2학기에는 일기도 바른 글씨체로 꼬박고박 남김없이 쓸 것이다. 선생님과 부모님 말씀도 잘 듣고 쓰레기도 아무데나 안 버리고 학교 시설들을 내것처럼 아끼겠다고 다짐하겠다.

"저는 여행을 참 좋아했습니다.
가족 여행으로 여러 나라의 풍물과
지리환경에 대해 익혀 왔습니다."

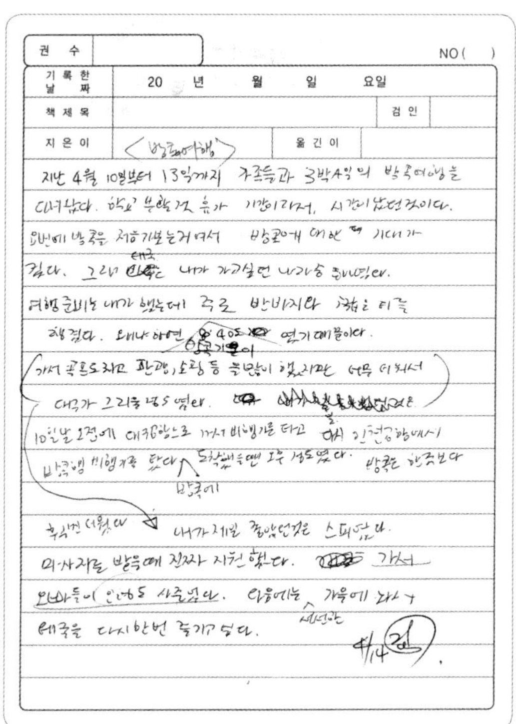
권 수 NO( )
기록한 날짜 20 년 월 일 요일
책 제 목 검 인
지 은 이 〈방콕여행〉 옮 긴 이

〈방콕여행〉

지난 4월 10일부터 13일까지 가족들과 3박 4일의 방콕여행을 다녀왔다. 학교 부활절 휴가 기간이라서, 시간이 났던 것이다. 요번에 방콕을 처음 가보는 거여서 방콕에 대한 기대가 컸다. 그리고 태국은 내가 가고 싶던 나라 중 하나였다. 여행준비는 내가 했는데 주로 반바지와 짧은 티를 챙겼다. 왜냐하면 방콘 기온이 40도였기 때문이다.

10일 날 오전에 대구공항으로 가서 비행기를 타고 다시 인천공항에서 방콕행 비행기를 탔다. 방콕에 도착했을 땐 오후 정도였다. 방콕은 한국보다 훨씬 더웠다. 가서 골프도 치고 관광, 쇼핑 등을 많이 했지만 너무 더워서 대구가 그리울 정도였다. 내가 제일 좋았던 것은 스피였다. 마사지를 받을 때 진짜 시원했다. 가서 오빠들이 인형도 사주었다. 다음에는 신선한 가을에 와서 태국을 다시 한번 즐기고 싶다.

〈내가 좋아하는 가수(빅뱅의 탑)〉

요즘 나는 노래를 아주 많이 듣는다. 내가 제일 좋아하는 그룹은 빅뱅이다. 빅뱅은 지금 현재 해외활동도 많이 하고 전세계적으로 사랑을 받고 있다. 빅뱅은 5명으로 이뤄져 있다. G Dragon, 태양, 대성, 탑, 그리고 한 명이 더 있다. 기억이 가물가물하다. 내가 제일 좋아하는 사람은 탑이다. 제일 잘 생겼다. 춤은 기본이고, 각자 자기만의 매력 보이스가 있다. 탑은 요즘 머리를 파랗게 물들여서 더 잘 생겨지고 있으니 탑의 싸인을 갖는 게 소원이다. 빅뱅이 3월 중순쯤 내가 제일 좋아하는 "런닝맨"에 나온 적이 있다. 그때, 진짜 재밌게 봤었다. 빅뱅이 계속해서 인기가 많고 세계적인 스타가 되면 좋겠다.

빅뱅 오빠들 장가 늦게 가시고 더 좋은 앨범과 활동 기대할게요!~~

〈我喜欢的歌手(Big Bang的T.O.P崔胜贤)〉

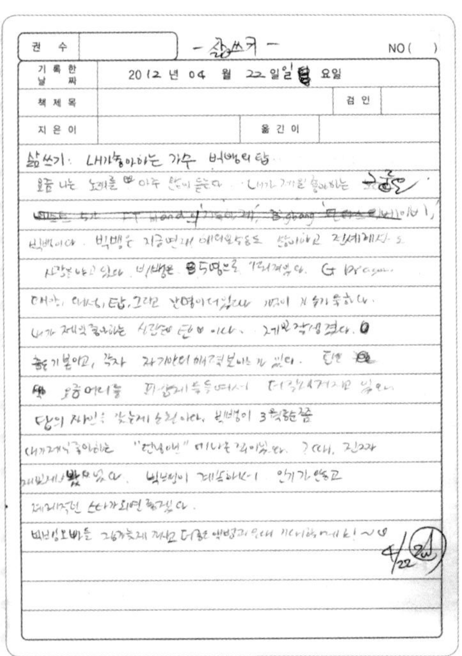
권 수 | - 삶쓰기 - | NO( )
기록한 날짜 2012 년 04 월 22 일 요일
책제목 | 검인
지은이 | 옮긴이
삶쓰기: 내가 좋아하는 가수 빅뱅의 탑

最近我听了许多歌，最喜欢的组合是BigBang。BigBang现在海外活动也非常多，在全世界很多地方都受到欢迎。BigBang由5名成员组成，G-Dragon、TaeYoung、Daesung和T.O.P，还有一名记不清楚了。我最喜欢的是T.O.P。是最帅的一个了。舞是最基本的，跳的很好，尤其是每个人的声音都有各自的魅力。T.O.P最近把头发染成了蓝色，显得更帅了。拥有T.O.P的一个签名是我一直以来的愿望。BigBang3月中旬左右出演了我最喜欢的“跑男”，真的非常有意思。希望Big Bang一直受欢迎，并且是在全世界都受到欢迎。

期待BigBang的哥哥们晚点结婚，能出演更多的电影和活动!~~

〈나의 어린 시절 10대 사건〉

어릴 때 친구들과 했던 놀이 중 하나로 '무궁화 꽃이 피었습니다'라는 것이 있다. 이 놀이에서는 한 명이 술래다. 술래가 자기 눈을 가리고 '무궁화 꽃이 피었습니다'를 외치면 나머지 아이들은 줄 뒤에 서서 조금씩 조금씩 술래에게 다가간다. 술래가 계속 '무궁화 꽃이 피었습니다'라고 외치고 뒤를 돌아본다. 그때 중심을 잃고 넘어지거나 갸우뚱하는 사람이 술래가 된다.

1학년 때 운동장에서 이 놀이를 하곤 했다. 하지만 하루는 술래를 '탁' 치고 뒤돌아서 뛰고 있을 때 아는 6학년 오빠와 '꽝' 부딪히고 말았다. 내 입술이 돌바닥에 땅하고 부딪히는 순간 피가 철철 흘러나오기 시작했다. 즉시 보건실로 갔으나 옆에 있던 선생님들이 흉터로 남으리라 장담하였다. 하지만 7년이 지난 지금, 내 입술은 말짱하다. 요즘도 많이 덜렁대고 넘어져서 다리에 흉터가 많다. 하지만 없어지리라 믿는다. 그래도 여자니까, 앞으로는 차분하게 행동해야겠다. 그때 같이 '무궁화 꽃이 피었습니다'를 하던 친구들이 궁금해질 때가 있다.

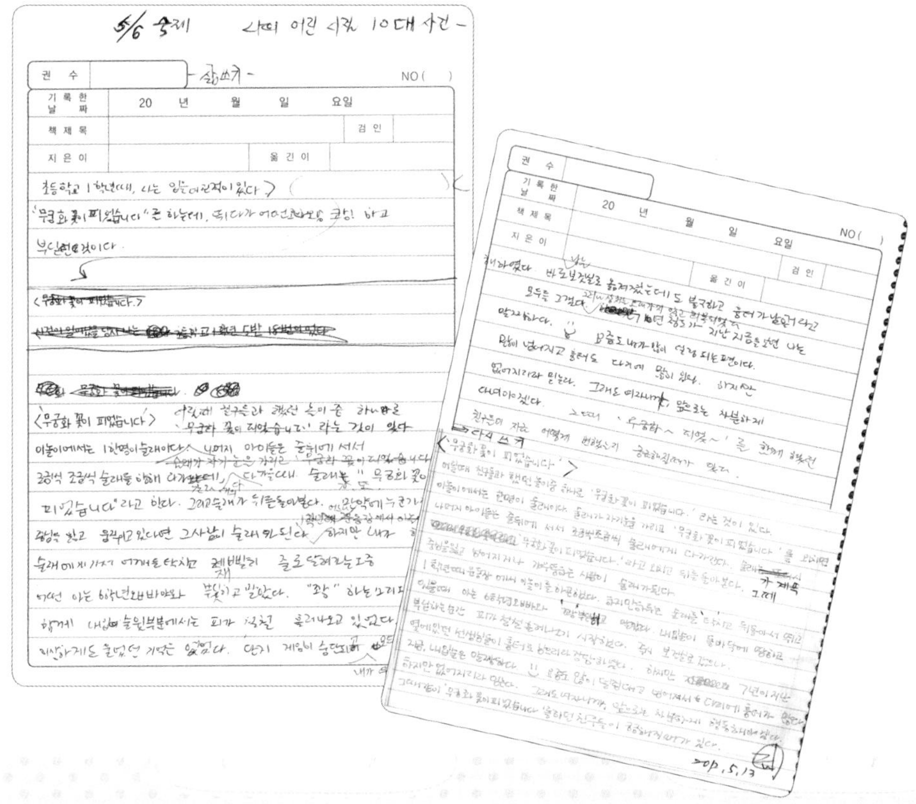

<An Incident of My Early Teen>

When I was little, one of the games I played with my friends was called "The Mugunghwa Flower Has Blossomed." In this game, one person becomes a tagger. The tagger has to yell out "Mugunghwa Flower has blossomed," while covering his or her eyes and while the rest of the players subtly move toward the tagger from the starting line. The tagger constantly yells out "Mugunghwa Flower has blossomed," and looks back, and when one of the players tags him or her without getting caught and returns to the starting line, the game ends. Whoever gets caught moving while the tagger looks back, he or she becomes the new tagger.

I used to play this game in 1st grade at the school playground. One time, I bumped into a 6th grader boy while turning after tagging the tagger to run back to the starting line. I fell, and when my lips met the hard ground, they began to bleed. I was immediately taken to the school nurse, and the teachers next to me said that the scar would become permanent. Those teachers predicted wrong. Now, seven years after that incident, my lips are perfectly fine. I'm still a clumsy girl with many scars on my legs, but I believe those scars will disappear as I age. To become a lady, I would have to start being more ladylike and cautious. Sometimes, I wonder how my friends with whom I used to play "Mugunghwa Flower Has Blossomed" are doing.

〈댄스파티〉

지난 금요일 학교체육관에서 댄스파티를 열었다. 고학년, 즉 8, 9, 10학년들을 위한 파티였다. 오후 6시에 모두 강당에 모였다. 기다렸던 터라 나는 마음이 조금 들떠 있었다. 음악이 흘러나왔다. 처음에는 아무도 춤을 추지 않았다. 서로 옆의 아이들의 눈치를 보고 있었다. 하지만 불과 15분 만에 나를 포함한 많은 아이들과 언니, 오빠들이 흥겹게 춤을 추기 시작했다. K팝이 흘러나왔고, 어떤 음악은 우리가 모르는 음악이어서 좀 낯설었다. 'Fatastic Baby', '붉은 노을', 이런 빅뱅의 노래들은 전주가 나오기 시작할 때부터 춤을 추었다. 우리는 미국이나 외국에서 이런 파티를 많이 해봤기 때문에 부끄럽거나 그런 건 없었다. 화장을 하고 머리도 하고 드레스는 기본이었다. 나는 빨간색 원피스를 입었다. 역시 왕자들은 옷이 날개다. 괜히 철들어 보였기 때문이다. 여자들은 파티 시간 전부터 꽃단장을 했다. 3시간 동안 춤을 추었다. 요

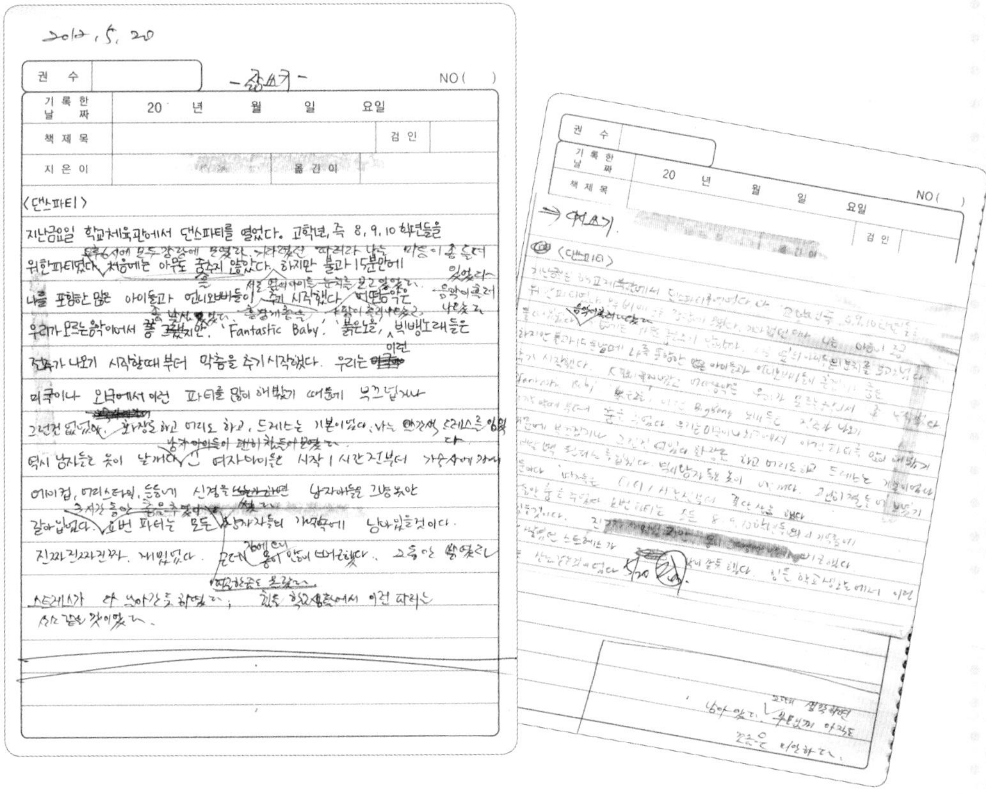
2012. 5. 20

권 수 | -춤쓰기- | NO( )

기록한 날짜: 20 년 월 일 요일

책 제 목 | 검 인

지 은 이 | 옮 긴 이

〈댄스파티〉

지난금요일 학교체육관에서 댄스파티를 열었다. 고학년, 즉 8, 9, 10 학년들을

위한파티였다. 처음에는 아무도 춤추지 않았다. 하지만 불과 15분만에

나를 포함한 많은 아이들과 언니오빠들이 추기 시작했다.

우리가 모르는음악이어서 'Fantastic Baby', '붉은노을', 이런 빅뱅노래들은

전주가 나오기 시작할때부터 막춤을 추기 시작했다. 우리는

미국이나 외국에서 이런 파티를 많이 해봤기 때문에 부끄럽거나

그런건 없었다. 화장을 하고 머리도 하고, 드레스는 기본이었다. 나는 빨간색 드레스를 입었다.

역시 남자들은 옷이 날개다. 여자아이들은 시작 1시간 전부터 가슴사에 가서

메이컵, 머리스타일, 등등에 신경을 남자애들은 그냥 봤안

갈아입었다. 이번 파티는 모든 남자자들의 가슴속에 남아있을것이다.

진짜진짜진짜 재밌었다. 스트레스가 다 날아간듯 하였다. 최초 학교생활에서 이런 파티는

처음 같은 것이었다.

번 파티는 모든 8, 9, 10학년들의 기억 속에 남아 있을 것이다. 진짜 재밌었지만, 몸이 그 다음 날 많이 뻐근했다. 그동안 쌓였던 스트레스가 날아갈 듯했다. 힘든 학교생활에서 이런 파티는 산소 같은 것이었다.

<The Dance Party>

There was a dance party in the school gym last Friday. It was a party for the upper-class 8th,9th and 10th graders. At six o'clock, everyone gathered in the auditorium. I was brimming with excitement for the event. The music started to play, and everyone looked at one another silently asking who would be the first to muster the courage to dance on the dance floor. After 15 minutes of awkward stares, everyone was infected by the groove of the music and began dancing. There was K-pop playing and as well as some songs we weren't familiar with. Songs like "Fantastic Baby," "Rosy Sunset" by Big Bang got us dancing even before the verses started. We encountered many events like this when abroad, so it was not foreign to us. Applying full make-up and wearing fancy dresses were the basic procedures. I wore a red dress. When I saw everyone dressed up nicely, I felt like a grown up. Girls got ready for the party hours before it started. I danced for three straight hours. It was a party to remember for all the 8th, 9th and 10th graders. I had a blast but my body was sore the next day. I felt like I'd shaken all my stress out of my body while dancing. A party like this is oxygen for us to inhale through the suffocating school life.

〈생전 처음 입원하다〉

한 달 전 일이었다. 그날따라 유난히 학교에 도시락을 싸가고 싶었다. 그래서 엄마께서 유리로 된 도시락에 밥과 반찬들을 싸주셨다. 점심시간이 끝나고 다음 수업으로 가게 되었는데, 그때 나도 모르게 갑자기 한 친구를 고양이가 개쫓듯이 장난삼아 쫓기 시작했다.

그러자 갑자기 한 친구가 뒤에서 내가 밤을 확 잡아 재꼈다. 순간 나는 손가락이 유리도시락과 부딪히는 것을 느낄 수 있었다. 쨍그랑소리와 함께 나는 바닥에 넘어졌다. 원래 좀 덜렁대며 잘 넘어지는 편이라 친구들이 그렇게 많이 놀라진 않았다. 하지만 내가 일어나지 않자 친구들은 이상하다는 표정으로 고개를 숙이고 있던 내 머리를 들며 얼굴을 살폈다.

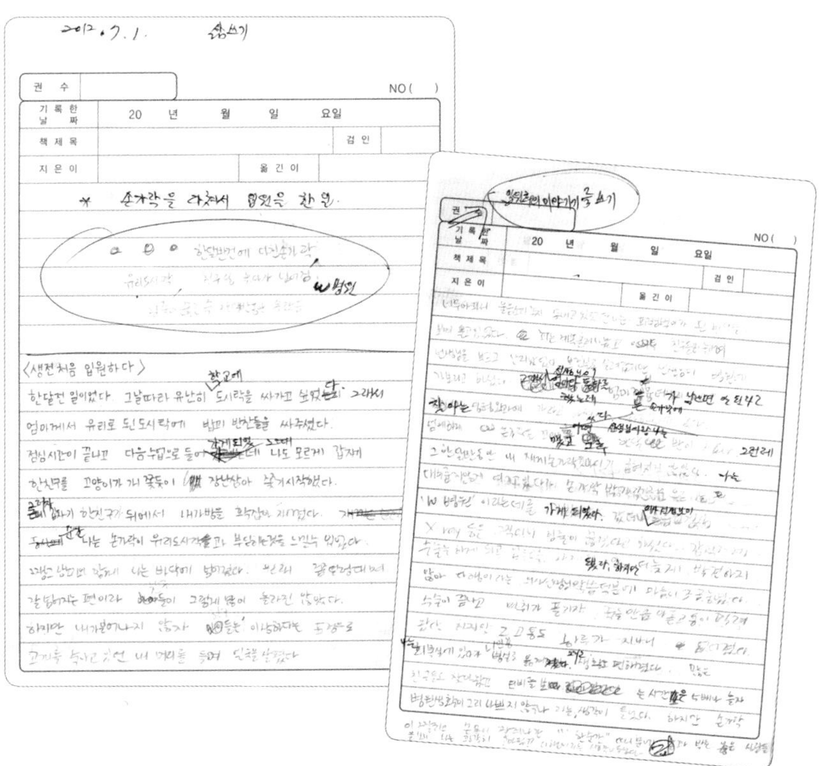

2012.7.1. 숨쓰기

권 수	

NO(　)

기록한 날짜	20 년 월 일 요일		
책 제 목		검 인	
지 은 이		옮 긴 이	

* 손가락을 다쳐서 입원을 한 일.

〈생전처음 입원하다〉

한달전 일이었다. 그날따라 유난히 학교에 도시락을 싸가고 싶었다. 그래서

엄마께서 유리로 된 도시락에 밥과 반찬들을 싸주셨다.

점심시간이 끝나고 다음수업으로 들어가게 되었는데 나도 모르게 갑자기

한친구를 고양이가 개 쫓듯이 장난삼아 쫓기시작했다.

너무 아파서 울음소리조차 못내고 있었던 나는 피범벅이가 된 바닥을 보며 울고 있었다. 피는 계속 흘러나왔고 친구들은 놀라며 선생님을 부르고 난리났었다. 보건실로 실려갔지만 선생님이 병원에 가보라고 하셨다. 그래서 선생님이 엄마와 통화를 했는데, 엄마는 손가락에 흉터가 남으면 안 된다고 잘 아는 성형외과에 가라고 했다. 선생님이란 나는 성형외과에 갔다. 섬세하게 손가락을 꼬맸고, 그 후 한 달 반이 지났다. 그런데 그 한 달 반 동안 내 새끼손가락 한 마디가 굽혀지지 않았다. 나는 대수롭지 않게 여기고 있다가 손가락, 발가락 전문으로 하는 'W 병원'이라는 데를 가게 되었다. 갔더니 의사 선생님이 초음파 검사, X-ray 등을 찍더니 힘줄이 끊겼다고 하셨다. 갑작스레 수술을 하게 되고 입원을 하게 됐다. 하지만 더 늦지 않게 발견되어 다행이라는 의사 선생님 말씀 덕분에 마음이 조금 놓였다. 수술이 끝나고 마취가 풀리자 죽을 만큼 아픈 고통이 밀려왔다. 하지만 그 고통도 하루가 지나니 없어졌다. 나는 회복실에 있다가 1인용 병실로 옮겨졌다. 그리고 생활도 편해졌다. 많은 친구들도 찾아왔고 티비를 보는 시간은 5배나 늘자 '병원생활이 그리 나쁘지 않구나'라는 생각이 들었다. 하지만 손가락이 짤리고 손목이 짤려나간 '한순간' 때문에 손과 발을 잃은 사람들을 보니 나는 굉장히 고마웠고 다행이라는 생각이 들었다.

할아버지, 할머니와 엄마와 아빠, 큰오빠

〈나와 자두 이야기〉

내가 과일 중에 그나마 제일 즐겨 먹는 과일이 자두다. 자두는 어렸을 때부터 즐겨 먹었던 과일이다.

유년 시절 할머니와 찍은 사진에 보면 거의 자두를 먹고 있다.

자두는 새콤달콤한 맛에 아주 귀엽게 생겼다.

손에 딱 들어오는 크기라서 더 끌리는 걸 수도 있다.

겉으론 빨갛지만 한 입을 베어 물면 달콤한 즙이 나오면서 노란 속살을 드러낸다. 만지면 탱글탱글하고 보면 콱 어리물고 싶은 사두는 내게 유일하게 알러지가 없는 과일이다. 그래서 더 잘 먹게 되는 걸 수도 있다. 요즘은 여름이라 자두가 많이 나오는데, 말랑말랑하고 새빨간 걸로 잘 골라 먹으면 10개 이상도 먹을 수 있다.

앞으로도 자두를 향한 나의 애정은 식지 않을 것이다.

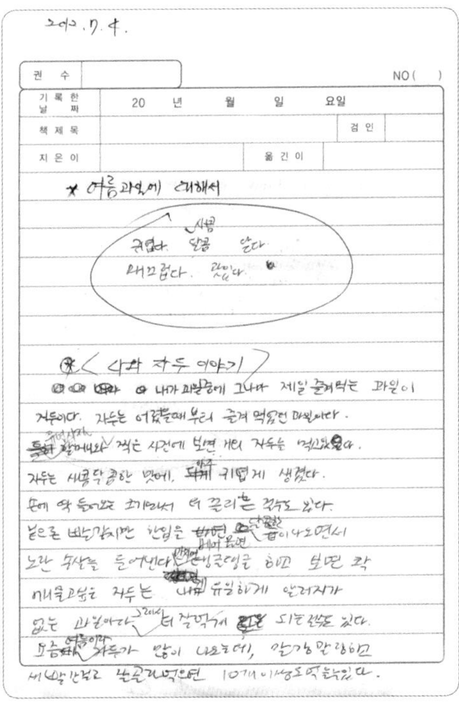

권 수		NO( )
기록한 날짜	20 년 월 일 요일	
책제목		검 인
지은이		옮긴이

〈나와 친구들〉

나는 혈액형이 O형이다. O형은 친구들을 잘 사귄다고 한다. 그렇다. 나는 주위에 친구들이 꽤 많은 편이다. 게다가 나는 프랑스와 미국에 유학생활을 했기 때문에 거기에도 친구들이 꽤 많다. 친구들과의 추억은 쉴새없이 많다. 친구들과 보내는 1초 1초가 내겐 다 모두 소중한 추억이다. 그 추억들은 사진으로 남아 있는데, 사진을 보고 있으면 그때 일들이 파릇파릇 기억이 난다. 친구란 내게 샤프심 같은 존재이다. 아무리 비싼 샤프라도 샤프심이 없으면 그 샤프는 쓸모없는 것이다.

샤프에 샤프심이 필요하듯 내게는 친구들이 필요하다.

친구에게서 배우고, 친구와 슬픔, 행복을 나누며 살아갈 수 있다는 게 나는 제일 행복하다. 나는 내 친구들을 진심으로 사랑한다. 그 친구들이 없었다면 지금의 당당한 내가 없었을 것이다. 나는 앞으로도 좋은 친구를 사귀고, 나도 좋은 친구가 될 것이다.

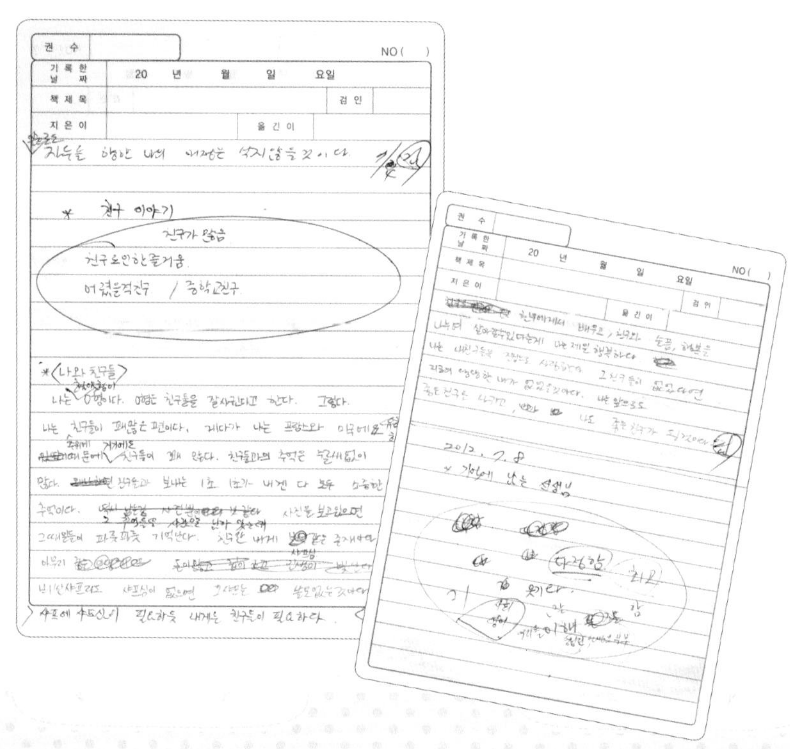
권 수 NO( )
기록한 날짜 20 년 월 일 요일
책제목 검인
지은이 옮긴이
* 친구 이야기
* 〈나와 친구들〉
샤프에 샤프심이 필요하듯 내게는 친구들이 필요하다.

권 수 NO( )
기록한 날짜 20 년 월 일 요일
책제목 검인
지은이 옮긴이
2012. 7. 8
* 기억에 남는 선생님

〈다정했던 햄린 선생님 부부〉

대구국제학교에서 제일 잘나가는 선생님은 아마도 햄린 쌤 부부가 아닌가 싶다. 미터스 햄린은 사회를, 미쓰 햄린은 영어를 가르친다.

그 부부에게는 같은 학교 다니는 8학년 아들, 3학년 아들, 2학년 딸이 있다. 우리 학교에서 햄린 가족은 최고의 가족으로 눈꼽혔다.

햄린 부부는 서로를 향한 배려와 사랑도 철철 넘친다. 예를 들어 남편은 키가 크고, 부인은 작아서 더 귀여운 것 같다. 그 부부가 있어서 내 수업시간들이 재밌었던 것 같다. 덕분에 나는 원래 사회를 싫어하는데, 관심을 가지게 되었고, 영어 성적도 많이 올랐다. 비록 한 해만 하고 매인(Maine)으로 가셨지만 항상 내 마음속에 있을 것이다. 아이들의 마음을 잘 이해하고 화도 거의 안 내시는 햄린 부부는 우리 학교에 있어 엄청난 선물이었다.

재치 있으시고 매력도 넘치는 햄린 쌤은 늘 미국에서도 교사생활을 하는 동안 별 어려운 일이 없으리라 믿는다. 미국에서 햄린 쌤들을 선생님들로 둔 아이들은 복이 엄청 많다. 왜냐하면 햄림 쌤들만큼 훌륭하고 멋진 선생님들은 드물 거니까.

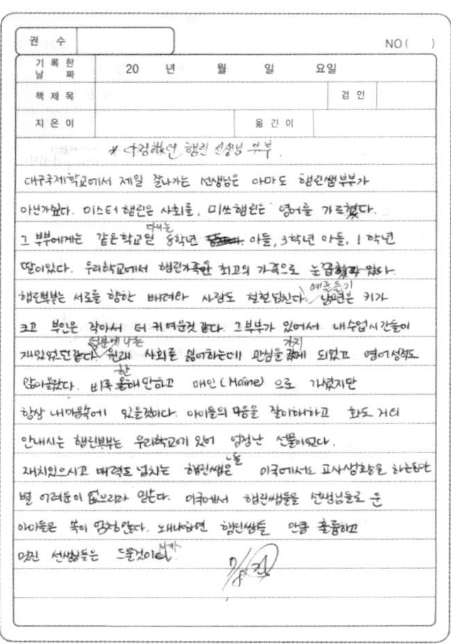

권 수 NO( )

기록한 날짜	20 년 월 일 요일		
책제목		검인	
지은이		옮긴이	

* 다정했던 햄린 선생님 부부

대구국제학교에서 제일 잘나가는 선생님은 아마도 햄린쌤부부가 아닌가싶다. 미스터 햄린은 사회를, 미쓰햄린는 영어를 가르친다.

그 부부에게는 같은학교 다니는 8학년 아들, 3학년 아들, 1학년 딸이있다. 우리학교에서 햄린가족은 최고의 가족으로 눈꼽혔다.

햄린부부는 서로를 향한 배려와 사랑도 철철넘친다. 예를들기 남편은 키가 크고 부인은 작아서 더 귀여운것 같다. 그부부가 있어서 내수업시간들이 재밌었던같다. 덕분에 나는 원래 사회를 싫어하는데 관심을 가지게 되었고 영어성적도 많이올랐다. 비록 한해만하고 매인(Maine)으로 가셨지만 항상 내마음속에 있을것이다. 아이들의 마음을 잘이해하고 화도 거의 안내시는 햄린부부는 우리학교에 있어 엄청난 선물이었다.

재치있으시고 매력도 넘치는 햄린쌤은 늘 미국에서도 교사생활을 하는동안 별 어려움이 없으리라 믿는다. 미국에서 햄린쌤들을 선생님들로 둔 아이들은 복이 엄청많다. 왜냐하면 햄린쌤들 만큼 훌륭하고 멋진 선생님들은 드물것이니까.

<The Warmhearted Mr. & Mrs. Hamlin>

If you were to ask who are the most popular teachers in Daegu International School, the answer would be Mr. and Mrs. Hamlin. Mr. Hamlin teaches Social Education, and Mrs. Hamlin teaches English.

Mr. and Mrs. Hamlin have three kids attending Daegu International School who are in 8th, 3rd and 2nd grade. The Hamlins were known as the best family in DIS.

Mr. and Mrs. Hamlin shows great respect and affection for each other. For example, the fact that Mr. Hamlin is very tall and Mrs. Hamlin is short makes them look more adorable. They made the classes entertaining and fun. Because of them, I got interested in Social Education and improved my English grade. Although they went back to Maine after one year, they will always be in my heart. Teachers like them who get along with students and not get mad are pleasant gifts for any student.

I'm sure Mr. and Mrs. Hamlin are doing well back in America. The kids in America who have them as teachers are lucky, because it's hard to come across great teachers like them.

2006~2008 미국 조지아주 아틀란타 Mount Vernon Presbyteian School에서

〈'Wicked'를 보고〉

나는 어제 친한 친구와 함께 서울에서 하는 뮤지컬 〈위키드〉를 보러갔다. 이 뮤지컬은 미국 브로드웨에에서 1위를 했던 작품이다. 그 뮤지컬은 사람의 겉모습만 보고 판단하면 안 된다는 교훈이 들어 있다. 한 마녀의 이야기다. 그 마녀는 살이 초록색이고 못 생겨서 사람들이 그 마녀의 성격을 오해한다. 하지만 그 마녀가 좋아하는 남자는 시간이 지나면서 초록색이라는 개념을 뚫고 진실한 그 마녀의 착한 마음을 보고 사랑에 빠지는 이야기다. 이 뮤지컬은 내가 본 뮤지컬 중에 최고였다. 정말 감동적이었다. 게다가 배우들이 노래도 엄청 잘 불렀다. 3시간 공연이었지만 지겨운 줄 몰랐다. 한두 달 간 이 뮤지컬에 빠져 있을 것 같다. 기회가 된다면 이런 뮤지컬을 볼 시간이 더 있었으면 좋겠다. 공연의 마지막에 반전이 있었는데 소름이 쫙 끼쳤다. 하지만 난 조금은 예상했었다.

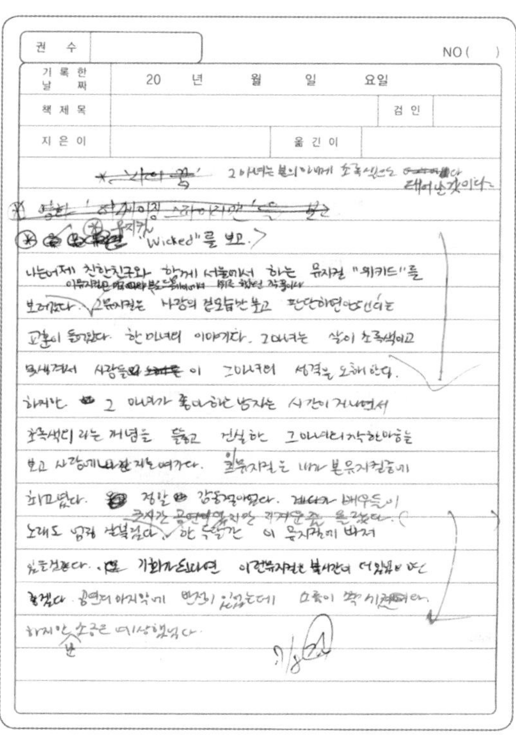

권 수		NO( )

기록한 날짜	20 년 월 일 요일		
책 제 목		검 인	
지 은 이		옮 긴 이	

"Wicked"를 보고.

나는 어제 친한 친구와 함께 서울에서 하는 뮤지컬 "위키드"를 보러갔다.

<After Watching 'Wicked'>

Yesterday, I went to Seoul to watch a musical called "Wicked" with my close friend. This musical was number one in Broadway in America. The moral of the musical is to not judge a book by its cover. It is a story about a witch. This witch has green skin and an ugly appearance that causes people to think less of her. But as time passes, the man that the witch loves sees the inner beauty of her. The "Wicked" is by far the best musical I have ever watched. It was heartwarming. On top of a good story, the actors and actresses did a tremendous job in singing and acting. The musical was three hours long, but I lost track of the time. For two or three months after watching the musical, I was hooked. I hope I get more free times to watch musicals like this. There was a twist in the end of the musical, but I somewhat predicted the ending.

2010 프랑스 Ecole des Roches School 여학생 럭비 선수

〈신기한 꿈 이야기〉

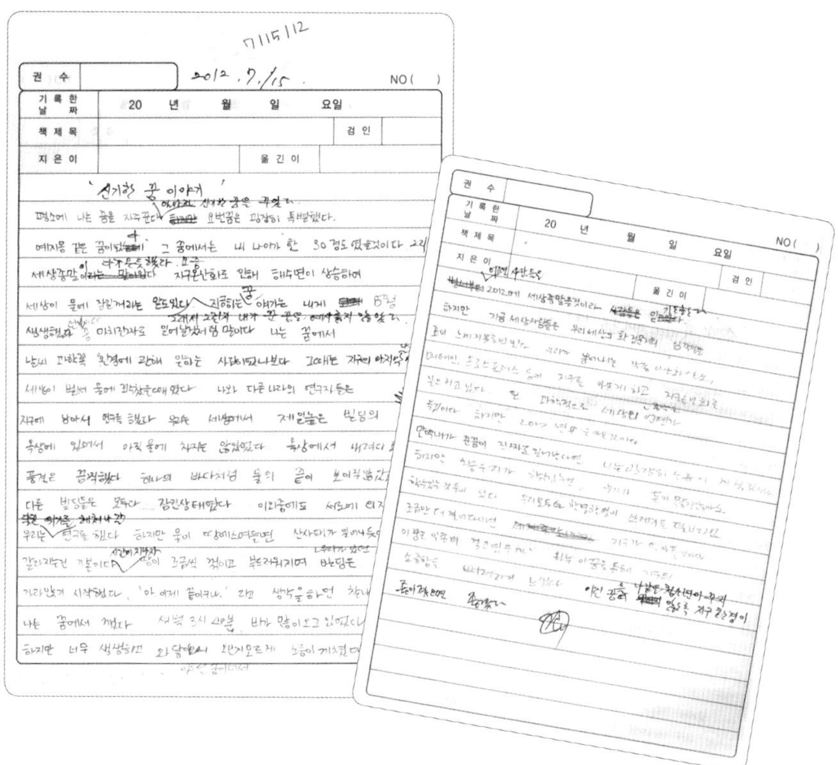

평소에 나는 꿈을 자주 꾼다. 얼마 전 신기한 꿈을 꾸었다. 요번 꿈은 굉장히 특별했다. 예지몽 같은 꿈이었다. 그 꿈에서는 내 나이가 한 30 정도였을 것이다. 그리고 그 세상 종말이 다가온 듯했다. 요즘 지구온난화로 인해 해수면이 상승하여 세상이 물에 잠길 거라는 말도 있다. 그래서 그런지 내가 꾼 꿈은 예사롭지 않았다. 지금하는 꿈 얘기는 내게 엄청 생생했던 꿈이다. 마치 진짜로 일어난 것처럼 말이다. 나는 꿈에서 날씨 과학쪽 환경에 관해 일하는 사람이었나보다. 그때는 지구의 마지막 날이라 세상이 벌써 물에 꽉 찼을 때였다. 나와 다른 나라의 연구자들은 지구에 남아서 연구를 했다. 우리는 세상에서 제일 높은 빌딩의 옥상에 있어서 아직 물에 차지는 않았었다. 옥상에서 내려다보는 풍경은 끔찍했다. 하나의 바다처럼 물의 끝이 보이질 않았고 다른 빌딩들은 모두 다 잠긴 상태였다. 이 와중에도 서로에 의지하며 우리는 닥친 위기를 헤쳐나갈 연구를 했다. 하지만 물이 땅에 스며들면 산사태가 일어나듯이 갈라지는 건 기본이다. 시간이 지나자 땅이 조금씩 꺾이고 부드러워지며 우리가 있던 빌딩은 가라앉기 시작했다. "아, 이제 끝이구나"라고 생각을 하던 찰나에 나는 꿈에서 깼다. 새벽 3시 40분, 비가 많이 오고 있었다. 하지만 너무 생생하고 와닿았던 꿈이어서 왠지 모르게 소름이 끼쳤다.

어떤 사람들은 2012년에 세상 종말이 올 것이라 믿고 기도한다.

하지만 지금 세상 사람들은 우리 세상의 환경문제의 심각성을 깊이 느끼지 못하고 있다. 우리가 뿜어내는 각종 이산화탄소, 메탄, 프로스포러스 등이 지구를 아프게 하고 지구온난화를 일으키고 있다. 과학적으로 세상 종말은 언젠가 올 것이다. 하지만 2012년은 아닐 것이다.

만약 내가 꾼 꿈이 진짜로 일어난다면, 나는 굉장히 소름이 끼칠 것이다.

하지만 지금 우리가 할 수 있는 건, 누구나 돈이 많지 않아도 할 수 있는 것들이 있다. 우리 모두 한 명 한 명이 쓰레기를 덜 버리고 조금만 더 걸어다니면 지구가 덜 아플 것이다. '이 꿈은 일종의 경고였을까?' 하는 이 꿈을 통해 지구의 소중함을 뼈저리게 느꼈다. 이런 꿈을 나 같은 청소년이 꾸지 않도록 지구환경이 좋아졌으면 좋겠다.

2010년 프랑스 유학 시절 친구들이랑

<The Story of an Interesting Dream>

I dream while I sleep frequently. About a few days ago, I had an interesting dream that unsettled me as if it were an omen. In this dream, I was in my thirties and the world had come to an end. Global warming is an issue nowadays saying the world will sink due to sea level elevating. Because of the current issue, I knew my dream wasn't an ordinary dream. I can still vividly recall the dream which I'm about to tell you. So vivid it was that it could've come from real life, and the sight and sound of it wouldn't be any different. In the dream, I was a meteorologist. It was the final day of the apocalypse, and the world had already begun sinking. But other meteorologists from different countries remained with me on Earth to further research the sorrowful phenomenon. We stood on the rooftop of the tallest building in the world, which hadn't yet been conquered by the rising waters. The rooftop's view terrified me: like a single vast ocean, the water was endless and all the other buildings had drowned. Despite our miserable surroundings, we depended on one other and continued to search for solutions. As was expected, the already most grounds softened further and the buildings began to crumble. In the very second that I was ready to embrace the world's end, I woke up from a dream. The rain was coming down at 3:40 A.M. Although the knowledge that the experience was a mere dream brought me relief, I got goosebumps from retracing the unbearably vivid dream.

Some people pray because they believe the world is going to end in 2012.

A lot of people don't know the seriousness of our environmental issues. All the carbon dioxide and biogas that we have spewed into the sky are harming Earth and causing Global Warming. Scientifically speaking, the world will have its end someday –just not in 2012.

The coming to fruition of my dream about the world's end would certainly be a bizarre turn of events.

What we can do right now for the environment can be done whether one is poor or rich. If we reduce littering and start walking more, the world will be in less pain. It feels as if this dream foreshadowed all our dooms. This dream compelled me to reflect on how we should treat the world. To reduce the effect of this terrifying dream of mine, I hope that the world environment changes for the better.

Since I was a little, I've enjoyed drawing my thoughts. I expressed my body and mind through sketching the "Structures of Thoughts." It is really entertaining to look through them. Did I really draw like this?

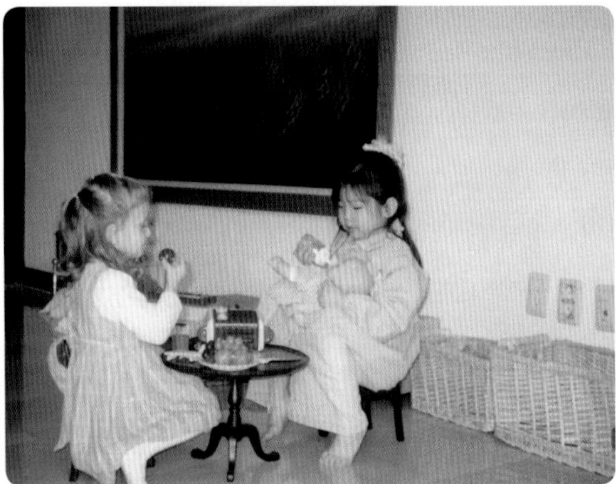

프랑스 친구랑 소꿉놀이

〈神奇的梦〉

2012. 7. 15.

我经常做梦，在不久前就做了一个神奇的梦。这个梦很特别，像是预言一样的梦。梦里的我，是30岁左右的样子。并且在那个世界，末日好像就要来了。最近因为全球变暖，导致了海平面上升，都说世界会被淹没。所以这个梦并不一般。现在要说的梦非常的生动，就像真的要发生一样。在梦里，我是从事天气科学方面与环境有关的工作。世界末日就要来的那个时候，整个世界已经都泡在了水里。我和其他国家的研究员们留在了地球上，在世界上最高的建筑物的屋顶上做研究，水还没有漫到这里。从屋顶上往下看，下面的样子令人害怕。整个的都是海，看不到边际。其它建筑物都被水淹没了，我们在这里相互支持，研究如何解决这迫在眉睫的危机。但是水肆虐在土地上，就像泥石流爆发一样，到处被撕成一片片的。随着时间的流逝，土地一点点的被吞噬、被融化。我们所在的建筑物也开始下沉。"啊，就这样结束了呀"，想道这的一刹那，梦醒了。凌晨3：40，雨下的很大。但这梦太真实了，身上不由得起了一身鸡皮疙瘩。

有些人相信2012年就是世界末日，并一直在祈祷着。

可是现在的人们，对世界环境问题的严重性并没有强烈的感觉。我们排出的二氧化碳、甲烷、氟氯烃等，会让地球受伤、会使全球变暖。这些会让世界末日到来，但是不会是2012.

如果我做的梦真的实现的话，我真的会起鸡皮疙瘩。

我们现在能做的是，即使是没有太多的钱，我们每个人都少扔一点垃圾、稍微努力一点的话地球就会少一点疼痛。这个梦会是一种警告吗？通过这个梦，我深切的感觉到了地球的重要性。为了不让像我一样年龄的人再做这样的梦，要是地球的环境能变好该多好。

2 가족·사랑

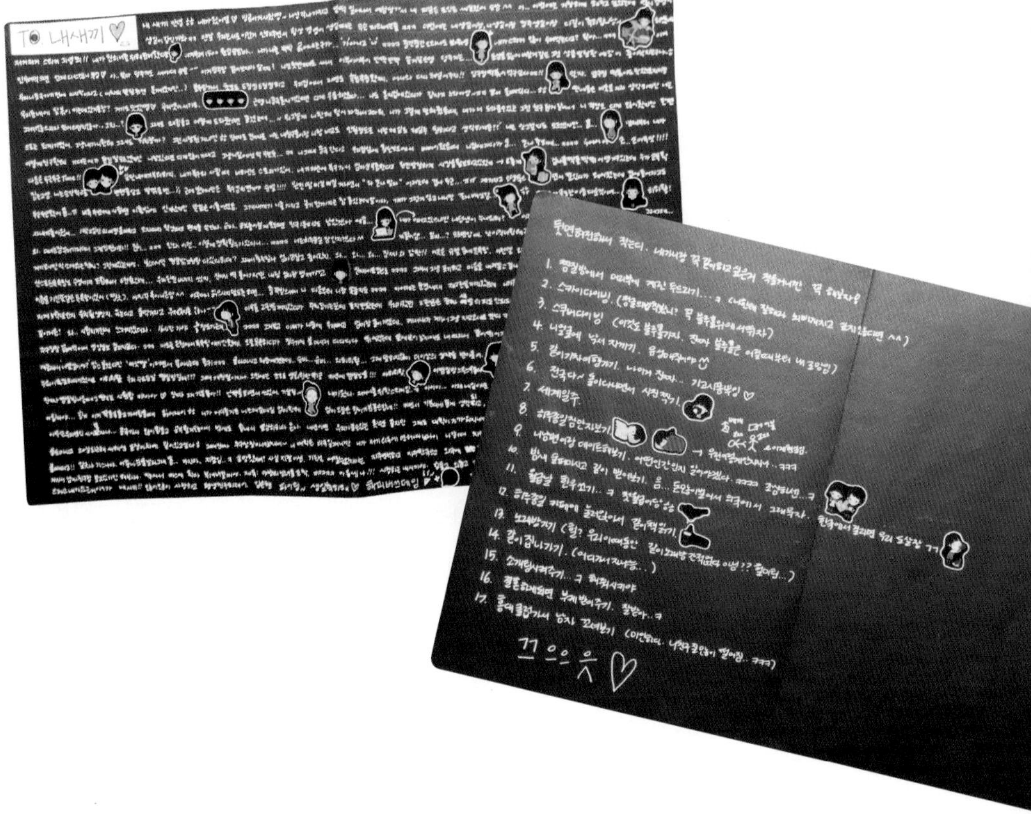

"제가 쓴 편지 읽어 보세요.
재미있지요. 마치 디자인한 것 같은 편지. 내 마음을 디자인한 그림 편지에요.
한 때 디자이너가 되는 꿈을 가진 적이 있었어요."

〈은향이네 가족 신문〉

은향이네 가족 신문

이달의 행사

10월 23 - 할아버지 생신

10월 24 - 아버지 생신

10월 24 - 은향이 시험(중간고사)

10월 1 - 국군의날

한마디 부탁해요

뭐가 보이니? 김은향

2위

뭐가 보이니?

갈매기들이 날아가는게 보여

정말?

나는 준비물을 안챙겨서

혼났다

뭐가 보이니?

인상찌뿌린 선생님얼굴이 보여

정말?

정말?

그게 사랑 아니니?

그게 사랑 아니니?

친구야

1위

친구야

나는 네 얼굴을 몰라

친구야

나는 네 이름을 몰라

친구야

나는 네 성격을 몰라

하지만

하지만

이 친구 한마디가

우리의 우정 꽃을

피운다는거 아니 친구야?

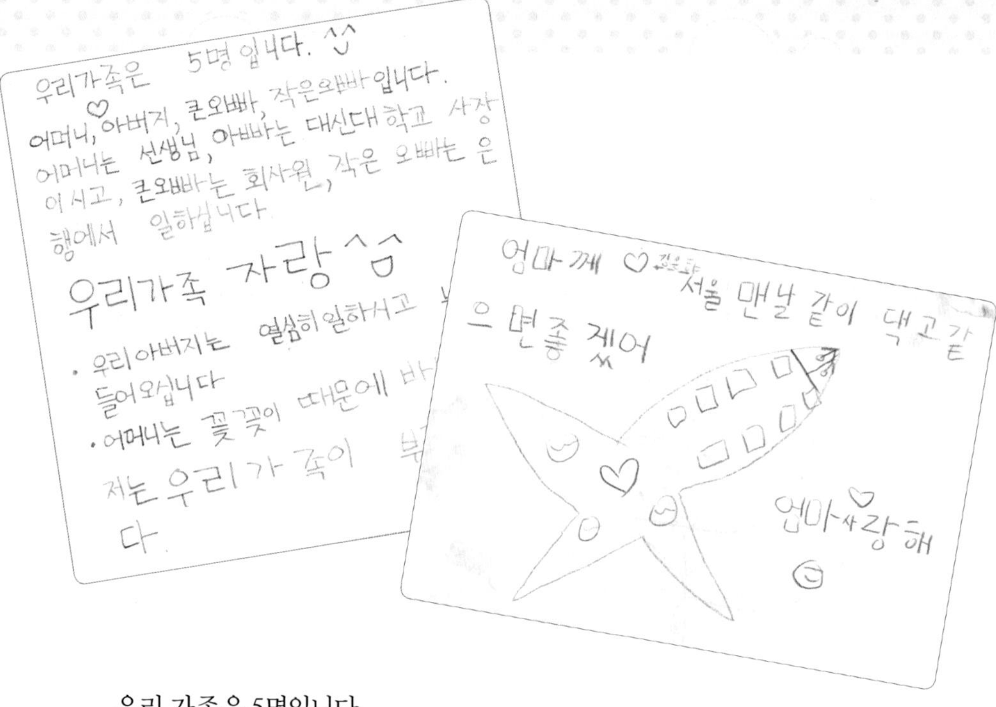

우리 가족은 5명입니다.

어머니, 아버지, 큰오빠, 작은오빠입니다.

어머니는 선생님, 아빠는 대신대학교 사장이시고, 큰오빠는 회사원, 작은오빠는 은행에서 일하십니다.

오빠들은 나의 소파

어버이날
은향이가 그린 카네이션을 아빠에게 보냅니다.

나의 소개

1. 혈액형: O형

나이: 8살

이름: 김은향

취미: 책 읽기

꿈: 선생님

운동 좋아함(줄넘기)

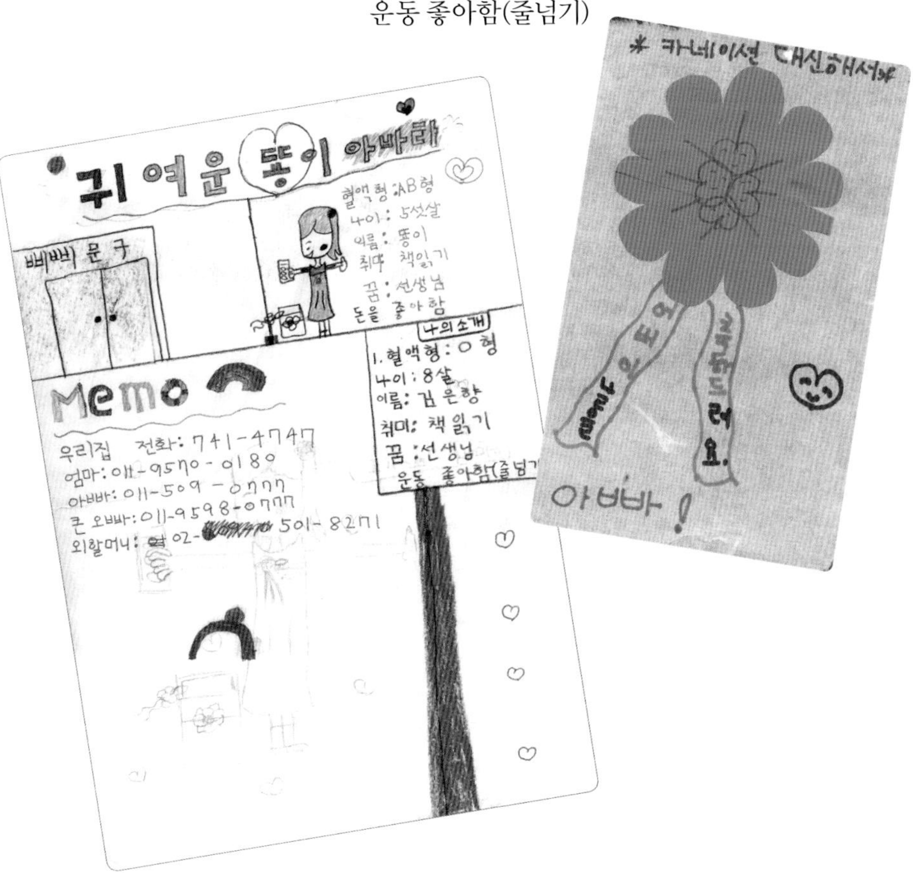

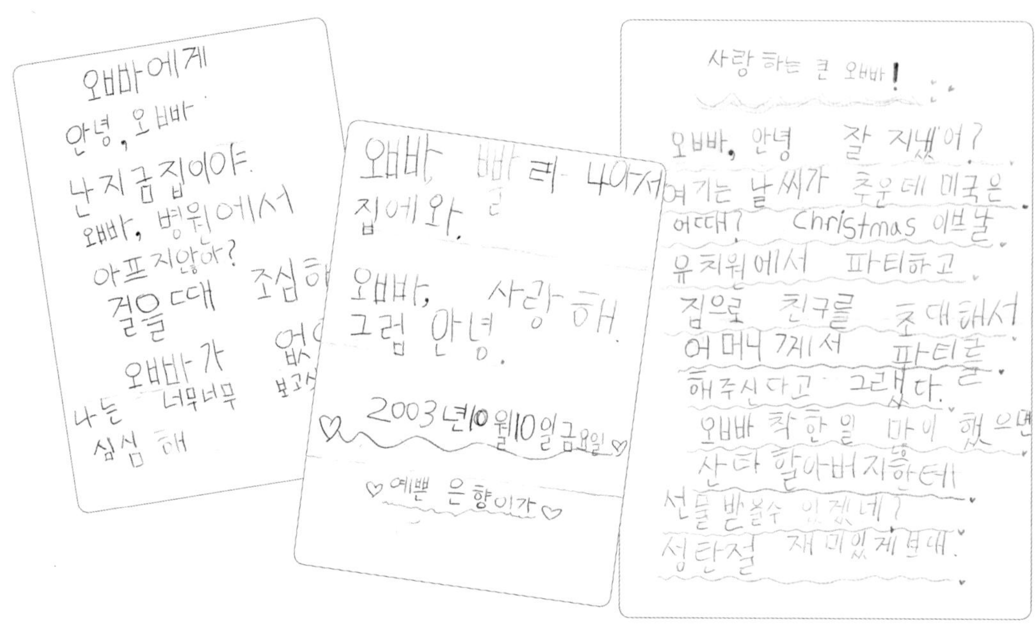

오빠에게
안녕, 오빠
난지금집이야.
오빠, 병원에서
아프지않아?
걸을때 조심해
오빠가 없
나는 너무너무 보고
심심해

오빠, 빨리 나아서
집에와.
오빠, 사랑해.
그럼 안녕.
2003년10월10일금요일
예쁜 은향이가

사랑하는 큰 오빠!
오빠, 안녕 잘 지냈어?
여기는 날씨가 추운데 미국은
어때? Christmas 이브날
유치원에서 파티하고
집으로 친구를 초대해서
어머니께서 파티를
해주신다고 그랬다.
오빠 착한 일 많이 했으면
산타 할아버지한테
선물 받을수 있겠네?
성탄절 재미있게 보내.

사랑하는 큰 오빠!

오빠, 안녕 잘 지냈어?

여기는 날씨가 추운데 미국은 어때?

Christmas 이브날, 유치원에서 파티하고,

집으로 친구를 초대해서 어머니께서 파티를 해주신다고 그랬다.

오빠 착한 일 많이 했으면 산타할아버지한테 선물 받을 수 있겠네?

성탄절 재미있게 보내.

큰오빠 시카고대학교 졸업식

가훈: 빛과 진리를 따라 가자!

뜻: ☆☆=예수님

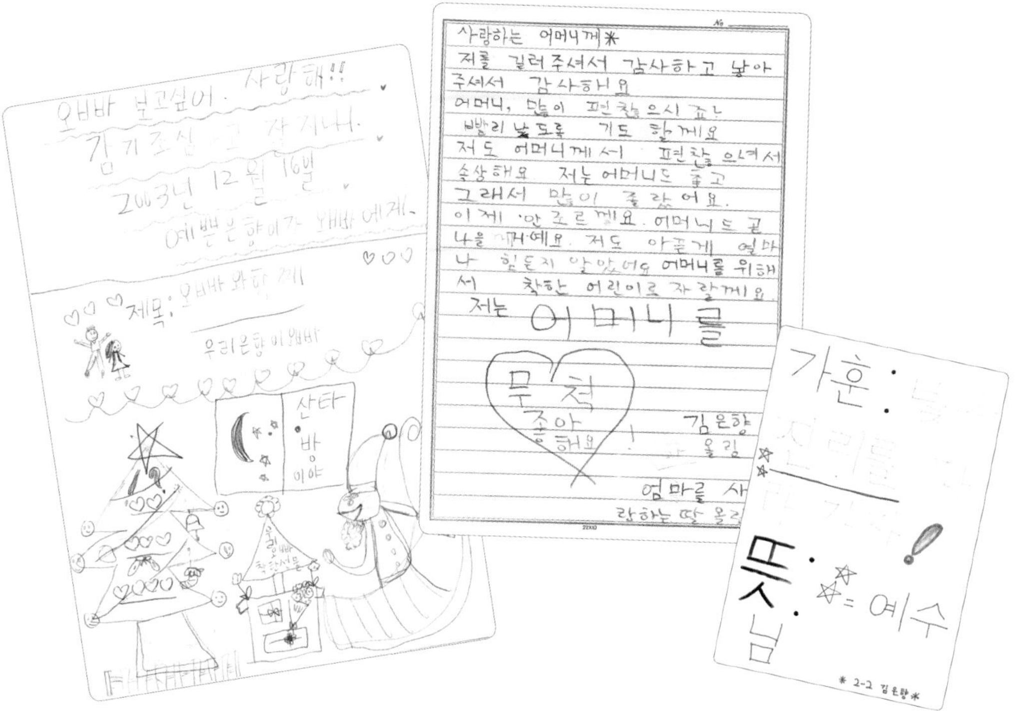

오빠 보고싶어. 사랑해!!
감기조심하고 잘 지내.
2003년 12월 16일
예쁜 은향이가 오빠에게.

제목: 오빠와 함께
우리은향이 오빠

산타 방이야

사랑하는 어머니께*
저를 길러주셔서 감사하고 낳아
주셔서 감사해요
어머니, 많이 편찮으시죠?
빨리 낫도록 기도 할께요
저도 어머니께서 편찮으셔서
속상해요 저는 어머니도 좋고
그래서 많이 울었어요.
이제 안 조르게요. 어머니도 곧
나을 거예요. 저도 아플게 얼마
나 힘든지 알았어요 어머니를 위해
서 착한 어린이로 자랄께요.
저는 어머니를
무척 좋아해요!
김은향 올림
엄마를 사랑하는 딸 올림

가훈: 빛과 진리를 따라 가자!
뜻: ☆☆=예수님
* 2-2 김은향 *

가족과 함께 할머니에게 앉겨 있는 은향이(백일사진)

〈너무나 멋진 우리 엄마〉

어머니께

어머니, 어린이날 선물 주셔서 감사드려요.

그리고 길러주셔서 감사해요.

어머니께서 사주신 인형 예뻤어요.

사랑해요!

은향 올림

엄마, 생일 축하해요.
지금 돌이켜 보면
나의 엄마는 하늘이다.
태양빛이다.
가녀리지만
밀려 오는 파도처럼
사랑으로 나를 감싸고 안아 준다.
I ♥ 엄마

Mam and Dad,

Merry Christmas.

어머니 발을 씻는 효녀 은향이

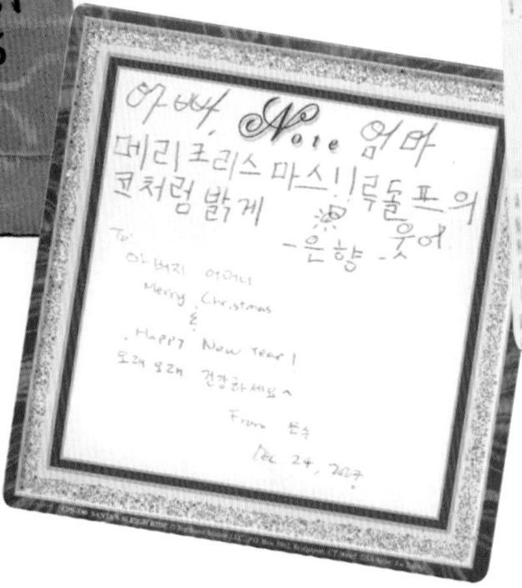

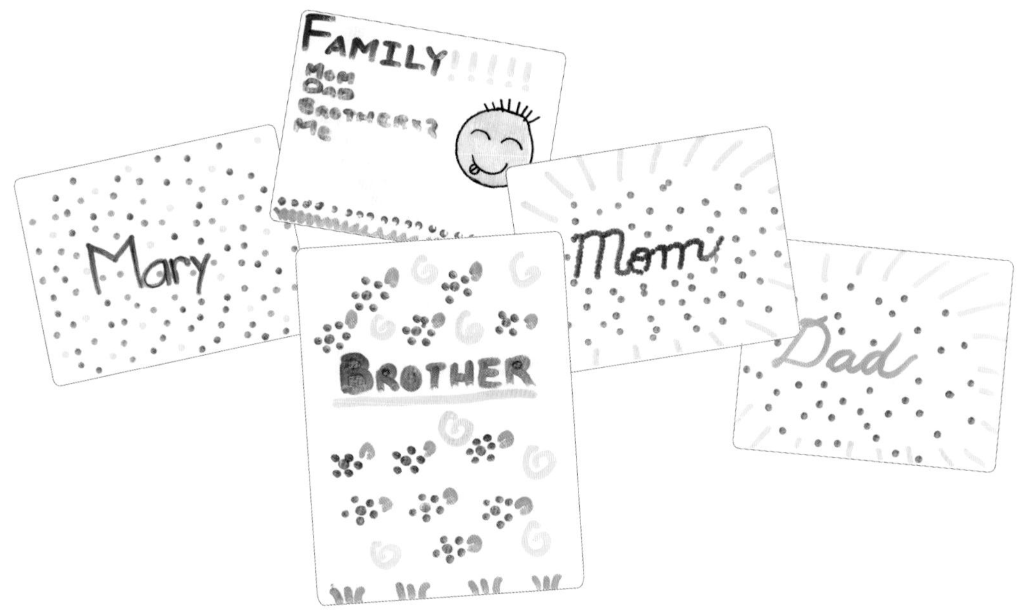

옛날 내가 쓴 카드의

먹물 빛이 어느 덧 차츰 바래져 간다.

그만큼 가족에 대한 사랑과 믿음은

더욱 두터워진다.

나의 유치원 친구들이랑

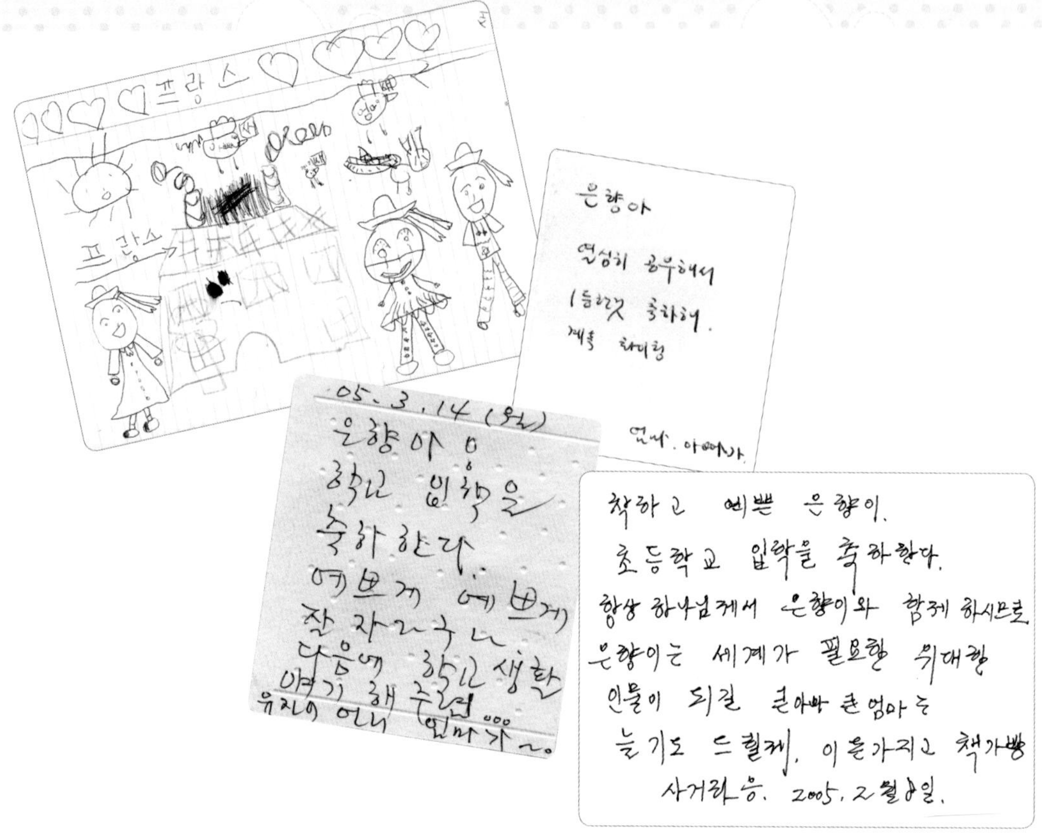

〈엄마가 보내준 편지(프랑스 유학 시절)〉

착하고 예쁜 은향이.

초등학교 입학을 축하한다.

항상 하나님께서 은향이와 함께 하시므로

은향이는 세계가 필요한 위대한

인물이 되길 큰아빠 큰엄마는

늘 기도 드릴게. 이 돈 가지고 책가방

사거라 응.

2005년 2월 8일

〈프랑스로 보내온 엄마 사랑〉

엄마의 사랑스러운 딸

♡향

♡향이가 떠나고 나니

집안이 텅빈 것 같고 ♡향이 방은 White로 예쁘게 칠했는데

♡향이가 없어서 너무 너무 보고 싶다.

이젠 6月에 아주 온다고 생각하니 하루라도 빨리 왔으면 하고

엄마는 기다려진단다.

목사님 말씀대로 항상 기도하면서 하나님과 의논하고

하나님의 대답을 기다리는

하나님의 어여쁜 딸이 되기를...

TO: Kim, Eun Hyan

ECOLE DES ROCHES (La Colline)

Avenue Edmond Demollns

B.P. 710

27130 VERNEUIL SUR AVRE, FRANCE.

Tel: 02.32.60.40.46

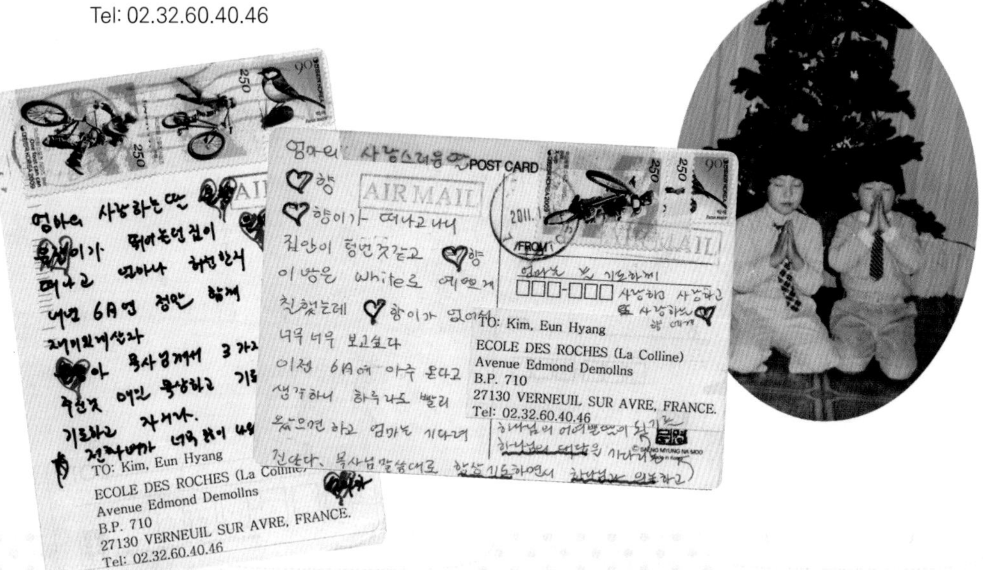

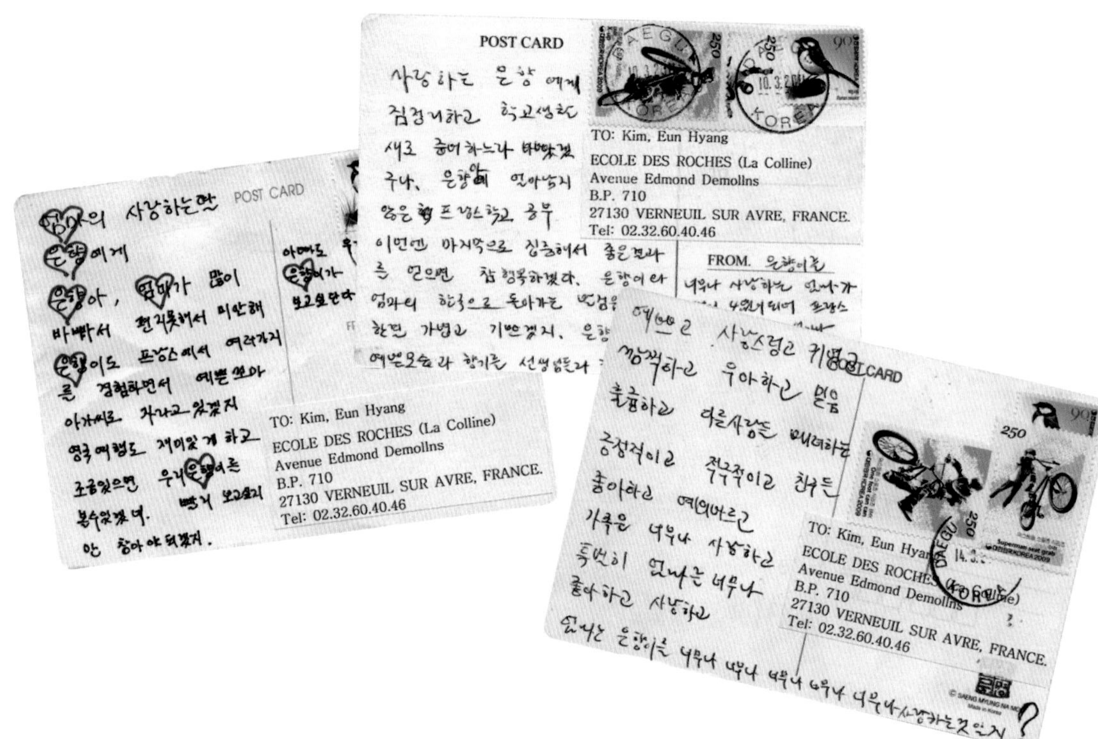

엄마의 사랑하는 딸

은향에게

은향아, 엄마가 많이 바빠서 편지 못해서 미안해

은향이도 프랑스에서 여러 가지를 경험하면서 예쁜 꼬마 아가씨로 자라고 있겠지.

영국 여행도 재미있게 하고

조금 있으면 우리 은향이를 볼 수 있겠네.

빨리 보고 싶지만 참아야 되겠지.

아빠도 우리 은향이가 너무나 보고 싶단다.

엄마!

〈끝없는 사랑〉

♡♡♡♡은향에게

은향아, 어제 우연히 TV에서 4나라의 최우수학교의 생활을 보여주는데

우리 민족사관학교는

두루마기와 치마저고리 같은 것을 입고

새벽 6시에 일어나 검도로 체력훈련, 중간에 악~

체육동아리훈련, 저녁은 새벽 2시 3시까지

무시무시하게 하는데 모두가 자발적으로 하기 때문에 성공하는 것 같아.

은향이에게도 조금은 도전이 되면 좋겠다.

아빠 엄마

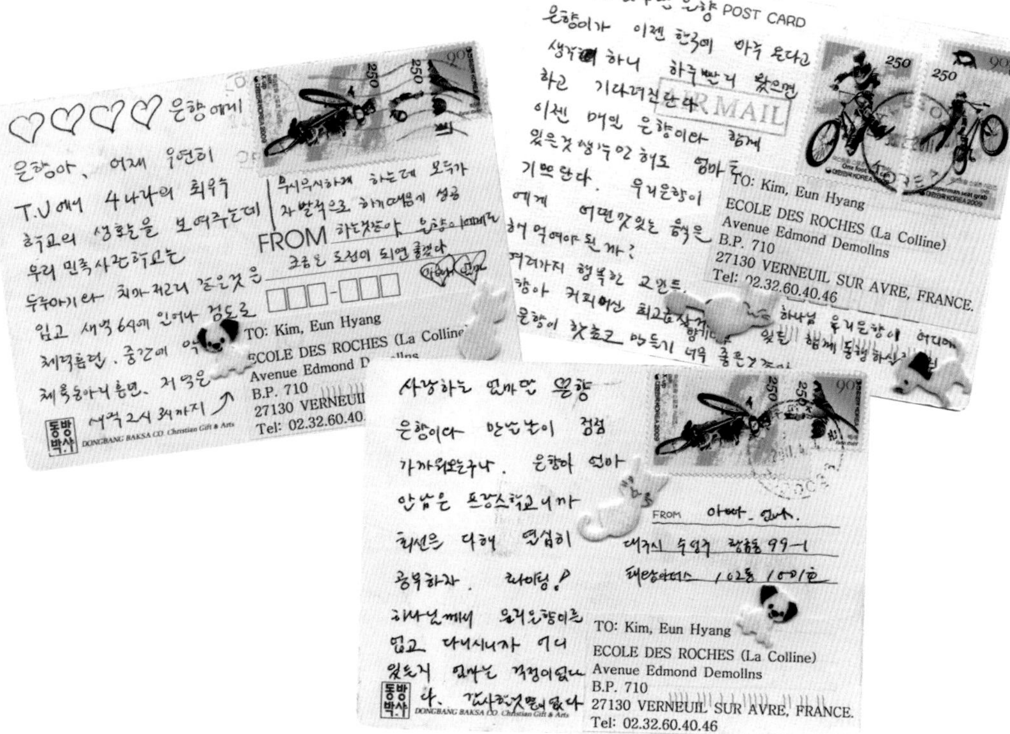

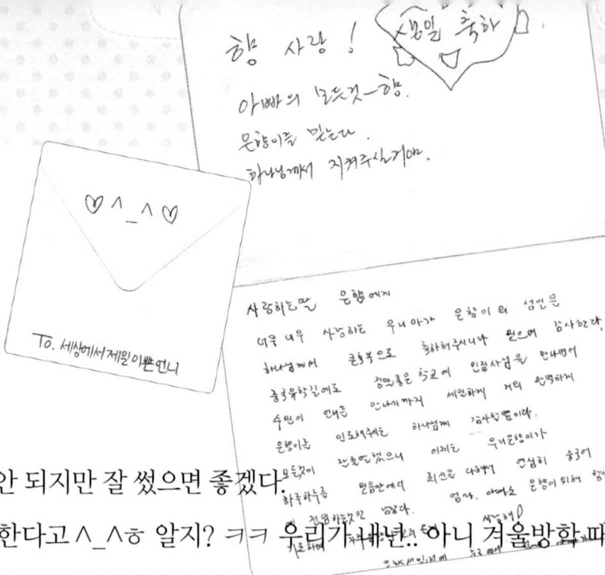

〈채연이가 보낸 편지〉

To. 내 사랑 언니 ♡

언니 나 채연이~!!

선물 잘 받았어?

언니가 나에게 준 선물과는 비교도 안 되지만 잘 썼으면 좋겠다.

〈3 뭐.... 하고 싶은 말은 그냥... 사랑한다고 ^_^ㅎ 알지? ㅋㅋ 우리가 내년.. 아니 겨울방학때도 즐거운 모습으로 reunion 하고 시프담...ㅎ 쫑리에서 잘 지내구! 잘해낼 거야ㅎㅎ 내가 언닐 좀 잘 알자낭ㅎㅎㅎ 언니랑은 뭐 후정 영원하자."

이런 말들도 구지 안 해도 될 것 같다. 왜냐하면! ^_^ 우리가 진짜 운명 친구라면 우리 노력 없이도 언젠간 어디서 좋게 만날 거야!

우리 서로에게 보낸 선물들과 편지 잘 보관해 두고 나중에 성공한 미래에 다시 읽어보장ㅎㅎ

우리 둘 다 노력할 꺼니깐 분명히 하고 싶고 해보고 싶은 것들 다 하게 될 거야=)

언니랑 지내면서 매우 편안하고 행복했음!!!

앞으로도 더 그럴거구ㅎ

나두 언니 잘되길 하나님께 기도할께!

우리 둘 다 예수님께서도 반할 만한 여자가 되장!!

미래에서 돌아봤을 때 자랑스러운 자기 자신이 되구!

나중에 또 만나면 그때는 더 재밌구

새로운 이야기두 하고

맛있는 것도 마니 먹장〈333 쇼랑해!!

-언니를 아주 좋아하는 동생 채연이가-

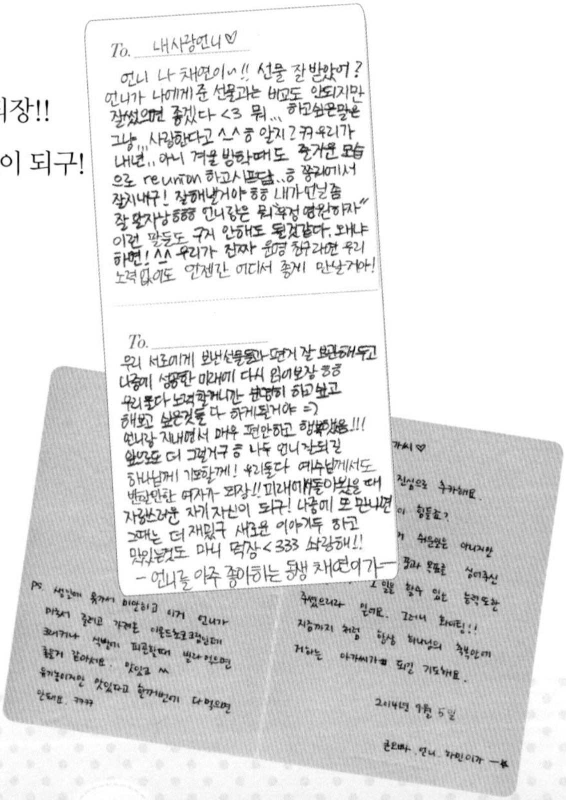

〈은향이가 언니에게〉

언니가 쓴 편지를 보고 편지를 쓴다.

언니. 언니가 썼지만 이쁜 은향 언니는 좀 그렇지 않다고

하하… 저 편지를 보면서 고데기를 준비하라고 이리 말해 주지 그랬어.

지금 이 상태로 동해 바다를 헤엄쳐 건너갈 수 있을 것 같아

이 카드가 너무 작아서 손이 떨린다.

그럼 2000

-非常非常 이쁜 미소가♥-

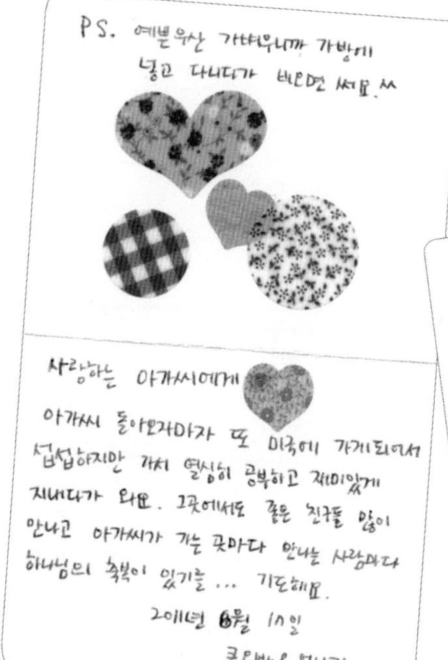
PS. 예쁜우산 가벼우니까 가방에
넣고 다니다가 비오면 써요.

사랑하는 아가씨에게
아가씨 돌아오자마자 또 미국에 가게되어서
섭섭하지만 가서 열심히 공부하고 재미있게
지내다가 와요. 그곳에서도 좋은 친구들 많이
만나고 아가씨가 가는 곳마다 만나는 사람마다
하나님의 축복이 있기를... 기도해요.
2011년 8월 17일
큰오빠 & 언니가

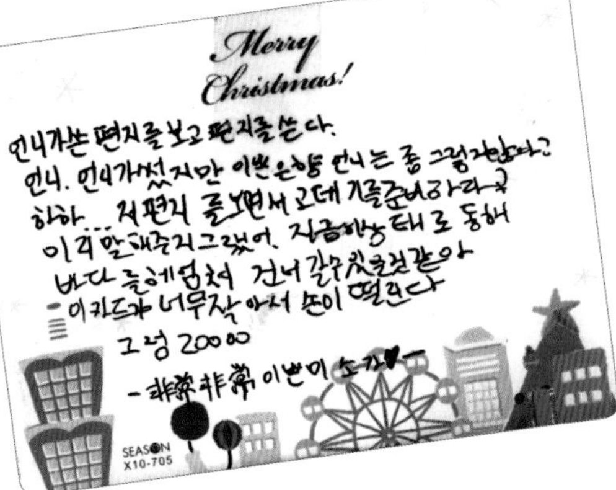
Merry Christmas!

언니가쓴 편지를 보고 편지를 쓴다.
언니. 언니가썼지만 이쁜 은향 언니는 좀 그렇지않다고
하하... 저편지를보면서 고데기를준비하라고
이리 말해주지그랬어. 지금이상태로 동해
바다를헤엄쳐 건너갈수있을것같아
이카드가 너무작아서 손이 떨린다
그럼 2000
-非常非常 이쁜미소가♥-

ALDARA
MARIA
CLARE

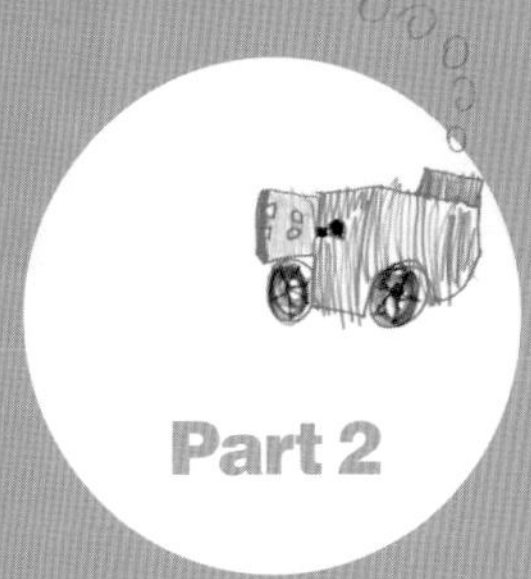

Part 2

은향의 갤러리

1 그림·낙서

"저는 어릴 때부터 생각하는 것을 그림으로 그리기를 좋아했어요.
'생각의 구조화'는 나의 꿈과 상상력조차 그림으로 표현했을 것 같은데
돌이켜 보니 진짜 재미있어요.
과연 내가 이렇게 그렸는가?"

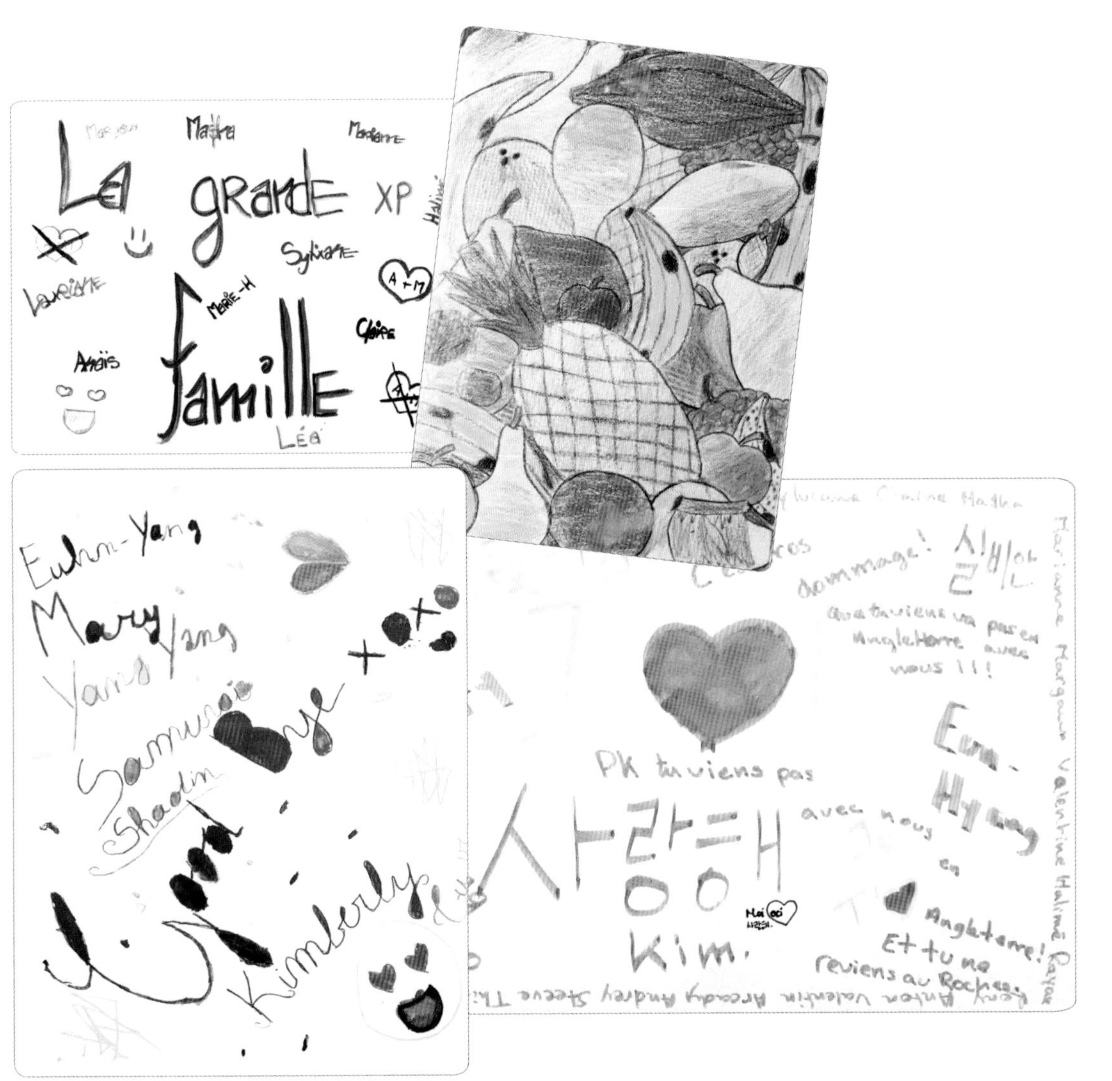

"친구들이랑 한 장의 종이 위에
꽃들의 마음을 함께 어울림 마당을 만들었네요."

<일본에 있는 화산, 옛날사람이 목욕했던 온탕>
온탕?
김은향

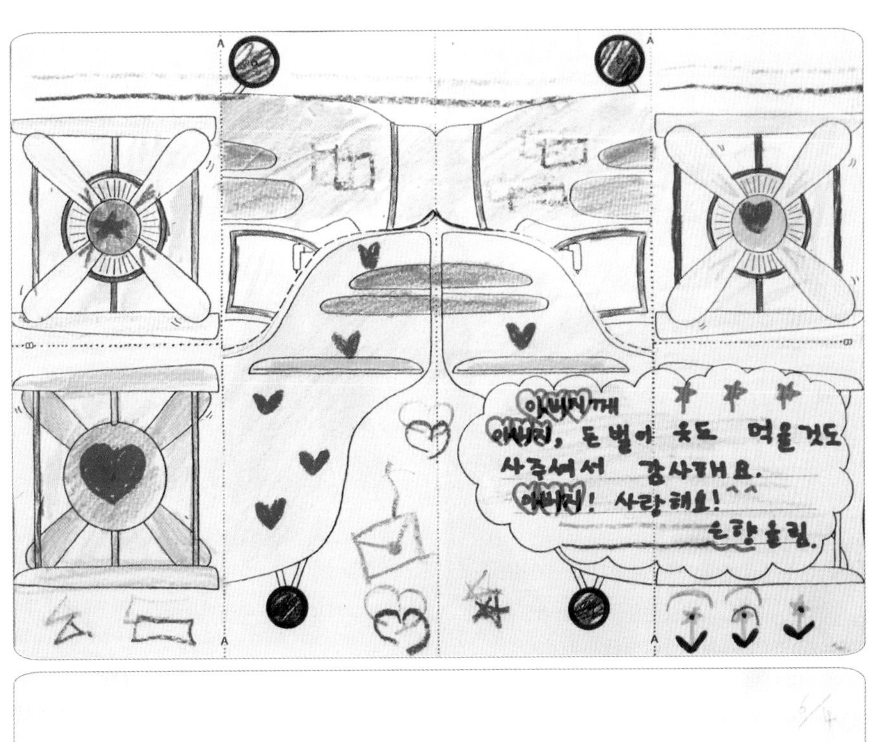
아빠께
아빠, 돈벌어 옷도 먹을것도
사주셔서 감사해요.
아빠! 사랑해요! ^^
은향올림.

동글동글
동글동글
바퀴도
연기도
동글동글
하얀 시계도
동글동글

아빠와 엄마에게 보낸 그림 우편

우리집

"은향이의 내면이
보이지 않아요"

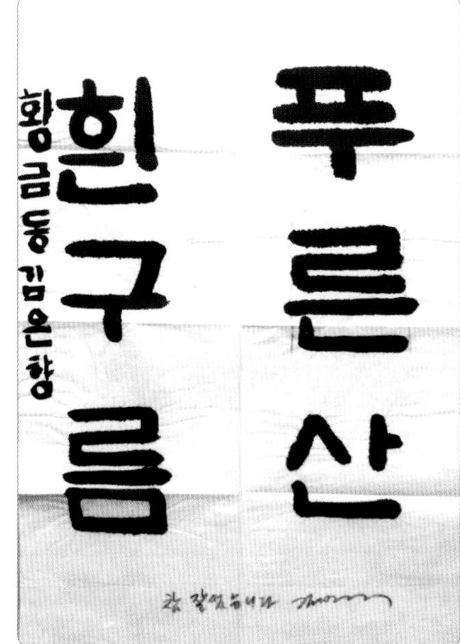

붓글씨

"그림은 저의 상상력의 아이콘입니다."

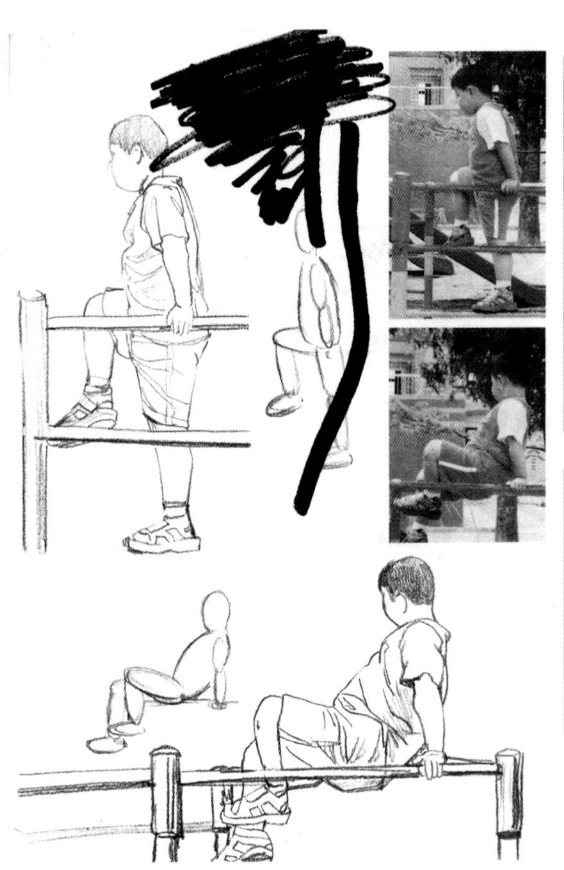

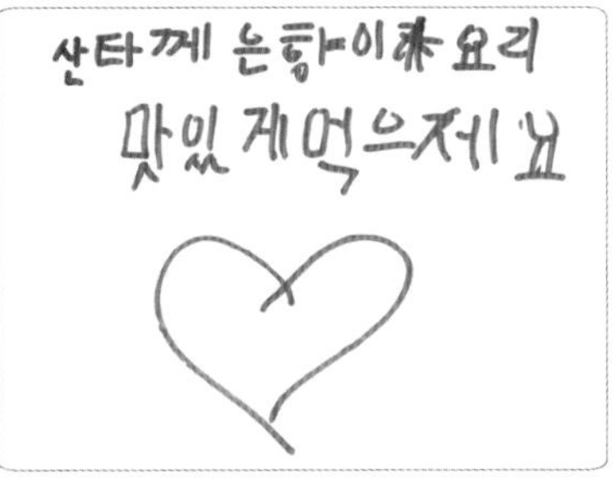

"스케치 정밀 묘사 그림 그리기 연습
우리집의 공간 지도 그림"

화가 김은향

은향이와 사탕 나라의 사랑

하늘을 나는 화원의 정원

오뉴월

태양 볕에

꽃들이 팔벌리며

사탕 나라

공간의 이중성-포개어진 평면

〈평면에 시간과 공간을 담기〉

김은향 8살때〈천사의 꿈〉

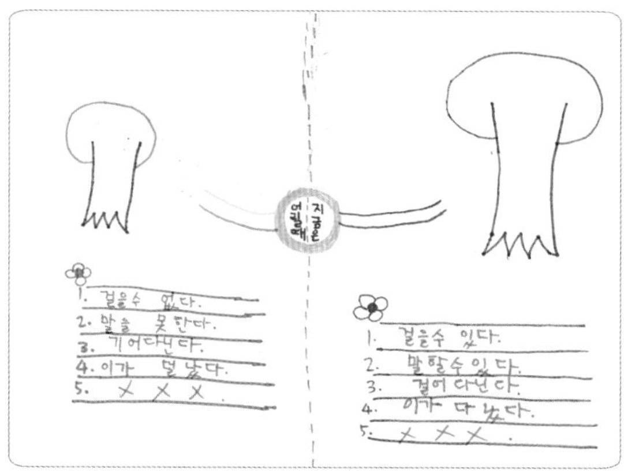

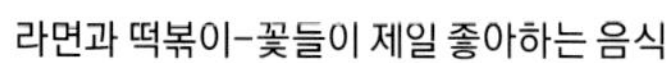
라면과 떡볶이-꽃들이 제일 좋아하는 음식

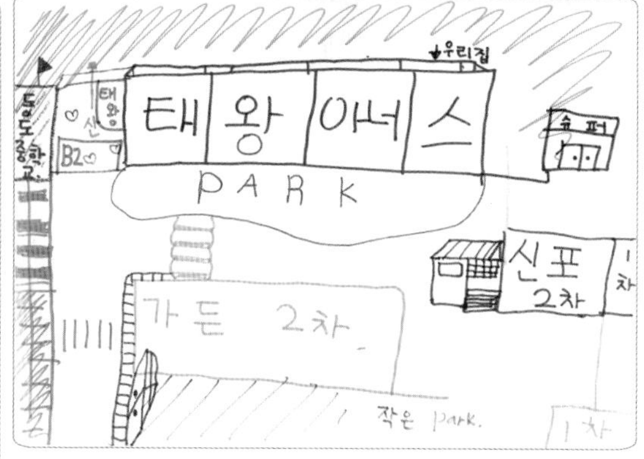

손을 다쳐서 병실 수술대에 누운 그림

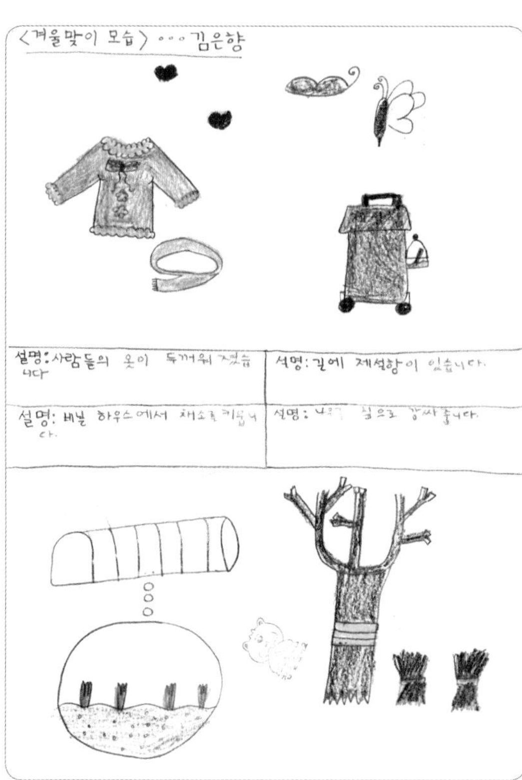

<겨울맞이 모습> ···김은향
설명:사람들의 옷이 두꺼워 졌습니다
설명:길에 제설함이 있습니다.
설명: 비닐 하우스에서 채소를 키웁니다.
설명: 나무를 짚으로 감싸 줍니다.

겨울맞이 모습

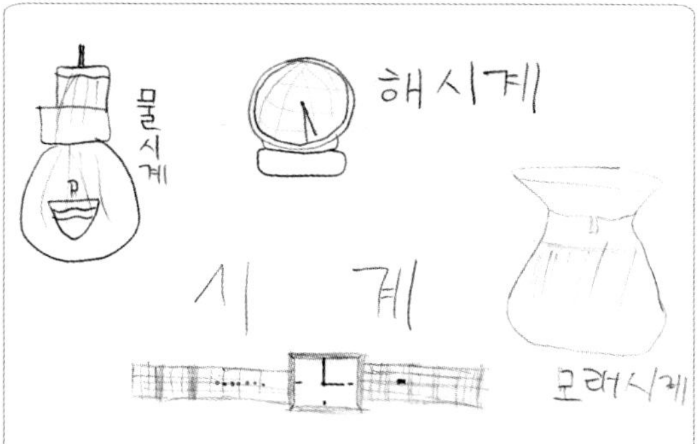

친구 예삐랑 놀기

정원 속의 곰과 꽃

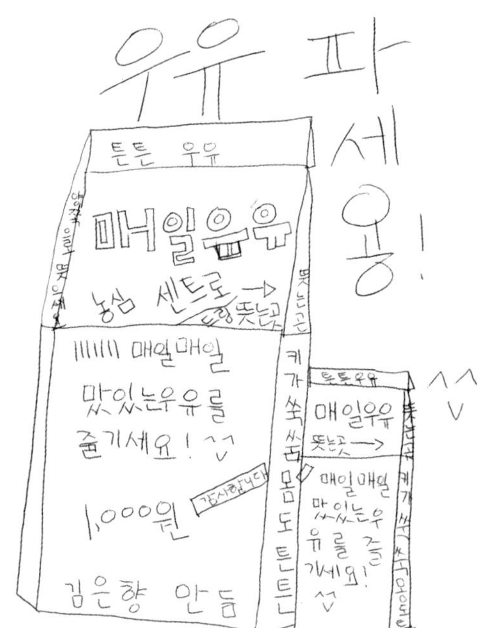

우유를 많이 먹어야 건강해져요.

운동회 줄당기기

레인보우-태양빛을 분석해 봅니다. 프랑스 메종 오브제 전시회

저 열심히 공부하죠?

어린 시절 가야금 연주를 좋아했어요

I ♥ 국악 모자이크

〈우정의 네트워크〉

미국에 친구들과의 우정

2 그래픽·만화

어린 시절부터 사물을 관찰하는 것을 즐겼던 것 같아요.

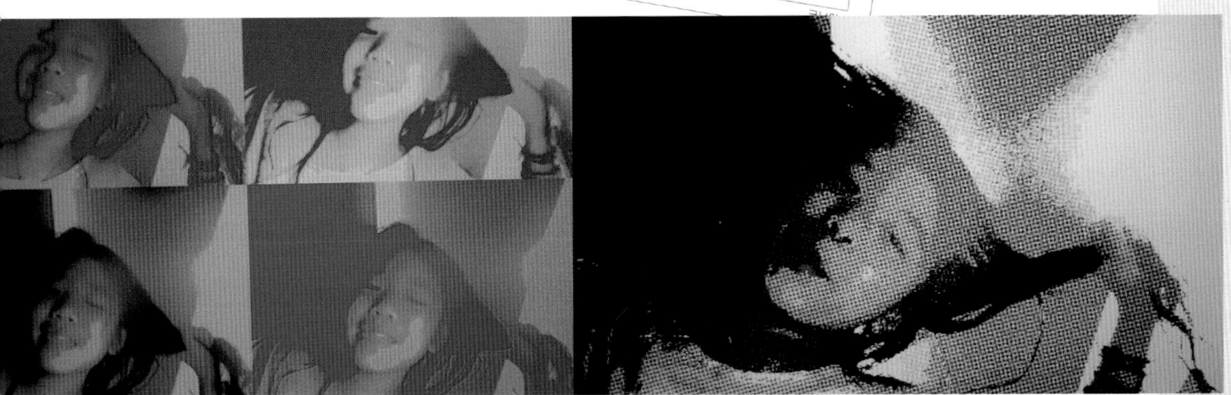

컴퓨터 그래픽으로 합성한 김은향 작품(2010).

〈그림일기〉

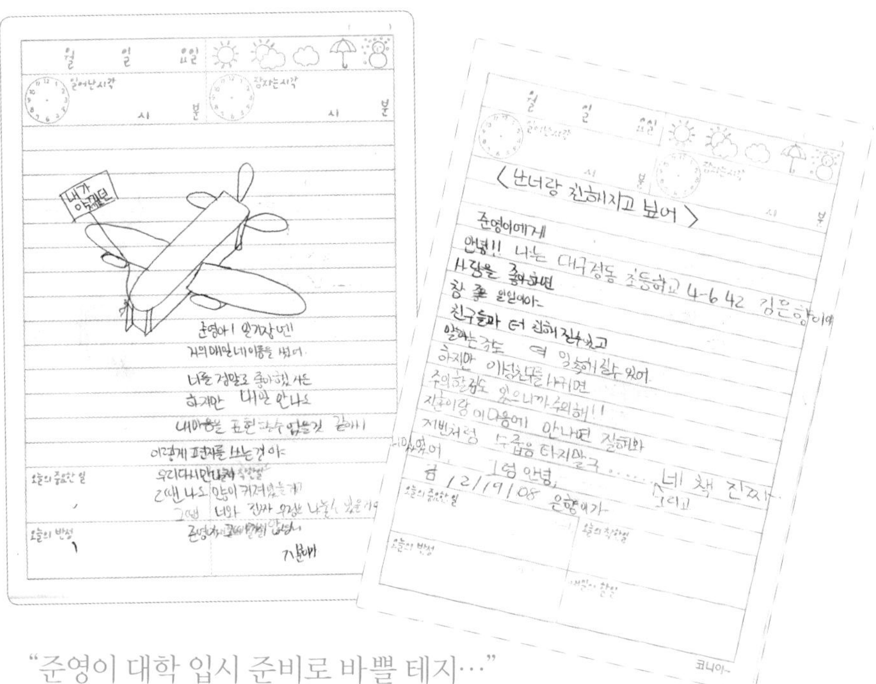

"준영이 대학 입시 준비로 바쁠 테지…"

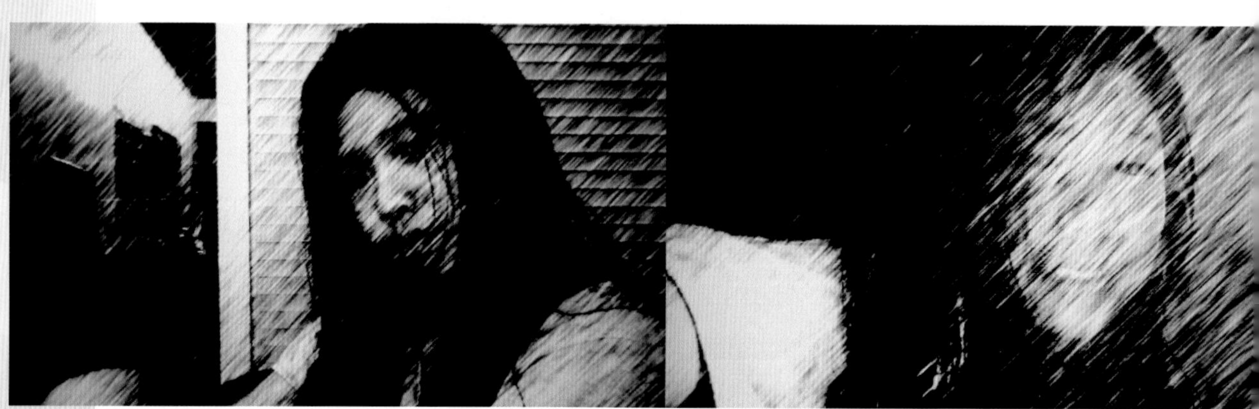

아티스트 백남준 같은 Neo-artist Kim.(2010).

"친구 정아가 그립고 보고 싶다."

생명의 나무. 김은향(2010)

"만화 그림을 자세히 보세요.
저의 얼린 시절의 이야기가 보석처럼 박혀 있어요."

환상(Kim, 2010)

생일 축하해
Excuse Me Miss
SHINee

Part 3

글읽기와 글쓰기

1 독후감

2009-03-20-금요일

독서감상문
리더십 1, 2를 읽고...

리더십 1, 2에나오는 등장인물들은 엄석대와 또다른 반장이다. 그들은 반을 이끌어 먼저 마지막 최종 체크포인트에 도착하는 사람이 이기는데. 석대는 이기는것만 생각하고 자기 팀원들은 생각하지 않는다. 하지만 그반면에 다른 반은 잘 무사히 잘 견디며 도착한다.

* 나는이것을 보고 나도 다른 반처럼 나자신만, 이기젹이 아닌 서로 아끼며 생각해주는 친구가 되고싶다

2009-03-20-금요일 〈『리더십』 1, 2를 읽고…〉

리더십 1, 2에 나오는 등장 인물들은 엄석대와 또 다른 반장이다. 그들은 반을 이끌어 먼저 마지막 최종 체크포인트에 도착하는 사람이 이기는데...

석대는 이기는 것만 생각하고 자기 팀원들은 생각하지 않는다. 하지만 그 반면에 다른 반은 잘 무사히 잘 견디며 도착한다.

* 나는 이것을 보고 나도 다른 반처럼 나 자신만, 이기적이지 아닌 서로 아끼며 생각해 주는 친구가 되고 싶다.

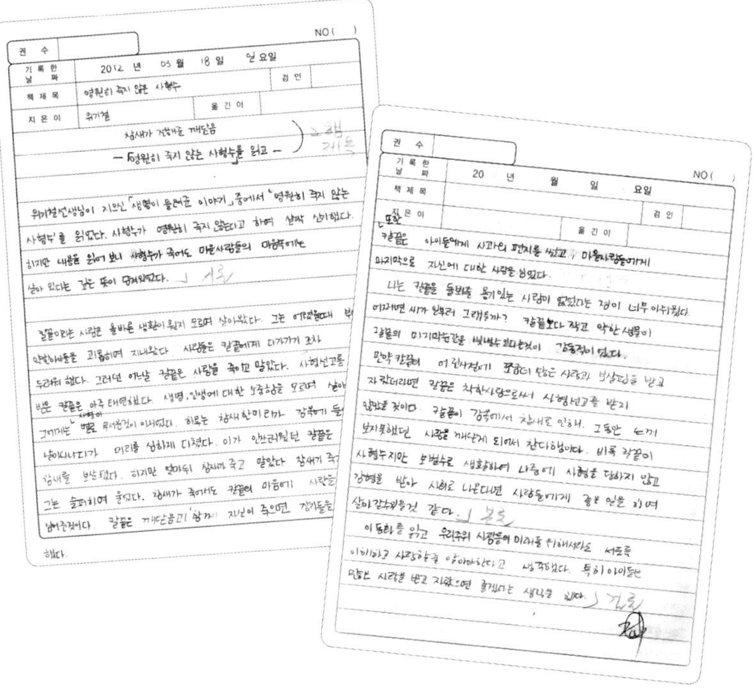

권 수	
기록한 날짜	2012 년 03 월 18 일 일 요일
책제목	영원히 죽지 않는 사형수
지은이	위기철

참새가 전해준 깨달음
— 영원히 죽지 않는 사형수를 읽고 —

2012년 03월 18일 일요일

참새가 전해준 깨달음—『영원히 죽지 않는 사형수』를 읽고

위기철 선생님이 지으신 「생명이 들려준 이야기」 중에서 '영원히 죽지 않는 사형수'를 읽었다. 사형수가 영원히 죽지 않는다고 하여 살짝 신기했다. 하지만 내용을 읽어 보니 사형수가 죽어도 마을 사람들의 마음 속에는 살아 있다는 깊은 뜻이 담겨 있었다.

칼끝이라는 사람은 올바른 생활이 뭔지 모르며 살아왔다. 그는 어렸을 때부터 약한 아이들을 괴롭히며 지내왔다. 사람들은 칼끝에게 다가가기조차 두려워했다. 그러던 어느날 칼끝은 사람을 죽이고 말았다. 사형선고를 받은 칼끝은 아주 태연했다. 생명, 인생에 대한 소중함을 모르며 살아왔던 그에게는 사형이 별로 무서운 것이 아니었다. 하루는 참새 한 마리가 감옥에 들어와 날아다니다가 머리를 심하게 다쳤다. 이것이 안쓰러웠던 칼끝은 참새를 보살폈다. 하지만 얼마 뒤 참새가 죽고 말았다. 참새가 죽자, 그는 슬퍼하며 울었다. 참새가 죽어서도 칼끝의 마음에 사랑을 심어준 것이다. 칼끝은 깨달음과 함께 자신이 죽으면 장기들을 기증하겠다고... 또한 칼끝은 아이들에게 사과의 편지를 썼고, 마을 사람들에게 마지막으로 자신에 대한 사랑을 심었다.

나는 칼끝을 돌봐줄 용기 있는 사람이 없었다는 점이 너무 아쉬웠다. 어쩌면 새가 일부러 그랬을까? 칼끝보다 작고 약한 생물이 칼끝의 마지막 순간을 빛낼 수 있다는 것이 감동적이었다.

만약 칼끝의 어린 시절에 조금 더 많은 사랑과 보살핌을 받고 자랐더라면 칼끝은 착한 사람으로서 사형선고를 받지 않았을 것이다. 칼끝이 감옥에서 참새로 인해 그동안 느껴보지 못했던 사랑을 깨닫게 되어서 참 다행이다. 비록 칼끝이 사형수지만 모범수로 생활하여 나중에 사형을 당하지 않고 감형을 받아 사회로 나온다면 사람들에게 좋은 일을 하여 살아갈 수 있을 것 같다.

이 동화를 읽고 우리 주위 사람들의 미래를 위해서라도 서로를 이해하고 사랑할 줄 알아야 한다고 생각했다. 특히 아이들은 많은 사랑을 받고 자랐으면 좋겠다는 생각을 했다.

2012년 04월 15일 일요일

라가도 『연옥의 교실』

어제 비행기를 타기 전에 추리소설 하나를 샀다.

너무 재밌어서 하루 만에 다 읽었다. 제목은 '라가도'이고 지은이는 모로즈미 다케이코이다. 플라북스에서 나온 책이다.

책 표지를 보면 공포스러우면서 음침한 모습의 그림이 그려져 있다. 자살한 리나의 아버지가 교실에서, 학살극을 벌였다. 하지만 아빠가 기억상실하는 탓에 경찰은 상황을 재현한다. 평범한 따돌림으로 인한 학살극이라고 처음에는 모두 주장하지만, 증인, 보모님들, 40명의 반 학생들이 알려주는 진실들이 얽히고설켜 시시각각 뒤집힌다. 나중에는 처음에 예상했던 추리와 정반대로 끝난다. 나는 이 책을 대낮에 방에서 읽고 있었는데도 불구하고 소름이 쫙 끼쳐서 거실로 나가서 읽었다. 다름에는 다른 미스테리 소설물도 사서 읽어야겠다. 이 라가도라는 책을 영화로 만든다면 진짜 대박날 것 같다.

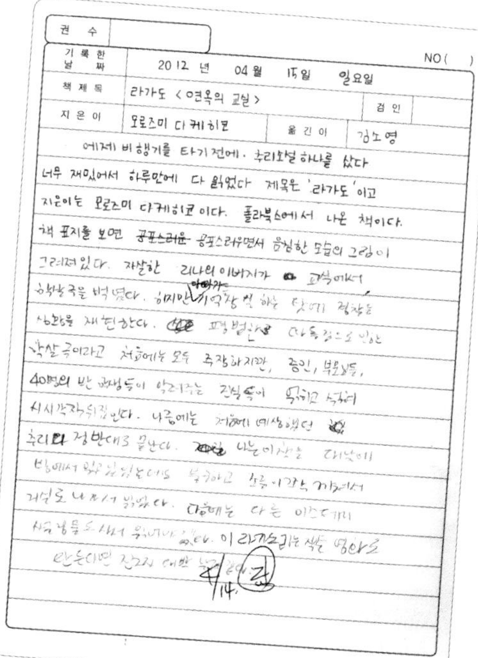

권수	

NO( )

기록한 날짜	2012 년 04 월 15 일 일요일		
책제목	라가도 <연옥의 교실>	검인	
지은이	모로즈미 다케히코	옮긴이	김소영

에제 비행기를 타기전에. 추리소설 하나를 샀다
너무 재밌어서 하루만에 다 읽었다 제목은 '라가도'이고
지은이는 모로즈미 다케히코 이다. 플라북스에서 나온 책이다.
책 표지를 보면 ~~공포스러운~~ 공포스러우면서 음침한 모습의 그림이
그려져 있다. 자살한 리나의 아버지가 교실에서
학살극을 벌였다. 하지만 아빠가 기억상실 하는 탓에 경찰은
상황을 재현한다. 평범한 따돌림으로 인한
학살극이라고 처음에는 모두 주장하지만, 증인, 부모님들,
40명의 반 학생들이 알려주는 진실들이 얽히고 설켜
시시각각 뒤집힌다. 나중에는 처음에 예상했던
추리와 정반대로 끝난다. 나는 이 책을 대낮에
방에서 읽고 있었는데도 불구하고 소름이 쫙 끼쳐서
거실로 나가서 읽었다. 다음에는 다른 미스테리
소설물도 사서 읽어야겠다. 이 라가도라는 책을 영화로
만든다면 진짜 대박 날 것 같다.
4/14.

87

Part 3. 글읽기와 글쓰기

기가 막히는 운명-『수난이대』를 읽고-7월 18일

요즘 세대에는 느낄 수 없는 전쟁의 고통과 극복의지를 이야기한 하근찬의 '수난시대'를 읽었다. 2대에 걸친 수난 이야기이다. 아들 진수가 돌아온다는 소식에 기쁜 마음으로 만도는 정거장으로 간다. 하지만 다리를 잃고 나무목발 하나로 지탱하며 서 있는 아들을 보고 가슴이 무너져내린다. 만도는 집으로 돌아오는 길에 술사발을 몇 잔을 해치우고 아들에게 어떻게 하다가 이렇게 됐는지 묻는다.

수류탄 쪼가리가 원인인 것을 알고 아버지는 절망해 하소연하는 아들을 위로한다. 일제시대 징용으로 끌려가 팔을 잃은 아버지 만도와 6.25전쟁에서 팔을 잃은 진수는 서로 서로의 팔과 다리가 되어 주며 외나무다리를 건넌다. 아들의 잘려나간 다리를 보는 아버지의 고통과, 팔을 잘린 아버지를 보는 아들의 고통이 뼛속까지 전해져 온다. '수난이대'가 전해주는 기막힌 두 부자의 운명은 독자들의 마음을 찡하게도 하지만, 우리 민족의 역사적인 고통도 전해준다.

만도와 진수는 앞으로 자신이 가진 장애를 극복하고 열심히 살았으면 좋겠다. 세계에서 유일하게 분단국가인 우리나라가 전쟁의 상처를 안고 가는 사람들이 아직도 있다.

만도와 진수가 겪었던 그런 고통은 우리 세대나 우리 후손들이 겪을 가능성이 없는 것은 아니다. 그런 불행을 두 번 다시 겪지 않을려면 통일을 해야 한다. 하지만 통일이라는 단어는 너무 쉽지만, 아주 먼 길이다. 우리 지도자들이 조금만 덜 이기적이고 욕심이 많지 않았으면 좋겠다. 통일로 가기까지 우리에게 장애물은 많을 것이다. 하지만 시간이 걸리더라도 조금씩조금씩 빨리 통일의 그 길로 나아갔으면 하는 바람 간절하다.

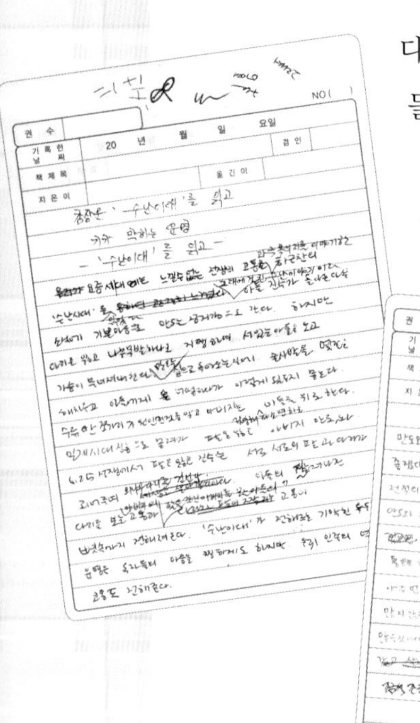

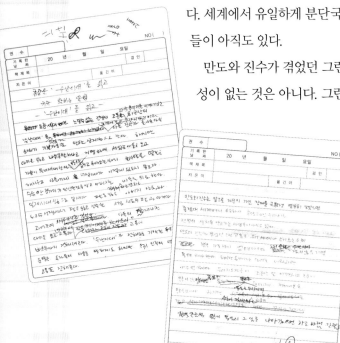

허영심이 불러온 비극-『목걸이』를 읽고-7월 22일

예나 지금이나 허영심을 가진 사람들이 있다. 모파상의 소설 목걸이는 그런 사람의 이야기이다. 르와젤 부인은 고가의 목걸이를 살 능력이 되지 않는다. 어느날 무도회 초대를 받자 친구를 찾아가 목걸이를 빌린다. 그녀는 사람들의 주목을 받으며 파티를 즐긴다. 너무나 빛나고 아름다운 목걸이였지만, 파티가 끝나고 나서 목걸이가 없어졌다. 당황한 남편과 르와젤 부인은 목걸이를 찾아보지만, 결국엔 찾지 못한다. 고가의 보석을 잃어버렸다는 생각에 친구에게 부부는 전재산을 처분하고 돈을 빌려 같은 목걸이를 사서 돌려준다. 그리고 10년 동안 힘든 일을 하여 돈을 벌어서 빚을 갚는다. 몇년이 흐른 뒤 그 보석의 값을 갚는다.

힘들게 일해온 탓에 마틸다 르와젤은 못 알아볼 정도로 변해졌다. 어느날 길을 가다가 친구를 만난다. 하지만 친구가 르와젤의 비참한 모습을 못 알아보자 사진이 누군지 말한다. 그리고 친구의 목걸이를 잃어서 똑같은 걸 산 목걸이값을 갚느라 이렇게 됐다고 한다. 그 말을 듣고 친구는 놀라지만 감동을 받으며 말했다. "그 목걸이는 가짜였소"라고.

인간의 허영심이란 자기가 가진 것에 만족 못하고 남의 것을 탐내거나 남의 것을 더 가지고 싶어하는 것이다. 사람들은 자신의 것을 사랑하고 자신이 가진 것에 감사할 줄 알아야 한다. 르와젤 부인 고가의 보석으로 치장하고 싶었던 것과 같이 사람들도 보통 비싼 물건을 갖고 싶은 것보다 더 많은 것을 갖고 싶어한다. 하지만 이 물질들이 우리에게 주는 행복은 한계가 있다. 이 소설을 통해서 나는 내가 가진 것에 만족하고 감사하고 내 모습 그대로 사랑해야 한다는 것을 깨달았다. 르와젤 부인 같은 사람이 되지 않기 위해 눈에 보이는 물질에 집착하지 않고 가진 것에 감사할 것이다.

<After Reading the 'Necklace'>

There are people with vanities. The book 'Necklace' by Guy De Maupassant talks about vanity. One day, a poverty-stricken woman named Mathilde Loisel was invited to a ball party and decided to borrow a necklace from her friend. The shiny necklace caught many people's attention. She enjoyed having all eyes on her. After the party ended, the necklace disappeared. She and her husband searched for it but could not find it. Thinking the necklace forever lost, she sold her house and took loans to buy the exact same necklace for her friend. She worked vigorously to pay off the debt for 10 years.

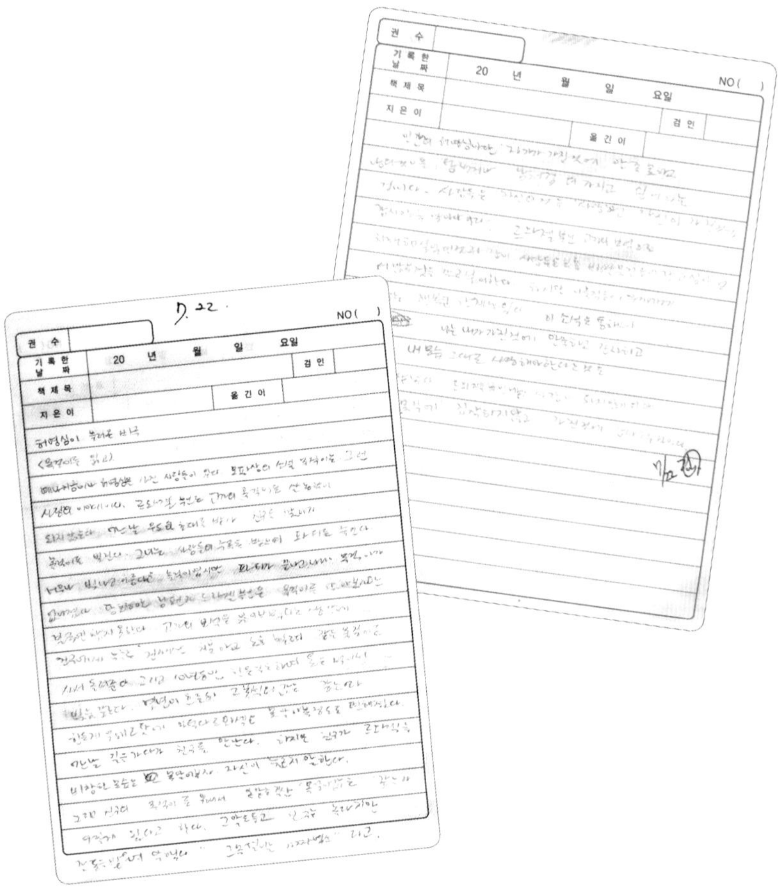

Because of those years of working hard, Mathilde's appearance changed until she was unrecognizable. One day, she bumped into her friend, but the friend could not tell who she was. After telling her friend who she was, she explained the reason for her change in appearance. When the friend heard about all the troubles she went through, the friend told her that the necklace was fake in a teary voice.

The vanity of humanity is not being satisfied with what you have and coveting something that is not yours. People should learn how to love and take satisfaction in what he or she has. Just like how Mathilde Leslie wanted to possess the expensive necklace, people want something more than they can afford. But these tangible objects can have only limited value for our happiness. This book has taught me how to accept and love what I have without desiring for more. To avoid becoming like Mathilde, I will not focus on tangible stuffs and be thankful for what I already have.

경동 초딩 김은향

2 일기

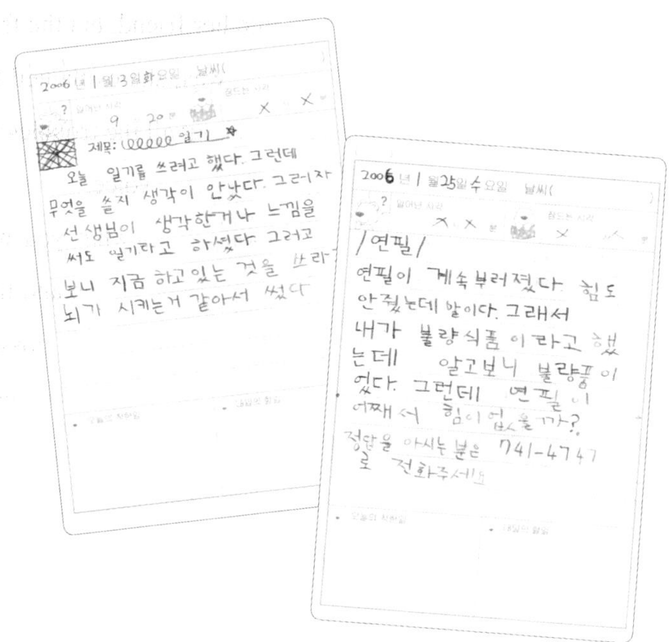

2006년 1월 3일 화요일 〈일기〉

오늘 일기를 쓰려고 했다. 그런데 무엇을 쓸지 생각이 안 났다. 그러자 선생님이 생각한 거나 느낌을 써도 일기라고 하셨다. 그러고 보니 지금 하고 있는 것을 쓰라고 뇌가 시키는 거 같아서 썼다.

2006년 1월 25일 수요일 〈연필〉

연필이 계속 부러졌다. 힘도 안 줬는데 말이다. 그래서 내가 불량식품이라고 했는데, 알고 보니 불량품이었다. 그런데 연필이 어째서 힘이 없을까?

정답을 아시는 분은 741-4747로 전화주세요.

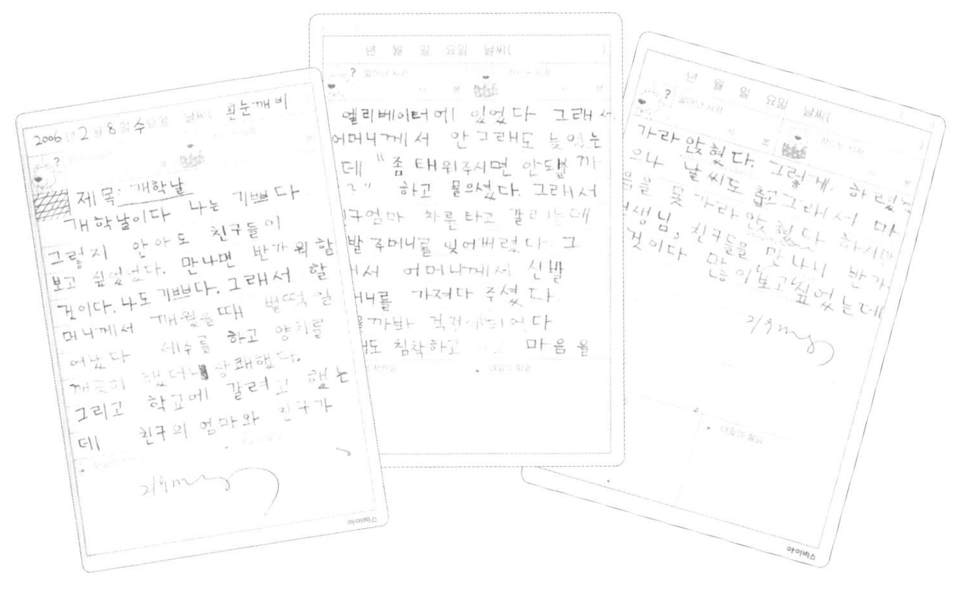

2006년 2월 8일 수요일 날씨 (흰눈깨비) 〈개학날〉

개학날이다. 나는 기쁘다. 그렇지 않아도 친구들이 보고 싶었었다. 만나면 반가워할 것이다. 나도 기쁘다. 그래서 할머니께서 깨웠을 때 벌떡 일어났다. 세수를 하고 양치를 깨끗이 했더니 상쾌했다. 그리고 학교에 갈려고 했는데 친구의 엄마와 친구가 엘리베이터에 있었다. 그래서 어머니께서 안 그대로 늦었는데, “좀 태워주시면 안 될까요?” 하고 물으셨다. 그래서 친구 엄마 차를 타고 갈려는데 신발주머니를 잊어버렸다. 그래서 어머니께서 신발주머니를 가져다 주셨다. 늦을까 봐 걱정이 되었다. 그래도 침착하고 가고 마음을 가라 앉혔다. 그렇게 하려했으나 날씨도 춥고 그래서 마음을 못 가라 앉혔다. 하지만 선생님, 친구들을 만나니 반가울 것이다. 많이 보고 싶었는데.....

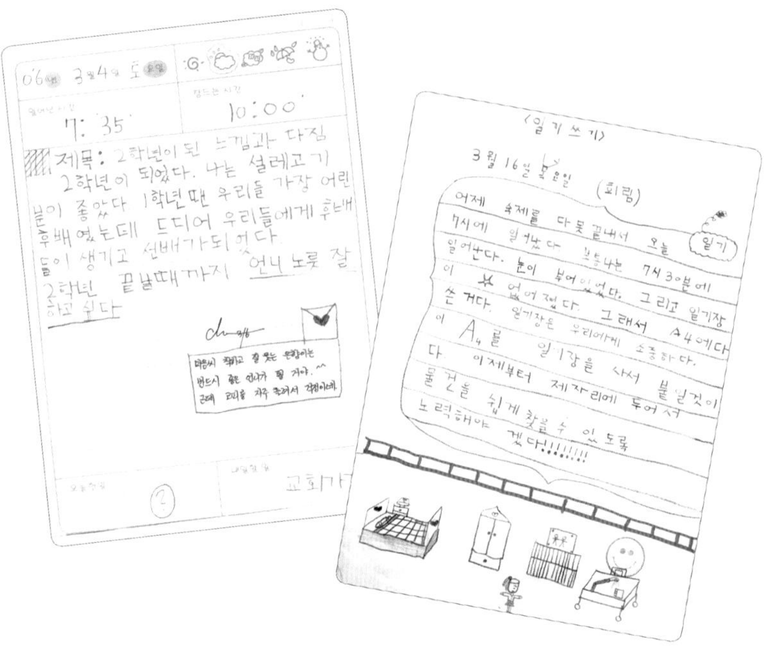

2006년 3월 4일 토요일 〈2학년이 된 느낌과 다짐〉

2학년이 되었다. 나는 설레고 기분이 좋았다. 1학년 땐 우리들 가장 어린 후배였는데, 드디어 우리들에게 후배들이 생기고 선배가 되었다.

2학년 끝날 때까지 언니 노릇 잘하고 싶다.

2006년 3월 16일 목요일

어제 숙제를 다 못 끝내서 오늘 7시에 일어났다. 보통 나는 7시 30분에 일어난다. 눈이 부어 있었다. 그리고 일기장이 없어졌다. 그래서 A4에다 쓴 거다. 일기장은 우리에게 소중하다. 이 A4를 일기장을 사서 붙일 것이다. 이제부터 제자리에 두어서 물건을 쉽게 찾을 수 있도록 노력해야겠다!!!!!!

2006년 3월 29일 수요일 〈짝궁〉

짝궁은 착하다. 하지만 우리반 모두의 짝들이 행복하면 좋겠는 생각도 든다. 내 짝궁은 쉬는 시간에 내가 책을 펴줘야 한다. 그것이 고칠 점이다. 짝궁이 별로 힘이 없는 것 같다. 비록 나도 고칠 점이 있겠지만.....

형균아, 우리 힘을 모아 사이 좋은 친구가 되자. 화이팅!

March 29, 2006 Title: **My Classmate Next To Me**

My classmate next to me is nice. I hope all my classmates are happy. I have to open a book for my classmate next to be even during break times. That is something to work on. He looks weak. I'm sure I have something to work on, too…

Hyung Gyun, let's work hard and be good friends!

3월 29일 수 요일

일어난 시각 시 분 잠자는 시각 시 분

제목: 짝궁

짝궁은 착하다. 하지만 우리반 모두의 짝들이 행복하면 좋겠는 생각도 든다. 내짝궁은 쉬는 시간에 내가 책을 펴줘야한다 그것이 고칠점이다. 짝궁이 별로 힘이 없는것 같다. 비록 나도 고칠점이 있겠지만......
형균아, 우리 힘을 모아 사이좋은 친구가 되자 화이팅!

오늘의 중요한 일 오늘의 착한일

오늘의 반성 내일의 할일

4월 18일 화요일 〈현장 체험 학습〉

오늘 현장 체험 학습을 어린이 회관으로 갔다. 그런데 다리가 아팠다. 왜냐하면 우리집 산을 넘어서 갔기 때문이다. 그기에서 밥을 먹었다. 할머니께서 김밥을 싸주셨다. 맛있었지만 내가 아파서 별로 그저 그랬다. 어린이회관 안에 들어가서 물건들과 물고기들을 관찰했다. 악어도 있었다. 가까이 갔는데도 입을 벌리지 않았다. 재미있었고 신기하였다.

April 18th Tuesday <A Field Trip>

Today, I went on a field trip to Children's Hall. My legs are hurting because I had to hike across the mountain from my house. I ate my lunch there. My grandma made kimbap for me. It was delicious but I could not enjoy much because of my legs. Inside Children's Hall, I observed the buildings and fish. There were crocodiles, too. They did not open their mouths when I went closer. It was fun and interesting.

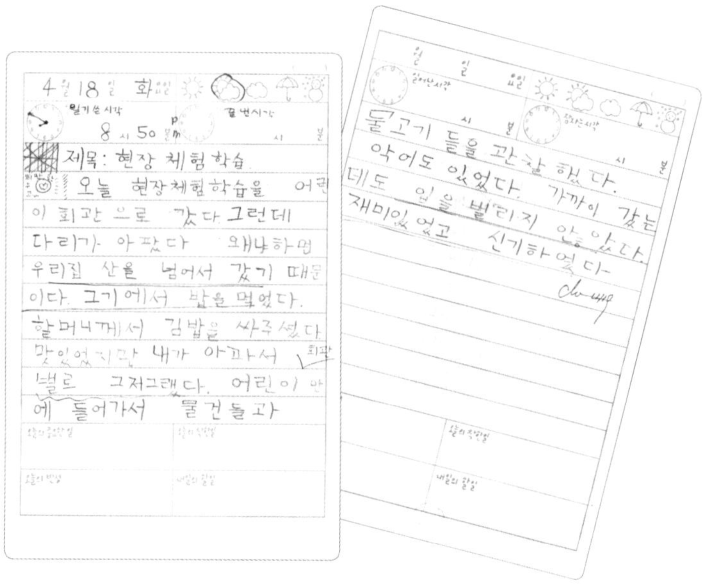
4월 18일 화요일
8시 50 pm
제목: 현장 체험 학습
오늘 현장체험학습을 어린
이 회관 으로 갔다 그런데
다리가 아팠다 왜냐하면
우리집 산을 넘어서 갔기 때문
이다. 그기에서 밥을 먹었다.
할머니께서 김밥을 싸주셨다
맛있었지만 내가 아파서
별로 그저그랬다. 어린이 안
에 들어가서 물건들과
물고기 들을 관찰 했다.
악어도 있었다. 가까이 갔는
데도 입을 벌리지 않았다.
재미있었고 신기하였다.

5월 10일 수요일 〈책읽기〉

안녕? 일기장아? 오늘 내가 읽은 책을 간단히 간추릴께. 나는 "토끼의 꼬리는 짧아"라는 책을 또박 또박 읽었어. 토끼와 친구들이 꼬리가 짤뚝짤뚝하게 짧다고 놀려서 도망을 깡충깡충 뛰며 달아났지. 씨익 소리가 나는 신문에 나왔대. 산양할아버지가 토끼의 친한 친구처럼 대해 주는 할아버지야! 깜짝 노랄 수밖에... 토끼도 화가 활랄활랄하게 나서 꼬리를 자르려다가 실수해서 꼬리가 더 짧아진거래.

재미있지? 나같은 깡총깡총 토끼를 위로해 주었겠지.

너는? 어 시간이 다됐네... 안녕!

May 10th Wednesday <Reading Books>

Hello, my diary. Let me briefly summarize what I read today. I read 'The Rabbit's Tail is Short'. The rabbit's friends teased how short his tail was, so he hopped away. It was held in a newspaper. The Grandpa from the forest befriended the rabbit. What a surprise…the tail got shorter for trying to escape.

Isn't it fun? He befriended a hopping rabbit like me.

How about you? Oh, the time is up already… Goodbye!

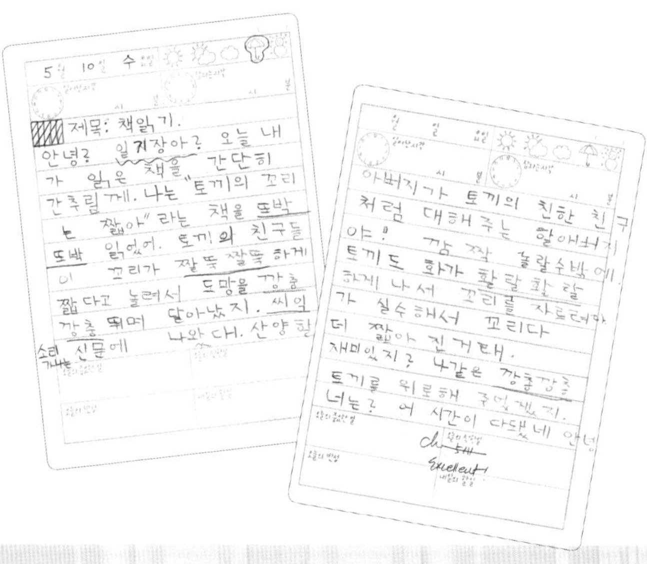

5월 13일 토요일 〈부모님께 감사편지 쓰기〉

부모님께

어머니, 아버지!

낳아주시고 길러주셔서 정말 감사해요.

말 수줍어 말할 때 교육을 바로시켜 해주시는 부모님!

이제부터 씩씩한 착한 아이로 자랄께요.

딸

May 13th Saturday <A Thank-You Letter To My Parents>

Dear my parents,

Mom and Dad!

Thank you for letting me in to this world and raising me.

You always correct me when I'm doing wrong.

I'll be a good kid.

From your Daughter

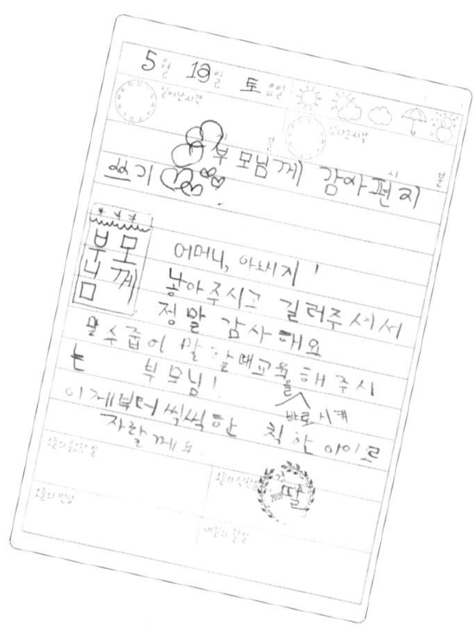

5월 13일 토요일

부모님께 감사편지 쓰기

부모님께

어머니, 아버지!

낳아주시고 길러주셔서

정말 감사해요

말수줍어 말할때교육을 바로시켜 해주시는 부모님!

이제부터 씩씩한 착한 아이로 자랄께요.

딸

8월 29일 금요일 〈4학년 1학기를 마치며〉

개학한 날 그저께 같은데 눈이
깜짝할 사이에 1학기가 끝났네

방학한 날이 그저께 같은데
눈이 깜짝할 사이에 방학이 끝났네

그래 1학기 괜찮았지만
그래 이제 괜찮지만

친구들의 마음 내 마음은
다 잘했을까와 잘할까의 바람이
담겨 있을 거야

선생님 한 학기 동안 고생하셨는데
우리 말썽꾸러기 가르치느라 고생하셨는데

이제 알겠어, 그래 알겠다.
왜 선생님이 우리를 가르키시는지

우리를 훌륭하게 만들려고 했을 거야
그래 그랬을 거야

내 마음 선생님을 존경하는 마음,
감사함이 들어 있고 한 번이라도
선생님의 어깨를 두드려 주고 싶은 마음

1학기 재미있었고
그래 보람찼고
혼나기도 했지만
그게 그저 사랑인 거야

다음부터 더 열심히 하는 게 내 마음속에
그거뿐이지.

2학기는 어떨지 가슴은 두근두근거린다.

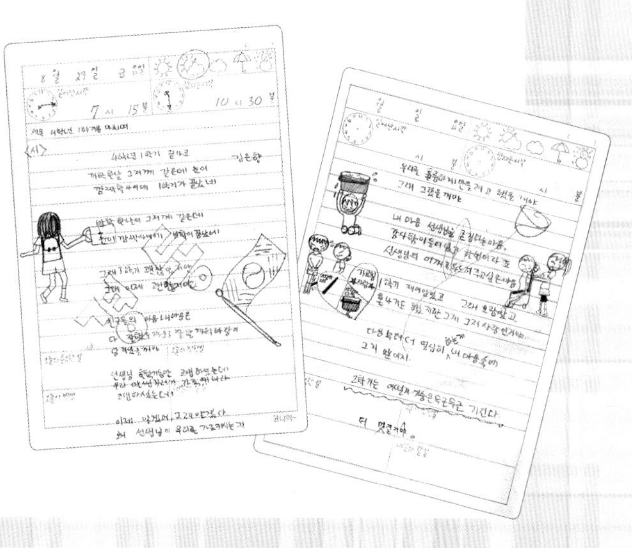

2008. 09. 15

오늘 나는 도쿄를 갔다가 왔다. 나는 도쿄를 금요일날 아침 6:00에 갔다가 오늘 왔다. 도쿄를 가서 나는 옷도 사고 맛있는 음식도 먹었다. 그 중에서도 내가 싫어하던 스시를 제일 많이 먹었다. 나는 일본에 오기 전 비행기 안에서 후지산(Fugi Mountain)을 못봐서 아쉬웠다. 도쿄에는 많은 것들이 많았다. 나는 금요일날 롯본기(Roppongi)를 갔고 토요일날은 오모떼산도(Omotte-sando)를 갔다. 그리고 일요일날은 원래 Disney World(디즈니)를 가야 했는데 줄이 너무 많아서 이세오빠(나의 엄마의 친구의 아들)와 함께 내가 묵는 Tokyo Dome Hotel (도쿄돔호텔) 앞 놀이공원에서 놀았다. 거기에는 귀신의 집, 80m에서 떨어지는 것, 페라슈트, 워티슬라이더 등이 있었다.

나는 귀신의 집을 들어갔는데 무서워서 1초 만에 나왔다. 그리고 자기가 돌리는 컵도 탔는데 이세오빠는 나와서 토할 기분이었다. 나는 일요일이 제일 재미있었다. 나는 일본을 또 가고 싶다.

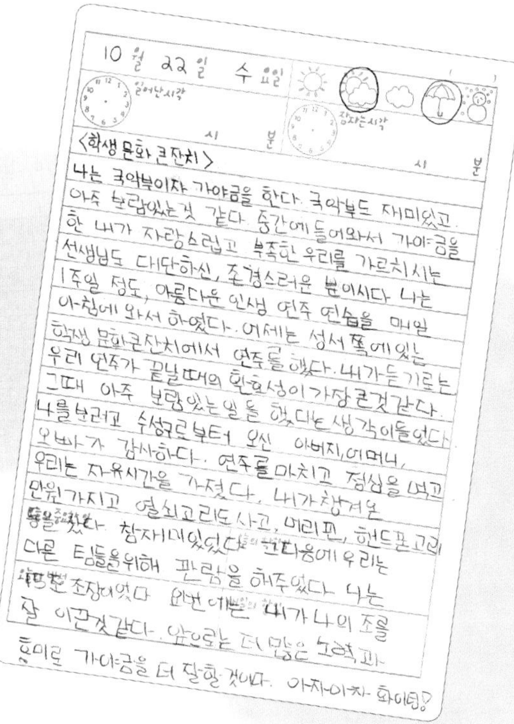

10월 22일 수요일
일어난시각 시 분
잠자는시각 시 분
〈학생문화큰잔치〉
나는 국악부이자 가야금을 한다. 국악부도 재미있고
아주 보람있는것 같다 중간에 들어와서 가야금을
한 내가 자랑스럽고 부족한 우리를 가르치시는
선생님도 대단하신, 존경스러운 분이시다 나는
1주일 정도, 아름다운 인생 연주 연습을 매일
아침에 와서 하였다. 어제는 성서쪽에있는
학생문화큰잔치에서 연주를 했다. 내가듣기로는
우리 연주가 끝날때의 환호성이 가장 큰것같다.
그때 아주 보람있는일을 했다는 생각이들었다
나를보려고 수성구로부터 오신 아버지, 어머니,
오빠가 감사하다. 연주를 마치고 점심을 먹고
우리는 자유시간을 가졌다. 내가챙겨온
만원가지고 열쇠고리도 사고, 머리핀, 핸드폰고리
등을샀다. 참재미있었다 그 다음에 우리는
다른 팀들을위해 관람을 해주었다 나는
15조 조장이었다 요번에는 내가 나의 조를
잘 이끈것같다. 앞으로는 더 많은 노력과
흥미로 가야금을 더 잘할것이다. 아자아자 화이팅!

10월 22일 수요일 〈학생문화큰잔치〉

나는 국악부이자 가야금을 한다. 국악부도 재미있고 아주 보람 있는 것 같다. 중간에 들어와서 가야금을 한 내가 자랑스럽고 부족한 우리를 가르치시는 선생님도 대단하신, 존경스러운 분이시다. 나는 1주일 정도, 아름다운 인생 연주 연습을 매일 아침에 와서 하였다. 어제는 성서쪽에 있는 학생문화큰잔치에서 연주를 했다. 내가 듣기로는 우리 연주가 끝날 때의 환호성이 가장 큰 것 같다. 그때 아주 보람 있는 일을 했다는 생각이 들었다. 나를 보려고 수성구로부터 오신 아버지, 어머니, 오빠가 감사하다. 연주를 마치고 점심을 먹고, 우리는 자유시간을 가졌다. 내가 챙겨온 만원 가지고 열쇠고리도 사고 머리핀, 핸드폰고리 등을 샀다. 참 재미있었다. 그 다음에 우리는 다른 팀들을 위해 관람을 해주었다. 나는 15조 조장이었다. 요번에는 내가 나의 조를 잘 이끈 것 같다. 앞으로는 더 많은 노력과 흥미로 가야금을 더 잘할 것이다. 아자 아자 화이팅!

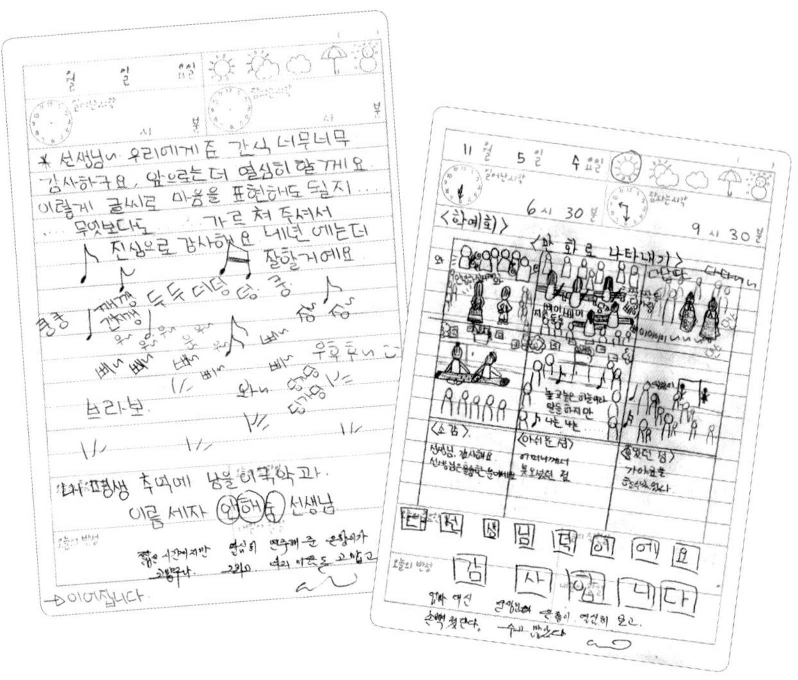

11월 16일 일요일 〈좋은 책을 읽고〉

나는 책을 읽었다. 책 제목은 난 '너랑 친해지고 싶어'이다. 그 책의 내용은 준영이가 전학을 왔다. 그런데 그 반에는 멋있는 남자 지훈이가 있었다. 그 아이는 인기는 많았지만, 말은 없고 여자 아이들에게 관심이 없다. 어느날 승민이라는 남자 아이와 짝이 되었는데 그 아이가 준영이를 좋아했다.

알고 보니 지훈이도 준영이를 도와주니 삼각관계인 것이다.

준영이는 나중에 지훈에게서 파스텔을 받았다.

그것을 경희가 보고 샘이 나서 싸움이 일어났는데, 여우 같은 경희가 준영이 친구에게 덮어씌웠다. 그 아이들은 억울했다. 싸움이 끝나고 지훈이가 전학을 가기 전날 경희는 슬퍼서 학교에서 울었다. 그리고 그날 첫눈이 온 그날 지훈이는 준영이에게 자기가 아끼던 장난감을 주며 편지도 주었다.

그 편지에는

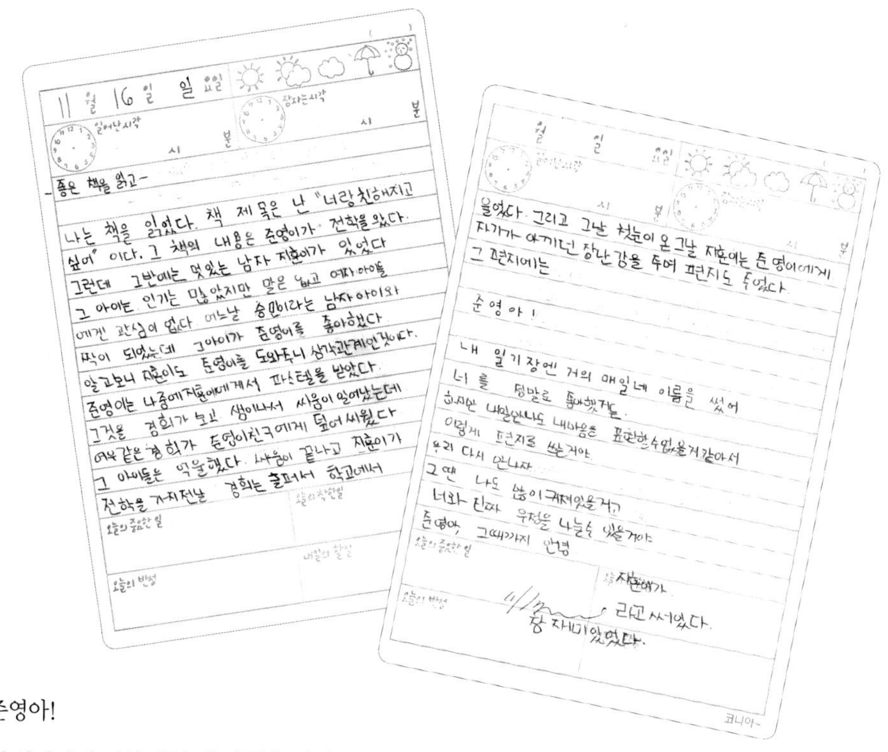

11 월 16 일 일 요일

일어난 시각 시 분

잠자는 시각 시 분

-좋은 책을 읽고-

나는 책을 읽었다. 책 제목은 난 "너랑 친해지고 싶어" 이다. 그 책의 내용은 준영이가 전학을 왔다.
그런데 그반에는 멋있는 남자 지훈이가 있었다
그 아이는 인기는 많았지만 말은 없고 여자 아이들에겐 관심이 없다 어느날 승민이라는 남자아이와
짝이 되었는데 그아이가 준영이를 좋아했다
알고보니 지훈이도 준영이를 도와주니 삼각관계인것이다.
준영이는 나중에 지훈에게서 파스텔을 받았다
그것을 경희가 보고 샘이나서 싸움이 일어났는데
여우같은 경희가 준영이친구에게 덮어 씌웠다
그 아이들은 억울했다 싸움이 끝나고 지훈이가
전학을 가지전날 경희는 훌퍼서 학교에서

오늘의 중요한 일

오늘의 착한일

내일의 할일

오늘의 반성

울었다. 그리고 그날 첫눈이 온 그날 지훈이는 준영이에게
자기가 아끼던 장난감을 주며 편지도 주었다
그 편지에는

준영아!

내 일기장엔 거의 매일 네 이름을 썼어
너를 정말로 좋아했거든
하지만 내일만나도 내마음은 표현할수없을거같아서
이렇게 편지로 쓰는거야.
우리 다시 만나자
그땐 나도 많이 커져있을거고
너와 진짜 우정을 나눌수 있을거야
준영아, 그때까지 안녕

지훈이가

라고 써있다.
참 재미있었다.

코니아-

준영아!

내 일기장엔 거의 매일 네 이름을 썼어

너를 정말로 좋아했거든

하지만 내일 만나도 내 마음을 표현할 수 없을 거 같아서

이렇게 편지로 쓰는 거야.

우리 다시 만나자

그땐 나도 많이 커져 있을 거고

너와 진짜 우정을 나눌 수 있을 거야

준영아, 그때까지 안녕

지훈이가

라고 써 있다. 참 재미있었다.

12월 30일

나는 오늘 내 꿈을 확실히 결심했다.
내 꿈은 화가이다.
나는 팬더를 좋아한다.

내가 좋아하는 책
친구가 만들어준 책인데....
제목은 '팬더의 사랑'이다.

등장인물: 꼬치 까리 꼬용 꼬미 꼬무

나를 깨닫게 해준 건 그 한 마디이다.
"아무 것도 해보지 않고 못한다고 하지 말 거라"이다.
그래서 나는 기말고사를 잘칠 자신이 펄펄 넘친다.
나는 용기를 낼 것이다.
나는 중이(중학교 2학년)화가이고 꼭 잘될 것이다.

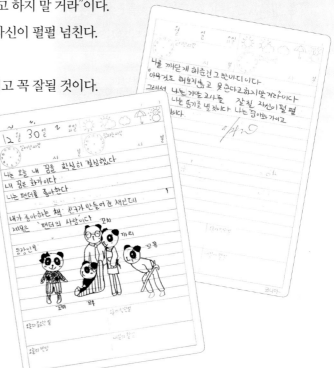

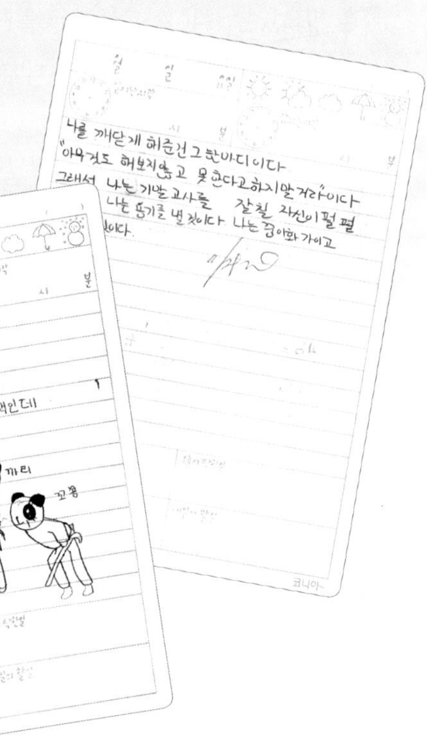

12월 30일
나는 오늘 내 꿈을 확실히 결심했다
내 꿈은 화가이다
나는 팬더를 좋아한다
내가 좋아하는 책 친구가 만들어준 책인데
제목은 '팬더의 사랑'이다 꼬치
까리
꼬용
등장인물
꼬미
꼬무

나를 깨닫게 해준건 그 한마디이다
"아무것도 해보지않고 못한다고하지말 거라"이다
그래서 나는 기말고사를 잘칠 자신이펄펄
나는 용기를 낼것이다 나는 중이화가이고
...이다.

2008년 12월 14일 토요일

오늘은 토요일이다.

나는 아직도 감기가 안 떨어져서 큰일이다.

하지만 나는 오늘 공정한 일을 했다.

우리 아버지와 이모께서 일을 하시니까 나도 함께 도운 것이다.

어른이다. 자기만 하면 안 되니까 돕는 게 당연한 일이라고 생각한다. 나는 그것 때문에 칭찬을 받았다. 기분이 참 좋았다. 나는 그때 이런 생각을 했다. '매주 토요일은 꼭 이런 일을 한 번씩 해야겠다'라고 말이다. 기분이 오늘은 칭찬도 받고 돕기도 도왔는지 참 좋았다. 오늘 같은 날이 매번 왔으면 좋겠다.

오늘 나는 친구들과 비사치기를 했다.

처음에는 어쩔 줄 몰랐지만 차츰차츰 해가기 시작했다.

팀은 이렇게 짰다.

소강이팀: 민영이, 예린이, 은동이, 소강이, 대강이

내팀: 소현이, 수현이, 나, 정아, 예진이

처음에는 우리가 차서 우리가 처음 라운드에서는 이겼다. 너무 기뻤다. 계속 놀다가 점수를 보니 3:6이였다. 9번을 한 것이다.

나의 최고 기록이다. 비사치기는 12 정도까지 하는 것이 적당하다. 2명이면 쉽고 8에서 12명이면 적당하면서도 재미있고 빠르게 할 수 있다. 그래서 나는 이렇게 오늘 놀았다. 참 재미있었고 옛날 사람들은 참 재미있는 것들을 많이 한 것 같다.

*느낀 점: 우리 조상들의 삶을 통해 많은 재미있는 게임을 배울 수 있다.

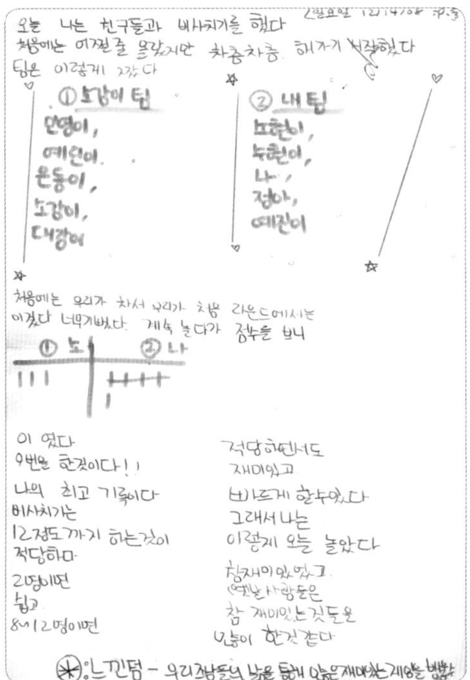
오늘 나는 친구들과 비사치기를 했다
처음에는 어쩔줄 몰랐지만 차츰차츰 해가기 시작했다
팀은 이렇게 짰다

① 소강이 팀
민영이,
예린이,
은동이,
소강이,
대강이

② 내 팀
소현이,
수현이,
나,
정아,
예진이

처음에는 우리가 차서 우리가 처음 라운드에서는
이겼다 너무기뻤다 계속 놀다가 점수를 보니

① 소	② 나
III	IIII I

이 였다
9번을 한것이다!!
나의 최고 기록이다
비사치기는
12정도까지 하는것이
적당하다
2명이면
쉽고
8에12명이면
적당하면서도
재미있고
빠르게 할수있다
그래서 나는
이렇게 오늘 놀았다
참재미있었고
옛날사람들은
참 재미있는것들을
많이 한것같다

※느낀점 – 우리조상들의 삶을 통해 많은재미있는게임을 배웠다

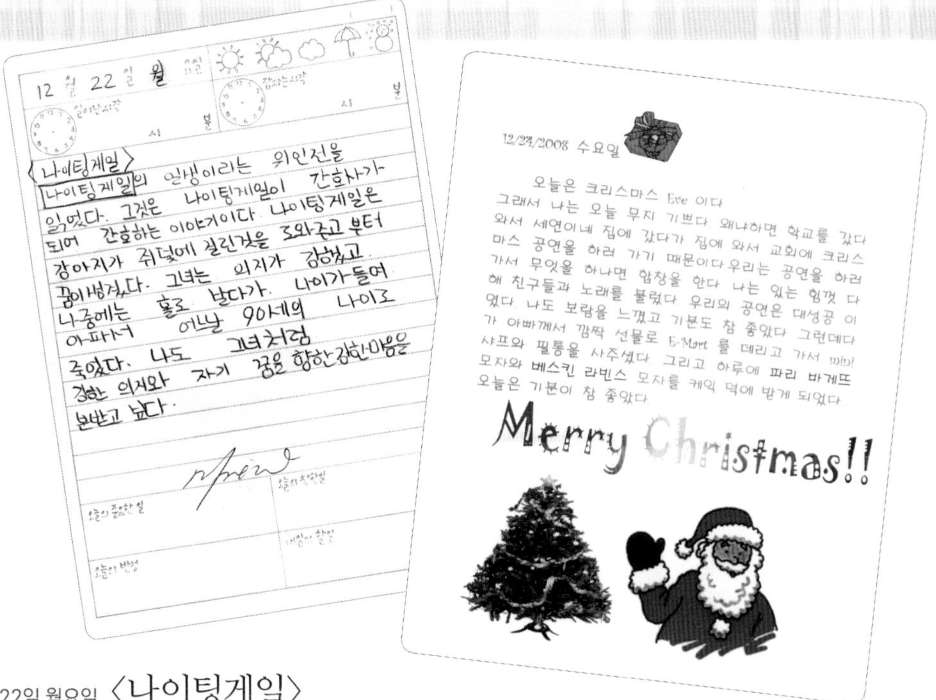
12 월 22 일 월

〈나이팅게일〉

나이팅게일의 일생이라는 위인전을 읽었다. 그것은 나이팅게일이 간호사가 되어 간호하는 이야기이다. 나이팅게일은 강아지가 쥐덫에 걸린것을 도와주고 부터 꿈이생겼다. 그녀는 의지가 강했고 나중에는 홀로 살다가 나이가 들어 아파서 어느날 90세의 나이로 죽었다. 나도 그녀처럼 강한 의지와 자기 꿈을 향한 강한마음을 본받고 싶다.

12/24/2008 수요일

오늘은 크리스마스 Eve 이다
그래서 나는 오늘 무지 기쁘다 왜냐하면 학교를 갔다 와서 세연이네 집에 갔다가 집에 와서 교회에 크리스마스 공연을 하러 가기 때문이다 우리는 공연을 하러 가서 무엇을 하나면 합창을 한다 나는 있는 힘껏 다해 친구들과 노래를 불렀다 우리의 공연은 대성공 이였다 나도 보람을 느꼈고 기분도 참 좋았다 그런데다가 아빠께서 깜짝 선물로 E-Mart 를 데리고 가서 mini 샤프와 필통을 사주셨다 그리고 하루에 파리 바게뜨 모자와 베스킨 라빈스 모자를 케익 덕에 받게 되었다 오늘은 기분이 참 좋았다

12월 22일 월요일 〈나이팅게일〉

나이팅게일의 일생이라는 위인전을 읽었다. 그것은 나이팅게일이 간호사가 되어 간호하는 이야기이다. 나이팅게일은 강아지가 쥐덫에 걸린 것을 도와주고부터 꿈이 생겼다. 그녀는 의지가 강했고, 나중에는 홀로 살다가 나이가 들어 아파서 어느날 90세의 나이로 죽었다. 나도 그녀처럼 강한 의지와 자기 꿈을 향한 강한 마음을 본받고 싶다.

2008년 12월 24일 수요일

오늘은 크리스마스 EVE이다.

그래서 나는 오늘 무지 기쁘다. 왜냐하면 학교를 갔다와서 세연이네 집에 갔다가 집에 와서 교회에 크리스마스 공연을 하러 가기 때문이다. 우리는 공연을 하러 가서 무엇을 하냐면 합창을 한다. 나는 있는 힘껏 다해 친구들과 노래를 불렀다. 우리의 공연은 대성공이었다. 나도 보람을 느꼈고 기분도 참 좋았다. 그런데다가 아빠께서 깜짝 선물로 E-Mart를 데리고 가서 mini 샤프와 필통을 사주셨다. 그리고 하루에 파리 바게뜨 모자와 베스킨 라빈스 모자를 케익 덕에 받게 되었다. 오늘은 기분이 참 좋았다.

2008년 12월 25일 목요일

오늘은 기다리고 기다리던 크리스마스이다.

오늘 나는 영화 〈벼랑 위의 포뇨〉도 보러가고 Out Back도 가고 오빠가 모래에 큰 아주 큰 곰인형을 부친다고 했다. 오늘은 정말 북적거렸다.

크리스마스라서 그런가보다.

나는 오늘 선물을 많이 못 받았으나 재미있었고 멋진 날이었다. 나는 크리스마스가 한 달에 1번이면 좋겠다.

모두에게 메리 크리스마스!!

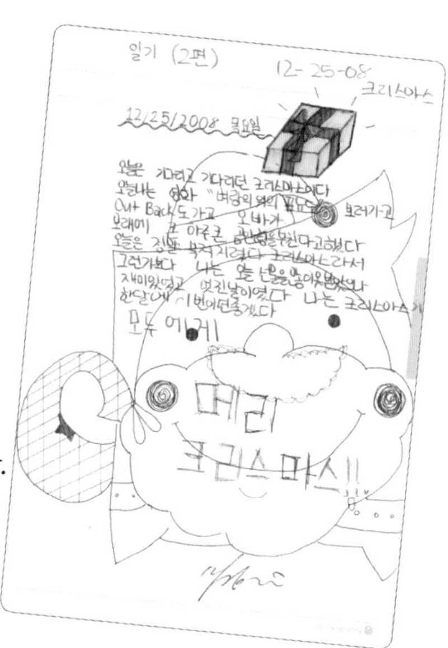

5월 28일 수요일 날씨: 비

오늘 나는 "네덜란드에서 보물찾기"라는 책을 읽었다. 그리고 나는 학교를 1학기 처음부터 다니지를 않아 학교생활이 약간 서툴다. 하지만 나는 내가 잘 적응할 것을 믿는다. "네덜란드에서 보물찾기"는 아주 모험적인 책이다. 아주 cool한 캐릭터들이 유명한 화가(진짜 화가 아님)의 그림을 찾으러 간다. 하지만 그 아이들이 가장 도둑이라고 생각한 사람은 마크 영 맨. 그리고 이 책을 쓴 사람은 곰돌이 co. 그림 강경효. 나는 피카소, 렘브란트, 모네와 등등의 화가들처럼 유명한 화가가 될 것이다. 하지만 내가 가장 걱정된 것은 내 수학 숙제다. 원래 어제 숙제였는데 못했다. 숙제는 배운 데까지(p.88) 못푼 것 푸라는 것이였다. 일단은 학교 갔다와서 할 것이 무지 많았다. 게다가 나는 1쪽부터 한 73쪽은 해야 한다. 나는 선생님이 화를 안 내시고 이해하시면 좋겠다.

^^* 선생님 죄송합니다. *^^

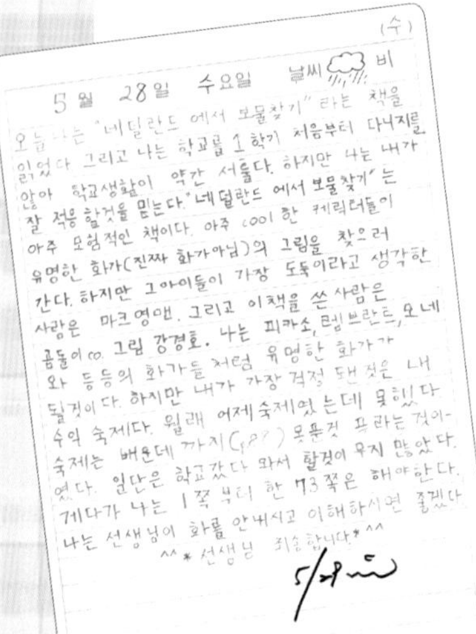

7월 6일 일요일 날씨: 더움

오늘은 무척 더웠다. 꼭 찜질방에 온 것 같았다. 하지만 교정을 해서 너무 차가운 것은 못 먹어 괴로웠다. 나는 한편 아이스크림은 싫었지만 이제는 무척 좋아한다. 나는 아이스크림 중에서도 셔벳이 가장 낫다. 나는 이빨교정을 빨리하고 내가 좋아하는 아이스크림 셔벳을 먹으면 좋겠다. 교정 그만하는 그날까지!!!

7월 25일 금요일

나는 오늘 은향이만의 필기체를 만들었다.
그것은 좁다리이다. "좁다리"는 ________ 에 맞추어 그 스페이스 안에서 쓰는 필기체이다.
예=♡이것좀 보세요♡ 그리 왜 좁다리이야면 나는 ________ 을 좁은 다리로 생각하였다.
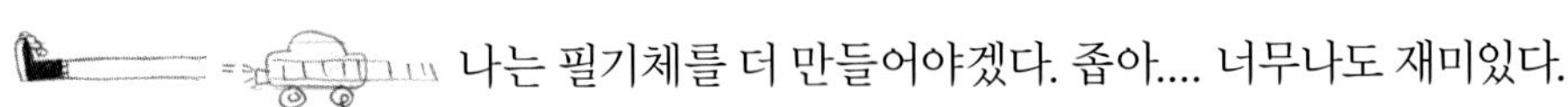 나는 필기체를 더 만들어야겠다. 좁아…. 너무나도 재미있다.

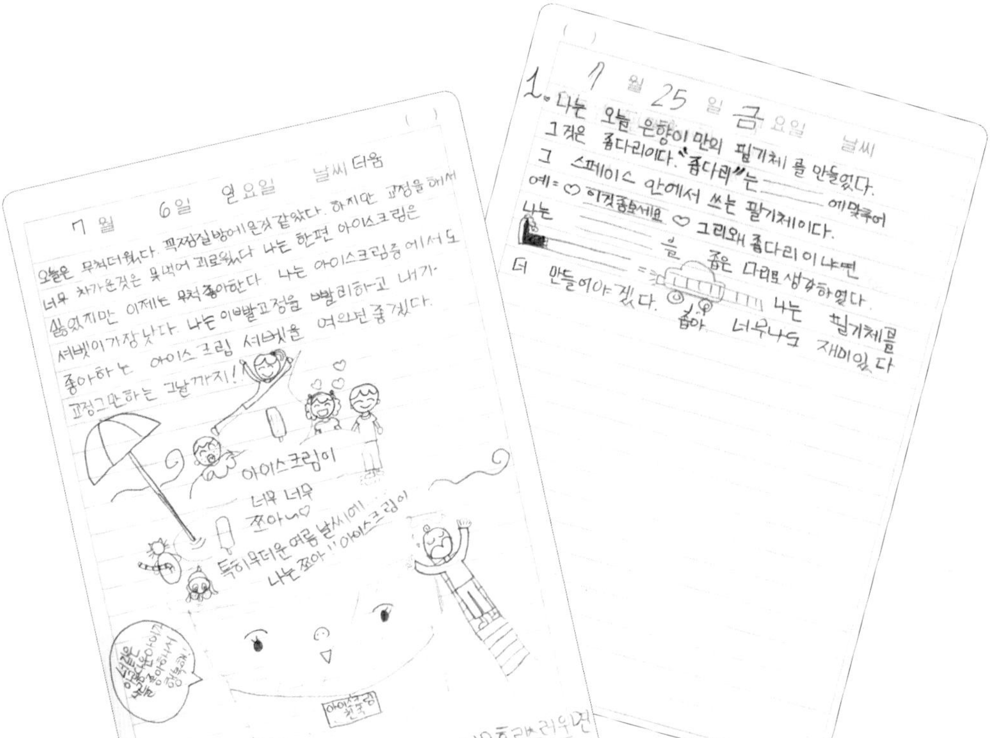

7월 27일 일요일

마지막으로 나는 구름체를 만들었다. 구름체는 구름처럼 둥실둥실 떠다니는 것을 표현한 것이다. 예를 들면=♡안녕하세요 저는 김은향이에요♡ 그리고 왜 구름체이냐면 둥실둥실 삐뚤삐뚤하게 써서 떠다니는 것처럼 하여 그렇다. 나는 좁다리, 사랑체, 구름체 중에서 좁다리가 제일 좋다. 필기체를 만드는 것은 즐겁다.

8월 1일 금요일

나는 왜 한국은 미국과 달리 공부를 하는지 모르겠다. 미국은 아이들이 키가 큰데....

한국은 크지 않다. 나는 대부분의 부모님들이 이해하면 좋겠다. 왜냐하면 아이들은 자유가 필요하고 운동이 필요하다.

8월 2일 토요일

나는 다음 주에 홍콩을 간다. 나는 너무 기대된다. 나는 여행 가는 것이 좋다. 경험도 하고 재미있게 놀고 맛있는 것 먹는 이런 재미 말이다. 나는, 노는 것을 좋아하고 그림 그리는 것이 좋다. 그러나 방학동안도 할 일이 너무너무 많아서 탈이다. 이제부터 보람차게 보내야겠다.

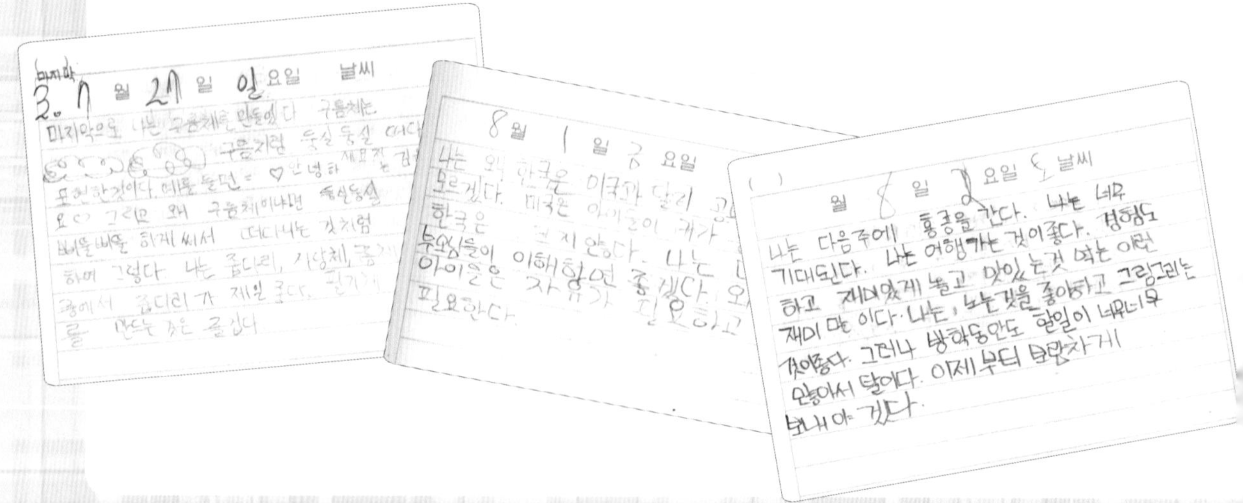

8월 23일 토요일

내일 모레는 꿈같은 개학이다. 그리고 오늘 베이징에서 야구대표팀이 금메달을 땄다. 아주 좋았다. 그리고 쿠바는 세계에서 야구를 잘한다고 알려져 있는 나라다. 그리고 김혜은 내 사촌 언니는 '태양의 여자'에 나온다. 언니는 MBC 아나운서였다. 신기했고 내일이 올림픽 마지막인데 잘해야겠다. 대한민국 파이팅!!

8월 24일 일요일

여름방학을 마감하며

나는 방학 동안 많은 일을 겪고 마음에 안 드는 일도 있었지만 아주 알차고 기쁜 방학을 보냈다. 나는 부산도 가고 많은 일을 했다. 하지만 어쩌면 내가 공부를 노는 것보다 더 많이 했을지도 모른다. 다음에는 더 알찬 방학을 보내야지~~

이제 학교 가니까 김은향 파이팅~~~

2009년 5월 7일 목요일

2일 전날에는 어린이날이었다. 나는 어린이날을 기념으로 엄마와 아빠와 오빠랑 부산에 갔다. 부산하면 회, 바다가 생각난다. 부산에서는 월요일 오후 첫날에는 오빠와 함께 바닷가에 가서 자연산 미역을 잡고 공놀이를 하며 놓았다. 그냥 어린이날이고 날씨가 아직 많이 한여름이 아니라 그런지 사람들이 별로 없었다. 저녁에는 TV에까지 나왔다는 유명한 멸치횟집에 갔다. 나는 멸치회는 맛있었으나 다른 것은 내 또래의 아이들에게는 맞지 안나보다. 우리 아버지께서는 "캬, 시원하다..." 하시며 아주 맛있게 잡수셨다. 나는 얼굴을 찌푸리며 "아빠만 그러겠지요..." 하며 속으로 생각했다. 호텔에 다시 들어가서, 쉴려고 하였는데 많이 안 먹어서 그런지 오빠와 다시 간단하게 먹으로 갔다왔다. 오면서 오빠는 "니, 안 춥나?"라고 물었다. 나는 춥다고 말했다. 부산이 밤에는 많이 추운가보다. 들어와서 취침을 취할려고 하는데 잠이 안 왔다. 하지만 결국에는 잤다. 다음날에는 그냥 선물 옷 몇 벌, 가방, 핀(머리), 접시세트를 받았다. 그리고 또 놀다가 음식을 사서 대구로 향했다. 가는 길 심심해서 책보다가 멀미가 나서 먼산을 봤지만 피곤했는지 잤다. 나의 어린이날은 그렇게 재밌게 끝났다. 이런 날이 또 오면 좋겠다.

2009년 5월 9일 토요일

나는 오늘 교회서 1시에 버스를 타고 성일교회로 향했다. 왜냐하면 스타킹에 나온 버블쇼 아저씨가 라이브쇼를 했기 때문이다. 우리는 3층에서 보았다. 아쉽게도 십층에 있었기 때문에 도와줄 어린이가 아무도 안 입었다. ㅠㅠ 나는 좀 아쉬웠다. 아저씨는 버블(비눗방울)로 코끼리, 왕관, 목걸이, 눈사람을 만들었다. 하지만 우습게도 사람을 비눗방울 안에 들어가게 한다고 애들을 앞으로 나오게 했는데 실패를 한 것이다. 속으로 "왜, 스타킹에 나왔지?" 싶었다. 희한했지만 재미있었다. 이것을 보며 각각 사람은 자기만의 재능이 다 다르지만 있구나라고 생각했다.

2009년 5월 12일 화요일

ㅋㅋ 지금 현재는 11:25분이다. 나는 지금 쓸 게 없어서 내가 가장 심하게 감기 걸렸을 때에 대하여 말을 할 것이다.

가장 심하게 걸렸을 때가 나의 열은 99.6이었다. 병원에서 x-ray를 찍어보니 폐렴 위험성이 보이지만, 괜찮을 거라고 했다. 근데 뜻밖에도 병원에서 우연히 내가 옛날에 다니던 영어학원 쌤이 계셨다. 나는 너무 반가워서 인사를 한 5번은 했다. 그리고 주사를 맞고 닝겔을 맞았다. 나는 닝겔 맞는 것에 익숙해서 안 아프고 이 정도는 아무것도 아니다. 하지만 병원비도 돈이니까 이제는 건강하게 안 아프면 좋겠다.

*선생님 왈, 체온이 99.6 No~~ 39.6도 아닐까?

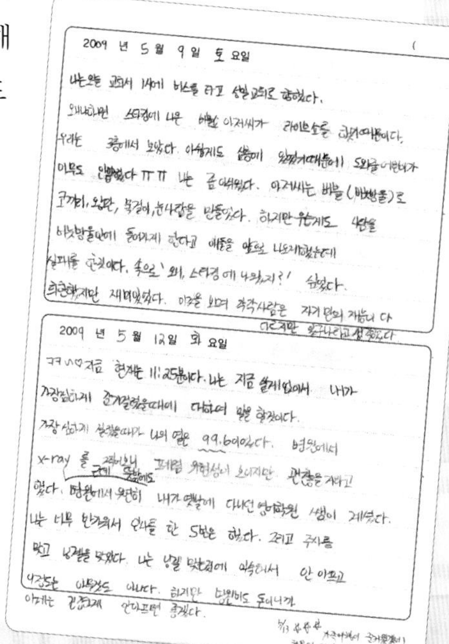

2009 년 5 월 9 일 토 요일 ( )

나는 오늘 교회서 1시에 버스를 타고 성일교회로 향했다.
왜냐하면 스타킹에 나온 버블쇼 아저씨가 라이브쇼를 했기때문이다.
우리는 3층에서 보았다. 아쉽게도 십층에 있었기때문에 도와줄 어린이가
아무도 안입었다 ㅠㅠ 나는 좀 아쉬웠다. 아저씨는 버블(비눗방울)로
코끼리, 왕관, 목걸이, 눈사람을 만들었다. 하지만 우습게도 사람을
비눗방울안에 들어가게 한다고 애들을 앞으로 나오게했는데
실패를 한것이다. 속으로 '왜, 스타킹에 나왔지?' 싶었다.
희한했지만 재미있었다. 이것을 보며 각각사람은 자기만의 재능이 다
다르지만 있구나라고 생각했다

2009 년 5 월 12 일 화 요일

ㅋㅋ ♡ 지금 현재는 11:25분이다. 나는 지금 쓸게없어서 내가
가장심하게 감기걸렸을때에 대하여 말을 할것이다.
가장 심하게 걸렸을때가 나의 열은 99.6이었다. 병원에서
x-ray를 찍어보니 폐렴 위험성이 보이지만 괜찮을거라고
했다. 병원에서 우연히 내가 옛날에 다니던 영어학원 쌤이 계셨다.
나는 너무 반가워서 인사를 한 5번은 했다. 그리고 주사를
맞고 닝겔을 맞았다. 나는 닝겔 맞는것에 익숙해서 안 아프고
이정도는 아무것도 아니다. 하지만 병원비도 돈이니까
이제는 건강하게 안아프면 좋겠다.

2009년 5월 14일 목요일 〈내일은 스승의 날....〉

내일은 스승의 날이다. 지금까지 나를 보살펴 주시고 그만큼 키워주신 1~5학년까지의 선생님께 감사한다.

나는 그래선지 영어선생님들, 지금 계시는 지난 담임선생님과 등등의 교과선생님께 꽃과 카드를 드릴려고 준비를 했다. 비록 지금 5-3반 선생님과 함께 한 시간이 짧지만 앞으로 더욱 더 즐거울 거라고 나는 믿는다. 그리고 친구들과 함께 일찍 가서 칠판을 꾸밀 것이다. 내일 선생님의 웃음과 교실 분위기가 기대된다.

20019년 5월 15일 금요일 〈오늘은 스승의 날!!!〉

오늘은 스승의 날이다. 오늘의 이벤트는 성공적으로 해냈다. 하지만 가장 좋은 것은 우리반만 거의 6교시를 영화 보며 놀았다는 것이다. 그 영화는 (?) 밀리언에어이다. ☆-영화요약-라말이라는 아이가 청년이 되어 아무도 풀지 못한 60억 달러가 걸린 것을 풀었다. 하지만 어려운 문제였기 때문에 경찰관이 라말을 체포해서 어떻게 맞췄냐고 묻는다. 이야기는 이렇게 시작된다. 장면들은 추억(옛)→현실(문제)로 계속 왔다갔다한다. 그는 자기가 겪은 추억과 본 것으로 문제를 푸는 것이였다. 그 와중 (?)티카라는 여자 아이를 찾으려고도 한다.

마지막에는 여자와 라말이 행복하게 눈치챌 것없이 만나며 끝나는데, 뒤로 이야기가 또 있는지는 모르겠다.

정말 인상 깊은 영화였다.

선생님, 모어주셔서 감사해요!!!

가르쳐주셔서 감사해요!!

사랑해요!!

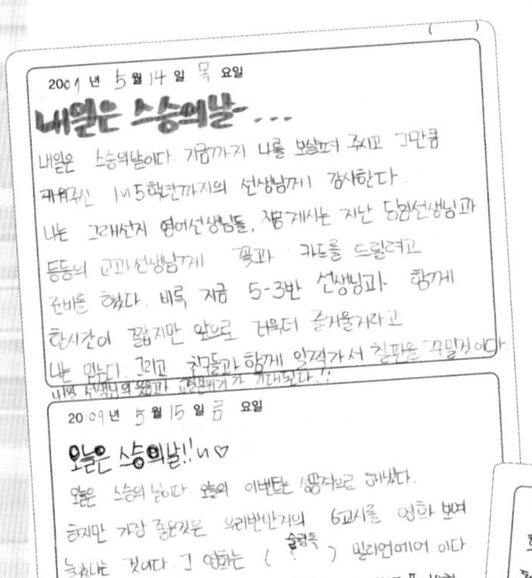
2001 년 5 월 14 일 목 요일
내일은 스승의날...
내일은 스승의날이다. 지금까지 나를 보살펴 주시고 그만큼 키워주신 1~5학년까지의 선생님께 감사한다.
나는 그래선지 영어선생님들, 지금 계시는 지난 담임선생님과 등등의 교과선생님께 꽃과 카드를 드릴려고 준비를 했다. 비록 지금 5-3반 선생님과 함께 한시간이 짧지만 앞으로 더욱더 즐거울거라고 나는 믿는다. 그리고 친구들과 함께 일찍가서 칠판을 꾸밀것이다. 내일 선생님의 웃음과 교실분위기가 기대된다.!!
20 09 년 5 월 15 일 금 요일
오늘은 스승의날!! ㅋ♡
오늘은 스승의 날이다 오늘의 이벤트는 성공적으로 해냈다. 하지만 가장 좋은것은 우리반만 거의 6교시를 영화 보며 놀았다는 것이다 그 영화는 (?) 밀리언에어 이다.
☆-영화요약-라말이라는 아이가 청년이되어 아무도 풀지못한 60억 달러가 걸린것을 풀었다. 하지만 어려운 문제였기 때문에 경찰관이 라말을 체포해서 어떻게 맞췄냐고 묻는다.
이야기는 이렇게 시작된다. 장면들은 추억(옛) → 현실(

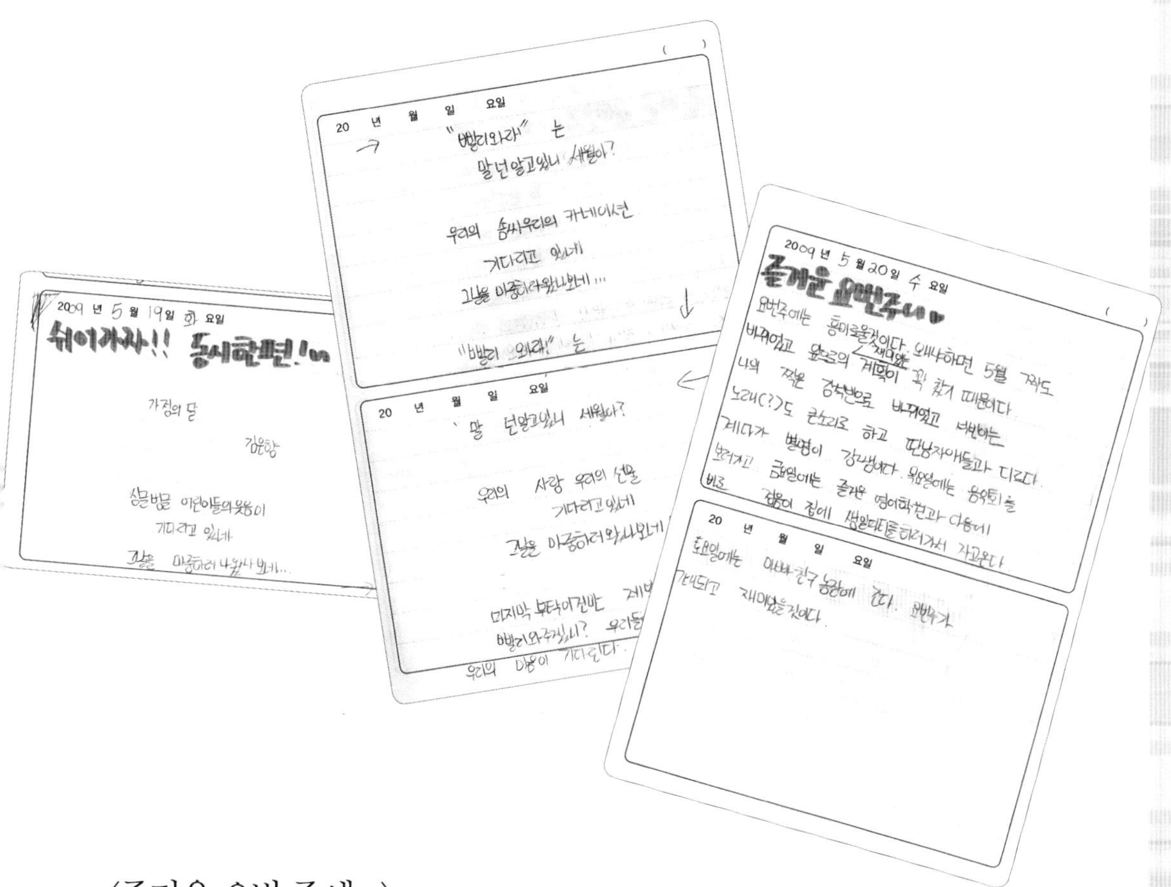

〈즐거운 요번 주에...〉

요번 주에는 흥미로울 것이다. 왜냐하면 5월 짝도 바뀌었고 앞으로의 재미있는 계획이 꽉 찼기 때문이다. 나의 짝은 강석빈으로 바뀌었고 석빈이는 노래(?)도 큰소리로 하고 딴 남자애들과 다르다. 게다가 별명이 강쌤이다. 목요일에는 음악회를 보러가고 금요일에는 즐거운 영어학원과 다음에 바로 정음이 집에 생일파티를 하러가서 자고 온다. 토요일에는 아빠 친구 농장에 간다. 요번 주가 기대되고 재미있을 것이다.

2009년 5월 21일 목요일 〈아무도 못보는 비밀 일기!!!〉

우리 반은 다 아는 비밀. 내가 누군가를 좋아한다는 사실.
고백은 받아봐도 이것은 처음이다....
나의 최고 비밀은 들통 났고 이 비밀은....
1) 우리 오빠는 청와대에서 일한다.
2) 1st 오빠는 31, 2nd 오빠는 29, 아빠는 61, 엄마는 55이다.
3) 나의 비밀. (제가요 저번에 이것에 대해 섰는데...)

하지만 이것으로 말미암아 나의 일깃감이 더 많아져서 좋다. 나만의 비밀이 있다는 게 뿌듯하다. 하지만 어떨 때는 답답하기 때문에 이불에 대고 소리를 지른다. 어차피 거의 다 아는 나의 사랑비밀, 가끔씩 스트레스나 소리를 지르게 하지만 다 말하고 싶다.

2009년 5월 26일 화요일 〈알뜰시장〉

오늘 우리는 알뜰시장을 했다. 하지만 그렇게 기대했던 알뜰시장이 꿈같이 지나가 버렸다. 게다가 처음부터 운이 안 좋았다. 초콜릿, 아이스크림, 빠삐코를 사고 컵데기를 버렸는데 터져서 손에 다 묻었다.

그래서 휴지를 감싸서 먹었다. 그리고 1~4학년이 좋고 예쁜 물건을 다 쓸어가서 살 게 없었다. ㅠㅠ

하지만 옷 3벌 등을 조금 샀다. 보니까 남자애들은 놀기만 하고 아무 것도 거의 산 거 같지가 않다. 하지만 내가 낸 한푼 한푼의 돈이 좋은 곳에 쓰일 것을 생각하니 뿌듯했다. 그리고 물건이 필요없이도 모처럼 좋은 일과 시간을 짧더라도 보낸 것 같다.

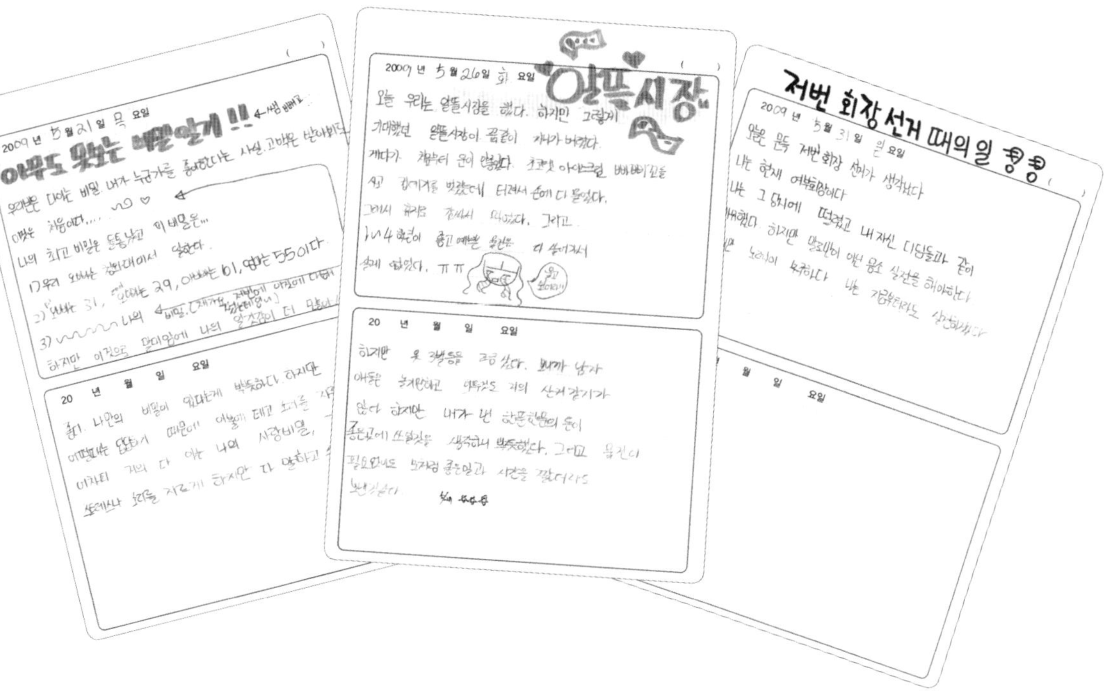

2009년 5월 31일 일요일 〈저번 회장선거 때의 일!!〉

오늘은 문득 저번 회장 선거가 생각났다.

나는 현재 여부회장이다.

나는 그 당시에 떨렸고 내 자신 디딤돌과 같이 비유했다. 하지만 말로만이 아닌 몸소 실천을 해야 한다. 하지만 노력이 부족하다. 나는 지금부터라도 실천하겠다.

2009년 3월 6일 금요일 〈미국 여행〉

나는 학교 방학 때 2달 간 어머니와 아버지와 미국 아틀란타를 다녀왔다. 그때도 재밌었지만 가장 기억에 남는 여행은 미국 말레시아에 갔던 기억이다. 말레시아는 정말 아름다웠다. 내가 5살 때 갔다왔는데 얼마나 좋았으면 지금까지 기억에 남는다. 말레시아에서는 한 1~2주 동안 있었는데 날씨도 하루 빼고 정말 좋고 맑았다. 호텔도 희한하게 호수에 떠 있는 집 한 채 한 채였다. 호텔 안에는 정말 아름다웠다. 호텔은 이렇게 생겼다.

이 구조는 생각만 해도 가고 싶을 것이다. 모험을 좋아하고 아름다운 풍경을 좋아하는 사람은 말레시아를 정말 좋아할 것이다.

3월 12일 목요일

나는 오늘 여름을 나타내는 문양을 발명해 보았다.

그리고 계절별....

겨울 봄 가을

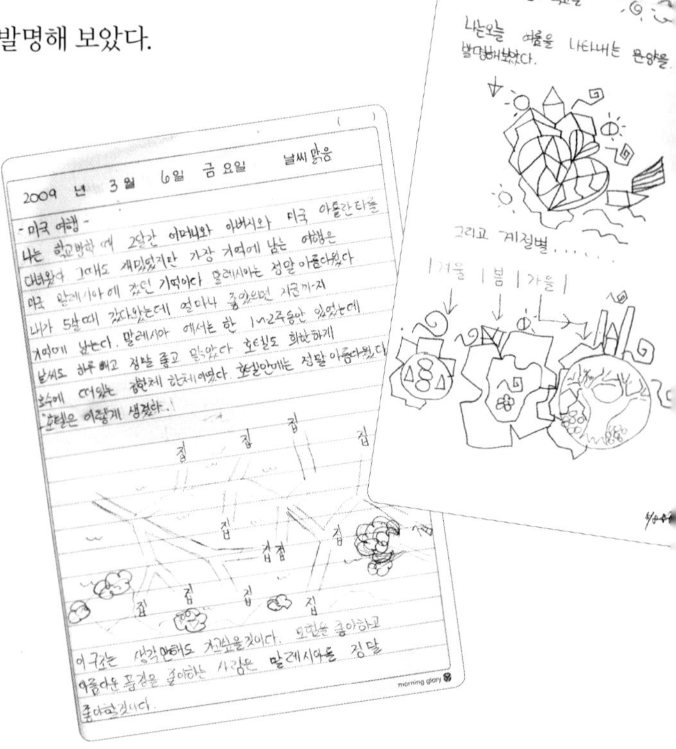

2009년 3월 21일 토요일

나는 오늘 너무 뿌듯했고 재미있었다.

오늘 학교 마치고 은소와 정음이와 함게 정음이네에서 놀다가 성경 공부를 하고 한샘교회를 가서 놀고 집에 왔다. 그리고 e-mart(이마트)에 가서 옷을 사고 쿠션과 베게, 운동화, 나의 새 수저 등등을 사서 저녁을 외식하고 왔다. 집에 와서는 개운하게 tub 욕조에서 복욕을 했다. 정말로 행복한 날이였고 재비있었다.

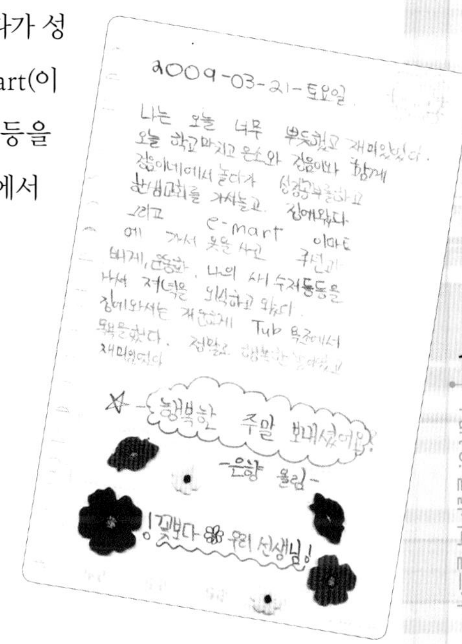

2009-03-21-토요일

나는 오늘 너무 뿌듯했고 재미있었다.
오늘 학교마치고 은소와 정음이와 함께
정음이네에서 놀다가 성경공부를하고
한샘교회를 가서놀고 집에왔다.
그리고 e-mart 이마트
에 가서 옷을 사고 쿠션과
베게, 운동화, 나의 새 수저등등을
사서 저녁을 외식하고 왔다.
집에와서는 개운하게 Tub 욕조에서
목욕을했다. 정말로 행복한 날이였고
재미있었다

☆-행복한 주말 보내셨어요?
-은향 올림-

!꽃보다 우리 선생님!

행복한 주말 보내셨어요?

-은향 올림-

2009년 3월 22일 일요일

선생님께

안녕하세요. 저는 5학년 3반 24번 김은향 여부회장입니다.

요즘은 화창한 날씨가 계속되고 있습니다.

저도 회장과 함게 우리반의 꽃을 피우겠습니다.

선생님,

이 봄의 Charm

행운을 떼어가세요.

***ㅎㅎㅎ은향이 덕분에 행복한 걸....

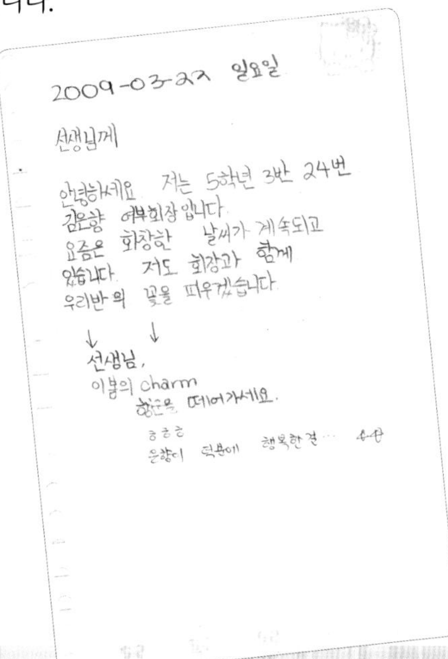

2009-03-22 일요일

선생님께

안녕하세요 저는 5학년 3반 24번
김은향 여부회장 입니다
요즘은 화창한 날씨가 계속되고
있습니다 저도 회장과 함께
우리반의 꽃을 피우겠습니다

선생님,
이봄의 charm
행운을 떼어가세요.

ㅎㅎㅎ
은향이 덕분에 행복한 걸…

2008년 3월 24일 화요일

나는 만화를 잘 그린다.

그 중에서 내가 좋아하는 3가지의 그림들은 ....

1) 사이 좋은 아이들-

2) 귀염둥이

3) 친구를 위하여 연주를-

동물들도 친구를 알고 사이좋게 지내면...

·언·젠·가·우·리·세·상·도·

·전·쟁·없·이·자·유·롭·고·평·화·롭·고·

·사·이·좋·게·살·수·있·지·않·을·까·?·

·그·렇·죠·선·생·님·!·

2008 년 3 월 24 일 화 요일 날씨

나는 만화를 잘 그린다.

그중에서 내가 좋아하는 그림은 3가지의 들

1) - 사이좋은 아이들 -

2)-귀염둥이-

3)- 친구를 위하여 연주를

년 월 일 요일 날씨

동물들도 친구를 알고 사이좋게 지내면...

·언·젠·가·우·리·세·상·도·전·

·쟁·없·이·자·유·롭·고·평화·

·롭고·사이 좋·게·살·수·있·

·지·않·을·까·?·

2008년 3월 26일 목요일

오늘은 다른 날과 특별히 다른 것이 없다.

그래서 이야기를 지었다.

(선생님, 컴퓨터로 작성을 했어요!!)

2008년 3월 28일 토요일

김연아가 세상 최고 신기록이라니 믿을 수가 없다. 나는 지금 너무 기쁜 것이다.

그렇지 않고서는 이럴 수가 없다.

하지만 더 기쁜 것이 있다. 내일 모레면 학교를 간다는 것이다.

나는 동생이나 같은 또래가 없어서 집에서는 심심하다.

그래서 학교가 놀이터 같다.

같이 놀면서 배우고 다치고 경험도 하고 학교는 누가 처음 시작했을까?

다른 아이들은 몰라 나는 기쁘다.

학교는 우리의 집 같은 장소이다.

5행시를 지어 보았다.

학생들은

교실이 감옥이고

선생님 말씀이 자장가래요.

생활이 재밌어야 하는데

님은 그게 좋은지 모르네요.

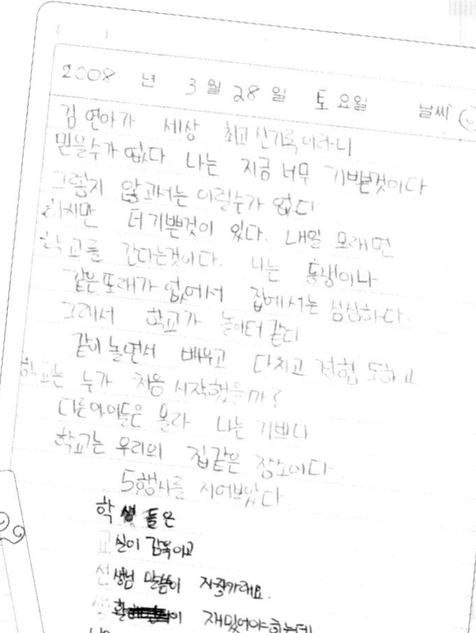

2008 년 3 월 28 일 토 요일 날씨

김연아가 세상 최고 신기록이라니
믿을수가 없다 나는 지금 너무 기쁜것이다
그렇지 않고서는 이럴수가 없다
하지만 더 기쁜것이 있다. 내일 모레면
학교를 간다는것이다. 나는 동생이나
같은또래가 없어서 집에서는 심심하다.
그래서 학교가 놀이터 같다
같이 놀면서 배우고 다치고 경험도하고
학교는 누가 처음 시작했을까?
다른아이들은 몰라 나는 기쁘다
학교는 우리의 집같은 장소이다
5행시를 지어보았다
학생들은
교실이 감옥이고
선생님 말씀이 자장가래요.
생활이 재밌어야하는데
님은 그게 좋은지 모르네요

2008 년 3 월 26일 목 요일 날씨

오늘은 다른날과 특별히 다른것이 없다.
그래서 이야기를 지었다 (선생님, 컴퓨터로
작성을 했어요!!)

4월 6일 월요일

오늘은 3.4조가 백엽상을 보러 다녀왔다.
너는 친구들과 함게 가는 것이 좋다.
하지만 아쉬운 점이 한 개 있다.
아이들이 내가 부회장이고 선생님이 아니라서
빨리 나오지 않다는 것이다.
나는 친구들이 선생님 말씀도 잘 듣고
다른 친구의 말을 들어야 할 때는
귀기울여 듣고 빨리 나오면 좋겠다.
나는 요번달의 당번 활동에 대해 만족스럽게 생각한다.
내한테 자신감을 주고 보람도 있고
무리도 안 가는 당번 활동이 운 좋게도 걸린 것 같다. ㅋㅋ
내 짝꿍 이재철도 비록 철없는 아이 같아서 한숨밖에 안 나왔는데
말을 잘만 들어도 재미있고 유머 감각이 있는 아이이다.
이처럼 나는 나의 학교 생활이 좋고
친구들이 겉모습만 보고 판단하지 않으면 한다.
재철이 파이팅!

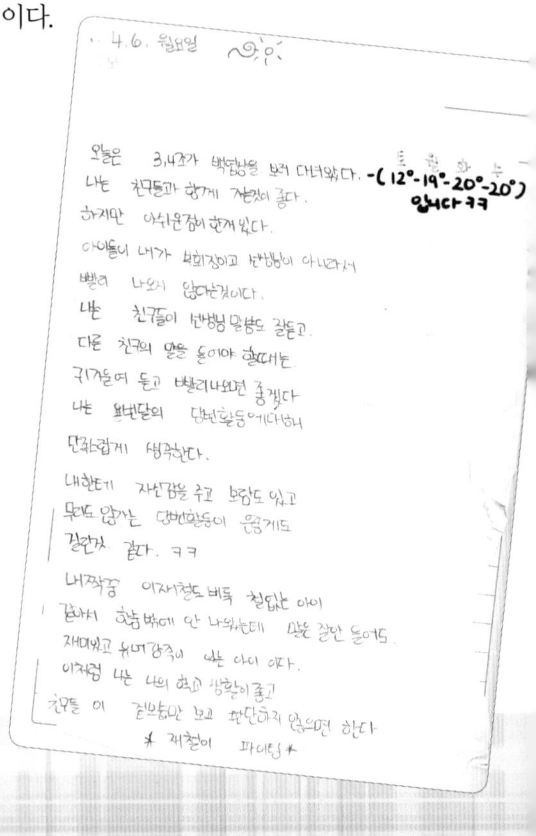
4.6. 월요일
오늘은 3,4조가 백엽상을 보러 다녀왔다. -(12°-19°-20°-20°) 입니다 ㅋㅋ
나는 친구들과 함께 가는것이 좋다.
하지만 아쉬운점이 한개 있다.
아이들이 내가 부회장이고 선생님이 아니라서
빨리 나오지 않다는것이다.
나는 친구들이 선생님 말씀도 잘듣고
다른 친구의 말을 들어야 할때는
귀기울여 듣고 빨리나오면 좋겠다
나는 요번달의 당번활동에대해
만족스럽게 생각한다.
내한테 자신감을 주고 보람도 있고
무리도 안가는 당번활동이 운좋게도
걸린것 같다. ㅋㅋ
내짝궁 이재철도 비록 철없는 아이
같아서 한숨밖에 안 나왔는데 말을 잘만 들어도
재미있고 유머감각이 있는 아이 이다.
이처럼 나는 나의 학교 생활이 좋고
친구들 이 겉모습만 보고 판단하지 않으면 한다
* 재철이 파이팅 *

2009.4.8 수요일

오늘은 학교에서 소변검사를 하는 날이다.

나는 그것을 대비해서 오줌을 참고 학교에 왔다.

1교시가 영어라서 못했지만, 그 다음에는 해냈다.

참은 보람이 있는 것 같다.

아직 하지 못한 아이들을 보니 조금 안쓰러웠다.

4학년 때는 신체검사를 하면서 소변검사를 했다.

하지만 5학년은 아니라서 다행이다. (신체: 비공개)

5학년 생활은 재미있다. 하지만 아직 반 아이들이 이름은 알지만 서로를 잘은 모르는 것 같다.

내한테는 F4가 있다.

허희수, 장은소, 나, 그리고 손정음이다.

우리는 점심때나 쉬는 시간 때 모여서 그림을 그리고

서로 점수를 매기곤 한다.

우리는 영원한 친구이다. (과연?!)

선생님도 하실래요!!????

2009년 4월 12일 토요일

선생님 앞장에 선생님께서 끼워달라고 하셨지요?

저희가 한번 생각을 했는데 끼워드릴께요.

좋으시죠?

저희와 무엇을 할 수는 없지만

F5로 선장하겠습니다.

오늘은 저의 이상한 꿈에 대하여 말씀드릴께요.

어제밤이였습니다....

친구들과 함께 학교에서 오고 있었는데

한 명이 없어졌습니다.

저희가 그것을 모르고 걷다가

우연히 제가 발견하게 되었습니다.

안타깝게도 그것은 정음이였습니다.

그 대신 한슬이와 경영이가 섞인 사람이(?) 옆에 있었습니다.

이 뜻은 정음이 대신 그 친구들로 된다는 말일까요?

저는 두렵습니다.

영원히 가야 할 텐데....

F4 아 참

죄송합니다.

F5 ㅋㅋ

보기 좋아요.

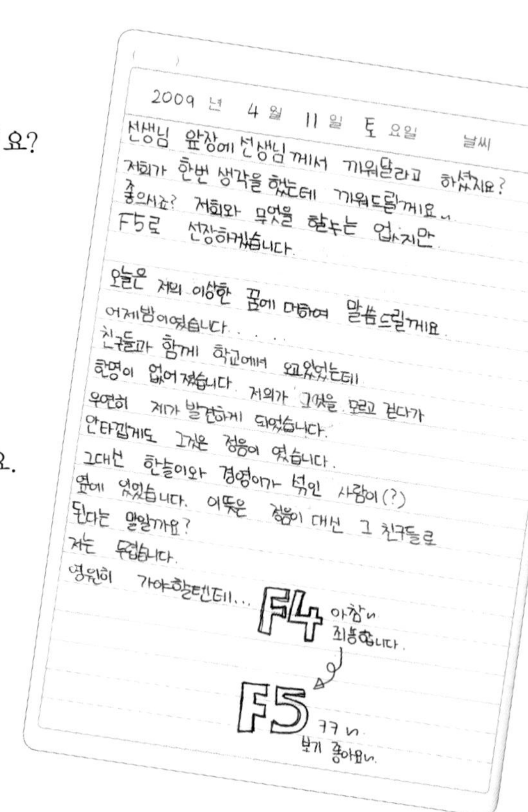

2009 년 4 월 11 일 토 요일 날씨

선생님 앞장에 선생님께서 끼워달라고 하셨지요?
저희가 한번 생각을 했는데 끼워드릴게요
좋으시죠? 저희와 무엇을 할수는 없지만
F5로 선장하겠습니다.

오늘은 저의 이상한 꿈에 대하여 말씀드릴게요
어제밤이였습니다....
친구들과 함께 학교에서 오고있었는데
한명이 없어졌습니다. 저희가 그것을 모르고 걷다가
우연히 제가 발견하게 되었습니다.
안타깝게도 그것은 정음이 였습니다.
그대신 한슬이와 경영이가 섞인 사람이(?)
옆에 있었습니다. 이뜻은 정음이 대신 그 친구들로
된다는 말일까요?
저는 두렵습니다.
영원히 가야할텐데... F4 아참 죄송합니다.
F5 ㅋㅋ 보기 좋아요.

2009년 4월 13일 월요일

선생님 쓸 게 없어서 선생님께 문제를 낼께요.

*PLEASE 풀어주세요!!

1. 은향이는 몇 번일까요?

① 23 ② 25 ③ 24 ④ 34

2. 은향이는 가족 구성원이 어떻게 될까요?

① 오빠, 나, 엄마, 아빠

② 오빠×2, 나, 엄마, 아빠

③ 언니, 나, 엄마, 아빠

④ 나, 엄마, 아빠

3. FINAL!!

요고 푸시면 아이큐 3000!!!

나의 생일은 무엇일까요? 정보 보지 마세요.

(　)년 ( )월 ( )일

-동그라미 쳐주세요!!

(어려웠음, 쉬웠음)

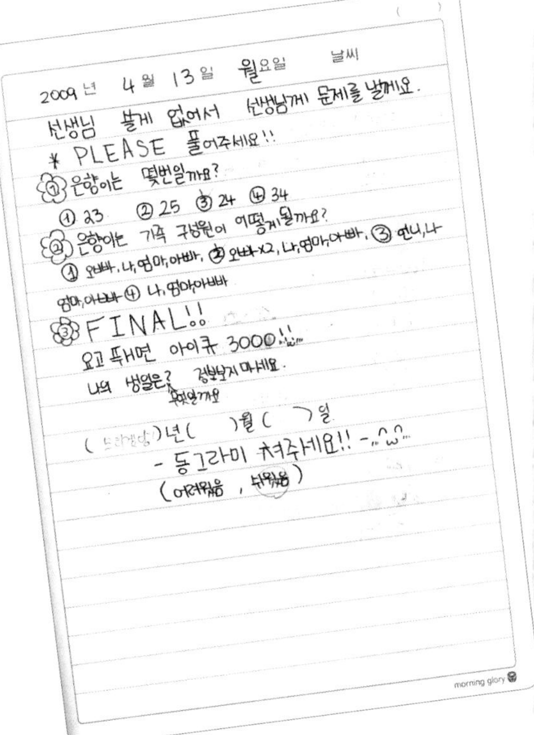
2009년 4월 13일 월요일 날씨

선생님 쓸게 없어서 선생님께 문제를 낼께요.

* PLEASE 풀어주세요!!

① 은향이는 몇번일까요?

① 23 ② 25 ③ 24 ④ 34

② 은향이는 가족 구성원이 어떻게 될까요?

① 오빠, 나, 엄마, 아빠, ② 오빠×2, 나, 엄마, 아빠, ③ 언니, 나

엄마, 아빠 ④ 나, 엄마, 아빠

③ FINAL!!

요고 푸시면 아이큐 3000!!

나의 생일은? 정보보지 마세요.

무엇일까요

( )년 ( )월 ( )일

- 동그라미 쳐주세요!!

(어려웠음, 쉬웠음)

2009년 4월 15일 수요일

F4 캐릭터 아이참~ F5~

실물이 더 예쁨~~

선생님두유~

2009년 3월 18일 토요일 〈시험공부〉

나는 시험공부를 이렇게 안 한 적이 없다.

1학년 때 문제집 6권, 2학년 때는 문제집 5권,

그리고 1학년 1학기, 2학기, 2학년 1학기는 다 All 100이었다.

요번에는 그렇게 안 될 것이다.

나는 꼭 좋은 점수 나오면 좋겠다.

하지만 점수가 잘 안 나와도 다음에 잘하면 된다.

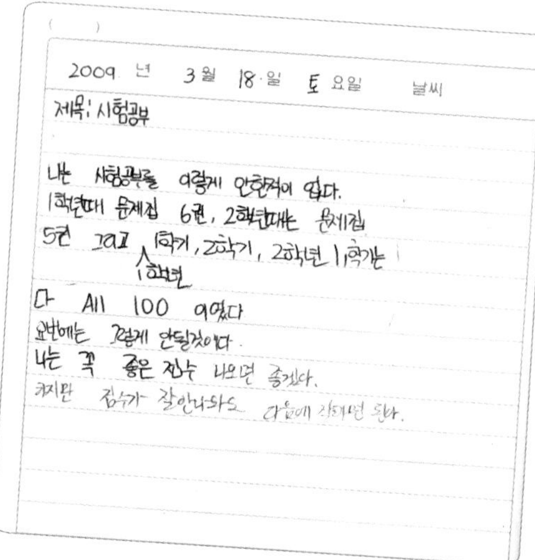

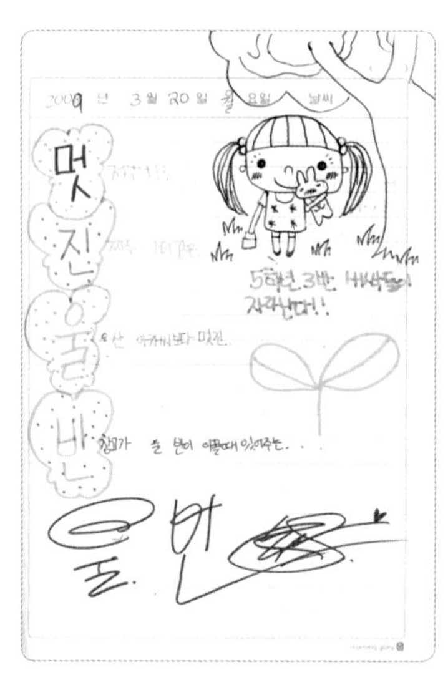

2009년 3월 22일 수요일

오늘은 수요일이다. 〈알다시피〉
오늘 나는 대구광역시 대구 어린이 미술대회에 참가했다.
막상하려니 잘 되지 않았다. 하지만 그것은 둘째 치고 어제 중간고사는 지옥 같았다.
앞에서 말했던 짐작과 같다.

나는 처음으로 나쁜 점수가 나올 것이다.
시험에는 내가 공부하지 않는 것도 나왔다.
하지만 난 실망하지 않을 것이다.
시험의 기회는 더 많기 때문이다.
나는 옛날이 부럽다.
시험공부를 빡시게 하지 않았을 것이다.
옛날은 좋으나 유기오전쟁이 싫을 뿐이다.
어른들이 우리 아이들도 자존심이 있고
마음과 생각이 있다는 것을 알면 좋겠다.
어른들은 무조건 공부이다.

아이들의 마음도 생각해 주세요.....

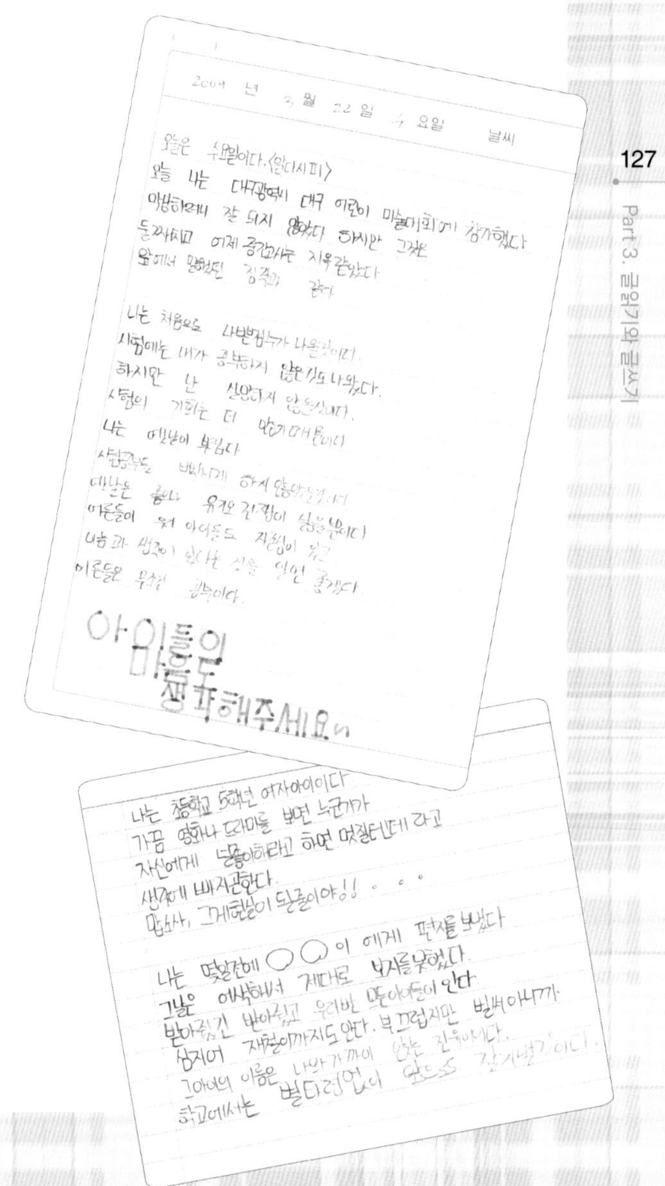
2009 년 3 월 22 일 수 요일 날씨
오늘은 수요일이다.〈알다시피〉
오늘 나는 대구광역시 대구 어린이 미술대회에 참가했다
막상하려니 잘 되지 않았다 하지만 그것은
둘째치고 어제 중간고사는 지옥같았다
앞에서 말했던 짐작과 같다
나는 처음으로 나쁜점수가 나올것이다.
시험에는 내가 공부하지 않은것도 나왔다.
하지만 난 실망하지 않을것이다.
시험의 기회는 더 많기때문이다
나는 옛날이 부럽다
시험공부를 빡시게 하지 않았을것이다
옛날은 좋으나 유기오 전쟁이 싫을뿐이다
어른들이 우리 아이들도 자존심이 있고
마음과 생각이 있다는 것을 알면 좋겠다
어른들은 무조건 공부이다.
아이들의 마음도 생각해주세요

나는 초등학교 5학년 여자아이이다
가끔 영화나 드라마를 보면 누군가가
자신에게 [illegible]하라고 하면 멋질텐데 라고
생각에 빠지곤한다.
맙소사, 그게현실이 될줄이야!! . . .
나는 몇일전에 ○○이 에게 편지를 보냈다
그날은 어색해서 제대로 보지를 못했다.
받아줬긴 받아줬고 우리반 모든아이들이 안다
심지어 재철이까지도 안다. 부끄럽지만 벌써 아니까.
그아이의 이름은 나와 가까이 앉는 진우이다.
학교에서는 별다른없이 [illegible] 잘지낼것이다.

2009. 4. 30

요즘 내가 싫은지 정음이가 내게서 멀어진다는 괜한 느낌이 든다. 문자를 해도 안 답장을 하고 내가 죄인처럼 느껴진다. 하지만 나는 그애들과 친구이기 때문에 다시 친해질 거라고 믿는다. 부디 정음이가 안 멀어졌으면 한다.

멀어졌다해도 알다시피 친해질 것이다.

우리 F5는 변함 없는 친구와 선생님(?)!이다.

파이팅!!

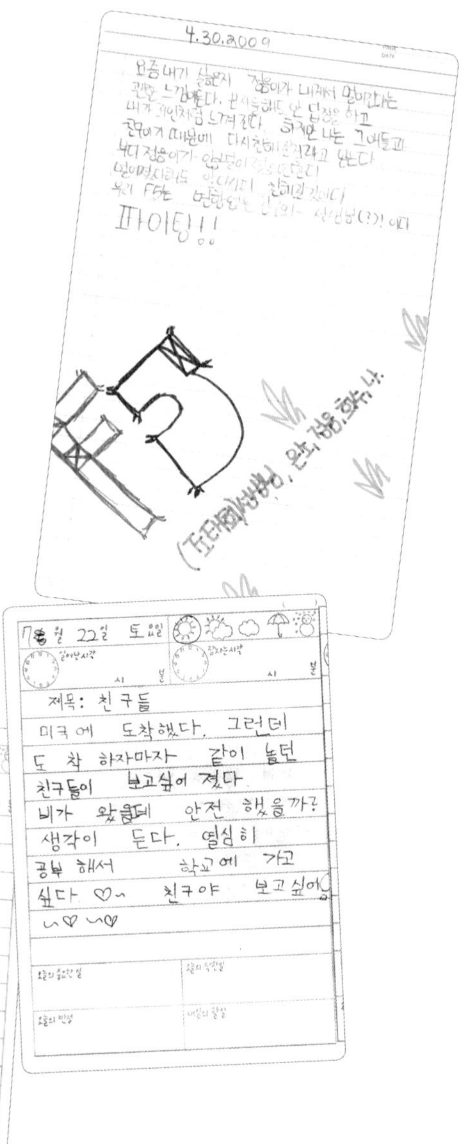

7월 22일 토요일 〈친구들〉

미국에 도착했다. 그런데 도착하자마자 같이 놀던

친구들이 보고 싶어졌다.

비가 왔을 때 안전했을까?

생각이 든다.

열심히 공부해서 학교에 가고 싶다.

친구야 보고 싶어.

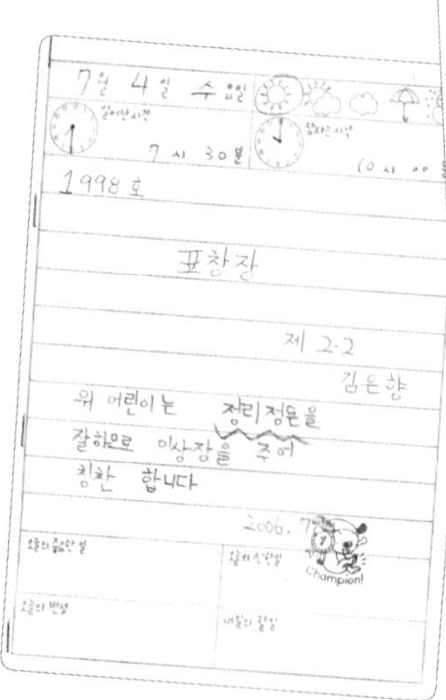

7월 30일 일요일 〈골프〉

나는 오늘 골프를 쳤다. 나는 골프를 잘 친다. 저번에는 연습장에 갔는데 선생님께서 "She is perfect."(애는 완벽해요. 가르쳐 줄 것이 없어요.)

그래서 놀랬다. 오늘 치고 싶지는 않았지만 쳤다. 더 잘 쳐서 '박세리'처럼 되면 얼마나 좋을까?

2월 15일 수요일 〈내가 공부한 학습지〉

오늘 우리가 공부했는 학습지를 윤주, 희진, 지연, 예림, 승연, 남협, 인태, 세린 그리고 나 이렇게 나눠주었다. 왜 이렇게 많은 사람이 나누어주었냐면 학습지가 많아서 그렇다. 하지만 나누어 주는 행동이 자랑스럽고 좋은 것 같다.

2월 16일 목요일 〈1학년을 마치면서〉

1학년을 시작한 지 일주일이 된 것 같다. 그 뜻은 너무 빨리 마치는 것 같다라는 말이다. 2005년도 정말 재미있었다. 친구들도 사이가 좋았던 것 같다. 2학년 가서는 더 좋은 친구들을 만나보고 싶다. 1학년 5반 화이팅!!

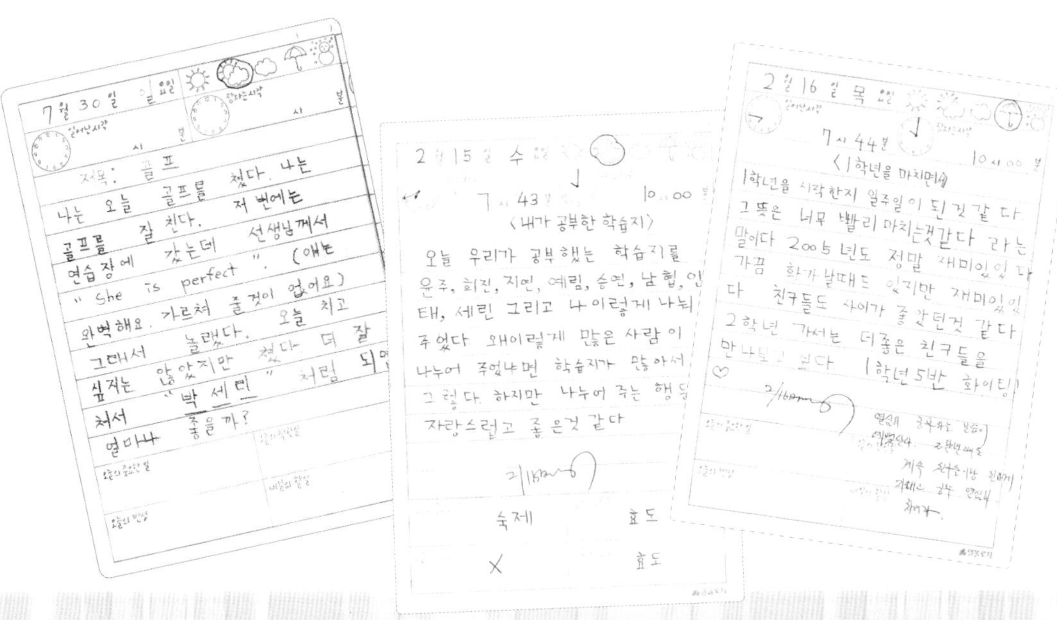

7월 30일 일요일
제목: 골프
나는 오늘 골프를 쳤다. 나는 골프를 잘 친다. 저번에는 연습장에 갔는데 선생님께서 " She is perfect ". (애는 완벽해요. 가르쳐 줄것이 없어요) 그래서 놀랬다. 오늘 치고 싶지는 않았지만 쳤다. 더 잘 쳐서 "박세리" 처럼 되면 얼마나 좋을까?

2월 15일 수요일
7시 43분 10시 00분
〈내가 공부한 학습지〉
오늘 우리가 공부했는 학습지를 윤주, 희진, 지연, 예림, 승연, 남협, 인태, 세린 그리고 나 이렇게 나눠주었다 왜이렇게 많은 사람이 나누어 주었냐면 학습지가 많아서 그렇다. 하지만 나누어 주는 행동 자랑스럽고 좋은것 같다
숙제 효도

2월 16일 목요일
7시 44분 10시 00분
〈1학년을 마치면서〉
1학년을 시작한지 일주일이 된것 같다. 그 뜻은 너무 빨리 마치는것 같다 라는 말이다 2005년도 정말 재미있었다 가끔 화가 날때도 있지만 재미있었다 친구들도 사이가 좋았던것 같다 2학년 가서는 더좋은 친구들을 만나보고 싶다 1학년 5반 화이팅!

2005년 7월 9일 토요일 〈교회에서〉

오늘 교회에서 조카를 만났다. 부끄러워서 나를 피한다.

나는 조금 눈이 글썽이었다.

지났지만 좋다.

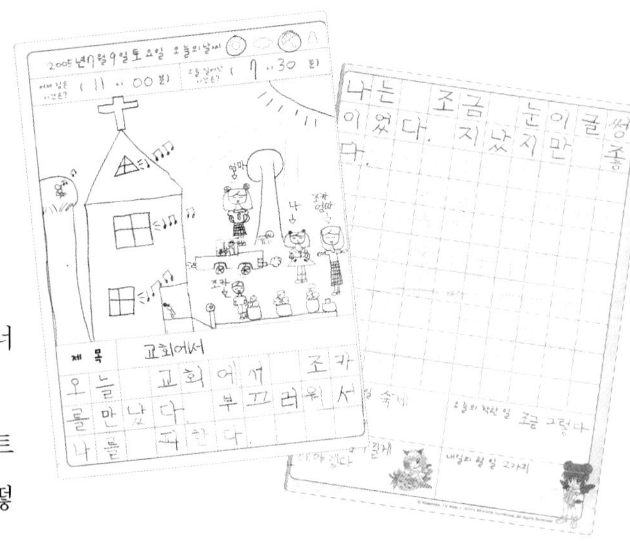

2012.10.15

오늘 소셜시험이 있었다.

ㅜ 망한 거 같애 ㅠㅠㅠㅠ

근데 저번만큼 망한 거 같지는 않아서 너무너무 다행이야 ㅜㅜㅎㅎ

요번 주가 마지막 Quarter 1주라서 스트레스도 너무 많이 받고 있고 도대체 뭘 어떻게 해야 할지 모르겠어.

학교 가기도 너무 귀찮아.

차라리 좋아하는 사람이라도 있다면 가고 싶은 마음이라도 생길 텐데....

그런 마음 zero ㅋ

에고고고고. 그래도 성적이 뭐가 나오든 내가 노력했다면 엄마아빠도 만족하신데... 쩝... ㅠㅠ

그래도 다음 Q2에는 잘해야겠당 ㅜㅜ

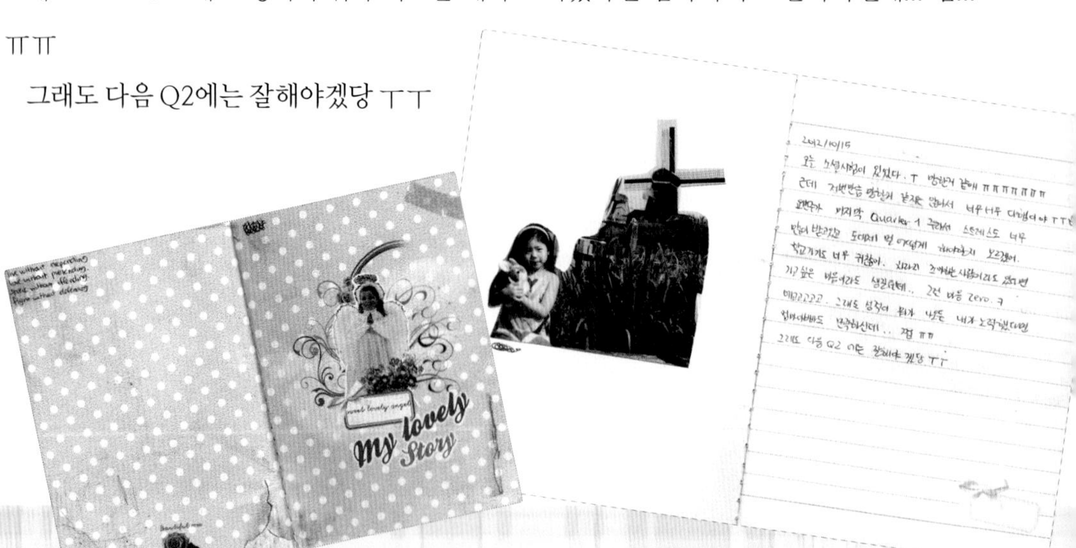

10.25

게르른가봐ㅠㅠ 한 일주일간 안 썼다. ㅎㅎㅎㅠㅠ

ㅋㅋ 그래도 오늘은 할아버지 일이니까.

내 이름 김은향도 할아버지가 지으셨으니 ㅋㅋㅋ 근데 나는 엄마 아빠가 연세가 있으셔서 그런지 죽음이나 기일 같은 거에 되게 예민한 거 같애 ㅠㅠ

...음... 나는 지금도 엄마 아빠가 일찍 죽으면 어떻게 하나라는 쓸데없는 생각을 할 때가 많아ㅠ

그래서 그런지 엄마랑 싸우는 날엔 항상 꿈에서 악몽을 꾸드라고.

힘들다.

10.26

오늘 DBS도 무사히 잘 끝나서 다행인 거 같애.

나는 혹시라도 잘 안 될까 봐 걱정을;;;

나 요즘 무지 거슬리는 사람이 생겼어.

근데 나도 그 거슬림이 뭔지 모르겠다....

10.29

오늘은 PAJAMA DAY!

나 악필 같애ㅠㅠ 원래 안 이런데.ㅜ 흑

학교만 오면 요즘 그냥. 물론 좋아하는 사람은 아니지만.

그냥 거슬린다고 멋 미친 미친 ㅜㅋㅋ

내가 병신인가ㅠㅠ

나 요즘 듣는 얘기가 더 많아서 그런가???

그냥 나도 내 감정을 모름.

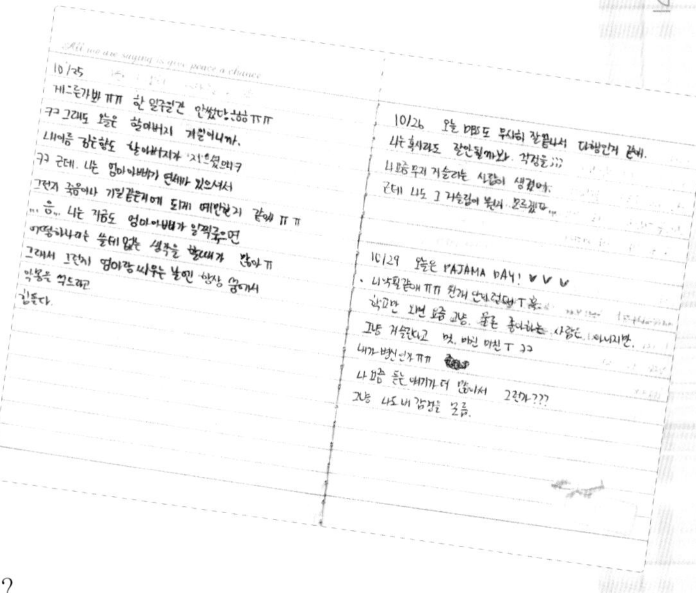

10.31

오늘이 할로윈
근데 우리는 모든 파티를 내일 할 꺼야.
오늘 별로 학교 가기가 싫었어.
그냥 쫌 그랬어. 그래도 그냥 어제 안 왔으니까.
오늘은 왔겠찌? 하는 마음에....

11.1

I Don't understand how I'm feeling well, I wouldn't go through so much detail but all the reactions and stuff made me feel more magretic to him. of course nothing....
그냥... 계속 보게 돼.
계속 그냥 그렇게...ㅋㅋㅋ
내가 이상한 거??

11.2

나 오늘 완전 많이 잤어ㅎㅎ
폭풍수면ㅠㅠ
ㅎㅎ ♡ 아이 조앙 ♡
12am~ 2Am까지 ㅋㅋ 흐흐 ㅠㅠㅠ
기분이 날아갈 듯,
이 기분이구나. 잠 많이 자면 ㅎㅎㅎ
에휴~ 근데 학교를 안 가서 아쉽기도.... 한가?
우와ㅋㅋ 천하의 메리가 학교 안 간 게 아쉽다니
확실히 문제 있음ㅋㅋㅋ

11.5

DBS 하는 날 좋아.

그냥 좋아.

아놔ㅋㅋㅋ 애들이 나보고 metromonal 카면서 카는데 완전 아닌데ㅋㅋㅋ -_- 하하

쩝. 내 감정을 모르겠어.. 머지??

11.11

있잖아.

나는

그

소문이

사실이면

좋겠어.

페북에서 온라인일 때 은근 기대하는데.

음악 듣다가 띠링해서 보면 벤즈 -_- 칫.

물론 벤즈도 친구지만...

빼빼로 따위 신경 안 써.

그냥 난 오빠와 그 소문이 맞는지만 진실을 알고 싶어.

왜냐면 나 혼자 기대하고 과대망상하고

좋아하는 게 바보같거든.

신경 쓰이고 그 차가운 말투 앞뒤가 안 맞는 스토리가 다 거슬리고 진짜 매일매일 신경 쓰여.

해나 언니한테 말해야겠다.

대구 국제중학 단체 촬영

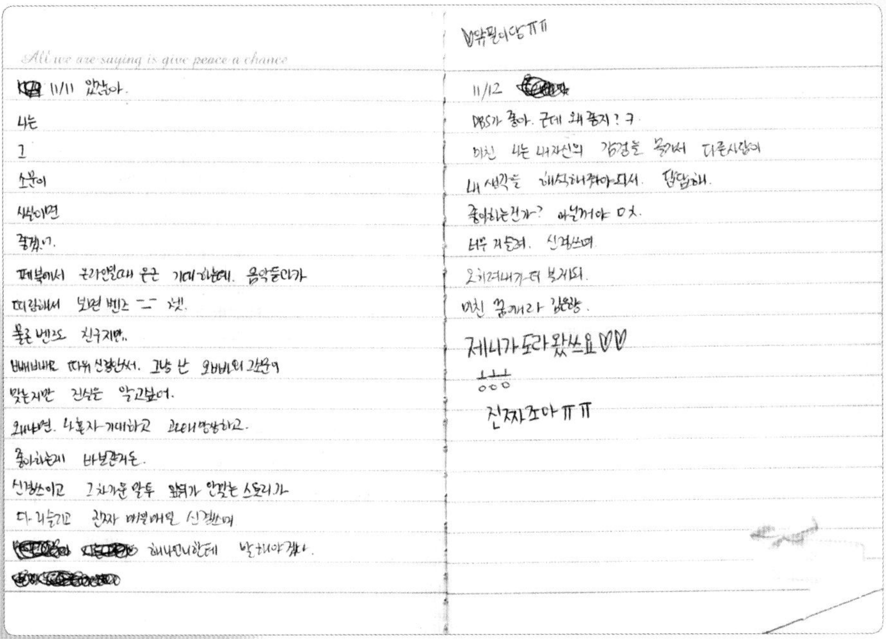

11.12

DBS가 좋아. 근데 왜 좋지? ㅋ

미친 나는 내 자신의 감정을 몰라서 다른 사람이 내 생각을 해석해줘야 돼서 답답해.

좋아하는 건가? 아닐꺼야 ㅇㅊ

너무 거슬려. 신경 쓰여.

오히려 내가 더 보게 돼.

미친 꿈깨라 김은향.

제니가 도라왔쓰요♡♡

ㅎㅎㅎ

진짜조아ㅠㅠ

3
편지

〈글씨체가 점점 못나서 미안ㅠㅠ〉

엄마, ♡♡

나 은향인데 할 말이 좀 있는데 직접 말할 시간도, 용기도 없네ㅠ

어젯밤에 너무 심하게 막해서 미안해.

진짜 나도 너무 외롭고 서러운데 엄마가 내한테 하는 얘기를 들으면 왠지 이해하지 않는 것 같았어.

엄마 아픈데 괜히 내 감정만 너무 앞선 건 아닌가 걱정이다. 너무 울어서 잠도 포기했어.

엄마가 내 5개월만 더 있는 만큼 안 놀고 열심히 하라는 마음 이해해. 하지만 나 진짜 친구들이랑 얘기 계속은 아니더라도 가끔 하면서 외로움도 달래고.

음악도 들어야 돼ㅠㅠ 엄마, 나 믿지?

나 진짜 폰 중독 그런 거 아니야.

진짜 열심히 해왔고 앞으로 그럴꺼고.

엄마나 나 믿고 따라주는 만큼 더 열심히 할꺼야.

엄마, 내 부탁 들어줘.

나 진짜 너무 슬프고 우울해ㅠ

나도 좀 웃게 해줘ㅜㅜ

엄마, 나 좀 살려줘♡

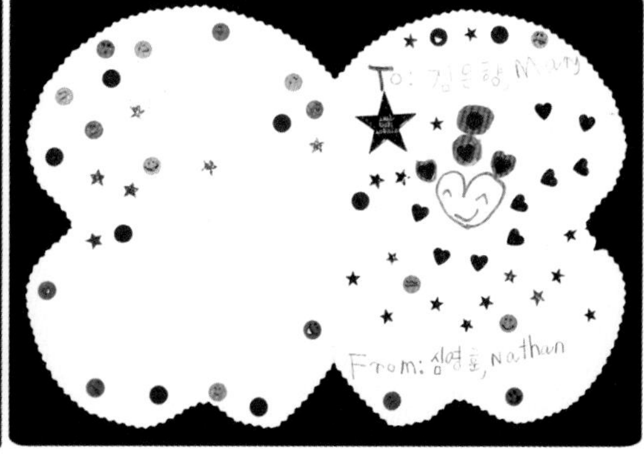

생일파티(미국에서)

아빠, 엄마

메리크리스 마스!!

로돌프의 코처럼 밝게 웃어

-은향-

오빠 ♡ 사랑해

아파트 4층에서 잘 살고 있어?

그런데 잠이 와서 잘게

그럼 안녕

11월 11일 토요일 은향

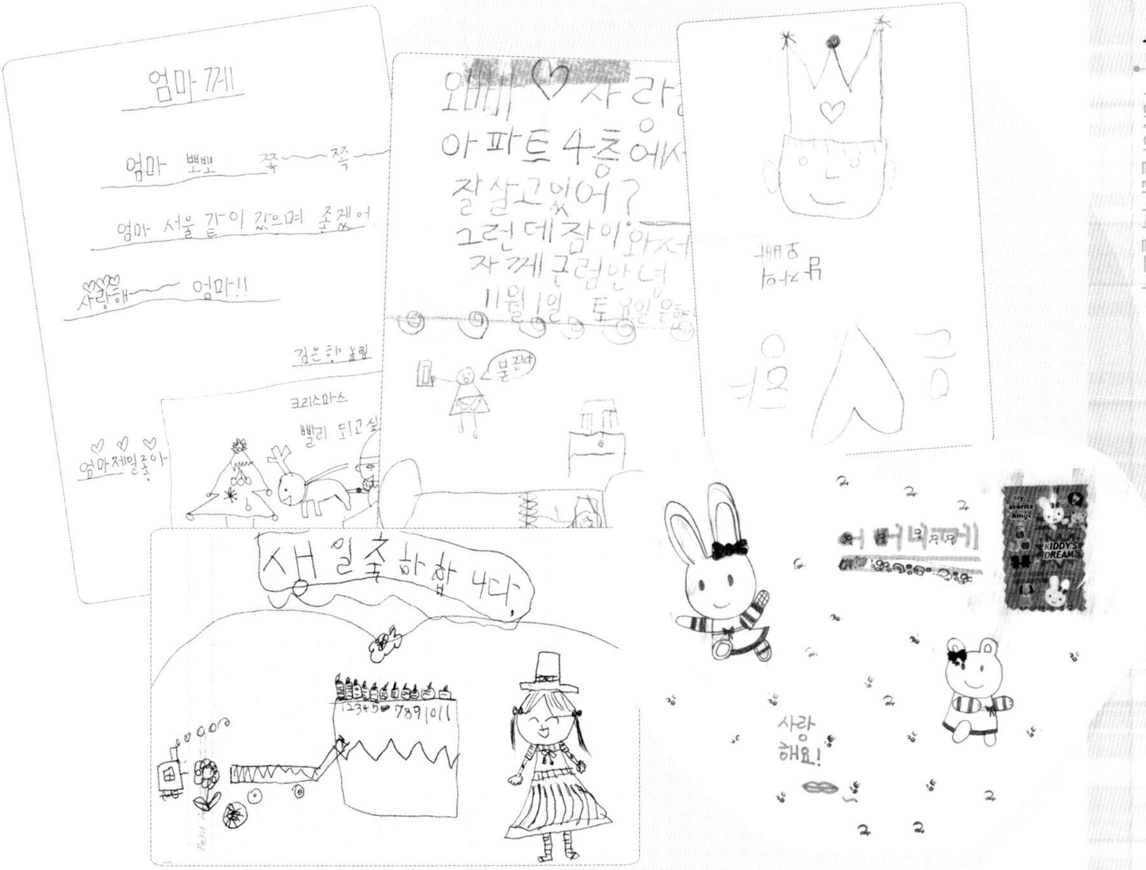

선생님께

선생님! 저 은향이에요. 글씨 보면 아시죠?

편지쓰는 마음 가지고 쓰는 거죠.

어머니께선 편찮으셔서 인사 못 했다고 미안한 표정이에요.

〈은향아~♡〉

'어린이날' 축하해~

은향이는 좋겠다~ 어린이라서…

왜냐구? 예수님께서 어린이를 많이 많이 사랑하시거든…!

성경책에 보면 어린아이들이 예수님 근처에 오고 싶어서 놀고 있으니까 제자들이 시끄럽다고 못 오게 했거든. 그때 예수님께서 "어린 아이들이 내게 오는 것을 금하지 말라"(막지 말라는 뜻이야) 하시며 아이들은 안아 주셨고, 또 다른 성경에는 어린 아이와 같은 순전한 믿음을 가지라고 하셨어(순수하고 깨끗하고 잘 믿는 믿음 말이야~!).

은향이가 예수님이 기뻐하시는 믿음 가지도록, 하나님이 원하시는 사람으로 자라도록 선생님은 생각날 때마다 기도한단다.

은향이도 그렇게 기도하자~!

'어린이날' 오빠랑 재밌게 놀겠네.

부럽네…

2006 어린이날을 맞아 최선생님이

은향아 ~ ♡
'어린이날' 축하해 ~ ^^*
은향이는 좋겠다~ 어린이라서…
왜냐구? 예수님께서 어린이를 많이 많이 사랑하시거든…!
성경책에 보면 어린아이들이 예수님 근처에 오고싶어서 놀고있으니까, 제자들이 시끄럽다고 못오게 했거든. 그때 예수님께서 "어린 아이들이 내게 오는 것을 금하지말라" (막지말라는 뜻이야) 안아주셨고, 또 다른 성경에는 "어린 아이와 같은 순전한 믿음을 가지라"고 하셨어 (순수하고 깨끗하고 잘믿는 믿음 말이야 ~!)
은향이가 예수님이 기뻐하시는 믿음 가지도록, 하나님이 원하시는 사람으로 자라도록 선생님은 생각날 때마다 기도한단다.
은향이도 그렇게 기도하자 ~!
'어린이날' 오빠랑 재밌게 놀겠네.
부럽네.. ^^*
2006. 어린이날을 맞아 최선생님이

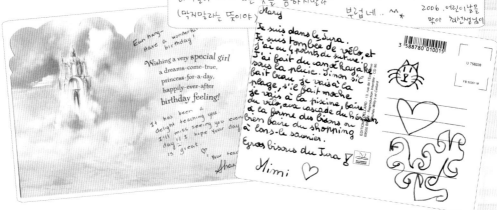

Eun hang-
Have a wonderful birthday!

Wishing a very special girl
a dreams-come-true,
princess-for-a-day,
happily-ever-after
birthday feeling!

It has been a delight teaching you. I'll miss seeing you every day!! I hope your day is great.
♡, Your teacher

Mary
Je suis dans le Jura.
Je suis tombée de vélo, et j'ai eu 4 points de suture.
J'ai fait du canoë kayak sous la pluie. Sinon s'il fait beau je vais à la plage, s'il fait moche je vais à la piscine, faire du vélo, aux cascades du hérisson, à la ferme des bisons ou bien faire du shopping à Lons-le-saunier.
Gros bisous du Jura !
Mimi ♡

〈혜성이가 씀〉

김으냥씨 생일 축하해요~♡ 오랜만에 보는데도 하나도 안 변하고 잘 웃고 다니는 모습 매우 보기 좋습니다! 늘 긍정적으로 생각하고 좋게 좋게 웃고 넘기는 건 나도 좀 배워야겠는 걸…? 예림당에서 우연을 가장해서 (사실 내가 님 스토커임) 만났던 때도 2년 전이다; 그때부터 생각하면 사실 우리 더 친해지고도 남을 시간만큼 알고 지낸건데 수업도 겹치는 것도 몇 개 없고 이칸디ㅜ^ㅜ 아직 학교 시작한 지 한 달도 안 됐지만 앞으로 더 웃고 댕기고! 스트레스 받을 일 있을지 몰라도 지금처럼 웃고 털어버립시다. 자 이제 엄청난 멘트 나온다 기대해라. 매일매일이 행복하고 즐거운 시간이었지만 자기가 태어난 오늘만큼은 더 행복하게 보내자! 생일 축하해 친구^o^

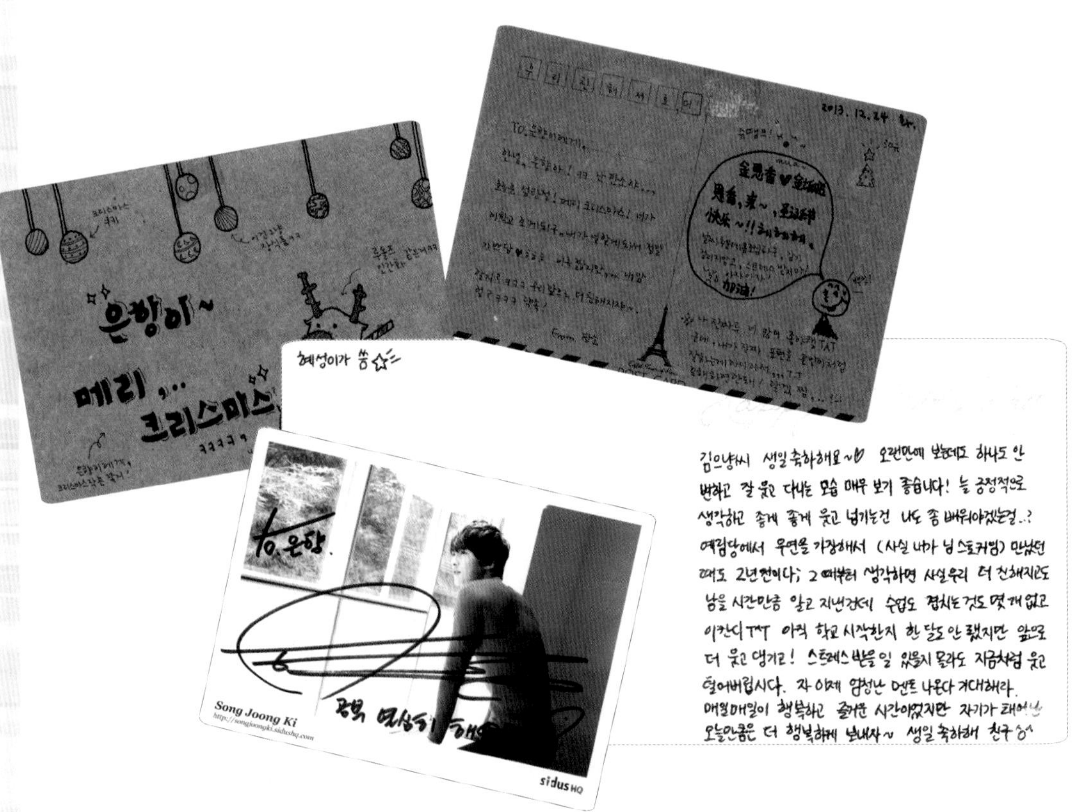

생일추카해

자칭 대구 촌닭 에게

P.S 힘내 우리 촌닭아

To. 은향이

나또한글씨체가 엉망이야 ㅋㅋㅋ 이해해줄꺼지? 너의 어제그 기도 편지는 정말 나에겐 엄청난 큰충격이였어.... 어떻게 너같은 아이가 존재하지? 너의 부모님이 10년 기도해서 나온게 너란게 진짜 와닿았어... 나너무 진지해? ㅋㅋㅋ 아그리고 그만좀아퍼 기시배야. 어떻게 맨날아퍼ㅡㅡ 속상하게 TT 살뺀다고 밤안먹지도 말고 아침꼭먹고 자기 4시간전부터 죄조금이면 음식은 삼가해! 너의 상한 위를 조금이라도 회복시켜야지T.T 아그리고 나도 들은건데 물은 목마를때 마시는게 가장 좋데 물을 많이마시면 몸의 온도가 1도 정도가 떨어지면서 변도안좋데 ㅋㅋㅋ 나왜이얘기 하는중? ㅋㅋㅋㅋㅋ 나 의사해도되겠다 그치!! ㅋㅋㅋ 지금쯤이면넌 수업이나 춤연습하고 있겠지? ㅋㅋ 내생각은 하고 있는거지? 잉 그래도 요즘은 너가 인간관계 때문에 안힘들어해서 보기 좋아!! 계속싸우지말고 잘지내~ ㅋㅋㅋ 아나는데 왜자꾸 쓸데없는얘기하는거야? ㅋㅋㅋㅋ 나이따가 어쩌면너 춤추는거 볼수있을지도 몰라 가서너 기세워줄께ㅋㅋ 우리안지 한2달정도 됐는데 서로에 대해서 너무잘안다♥ 너같은 남친좀... 하앍. 어맞다 요즘 케팝스타하고 마녀사냥진짜 재밌드라 ㅋㅋㅋ 시간될때아니면 기분안좋을 함봐바. 아맞다 나도 프랑스어 배울라고!! 아니면 같이 아랍어 배울래? 배우자!! ㅋㅋㅋㅋㅋㅋㅋㅋㅋㅋ 아왜케웃기지 ㅋㅋㅋ 아빨리 너보고싶어. 너랑 밤새도록 얘기하고싶다. 졸리면 같이자...자고...♥ 하앍 ㅋㅋㅋ 곧 크리스마스야... 올해도 남친없이 보내는군하... T.T 그래도 뭐 우리에겐 서로가있으니깐♥ 띄어쓰기도 이젠 안되고 있어ㅋㅋㅋㅋ 아!!! 수업끝났다♥ 나계속 샤이니-샹사병 이거이써고 파인애(?) 그목뵬 계속귀에서 맴돌아... 안되는데 나바이브팬인데 TT 사실이 종이 다채우고싶은데 할말은 생각이 안난다. 그냥너무고맙고. 꺅!!! 오글!!!!!!!!♥ 사랑해ㅋㅋㅋ 진짜 넌같은 친구 처음이야. 너란친구신세계♥ 하나님 은향이 한국가도 저 은향이랑 연락할수있게 해주세요. 한국갔다고 저 막 잊는거 아니겠죠? ㅋㅋㅋ 아그리고 은향이 어디에있든지 행복하게 해주세요♥ 내가 너 엄청 좋아하는거 알지? 나도 너 엄청아껴!! 너가 태민이랑 만약에 사겨도 너가 아까울 만큼(이건좀아닌가? ㅋㅋㅋ) 너 아껴♥. 진짜마니 사랑해♥ 오글거리지? 어쩔수없, 난널 사랑하니까♥

From. 은빈이

우와!! 은향 은빈 은자돌림이야!!

ㅋㅋㅋ 너랑나랑은 운명인가봄♥

내가글을좀못써T.T 이해하고 읽어줘

아그리고 클스마스 선물 뭐갖고 싶어?

중국의 한 古詩중에 떠나는 친구에게 축복해주는 말이있엉ㅎㅎ

金恩香!

海内存知己，天涯若比邻!

不要伤心 也不要难受!

祝你喜福，祝你快乐!

在韩国见! :) (笑)

To. 김은향, 메리킴! Mary Kim, 金恩香

안녕, 은향아?! 이렇게 막상 편지를 쓸려니까 많이 두근거린다, 히히히 :).
음... 생각해보니 니가 한국으로 갈 날도 몇일 안남았네,.. 기분이 좀 (육수로) 꿀꿀^^ 하다 T.T.
비록 미소처럼 같은 [illegible] 아니었지만 난 너가 very very 真的 喜欢했엉 ㅎㅎ (북흐).
그동안 미소 잘 챙겨줘서, 또 많이 참아줘서 고마워 ^^. 아! 그리구 날 좋은 친구라 생각하고 니 얘기도 해줘서 고마웡 ^^.
항상 혼자 짊어지려해서 많이 힘들어 보였는데 넌 정말루 괜찮은 朋友니깐!
그런 스트레스 받지마 T.T 千万 받지마 T.T
한국가서 좋은 친구 많이 사귀고 꼭꼭꼭 혼자 좀 想太多하기! 爱自己하기!!
알겠지잉! 사실은, 니가 좀더 중국에 있었으면 좋았을걸 한다 T.T..
그래두 한국에서 만날수 있으니까! 맞지잉! ㅎㅎㅎ
종종 페북으로 연락줘! 나도 (자주는 못하지만 ㅠ.ㅠ) 보면 꼭꼭 다시 연락할께!
꼭꼭꼭이다? 한국가서 꼭 다시 만나고 꼭 페북해주고 힘들때 카톡해 ㅋㅋ!
안그럼 나 삐짐. 흥!
이상하게 넌 느낌이 좋았어... 북경에서 미소랑 너의 앞날을 축복해 주마, 닝겐!
쿠쿠.. 와타시하 은향짱이 좋다데스요, 아레야레, 쿠쿠..

From. 김판소, 金[illegible]

To. 은향이♡

사실... 편지를 썼었는데 ㅋㅋㅋ 글씨체가 너무 이상해서 다시 쓰는중이야!!
우선 메리크리스마스~ 우리 모두 솔로들의 파티를 열자ㅋㅋㅋ. 이 양말은 선물이야!! 초라해도 좋아해 줘TT. 너 선물!!! 진짜 좋아!!!
나 화이트 필요했었거든 ㅋㅋ TT.
이런 센스쟁이♡
우리 서로 기도하면서 잘살자!!
편지도 너무 고마워 TT.

From. 은빈이

© bentoy

장난이야ㅋㅋ
기분나빴다면 미안ㅠ
내일부터할래?
우리시험엄청잘봐서 시험끝나는날
맛있는거 먹으러가자! ㅎㅎ
기분좋게~♡

Marry Christmas Marry 가♡
생일 축하해 은향아! 처음으로 축하해주는
너의 생일이라 신경좀 많이 썼다. Krystal 이랑 연기까지
해가면서 니 락커 비번 알아내고 ㅋㅋㅋㅋ 내가 짱이지?
DIS 처음와서 모든게 어색하고 적응하느라 힘들때 옆에
같이 있어줘서 너무 고마워♡ 사랑하구 앞으로 더더더
친해지자♡ 다시한번 생일축하해애애애

Ja기 야아아아으아아악

시험D-1이다ㅋㅋㅋ

멘붕이 왔음돠 (feat 개뤼씨)

여튼ㅋㅋㅋ 시간짱빨리간다ㅜ

열심히 공부하고 시험 끝나는 날

겁나게놉세ㅎㅎ

기도 항상 하시고요 이쁜아.

잠도 푹 자고!

열공해 ♡

P.S 아이디어가 없어서ㅜㅜ

그래도 좋아해줄 거지?

-인천의 흔한 북경 유학녀-

To. 은봉이

은향아 이편지가 좋은 내용은 아니지만 답장을
해야될것 같아서 쓸게. 너가 눈물도 많고 맘도
여린 애라는거 알아. 근데 본의아니게 내가 신경쓰게
하는 일이 되는것같아 안그래도 힘든 너한테 힘이
못되어줘서 미안해. 근데 내가 요즘 계속 스트레스가
쌓이는데 그걸 못풀고 있는거나; 차반시험 걱정이나,
아무래도 벌써 고고고 하니까 지금상황이
여유롭지가 못해. 해야할건 많은데 어떻게
해야될지도 모르겠고, 좋다가도 많이 착잡하고
우울해지고 그래… 나도 막 놀란다 내가 이렇지
않았었는데 변한것같아서 조금.
왜 서로에게 힘이 되주지는 못할망정 힘들게만
하는지 모르겠다. 나도 웃고 싶어.
그냥 걱정없이 웃어보고싶고 놀고싶고 부담같은것도
없어졌음 좋겠어. 너도 힘든일 다 사라졌음 좋겠고
좀 행복해지자 우리. 안에 먹구름이 잔뜩 껴있으면

겉으로 웃어도 웃는게 아니잖아. 그런거말고
진짜로 웃었으면 좋겠어 진심으로.
말이 좀 앞뒤;; 미안 글씨체 엉엉이 같아서 미안.
그리고 너처럼 이쁜 종이에 적기엔 내용이 별로라서
그냥 노트에 썼어 나중엔 진짜 예쁜 카드에 쓸게.
이쁜 은향아ㅋㅋ 고마워

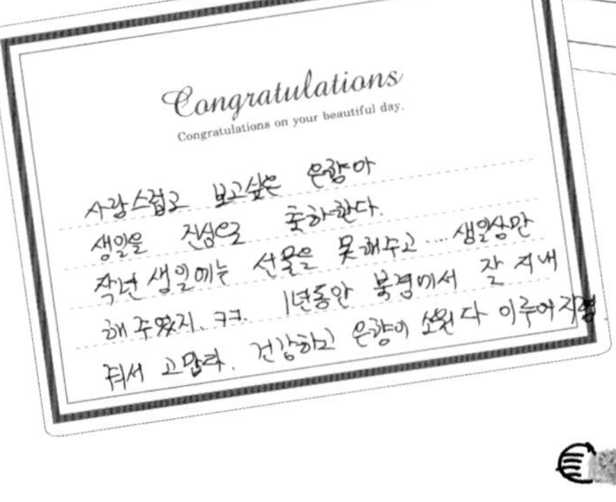
Congratulations
Congratulations on your beautiful day.

사랑스럽고 보고싶은 은향아
생일을 진심으로 축하한다.
작년 생일에는 선물을 못해주고 … 생일상만
해 주었지. ㅋㅋ. 1년동안 북경에서 잘 지내
줘서 고맙다. 건강하고 은향이 소원 다 이루어지길

요즘 한국에서 다시 적응하느라 바쁘고 고생이 많지?

지금의 노력이 고국에서는 환하게 웃을 수 있단다! ㅎㅎ

빡세게 열심히 해서 좋은 결과로 부모님께 기쁨 드리고

하나님께는 영광 돌리는 은향이 되길 늘 기도할게!....

사랑한다! 화이팅!

2014.9.5 민집사님이

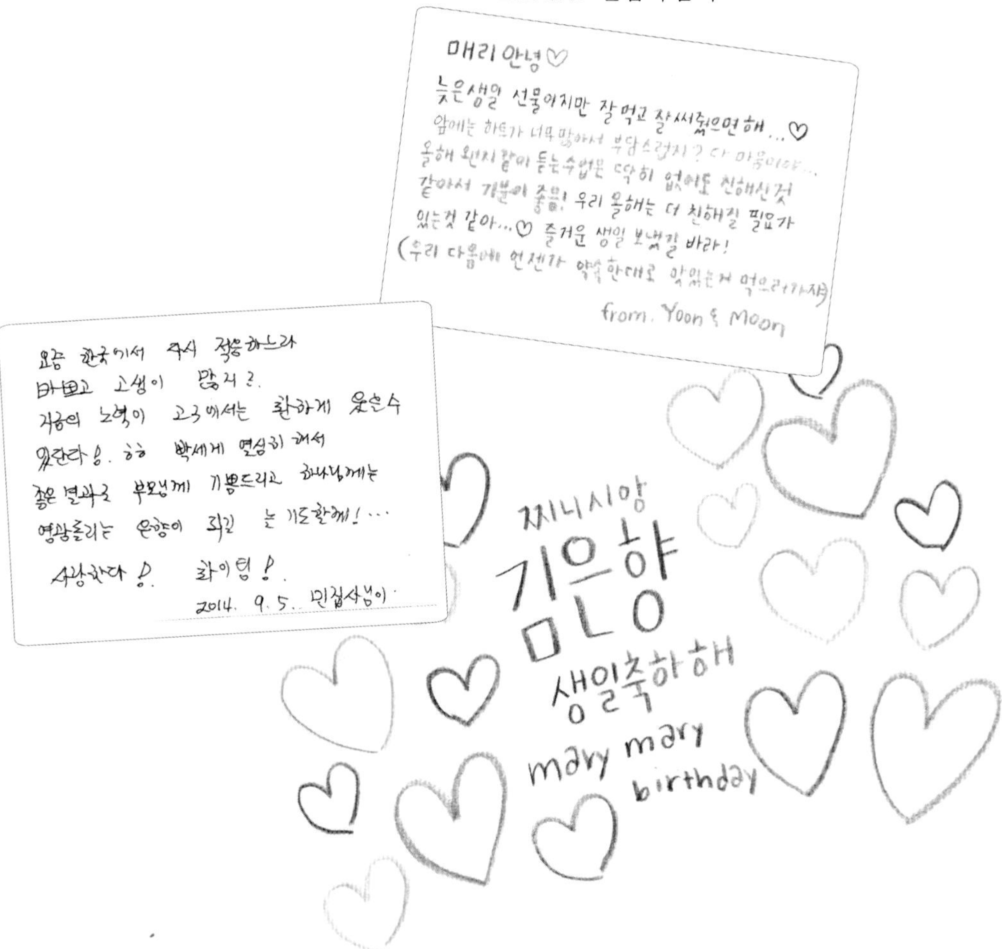
매리 안녕♡

늦은생일 선물이지만 잘 먹고 잘 써줬으면 해...♡

앞에는 하트가 너무 많아서 부담스럽지? 다 마음이야...

올해 왠지 같이 듣는 수업은 딱히 없어도 친해진 것 같아서 기분이 좋음! 우리 올해는 더 친해질 필요가 있는 것 같아...♡ 즐거운 생일 보내길 바라!

(우리 다음에 언젠가 약속한대로 맛있는거 먹으러가자)

from. Yoon & Moon

요즘 한국에서 다시 적응하느라 바쁘고 고생이 많지? 지금의 노력이 고국에서는 환하게 웃을수 있단다! ㅎㅎ 빡세게 열심히 해서 좋은 결과로 부모님께 기쁨드리고 하나님께는 영광돌리는 은향이 되길 늘 기도할께!...

사랑한다! 화이팅!

2014. 9. 5. 민집사님이

From. 세상에서 두번째로
이쁜 채연이가

To. 은향이에게^^.
안녕?? 잘 지내니 ㅋㅋㅋ 너한테 편지 써보는 건 첨이다... 이걸 생일편지라
해야하나... 하하하^^ 너를 교회 수련회에서 처음 봤게 ㅋㅋㅋ 같은 팀
돼서 게임도 같이 해서 이기고 물놀이 가서도 물 많이 먹이고...ㅎㅎ
너 처음 봤을 때 중1 인줄 알았어...ㅋㅋㅋ 어리게 봐줘서 고맙지?^^
막 수련회 때 체해가지고 계속 물 마시고 초록색 후드 집업 입고 음악 듣으
면서 토 없다고 음악 안 들으면 잠 안 온다고 ㅋㅋㅋ 그러다 놀아주다가
자고 내 파스 챙겨서 가져가고...ㅎㅎ 추억 돋는구만.. ㅋㅋ 손가락 다쳐서
W병원 다닌 것도 기억이 나고 참..^^ 이런 애가 공부 잘하고 막둥이 딸내미
에다가 이쁘고.. 완전 엄친딸이 있어..ㅋㅋㅋ 한국에 계속 있을 줄 알았는
데... 중국으로 간다는 말 듣고 좀 놀랐어 그것도 혼자... 조심히 잘 다
녀와~^^. 밤엔 막 돌아다니지 말고!! 알았냐? 중국어 잘하냐
나도 학교에서 배우고 있긴 있다만.. 좀 어렵던데... ㅋㅋㅋ 열공하고!!ㅎㅎ
중국어 좀 알려줘... 이해해줘^^ ㅋㅋ 아! 그리고 내가 추천해준 음악도 진짜
잘 듣고 있어 ㅎㅎ 고맙다잉^^ 또.. 뭐써야 하지 ㅋㅋㅋ 내가 한 [illegible]
했자나 갔다와서 머 먹고 싶은 거 있으면 말해 사줄게 ㅎㅎ 너는
빨리 아이스크림이나 사주고 [illegible] ㅋㅋㅋ [illegible]... 이제
여름도 막 바지에 다르고 조금씩 추워지려고 하나보다.. ㅋㅋㅋ
감기 조심하고!! 난 벌써 바보도 안 걸린다는 감기에 걸렸단다 TT
명심하고!! ㅎㅎ... 그리고 노래방도 가치가자~ 내가 신나게
해줄 자신 있다며 ㅋㅋㅋ 기대되는구만^^ 막 놀리면 때려 카고...
ㅎㅎ 이거다 보니 많이 적었네 ㅋㅋㅋ 어제 오늘 보고.. 한달에 한번
온다고 했나? 그때 볼 수 있으면 보겠네.. 몸조리 잘하고 날씨가
갑자기 추워 졌는데!!... 거기가서도 열심히 하고 잘지내고 잘 할수
있을 거야!! 김은향이~~ fighting!! 이거 맞나? ㅋㅋㅋ
한국이 그립거나 내가 생각나면 가끔씩 읽어봐 ...이키고잉^^
잘지내고 잘 다녀와라 은향아...^^ 울지말고 ㅋㅋㅋ...TT..
중국가서도 담에 또 보자아 ^^ ㅎㅎ — 2013. 8. 25. 일
심심하면 연락해^^.. 바보, 동범이오빠가 —
페북으로 ㅋㅋㅋ

은향이한테! 긁적긁적

은향아~ Happy Early Birthday!!!
난 지금 뼈 빠지게 중국어 숙제를 하면서 널 위해 편지를 적고 있어~!
그래도 너랑 중간에 만나서 재밌고 즐거웠다!
편지도 감동이였구……
내가 널 위해 특별한 선물을 준비했어.
기대하는 게 좋을 꺼야.

천사같이 예쁜 엄마랑

은향이 한테 ~ 긁적 긁적

은향아 ~ Happy Early Birthday !!!
난 지금 뼈 빠지게 중국어 숙제를 하면서 널
위해 편지를 적고 있어 ~ :D 그래도 너랑 중간에
만나서 재밌고 즐거웠다! 편지도 감동이였구....
울먹ㅋ 내가 널 위해 특별한 선물을 준비했어!
기대하는 게 좋을꺼야
그리고 너한테 말하고 싶은 것은.... 살 빼지
마!!! 다이어트는 나중에 생각하자고- ㅋㅋㅋ 달밤에 체조를 맨날
하다니... 충격이었어.... 띠로리 나는
맨날 뭐먹을까 고민 하고 있는데... 크흡 TT 메리~~
중국 가서 돌도 씹어먹을 기세로! 코피 팡팡 터지게 열공! 하구
11학년 때 꼭! 돌아와야돼~ 엉엉 TT 너 만나고
나서 소소한 즐거움이 언제나 있었는데 너 가면
나 우짠다니? 그래... 뭐... 음... 수줍/// 사랑한다
~~♡ 보고시플꺼 ~ 한국 들어오면 꼭 만나!
생일 너므너므 축하해! 빠이~
- 혜나가 -

4

My Portfolio

Eun Hyang Kim's Writing Work

"I hope that you saw my hard working spirit and positive personality in this portfolio."

Personal Narrative

<My lucky barefoot> day

"Wake up!" Our house keeper shouted. I slammed my pillow and shoved it in my ears. I woke up in the morning feeling annoyed. I knew that today was the summer bible school day but remembered that I had math tutoring in the morning. That made me a little mad. I brushed my teeth very harshly, splashed my face with water, and rubbed the water off, hoping it will wipe off the other stressful thoughts too. Finally, I was all ready for the big thing. The summer bible school!

"Ding dong!" The door bell rang. Here's my math teacher. I growled. I liked studying math, but not on the day of a fun event. I was crossing my fingers that he wouldn't come, but he came anyways like how the sun comes out every day.

A few hours passed which felt like 1 year to me. "That's it for today." He remarked. I was yelling 'Yes' in my head. It was 1:30. I had to leave. I came out of my apartment and stood like an iceberg in the hallway. Pressing the elevator button, I was staring at the shiny Chanel logo, displayed on my mom's big black fancy bag. I was worried that I would be the only one bringing a Chanel bag.

I got off the elevator and headed to my church. I went into the building and walked up the stairs to get to the roof area. That's where the summer bible camp was held. There weren't a lot of people. I could only see a huge silver carpet taped up to the floor for us to sit on. I sat down on the carpet with my group and began to look around. I was relieved to see some other people coming with other kinds of fancy bags, such as Gucci and Louis Vuitton.

"Take your seats!!" Our teacher exclaimed as soon as everyone arrived. "In order to get points to win the first prize, you guys need to behave well," he announced. As soon as the students heard him, we all became silent as a wet mouse in a box.

My group didn't do anything for 5 minutes while waiting for our teachers to get started. We just watched the other teams performing. Suddenly, the announcer called on us to come up to the stage to sing. I was startled. I didn't want to go out on the stage and sing in front of other people. Unfortunately, one of my friends forced me to go out with her. She pulled my arm and tried to make me stand up. Blinking nervously, I didn't see my shoes! I got so annoyed and scared. The teacher was still waiting for our group. I had to think fast but all I could do was staring at my friend.

"Come on, come on, it's for our own good!" Ye Jin said nervously. I had to listen to her. We all scurried out on the stage. Looking at each other's face we got ready to sing and started dancing along the song 'Go Savior!' It was hilarious how I was out on the stage singing and dancing when I didn't even know the song. I looked at my friend in front of me. I was able to depend on her because she was in the "Kid's Dancing Team." I felt like becoming a turtle trying to catch up to the rabbit as I followed her dance movement. I realized my feet getting dirty and dusty as I danced barefoot. I felt horrible about everything that was going on!

Finally, our performance was done. I sighed with relief. Now we had to wait for the score from the announcer. My friend"Ye Jin" suddenly called out, "Ms. 000, I think we should have more points than the other teams. Mary came out barefoot!" I looked at Ms.000 with my eyes wide open. Ms. 000 checking on my feet responded, "Ok. We will give more points to this team!" As soon as she announced that, I heard, "I should have got out there without my shoes also……Awe man!" I felt awkward to see 30 eyes staring straight at my feet. We screamed with a big "Yahoo!"

I came back to my seat. I didn't really understand why the announcer gave us more points than the other teams. Still, I liked the fact that we got more points.

"Extra points for barefoot was just for you to come out." My group teacher whispered calmly. She told me to be attentive and patient because there were barely any kids who heard about the suggestion.

I thought in my head, 'I thought feet were just for walking, playing soccer, and running, but they can also bring a good luck too!! ^^*

〈영어로 쓴 픽션〉

Realistic Fiction

Hold on Tight

By Eun Hyang Kim

" Push! " Mr. Bucket told his wife. " I can't take it any longer. " Mrs. Bucket responded.

It was 24th of December, a peaceful Christmas Eve, until the town jumped on their chairs with a loud cry of a new born baby.

"Ungaeungaeungae!!!" the loud cry had suddenly covered the town. "Well, well, well, you've got a baby girl. She looks just like her mother."One of the town people said. Soon the Bucket's house was filled with people.

"Her name is Sel!" Mr. Bucket said proudly. "Sel, the most important girl in our family."

" Well of course! She is the girl, who will take down the tradition of her mother's sherbet." Mrs. Tug said with a smile on her face.

That night the laughs of the whole town brightened the dark night of Sel's first birthday and Christmas Eve.

"Are you ready for school, honey?" mom exclaimed from the kitchen.

"No! I have to look perfect for the first day of 4th grade! So stop jacking me up!" She yelled in somewhat frustrated voice. "What has gotten in to you? You're suddenly worried about how you look. And look! You're yelling at your own mother?"

" Mom, I'm not a 3rd grader anymore. I'm almost a teenager!!!!!!Not a baby!!!!"Sel screamed at her mom. Her room was painted mostly in lavender color. She had a lot of stuffed animals around her room and a huge crown nailed to the door. She knew that her mother was going to be upset about what she said, but it was the first day of her 4th grade. She was nervous.

She headed to school on her pink and white bike that was covered with sparkles all over. She wore a jean skirt with a ribbon tagged on the bottom, a bright lavender striped Polo Ralph Lauren t-shirt, black leggings, and brown gladiator Gucci sandals. She sang, "Ring the bell, ring the bell, and tell them that princess Sel is on her way!" She was very nervous about the school. She wondered 'What if there are girls much prettier than me?" Sel took a deep breath. She was busy thinking about all the possible things that could happen. When she was crossing the street, Sel didn't see a girl in her way. She bumped into the girl. It wasn't a pretty scene.

"Ouch!" Sel screamed. The bike screeched right in to the bushes.

The girl who fell freaked out saying, " Were you out of your mind? You almost got my new dress all dirty! Sel wanted to yell back at her when the girl's pretty face distracted her from doing it. Sel thought, 'With that kind of personality she has, she doesn't have a lot of friends.' The girl was wearing a light blue dress, a purple Long Champ hand bag instead of a back pack, and silver sandals which showed that she was probably from a rich family. The girl had brown eyes, short curly hair, and plus she was thin. 'Well... I can be better.' She thought. 'I have beautiful greenish blue eyes, long waved hair and I'm also thin.

9

Sel told herself, "Don't worry, Sel. I'm sure she's 6th grade or something."

Sel stared at the girl as she walked away in silence. She parked her bike behind the trees where kids parked their bikes. As she was walking in to the hallway of the building, she spotted the "Beauty Contest for college students" announcement that she'd seen all around the town.

"DING DONG DANG DONG!" Sel tried to find her class room which was 4-2. It wasn't easy for her to find it because it was her first day in this school. So she decided to ask one of the passing by students. "Excuse me, where is the class 4-2?" Sel asked.

The student answered. "Oh! You are in that class too? We can be buds. Follow me. We're in the same class! Oh, by the way my name is Helen. Were you popular in other schools? You look like a model!"

Sel was so happy that she found a potential friend. She also liked the fact that she has been called a model. Suddenly, Helen asked, "Do you happen to know this girl in our class who is really pretty? Today I think she wore a blue dress."

Sel answered with a surprise, " She is in 4th grade! Oh my god!!!! Impossible!!I hate her and I have never seen her before except this morning with the stupid accident!!"Sel yelled out. She couldn't resist her competitive feeling with the unknown girl.

Than Helen asked, "You hate her also? I hate her also...! Almost all the boys and girls hate her except these two boys. She is only kind to them because they are handsome. The 2 boys don't know who she really is. By the way, their name is Bill and Tom. Bill is in our grade and he's sooo handsome. Tom is in 5th grade and he's really popular between everyone. They are cousins. They live together with their entire family including their relatives. They have a gigantic house."

"Helen, how do you know all this?" Sel asked with amazement.

"Well...after all I've been here since forever. It's a great school. It's a small school but there are a lot of cool boys and some mean girls."

Just then, Sel had an idea. "I have a brilliant beyond brilliant idea!"Sel quoted.

"Well, what is it?" Helen asked.

"You'll see." Sel responded with a pretty big smile on her face."

"Gosh! How stupid I am! I said my name but I didn't ask yours! What's your name?" Helen asked Sel.

"I'm Sel. I live in the 8th house in Willie's Village. Where do you live?" Sel smiled as she responded.

"I live so close to you. I live in the 12th house. Wow! I feel like were meant to be friends." Helen said happily.

"Do you know that you're as pretty as that witch?...You know who?"Helen said all of a sudden.

"I am? Thanks. Well... you too...?!" Sel replied awkwardly.

"Are you kidding? Ha Ha~! We're here!" Helen exclaimed.

"Wow that's a one big class room. Bye~ summer vacation!" Sel said.

As soon as she came in, she spotted that the witch was in the same classroom." Iuuuuu who farted? It's coming from the desk over there." Sel shouted as she winked to Helen. They seemed to agree that it was mean of them to say that but they did it anyways.

"I can sort of smell something…" One of the girls said sniffing her nose near the witch's desk.

"You see?!" Sel exclaimed as she thanked the girl who helped in just in time.

Sel whispered to Helen, "Let the game begin!"

Sel never thought of doing such a thing like this. It was new for her. After school, when she said bye to Helen, Sel saw Bill and Tom walking with the girl back from school. Now, she got really sneaky. She decided to do something to her. She tiptoed to the bushes and overheard their conversation.

"Sally, are you free this Sunday?" Tom asked.

"Well yeah of course Bill! Come on Tom I have nothing to do with those kids." The witch Sally replied.

"Sally come on, you need to fix your character! You're not the only one in this world! Don't you realize how many kids who hate you? The whole entire 4th grade!" Tom said as he passed by the bushes.

"It's cool. Calm down, you two. 4 o'clock in front of the fountain on Sunday. Sounds good?" Bill said as he calmed down the other two 4th graders.

'Hum… I might be able to use this date to separate them. 'Hee hee.' Sel thought in her head with a smile.

That night Sel followed the boys to find out where they lived. She had the meanest and the craziest idea in the world. Sel headed back home feeling like a feather

"I'm home!!!!!!!" Sel yelled happily.

"Hey, where were you? I heard someone coming in and I knew it was you. What happened? You're so happy!" Mrs. Bucket asked Sel curiously.

"It's a secret!" she responded. As soon as Sel finished the sentence, she climbed up the stairs to the attic. It was her own little space, where she can dream of being a star and winning the kid's national beauty payent.

She pictured herself up on the stage wearing a beautiful dress with high heels that she dreamed of wearing. However her real dream was to take a picture with the star of the "Middle School Musical" Roy Colton.

As she daydreamed, she had a huge smile on her face.

She came down stairs to her own room and started jotting down her plan to break up the friendship between the boys and the witch in her note book:

My very first step of the plan of crushing the witch:

- *I will send a letter to Bill and Tom saying "We're not friends anymore. You suck!" And the boys will panic and stop talking to her.*
- *I will do some bad stuff on teacher's desk and say that it was her: Spilling water on her coat, Making her leave the cell phone on, pretend as if she tried to change her*

scores in her report card...etc

- *I will pretend to be injured in sport as soon as she will hit me in dodge ball.*

She was satisfied with her plan.

"I kind of feel bad for her.... No, may be not! She deserves it!" She started writing the letter to the Boys.

Dear Bill and Tom,

I can't go to the theater. I have stuff to do rather than meeting you guys. I was planning to tell you guy this but I never had a chance. I don't really want to hang out with ya'll anymore. Please don't even say hi to me tomorrow. I beg you. Sometimes I get really embarrassed.

Sorry and bye,

Sally

Sel was proud of what she had done. Now all she had to do was to copy the hand writing of the witch onto a neat paper. To get the witch's notebook, she pretended to pass by and she memorized her locker combination. When everybody left she had opened it and got her notebook. She started copying the letters down one by one.

Dear Bill and Tom,

I can't go to the theater. I have stuff to do rather than meeting you guys. I was planning to tell you guy this but I never had a chance. I don't really want to hang out with ya'll anymore. Please don't even say hi to me tomorrow. I beg you. Sometimes I get really embarrassed.

Sorry and bye,

Sally

She was so happy to have accomplished her first revenge.

"Dinner is ready!!!!" her mom called.

"Mom, I can't have dinner. I need to go somewhere fast!" As soon as Sel finished talking, she ran out of the house.

Sel is neither rich nor poor. She's just an ordinary girl who lives in the 8th house in Sesame St. of Willie's Village. So as usual, Sel went by the post office. Sel said "Hi" to the yogurt woman and grabbed an ice cream from her parents' ice cream shop on her way to the boys' house.

"I guess this is it!" Sel said standing in front of the boys' house.

The boys' house was a huge 4 story Mansion. She read the sign on the door,

"Mr. Hallows." She didn't know their last name but she had to stick to her choice.

"Wait! Something is weird. I sort of recognize this place." She said to herself. "No that can't be true...Impossible! Snap out of it Sel!" She looked around and found a mail box. She looked around to see if anyone was there. She slipped the letter in the mail box and ran away as if she was being followed by a killer.

That night, she hesitated to ask her mom about the boys' house. Sel has never heard about her childhood story. Now, she felt like that the house might have something to do with her childhood. She decided to ask her mom. It was the millionth time she asked about her own childhood, but it was obvious that her mom would say no.

"Um...mom, can I talk to you about a subject I've asked a lot of times?" Sel asked. Normally, finding a familiar house isn't really important to anyone, but for Sel it was.

"Sel, We've already talked about this. Even though I tell you you will never understand why we kept it as a secret."She said.

"But...no one ever told me. I really want to know. I bet that there are no kids in the world who don't know about their childhood." She responded.

"Sorry honey but even for the trillionth time I can't tell you."

Just then, her dad came back from the shop with a bunch of samples as usual. "I'm home!!!!!!!!!!Why is everybody so serious?"As soon as he came home, Sel's mom took his arm and pulled him in the room.

'Something's going on.' Sel thought in her head. 'I'd better overhear the conversation.' Sel knew that it wasn't a good thing to do, but she had no choice.

"We can't tell her that!" Her mother yelled.

"Don't you remember what kind of a disaster it was? Sel is too young to understand, and it's HER childhood. She has been a bright girl Garrett, and we don't want to ruin it... do we?"

"Wait! Does Sel know about the book of her childhood? Did you check if it's still there?" Her father replied to her mom as he jumped out of his chair.

"Shhhhhh...Be quiet! We don't want her to know about the book. Also it has been a huge shock to everyone. Let's not talk about it." Sel's mom said putting a finger on Mr. Bucket's lips.

"You know how much we were shocked with the fact that her childhood story came out as a book. It has been so many years since we read it for the last time. I need to put Sel into bed. I'll be right back." Her mom said.

"Creek!!" The door was about to open. The sound of the door was pretty helpful for Sel. Whenever she was playing on the computer, with the sound she can always turn it off but she has been stopped using the strategy. She thought that now she was too big.

However, now, this was the time to use the old "Sel way" strategy. This was the time that she had to run.

She hid herself in the basement. Her mom had told her not to go in there because there are rats.

"Wow, I've never seen this place before in my life! There are so many good things!" She suddenly forgot about the whole problem.

"Why don't mom and dad use all of these things? Wait... Why did they put all of my baby stuffs in the basement? There aren't rats in here. Why don't they want me to come down here?" Sel started having all kinds of questions in her head.

All of a sudden, her head hurt. She thought to herself, 'Why did they try to erase my childhood?'

Sel stayed in the basement hearing her mom call her name in worried voice. However, she promised herself not to go back up stairs until she finds the secret.

Suddenly the basement door opened. Sel had to hide somewhere. "What should I do? Where should I hide?" She spotted a big storage in the corner. She went behind the box and stayed still.

"Sel, if you're in the basement you'd better get out. I'll count to three and if you don't, you'd stay here for the night. 1..., 2..., 3.... That's what you want? You've got the night with rats here. Happy Birthday Sel!" Her mom yelled with a slam of the door. Sel have never seen her mom as mad as this before. Sel was scared and felt sorry for her parents looking for her.

"Ouuuuuchh!!!" she screamed with a grimace on her face. As she looked around to see what made her trip, she rubbed her ankle. She had tripped over a book.

"What's this? Hummm....Huh? Why does this book have my name on it?"

"The secret of Sel〉〉〉〉〉〉"

'No one wanted to talk about her childhood but now I will. When the baby was born everyone knew that she was special. She was loved by a lot of people. She was especially adored by her grandfather. Her grandmother died of cancer a decade ago.

When Sel was 3 years old, her family was on a trip to South Carolina with her relatives. At that time, the town where she went to was known for kidnapping and violence. Sel and her family and of course her relatives were at a restaurant and they noticed a stranger was following them. They kept turning around but they didn't see a thing. Suddenly, a guy with a weapon came out of nowhere saying, "Pass me the young girl. She is wearing a dress out of precious diamonds that cost more than a million." Actually they were fake diamonds. So they went in to a fight.'

"Wow! I actually had a grandfather! South Carolina isn't my home town!!" She was really amazed. The whole story sounded as if it never happened to her.

'Sel's grandfather started the fight. They did all kinds of crazy stuff. Her relatives ran with all their might except for her grandpa. Sel's grandpa was pretty healthy and he always carried a knife "in case of an emergency." Now this was an emergency. He brought out his knife and started swinging around with the baby beside him leaning against the wall. There were only Sel, grandpa, and the unknown kidnapper. The others ran off somewhere to hide. At first, the grandpa made a cut on the wrist of the guy. The second thing we know, at least I know is that her grandpa was lying on the ground with a knife stabbed in his chest. The love of the grandpa was stronger than anyone else. We couldn't even imagine how cruely the kidnapper killed her grandfather.. The baby was taken by the kidnapper and has been left in front of a house of someone. The rest it's up to you to imagine

-1995Carolina times, James Boper-

"Oh my god!!!" She whispered to herself with tears coming from her eyes. "After all these years I was stupid enough to believe that my grandpa died in a car accident before I was born! With whose permission! Who told them to lie about MY CHILDHOOD!!!!!! If it's true about the kidnapping WHO ARE REALLY MY REAL PARENTS?? WHERE ARE THEY?? I NEED TO KNOW THE TRUTH OF WHAT REALLY HAPPENED!!"

She didn't know whether she should be happy or not. She was 30 percent happy that she revealed the secret, 60percent she was mad about the secret, and 10 percent she was worried about a spending a night in the basement and wanted to go back up as if nothing happened. Sel wanted to talk to her mother about it. She felt like a adopted child who doesn't know their real parents.

She waited until her parents went in to their room to get out of the basement and go to the attic. She peeked through the cracked floor of the kitchen to see if her mom was there.

Sel thought in her head, 'This is the only chance!' She opened the door to the basement, checked again if anyone was there, passed by the living room, and peeked through the slightly opened door to her parent's room. Her plan was to act as if she'd been in the garage and to say that she couldn't find the huge pair of scissors.

"Knock, knock..." she tapped on the door while sweating as if she just got out of the pool.

"Come in." Her mother replied while reading a book. When Sel came in she spotted a glass of Vodka next to her mom. That meant that she was in the bad mood. It was a habit of her mom.

"Mom, I can't find the huge scissors... Do you know where they are?" Sel said with a smile on her face.

"You were in the garage? How come the light wasn't on?" Her mom replied coldly.

" Well...Wha...What happened is that I wanted to do some little garage adventure and I took the hand light...Yeah...!"Sel replied really nervously. She was worried about the answer she will respond to her. It was the first time she has ever thought that lying was so hard.

"Whewwwww...Ok. Go up stairs and get ready for bed." Her mom replied with a sigh but not a normal one. Sel was worried if her mom found out about the basement. She had a feeling that her mom knew it all already. However she believed that she was doing the right thing. Sel thought in her head, 'They already lied to me since I was a baby. Lying about a relationship between families is much bigger big deal...I guess."

That night Sel dreamed of meeting her grandfather. In the dream, her grandfather was telling her the real story. "Grandpa? Is that you? I missed you so much?" "Sel, we don't have much time. I will tell you the truth. Your parents are your biological parents. You have been raised for a month in other house right next to where the accident happened. You were born in San Francisco until you're your parents moved to Carolina to look for you. You have a very good friend who played with you while you stayed in the house of someone else. I'm happy that you are safe. They had to try to erase the secret for your own good. We thought that a huge shock for a young child wasn't part of a lovely, bright girl. Just like you. Would you forgive your parents and go toward your goal of winning the contest of your dreams?" The voice of Sel's grandpa faded out as the sun raised.

"Wait don't go! I..I ...will always remember you. I will do what you told me to if it's the only way to make you happy."

The next morning Sel woke up really early to sign up for the contest." Ahummmm~! Good morning mom!"Sel shouted for almost the whole world to hear. Sel quickly got ready for the signup. She wore black skinny jeans long bright green tank top, and the same sandals from yesterday. She tied her head to the left and swirled it to the top.

"Perfect! It's neat, cute, and comfortable." Sel was satisfied of how she looked like today.

When she arrived in school it was a half day. They only had class for 4 hours.

"Awesome! I am going to home early!" Helen shouted.

"Helen, can you come with me to the signup? Please~~~!!!" Sel asked her nervously. Helen had worn a pink dress with black tiny polka dots. She has unbelievable beautiful brown eyes and sort of long super curled blond hair.

"Ok. If you will be the one to crush the witch in the contest I can even make a team for you! I've been in this school since kindergarten. I know a lot of people!" Helen responded with confidence.

"Thank you so much! I'll give you half of the prize when I will win. We're all in this together...right!!??! Sel yelled with a hope.

"Of course! We're friends!" Helen said with a yahoo.

"So where do we have to go to sign up for it?" Helen asked.

"Right over there in the corner." Sel replied with a smile of gratitude.

Sel passed by the post office again and ended up in a small place with a lot people. They were all busy getting ready for something.

"This is the last call! Are there any more children who wants to sign up?" The secretary of the manager yelled in a tiring voice.

"Sel yelled," I do!!!! I would like to sign up!"

"One more...whewwwww.....and no more!~" The secretary said.

"Thank you for waiting girls and boys. Since we have too many people signed up, we will pick some people throughout the audition in ten minutes. You all need to sing and dance and smile the whole time. We will call out your names in the order of sign ups. There are altogether 46 people. We will pick the best 15 children! Please do your best!" The manager announced.

"Ohhh...no..... I can't sing in front of people. I love to sing but I feel like I'd faint when I stand in front of people." Sel worried as she talked to Helen.

"Don't worry! Remember yesterday in our music class? You sang great! The teacher was so impressed! Even Bill was out of his mind and the others also! You can do it! Face it! It's for your career also but for our pride...remember? The witch ...our promise...." Helen replied in a encouraging voice.

"Thanks Helen, I'll try hard to do my best... It's for us not for me... I can do it!!!! Yes I can! I will complete my grandpa's dream..." Sel replied as her tears came out and her voice faded out. She didn't know why she had brought up her grandpa.

About 2hours had passed while Sel told Helen about the story and Sel practiced under a tree with Helen.

"Number 46 Sel Bucket, please come up to the stage for the last auditioning girl." The manager announced.

"Good luck!!!" Helen said as she made thumbs up to Sel.

Sel didn't have time to thank her because the two boys and the witch was watching her also.

"A...a...a..." Sel started off with checking the microphone as usual. Sel had learned from her dad that in order to sing well we always have to check the microphone.

She started to sing as if she was singing for her grandpa. The song's title was "For you." It was Sel's favorite song but there is a very sad story of the singer hidden in the song.

"Thank you." Sel said as she wiped up the sweat from her hands.

For Sel 5 minutes felt like 5 years.

As soon as she finished the song, loud claps and whistles covered the stage. The real incident was that Bill and Tom were showing thumbs up at her.

"Those who made it through were number 1, 5, 7, 13, 15, 16, and 19... ....and lastly 46! Congratulations everybody!!!!!" The secretary announced.

Sel looked for Helen. She was talking with some friends.

"Hey, Helen thank you so much! If it weren't for you I wouldn't have been able to pass the audition." Sel said as she hugged her.

"I'm so proud of you!!! I knew that you would make it through!" Helen replied hyper.

"I'll be right back...I need to go see the boys....." Sel said. She wanted to go ask them if they knew her.

"Excuse me... Can I interrupt you guys for a second?" Sel asked carefully.

"Of course! We have time..." Tom said winking to Bill.

"I know that it's stupid to ask this but do you guys know me? I coincidently saw you guys going in to a big house which was really familiar to me. Also, I have noticed that you guys gave me thumbs up and we never talked before or did we?" Sel asked curiously.

"You really don't remember us? We're Tom and Bill. You stayed in our house for couple years because you were lost in a family trip I believe. We missed you a lot. Especially Bill. He played with you a lot. We were happy to be in the same school. My aunt misses you so much. You were like her daughter." Tom said.

"You sang really well just like yesterday....!" Bill yelled trying change the subject.

"I stayed in your house? You guys are Bill and Tom who were called "V Robot Boys" at that time?" Sel asked in amazement and with happiness.

"Now you remember! Yes, we're the boys who were your best friends." Tom said with a final sigh.

"No wonder!!! I missed you guys a lot!!!!" Sel replied under the hot sun.

"Why are you sweating like crazy? Do you have something to say, Sel?" Tom asked. Sel felt ashamed of herself doing such a bad thing to Sally and the boys. She didn't want them to be mad at her for doing that. After all they are best buds.

"I...I... need to go to the toilet..." Sel answered in a quivering voice.

"Go ahead...wait it seems like you're hiding something from us..." Tom claimed as he came close to her. Sel blushed like an apple as her heart beat loudly.

"I...I don't have anything I'm hiding. Just your imagination. Ha ha..." Sel whispered back.

"Ok... We'll be in the cafeteria behind the building. We'll meet you there.. Come on Bill... let's go!!!" Tom yelled at Bill who was talking with Sally who glanced at Sel.

'What am I suppose to do? Ok...I will count to three and say that I'm back from the toilet. Wow! A dandelion. I might be able to decide whether to tell them the thing or not by taking the petals off. Tell, not, tell, not, tell, not...tell...not, and TELL!!! I can do this. I can do this...' Sel thought in her head as she wanted to go home when she couldn't because she promised Tom to wait in the cafeteria.

"I'm back!" Sel said as if nothing ever happened. She soon decided to tell them if they asked her.

"Sel, so how are you? You don't look ok." Tom said

"..." Sel was looking at the table else while her mind was in somewhere else.

"Sel!" Bill said shaking tapping her shoulder.

"Yes, what...what happened? What did you say?" Sel finally answered jumping out of her chair.

"Are you sure that you have nothing to tell us?" Tom asked.

"Come on, Sel tell us. We've promised each other that we will not have any secrets in kindergarten." Added Bill.

"Ok...No panicking allowed! So what happened is that I saw these two boys which I was sure that they were popular, walking with Sally. For the first time, I was really jealous of someone."

"You were" Tom asked.

"Yeah...well and I decided to write a fake letter to you guys by the name of Sally. And I did...it's in your mail box right now...I think. I'm really sorry. It was a big mistake I did in a strike of lightening. I know that it's no use saying that I'm sorry ...but I'm sorry..." Sel said sorry for the last time in silence and ran away in tears.

"Wait...we've forgiven since forever and we don't even care...well we do about what you said but not the letter...!! We are not ashamed of you!" Tom said as he blushed.

"I really don't that I deserve forgiveness!!" Sel screamed as her shadow faded away in front of the cafeteria and in the corner.

"What should we do? We can't leave her like that. Plus, you know... " Bill said to Tom.

"I'll talk to her best friend in personal. I'll ask her to talk to her this evening after dinner. That way she can prepare the contest with some help and tell our forgiveness to her. Don't worry about it. You know her. I mean, she'll be herself again." Tom said with a bright smile trying to encourage his cousin.

Sel ran to her house and ate a delicious dinner. 'I will never be able to go see them again...oh my god I bet that Helen is mad! I hope that all the problems will go away! Oh no....the contest is tomorrow!!! Nothing's working for me today... at a time like this... I wish my sister was here. She'd always cheer me up with dumb childish jokes. Why did my mom send her to a French boarding school?' She whispered to herself in her head.

"Ding dong!" the door bell rang loudly and clearly.

Sel opened the door without looking at who it was.

"Wow~ you seem discouraged... Looks like you want to cry in your mom's chest like a baby...Am I right?'' A voice said. It was a very familiar voice. It was sweet, nice, and hopefully girly.

"You weren't mad at me because I left without telling you and plus in a hurry and I couldn't walk you home from school and I feel bad about everything??!!!??" Sel said without even stopping.

"Calm down Sel... Take a deep breath. I know what happened with the boys and why you ran. I'm here for you. Tom came to me to go talk to you. I also noticed that you need a lot of help with the contest right? Helen said calmly as she looked at the mess in her room.

"I need a lot of help. Even though I'd have 10 arms I still wouldn't be able to finish the preparation. I'm doomed. After all the things I prepared. It will all be a mess." Sel said with a worried face.

"Come on Sel, let's get ready for the show! I think that you will win if you wore not fancy but cute. I mean original but very cute. And you might want to sing a song that goes really good with the clothes. I recommend you to wear the jacket you wore in your profile photo in facebook. It's totally awesome. And..." Helen suddenly stopped.

"I'm still listening. Why did you stop?" Sel asked scarily. Helen was suddenly pale as a ghost.

"Be...be...behind...behind y...you. There is a GHOST!!!!!!" Helen screamed.

"Yeah...sure...Helen...that's sooo possible!!!!" Sel said trying to look strong.

"Awww...man! You're not a scardy cat. You're not like other girls...That's good. I like your personality. Oh...and I won't help you anymore. It's your contest after all. I'll see you in front of the clock tower at 8:30 in the morning. Sleep well!! It's the contest and the day to crush the witch. We believe in Y, O, and U... YOU!!!!!! See you tomorrow!" Helen said.

'I will win this contest for my grandpa, Helen, my family and the mega-super dooper mean WITCH!!! 'Sel said to herself in her head.

She once again took out her little thinking notebook and started to right the plan of tomorrow!

*For the big day of tomorrow!!*****(five stars, very important!)*

- *I will wear my pink and purple checkered skirt with white leggings that comes five centimeters above my knees.*
- *I will wear my white blouse that comes down to my*

elbows and I will fold the part where there are the buttons. I will also wear my pink sweater with a star on the back on top of the blouse. The blouse show about 30% and the sweater will show about 70%.

- *I will French braid my hair in 2 knots.*
- *I will bring my white converse bag with some make ups that my mom let me borrow for the day, some sweets, a camera and of course some money for afterwards. (AND MY IPHONE)*
- *I will bring some clothes for "in case of an emergency."*
- *Lastly my big goal I will win the contest.*
- *Remember Sel, Your dream is to be a singer...*

"I'm all set for tomorrow." Sel said

"Sel, come down stairs!" her mother called her from downstairs in a happy voice.

"I'll be there in a second!"Sel replied as she out her notebook in the drawer in her desk. The drawer was for all her special stuff. Her first diary, first candy wrapper, her thinking notebook, and love letters etc. It was her own little treasure box.

Sel walked carefully down stairs. "I'm down, what's wrong?" Sel asked her mother as she stretched.

"We wanted to have a party for you. I heard from Bill that you're having the contest! Ooopsy daisy! (My big dumb mouth!) Never mind about Bill. He's just my friend. Ha ha!" Her mom said as she looked at her father who was glancing back at her in a scary look.

"Dad, mom, you guys don't have to hide these things from me. I know about my grandpa, Bill and Tom. I coincidently overheard the conversation and I went in the basement. I was going to get out when I got my eyes attracted by so many wonderful things in the basement. Just then, I heard mom calling me. I had to hide somewhere. I do regret of not getting out as soon as you left the basement. Anyways, I tripped over a book. I started reading it because it had a funny title. "The Secret of Sel." At first, I thought that it was just a fairy tale. However it wasn't a fairytale. It had my birth date and all the information about me. I had to keep reading. I started hating you guys and feeling disappointment in you guys. I was also worried that the parents I lived all my life wouldn't be my biological parents. But, about 2days ago, grandpa talked to me in my dreams. He explained everything. He was really proud of me. He wanted for me to be strong and bright. So I did it. It was my turn to do him a favor. Well... you can still scold me if you want. I'm...sorry." Sel said with a face about to cry.

The living room was silent for more than a minute or two. His father was coughing with his arms around her mother in tears. Sel was looking down with tiny tears dropping on the floor like a rain drop.

Suddenly her dad asked her, " Why weren't you mad at us during all this time?"

"I would have, though I wasn't. I was busy thinking about the contest and I thought that it was just life. It was too stupid to be all mad about this. I believe that there are more things to worry about in the future than today. Am I right? So I wish that my mom will stop crying and scold me or have the party. Sounds good?" Sel cheered up her parents.

"Let's get the party on the road!" Her mom said wiping her tears off.

Sel ate a big cake like a queen with chocolate pudding and a big teddy bear from her parents.

Sel felt like flying away because she was so happy.

"I'm going to bed! I need to sleep like a sleeping beauty for tomorrow!" Sel told her parents before going upstairs.

"Ok, good night, sleep tight, and don't let the night bugs bite!" Her parents told their daughter with a laugh.

Sel went in to her room and tucked herself in bed until the sun rise.

"Good morning, everyone? It's the big day!" Sel said with lots of happiness. But, weirdly no one answered. She couldn't hear neither her mother boiling her tea nor her dad turned on television. Except on the refrigerator there was a small note that said,

Hey Sel, mom and dad are out doing the groceries. Good luck in the contest and hope you get a good result!

We wish you luck and love you!

Love,

Mom and dad

'Wow! Mom and dad doing groceries! I hope they get some yummy stuff for me also!' Sel thought. She was all ready for the contest! She had packed her clothes "in case of an emergency" and the things that she wrote in her thinking notebook. She got dressed and headed for the clock tower where she told Helen to be.

"Helen!!! You look so pretty today! Wow you dyed your hair in light brown. You look better than last time...You were basically white because you were so blond." Sel said as she looked at her hair.

"Yup! I know! Bad old blond days... I'm not blond anymore...Am I?" Helen has worn a pink tank top with skinny jeans and she has cut her hair up to her shoulders. She also straightened it. She looked beautiful but lack of 10%.

"You look so pretty and cute today...I love it! I'm sure that you can crush the witch. She is completely out of her mind. You know what she wore? Look!! She wore a black tank top without straps and a black mini, tiny, skirt. That's not a fourth grader. Will you be ok?" Helen asked in a worried voice.

"Sure, who am I?! Nothing will happen. The beauty contest isn't only for well dressed people and pretty people. It's for people who are pretty, a good talented singer or a dancer, healthy, well dressed, and who gets the most votes by the audience. I better go in and get ready. And...if you see the boys tell them I'm sorry for the yelling. I was just sensitive. It just came out. Also tell them that I really want to apologize. Also if they want to forgive me tell them to give me thumbs up afterwards. Just like yesterday." Sel replied to Helen with a huge smile. She never looked so happy before.

"And hello to the beauty contest number 1! Here are some rules! You need to be healthy, pretty, well dressed, and talented. You have to prepare a cassette of what you will sing. Good luck everyone!" The manager said as the smoke came out and he disappeared in to the smoke.

" Hello my name is Sally Tuckson. I'm dreaming of being the star that everyone wants. I measure 151cm and will always be the star of everybody. Please enjoy!" Sally said as she gave a wink to everybody. She danced and sang really well. However, Sel was on fire.

It was Sel's turn. "Hello peoples and thank you for coming here even though it's boiling hot. I've always dreamed of being a young star that can represent at least 40% of California's West side academy school! Enjoy and hope all your dreams come true like me!!" Sel announced with a kiss to the audience. The audience seemed to like Sel's opening better than Sally's opening.

Sel sang and sang until the tape suddenly stopped. She felt really sad and worried. She wanted to get out of here. However, the audience was still clapping in her song's rhythm. She used the clap to sing the rest of the song. She also had to try to spot the boys and quick. She had spotted the boys with Sally once again. But the song and the singing calmed her down. Songs always make Sel calm down.
The boys looked annoyed by Sally.

The time went fast and it was finally the time to announce the votes. "In 5th place there is Henry Gott. In 4th place there is Diana Durkinshna. In 3rd place there is Sally Turkson. And in second place there is Garrett Luvert." The manager announced. Sally looked really upset to not be the first and also mad. She suddenly glanced at Sel. Sel quickly turned back. She looked really stressed up on the stage with a bronze medal. "And to continue, in first place there is Sel Bucket who got over the emergency without getting shocked! Congratulations everybody! For Sel our winner of summer 2010, we will give her a trophy with my sign on it. Thank you for participating and see you this winter!" The manager announced.

Sel was so happy to be in first. Also she felt really sorry for Sally for the first time. She also has done a lot of things to her. She thought, 'Maybe it was all thanks to Sally who turned off the cassette that I got to win.'

"Or you need to say…!" Helen suddenly said hugging me.

"Thank you my princess BFF Helen! I will give you my medal. This medal is for great friendship… and it belongs to Helen!!" Sel said as she gave Helen also a hug.

"Thumbs up! " A very familiar voice said.

"Tom?" Sel suddenly turned around.

"So I gave you thumbs up…congrats!! You crashed her right down the trash can… and as I said…It's really no big deal. So why don't we have some ice cream? It's steaming hot!" Tom said as he looked around trying to look for his cousin Bill.

"I'm sorry for the last time. And I need to change. I'll be right back." Sel said. -

"You know, I started to like Sel a lot. A lot more than I expected myself to.

"I will be with her for the entire school year. I hope." Helen said.

"You won't be able to. She's staying here for a month. It's impossible. Haha that's not the answer you want is it? Haha… I have discussed with her mom, and she said that she can stay in this school!" Tom announced to some of his friends and Helen who was with Diana the girl who ranked 4th place.

"I'm back! Wow! These are all my fans who want my autograph? ha! Kidding!" Sel said.

"Well I guess all WE have to do is go straight to our goals! Just like Sel! She stepped on the very first road to her goal! So everyone will encourage each one us until the day we get famous? One two three we shout hurray. 1…, 2…, 3… HURRAY!!!!!!FOR OUR DREAMS!!!"

김은향

Persuasive Essay

Pro Uniform

By Eun Hyang Kim

Introduction

The topic is whether there should be school uniforms or not. In the world there are some people who are for it and are some people who are against it. Ones who are against it are mostly students. They hate uniforms. They think that they are ugly enough to be in a museum of old fashion. The main thing they usually talk about is liberty. They say that they need freedom. They need to express themselves.

On the other hand, there are some people who are for school uniforms. They are usually adults and principals of the schools. Some parents want to save money from buying their kids' clothes. The principals want to get money and represent the school by making them wear uniforms.

Today, I am on the side for school uniforms to be allowed in schools. There are 6 reasons. I will talk about my view from both sides. In this write-on debate, there are two sides, the pros side and the cons side. In section 1, we talk about the "focus and time" of the students while wearing uniforms. In section 2, we talk about how we are equal while wearing uniforms as in "equity." In section 3, we show how much money we can save when we wear uniforms. In section 4, we talk about the safety of uniforms. In section 5, we say that it changes the behavior of one's personality. In section 6, we talk about the pride of the school when we have uniforms. In section 1 of the cons side we talk about the individuality of a student. In section 2, we talk about freedom of one's child. In section 3, we show how we can save parent's money on children's uniforms. In section 4, we tell how it helps discipline. In section5, we say that it is much more comfortable. In section 6, we can know that it's safe.

Focus and Time

We are talking about whether there should be school uniforms or not. There should be school uniforms because it helps student focus and save time. In my research, they claimed that the uniform has been very effective for focusing on work. It helps children focus more on work and not on shopping. They also said that it saves time in the morning not picking out clothes. One of the people from the internet replied saying, in the morning;

we can just grab our uniforms and go to school. They do not need to worry about their lateness for school. "It only took 30 minutes. Before I had a uniform it would take about an hour or so deciding on what I was going to wear," said Ayana, a seventh-grader. "It was very exciting to see all the kids in uniforms, because it keeps them focused on school and there was more of a sense of unity between the kids," Principal Judy Austin said Tuesday. "Uniforms are great for teens because it keeps them focused off of clothes and appearance and puts it more on school," Washington said.

I totally agree with the fact they stated in the research I have done. It saves time from the morning and it makes people focus more on work than how they look. They can't focus on work when they keep staring at other kids' clothes. They can grow jealousy and all kinds of other stuff. Girls spend a lot of their time picking out clothes. Time is like a treasure. Whenever a minutes passes we can't get it back. We never know when we'll die. We always need to use our time wisely.

My opponent quoted that it's bad because focusing on work depends on each one personality not on clothes. Everyone can work hard to focus on work without uniforms. Also, time, if their parents support their children to wake up early and pick out clothes quickly, there wouldn't be any problem.

In conclusion, I think that my opponent's claim is wrong. Actually, for some kids, it is very effective because, not all kids can change their personality quickly. Also, it prevents the girls and the boys to stop thinking about their clothes. I don't really think that their children want to wake up early in the morning and even though it can last for few days but not for a year. We're just wearing these uniforms for school. It's less than 10 hours a day, and less than 365 days. I think that uniforms help children focus more on work and saves also precious time. That is why I think schools should require school uniforms.

Equity

The next topic we will discuss is about equity. Uniforms make every students look equal which may prevent students from teasing each other saying," You're poor! I'm not!!" These problems happen because the students are mostly judged by how they wear. (DEN, pg.8, arg.1) One of the people from the internet said, "Children often ostracize, belittle and tease students who wear clothing items that don't meet certain standards of appearance and brand. At times the teasing can progress to physical and emotional assault. Students who are made fun of because of their clothes may resort to violence out of anger toward their persecutors. Wearing school uniforms evens the playing field, so to speak. Students certainly can find other ways to exclude others, but at least reason of wearing the "wrong" clothes has been removed. From the same site a girl named Jerrica said "Anyway, School is for learning after all, not fashion. I like how everyone looks equal. That's how it should be." A internet person from this cite: http://www.ehow.com/how-does_5438137_do-uniforms-keep-school-safer.html

If we wear normal clothes we won't be equal which can lead to certain problems. The word equity represents the word equal. If we're not equal, we can easily tell whether we are poor or not by looking at their clothes. Most people tell their environment by whether they have some brands or not which now leads to a big problem in schools called "bullying." I believe that in each school there is at least 1 person who is getting picked on because they're too poor or too rich. Therefore, in each school there should be uniforms.

On the other hand, my opponent says that it's wrong. They said that the bullies will and always try to find something else to pick on like hairstyle. Their parents and their environment is naturally like that for them to be like that also. We can't do anything about it.

In conclusion, I think the opposite of my opponent. I think there still should be uniforms because it's better to prevent at least from getting picked on for richness then getting picked on for everything. I also believe that bullies can pick on whoever they want. So we never know if we will even get picked on. However the sure thing is that we want to decrease the amount of people getting bullied. For these reasons I suggest that schools should have uniforms.

Economic

The following topic is Economic. The main thing is that the uniforms save lots of money. In this website from the internet

http://answers.yahoo.com/question/index;_ylt=At30_6zL8EyTYobGW_XLxl4jzKIX;_ylv=3?Qid=20080423120936AAA1BFD

They said, "It saved us a lot of money in the long run. AND we never heard, "But so-and-so has _______ brand jeans, shoes, etc." I also think it is correct that non uniforms save much more money. Another person who agrees with our statement said, "While it is true that school uniforms cost money, it is equally true that in Western society the peer group, fashion industry and other societal pressures pressures on kids to wear the 'right' trainers the 'cool' trousers or the particular style of top that is in fashion this month can lead to ostracism, bullying and emotional stress for those pupils whose parents are unable and unwilling to pay the price." I agree with the statement that the person said because it is hard for the parent to buy all the clothes that their kids want just because they don't have the same clothes.

If we wear normal clothes it's true that it will be much more expensive than school uniforms. We go to the shopping mall with our parents to buy brand clothes which are much prettier and expensive. However, alumni can donate their uniforms to current students. Uniforms can be worn easily for 1 or 2 years if they're clean. However we get tired of our everyday normal clothing and it becomes a habit of buying new clothes when we already have a lot. Therefore uniforms save money.

On the other hand, my opponent said that it is absolutely wrong because in rich peoples' school they need to buy new pairs of uniforms even though there is a tiny thread popped. Also normal clothes there are some people who adore their clothes who don't need to buy new clothing.

I do not agree with my opponent's statement because we can always order the schools to let them wear the same uniforms but they need to sew it on their own. Also I don't really think that a lot of girls will like the fact that they can't shop for a year. It's very hard thing for girls especially. For these reasons I think that uniforms need to be required in schools.

Safety

Staying on the same topic of our debate, schools should have uniforms because of safety also. According the one of the research I have done, they say that it is easier to know who is from which school. Also the adults and doctors said that it also depends on how they wear the kidnappers react. Mostly the kidnappers try to get children wearing clothes which don't cover much part of the body. In this site, http://712educators.about.com/cs/schoolviolence/a/uniforms.htm they claimed that uniforms prevents gang colors, etc. in schools. These are one of the reasons; Decreasing violence and theft because of clothing and shoes, Helping schools recognize those who do not belong on campus. A girl from the internet also said that "Overall, the crime rate dropped by 91%

School suspensions dropped by 90%

Sex offenses were reduced by 96%

Incidents of vandalism went down 69%

With effects like that, it's exactly what America needs considering how far behind we are from the rest of the world."

To begin with, normal clothes can be very unsafe. A lot of kidnappers try to look for people who wear clothes which doesn't cover most part of the body. They also kidnap mostly kids because they don't really know anything to do when they have this situation. Also in a natural disaster which we never know when will happen, it will be hard to gather up the classmates of each school if they're all in different kinds of clothes in the public. Therefore, school uniforms make students' life safer.

On the other hand, there are some people who don't agree with me at all. They say, "There is no time to gather up in a natural disaster. Everyone will be busy thinking about themselves' life. Also in America or in other country which is huge have carpool. It's not really-super dangerous."

I do not agree with my opponent because in a natural disaster, if we all panic no one will be alive. We have to remain calm and listen to the adults. If everyone panicked, no 911 will come because they're panicking with us also. There aren't a lot huge countries that have carpool. We need to think about all of us. Therefore school uniforms should be allowed in schools.

Behavior

We are still debating on whether schools should require students uniforms. I think that there should be uniforms with a solution of "Behavior." According to the research I have done on behavior, the public and the psychologist says that the uniforms make the mind calmer than wearing normal clothes. say that a lot of children wearing uniforms are well behaved in school during class.

Here are some students who agree with this topic. They say,

Jenna says, "When I began teaching in different schools I found that students who wore uniforms had more respect and were better students than those who wore their "street" clothes. Yes, they can be uncomfortable and I sure looked like crap in mine but, I found students were able to fit in better and there were less behavioral problems. Once you get past wearing uniforms, you'll see what a great asset they are!!!"

Eric says, "My school has a shirt uniform not pants. I think they are a good idea, my schools violence and bullying has dropped 67%."

Vic-g says, "I have lived most of my life not having to wear uniforms; however, I have seen many people criticize other kids for not having fashionable clothes. A lot of people themselves have done it, me included." There are plenty of other ways to express yourself; the most important way is through your voice."

If we had to wear normal clothes to go to every school, no one will be behaving well because they are all busy thinking about clothes of different people. Sometimes they can get in to serious fight teasing kids about their clothes. Psychologists said that uniforms can also calm students' exited body down. Therefore uniforms make students behave well.

My opponent thinks it's wrong because a lot of people gets A whether they have uniforms or not. Uniforms mostly represent the school not behavior. Uniforms are for different purposes not for making them behave well. The students will be glad to have the uniforms that make you behave well.

In conclusion, I do not agree with this statement he just made because uniforms are also here to calm down the minds of those who grow jealousy each day because of their pretty friend's cloths. For these reasons I think that schools should have uniforms.

Pride

Continuing with this topic, there should be uniforms because they also have to keep the school's pride. By looking at the research I have done on Pride, most of the schools would like to keep the school's pride and to tell the people that we are from this school. A person from this site http://www.thisisexeter.co.uk/news/School-uniform-s-question-pride/article-216600-detail/article.html said that, "Finally, they argue that uniform is vital in fostering a spirit of community, a sense of pride and identity with the school that you attend"

I think the school has a right to spread the word of the school across the town by making students wear uniforms. Also when they go on a field trip to somewhere, when they wear a uniform, they can be also appreciated by a lot of people. They look elegant and hard working student. In my experience, when I was on a field trip to somewhere in France, I felt people looking at our group and I was positive that it wasn't a bad look it was a good look. Sometimes we often hear that we have lots of love on nature because we were on the newspaper. How did we save the school? We were wearing uniforms! They just took a picture of us and we represented the school! Therefore if we wear normal clothes we would be against our school's pride. We should wear these clothes for our school and to represent the school.

My opponent said that why don't teachers wear uniforms like us? If they want the school to be famous why use us instead of them? They said that it's unfair and they make them use uniforms not for us and the pride but for money.

I think that it is wrong about what my opponent said. Our teachers do want money but they love us. They don't want to hurt us. If they want money, why don't they just work in a shop? It is much easier. They're doing this job for us and the future not for money. It is also for the school's pride. They want to lead us to the right place because they much more experience than we do. For these reasons I think that students should require school uniforms.

Individuality

We are debating the resolution whether the school uniforms should be allowed or not. I don't think that there should be uniforms because they won't be able to express ourselves. One of the people from this site http://www.buzzle.com/articles/facts-against-school-uniforms.html have said, "School uniforms inhibit student's individuality. Young people often express their feelings through the clothing that they wear. Uniforms will take away this form of expression. Why should school districts try to make everyone look the same?"

To start with the statement of "It prevents us from expressing ourselves" is wrong.

However, I do think it's a little true because it is annoying to wear uniforms to go to school. However, kids have almost all their life to spare time expressing their selves. If they want to do it when they're young, they can do it after school or during the weekends. It's not like they will wear it forever. Therefore there should be uniforms with the reason of "individuality."

My opponent said that my statement was wrong. They said that mostly during the puberty, girls and boys want to express themselves in front of them and not alone.

In conclusion, I think that it is wrong about what my opponent said. As they want to be with boys and girls, they can meet them outside of school and they won't be able to focus a lot thinking about them. Therefore there should be uniforms.

Freedom

We are arguing with our opponents whether the students should wear uniforms or not. There shouldn't be uniforms because it prevents freedom for children. According to the research, the public said that it will stress the young children, and that they should have the right to wear whatever they want to wear. They also said that it is like as if they were in a prison. They said that it might even cause economic issues. For example, some of the shops for kids closing down because there are no more kids buying new clothes.

A person who has the ID of speakhermmind said,

"i feel like uniforms take away from the child being one individual. people need too express themsives and if making a child wear what someone else is wearin makes them want to do what others wont do..like joins gangs, act out in class, to b notice from one another. this also takes away from the parents who make money to buy their kids uniforms. more money is spent.. uniforms dont stop voilence as a matter of fact it brings more violence betwee schools, because the uniforms single them out.."

—Guest speakhermmind

Also these are some people who don't agree with the topic we have talked about so far.

Allyse says:

"When I think of this argument, I think of the core democratic value liberty. A part of liberty is personal freedom: each person is free to act, to think, and to believe in which no one can legitimately stop. School uniforms invade a student's freedom of choice, and how they act. Don't schools teach students how are country is a free one? When school boards choose what students wear, it limit's a students freedom. "

bella says:

"isabel is right dn't grown ups remember wen they were lil and they hated uniform put urselves bac in our shoes and feel wat we feel. It feels like ur taking our freedom from us. We need to be able to express ourselves some pple like me r shy and the only way to get our voice out is through clothing and if they made cooler uniforms that show who we r we would wear them kids who dnt wear uniform pick on other kids that do so u think that solves violence no it doesnt it makes us rebel to get OUR VOICE OUT THERE!!!!!! listen to us our happiness matters to u know?"

If there are uniforms If there are uniforms there won't be freedom is wrong. Students for example in America are free after school and during the vacation. They have a lot of freedom compared to some of the countries. I also believe that if we're free nothing will be interesting and hard. It's always after difficulties that comes happiness. School uniforms aren't the only ones that might prevent freedom. It's just the students who think like that. Therefore there should be school uniforms.

My opponent said that I was wrong because students won't be free. They will be like mice caught in the traps. They will be coming to school to learn stuff and to talk with their friends and to be free from home. If the children aren't free from anything they will be really stressed.

In conclusion I do not agree with the statement. It's wrong because I think that it is a bit exaggerated by saying that we're mice caught in traps. There may be the grade

33

problems or some other difficult problems but it is wrong to say that it is all the uniforms fault. Therefore I think there should be uniforms.

Economics

We are still arguing about whether there shouldn't be uniforms because; it takes a lot of money. Reference to the research, for example in a very rich private school, when there is a tiny thread popped that leads to buying a new uniform which takes a lot of money. One of the people Angella Benjamin, from Beltsville and also from the internet replied, "How many parents can spend $130 on one child for the entire school year? In answering my question, remember you have to shop for the four seasons. Parents, how many times can you afford to buy new clothing? What does a parent have to lose in putting their child in uniform? How much time does a child spend in the morning trying to find something to wear? For the entire school year, how many times does a parent shop? How much do they spend? Remember parents, all you need for a child are five uniforms for the entire school year." Angella Benjamin, Beltsville

A person also from the internet agrees with this topic. His name is sweede. He says: "School uniforms are expensive. While many students in public school may be able to easily afford uniforms, there are families with lower incomes who may have difficulty affording the required clothing. This can inflict an even greater problem on lower income families who may have enough troubles already. School uniforms may hold back self appearance through clothing, forcing children to find other ways to show who they are. Children who wear school uniforms are more likely to use makeup early, and many resort to extreme accessories or to change their uniforms to individualize themselves from others. For example, many girls shorten their skirts as a way to rebel against the strictness of school uniforms."

If we wore uniforms it saves money because we can do a cycle of uniforms. We can pass our uniforms down to our 후배들. It saves money and also it's free. We can buy new ones if we want to but, as long as it's free almost everyone will get the 선배들의 uniforms. Therefore there should be school uniforms.

My opponent doesn't agree with this statement. They said "What about the first students to come to a school? What will they do? They will have to pay everything."

I don't agree with this topic because the school can always give out free uniforms. If they are afraid to lose money, they can add some price to the afternoon activities. That way they do get the money back but the activities aren't forced to do.

Discipline

- We are still talking about the resolution whether schools should require students' uniforms. There shouldn't be uniforms because it helps discipline. According to the research, they say that two high school girls were really stressed about wearing uniforms that they became crazy and started doing all kinds of bad stuff. Also they said that if they push too much on one's clothes, it might lead to a huge problem. In another way of saying that they are bad, it isn't really a good idea to have uniforms because, even though some kids acted badly not everyone did it in order to have uniforms. Also, with an example from the bullies, even though the opponents say that it decreases bullying, they always pick on something else.

There are some similar quotes that some people made. Firstly there is a guy named Wes.

"School uniforms do not help. They are a lame and foolish attempt by educators to try and correct behavioral and academic problems. Do you honestly think that making everybody wear the same thing will erase their misbehavior?"

Bri says, School uniforms will not stopp harassment and bullying. If bullys want to harass you they will just find something else to pick on you about such as your face or hair. Therefore they really aren't a solution to bullies.

If we don't wear uniforms, It will effect discipline. Girls will be literally making the school into a fashion show. Also boys will be making the school in to a group of street boys. The girls won't stop wearing short skirts and t-shirts without straps. On the other hand, boys won't stop wearing baggy pants showing their underclothes and shirts that are all ripped up. Therefore there should be uniforms.

My opponent said that I was wrong about the statement. It may be baggy about the clothes they wear but it is just the way of expressing themselves. They also said that even though the girls wear short pants, they won't do anything bad about it. They might be just hot during the summer. We should let them wear whatever they want to wear.

I think the statement of my opponent is totally wrong. We never know what makes the pants so baggy and what is in their pockets. We can't even tell whether there are weapons or cigarettes in their pockets or not since they are already so baggy. For the girls, even though it's feeling hot, it's not a time to wear some clothes that doesn't cover a lot of the parts. Therefore there should be uniforms for school.

Comforts

For the before last time to sort of wrap up the situation, we will talk about whether school uniforms should be banned or not. There shouldn't be uniforms because we need to wear what is comfortable for us. According to the research, a lot of children can't concentrate on a thing or a work when they are wearing something very uncomfortable. They said that the uniforms can make students more sensitive because they are mad about the clothes for the whole school day. The experts said that the students need to be comfortable in order to work hard. A person from this website "http://lifestyle.iloveindia.com/lounge/pros--cons-of-school-uniforms-1248.html said, "Another ill effect of school uniform is that it deprives the children the comfort, which one experiences on wearing different type of clothing, as per individual choice. This discomfort might adversely reflect upon the academic performance of the child.

If we wore normal clothes it wouldn't be really comfortable. They said that they can concentrate more when they are wearing comfortable clothes...right? We can always make the uniforms much more comfortable. That's want they want isn't it? Sometimes home clothes either they aren't comfortable.

My opponent said that they are much more used to the home clothes than the freaky new uniforms. They say that they can't even move fast or freely to other places. We also have to think about handicapped people. It will be really hard for them.

In conclusion, I think that the statement is wrong. I think that they give out uniforms for us for our normal clothes won't be dirty not for it to be clean. After all it is for sports. It is impossible for it to be clean. If the opponents want normal comfortable clothes, we can imitate the clothes that the children wear like Polo Ralph Lauren and put the name tag of the school on it with khaki shorts. It is comfortable and no skirts or ties! All my opponent need is a comfortable uniform. If we make or change our present uniform in to a comfortable uniform, soon we'll be use to it and we'll be comfortable. With these reasons we should have uniforms in schools.

Safety

We are therefore for the last time talking about the resolution whether we should wear uniforms or not. There shouldn't be uniforms because of students' safety. According to the research, a young boy was killed because of his tie getting caught that between the doors. Also in a natural disaster they say that it is hard to run in the uniforms. A person from the internet with the ID of Fosters cocoo and the real name of Rashida Khilawala n –said, "like environment: School Uniforms create a false sense of security. If the student gets used to being respected for their mind and not looks, the "outside world" could come as quite a surprise to them." By Rashida Khilawala

If we wore normal clothes it wouldn't as safe as wearing uniforms. We can't stop the schools requiring uniforms because of silly examples such as the incident of the tie. It's a very rare situation. I think that if everybody will pay attention to what they are doing, they will be able to be safe. It's true that we never know what will happen but, we don't know what will happen either. Do we? Also it's better to keep track of the schools' students in uniforms in case of a natural disaster. As we said we never know. Therefore there should be uniforms.

My opponent claimed that my quote is false because, we never know when the natural disaster or a situation might fall. We should always think about what will happen in many ways before actually doing it. We never know tomorrow. Maybe right now someone is dying because of the same accident.

In conclusion, I don't think that our principals are making us wear uniforms to put us in danger. Also, if there was a same situation like this, why do they still allow it? For these reasons I think that we should allow school uniforms in schools.

Conclusion

In conclusion, we have talked about why we shouldn't have uniforms and why we should. To sum up this debate, I think the strongest side of the cons' side was Individuality. They've talked about how they need to be able to express themselves. They said that they won't have any time to express themselves if it weren't their childhood and with the boys and girls.

The strongest side of mine which is the pros' side is the Focus and time. In this topic we have talked about the qualities of the uniforms. Also we showed clearly how it helps the students focus more on work rather than on fashion. The word fashion distracts a lot of children to go out buy clothes with brands from work.

I think that we should go with "For uniforms" because; the strongest argument of the cons' side was individuality. I have a persuasive reason why it is wrong and we are right. They said that they should be able to express themselves. However, it is wrong. We have all the other years to do whatever we want. It's funny how we're making a big deal out of wearing uniforms for lea than 9 hours a day for less than 365 days. According to my strongest argument it has been scientifically proved by scientists and psychologists that it calms down our mind to help work harder for certain students. Even though it isn't effective for the whole world, certain students are better than nothing.

For these reasons I think that we should require school uniforms.

I won the 1st prize in the National Chinese Speaking Contest competing with other 6th grader. I felt so excited as if I was going to fly away. I was really proud of myself. I was wearing a white dress with a golden box in my hands. Can you find where I am in this picture?

내가 유치원을 다닐 때 6학년들과 함께 전국 중국어 말하기 대회에 나가서 대상을 수상했다. 엄마의 얼굴에는 웃음꽃이 피어 있었다. 난 내 자신이 자랑스러웠다. 나는 황금색 포장지로 둘러싸인 상자를 들고 있으며 하얀색 드레스를 입고 있었다. 나는 어디에 있을까요?

I was taking this picture with my third grade class at Mount Vennon Elementary School in Atlanta, Gerogia. I was sitting in front of my teacher. I had short hair, and I didn't like my hairstyle back then. I believe, however, this photo will be a good memory when I get older.

나는 3학년 때 반 아이들과 함께 사진을 찍었다. 나는 선생님 앞에 앉게 되었다. 나는 그토록 싫어하던 짧은 머리를 하고 있었지만 이 사진들이 내가 커서 좋은 추억이 되리라 믿는다.

Wow, this is a picture of my sports' team UNSS at Ecole des Roches School in Normandie, France. We won the 4th place out of more than 15 schools in rugby. Isn't that awesome??? Keep on watching us principal Kamminsky! We will brighten our school and spread our school's fame! Go UNSS! By the way, can you guess where I am?

이 사진은 현재 내가 프랑스에서 다니고 있는 학교 Ecole des Roches School의 스포츠 침 UNSS 사진이다. 우리가 살고 있는 지역의 학교들 럭비 시합을 하여 15개 이상의 학교를 물리치고 4등을 했다. 대단하지 않아요? 교장선생님, 계속 우리 계속 봐주세요! 우리 학교를 꼭 빛낼 게요. …… 왜냐하면 우리는 한 팀이니까! 그런데 나는 어디 있을까?

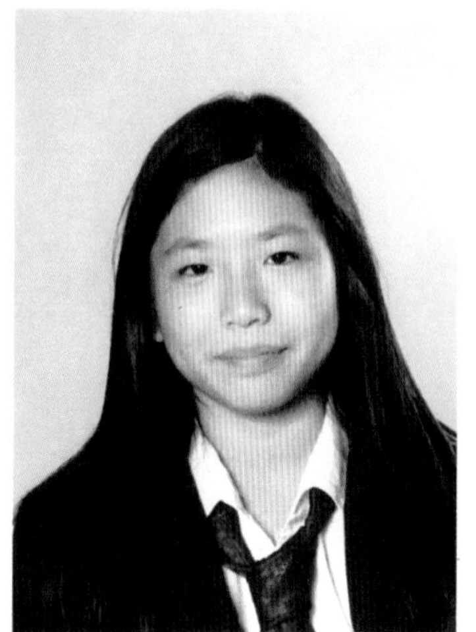

This is the picture of me in the uniform of my current school at Ecole des Roches School. I eagerly hope to attend Daegu International School next year to start off my middle school years in April 2011. I hope that you saw my hardworking spirit and positive personality in this portfolio. Thanks for your time and consideration.

Sincerely,

Eun Hyang Kim

저는 고3이지만 그동안 미국, 중국, 프랑스에 유학을 하면서
다양한 언어와 문화를 직접 체험하면서 익혔습니다.
돌이켜 보면 부모님 곁을 떠나서 언어와 문화가 다른 나라에서
공부하기란 쉽지 않았습니다.
한국의 부모와 형제, 친구들이 그리워 혼자 울기도 많이 했습니다.

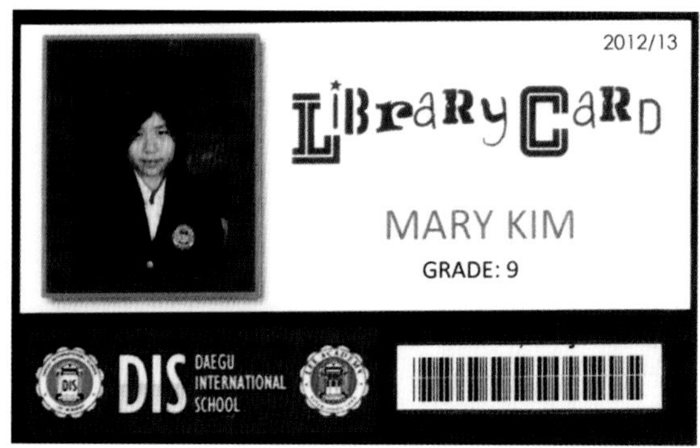

대구국제중학교 도서관 출입증(9학년)
Mary Kim, 김은향

힘에 겨울 때마다 책을 읽고 글을 쓰고
메모에 낙서와 그림을 그리며 책을 읽고 음악을 들었습니다.
참 먼 길을 돌아온 느낌이지만 이젠 전혀 새로운 세계로 뱃머리를
돌려야 할 시점입니다.

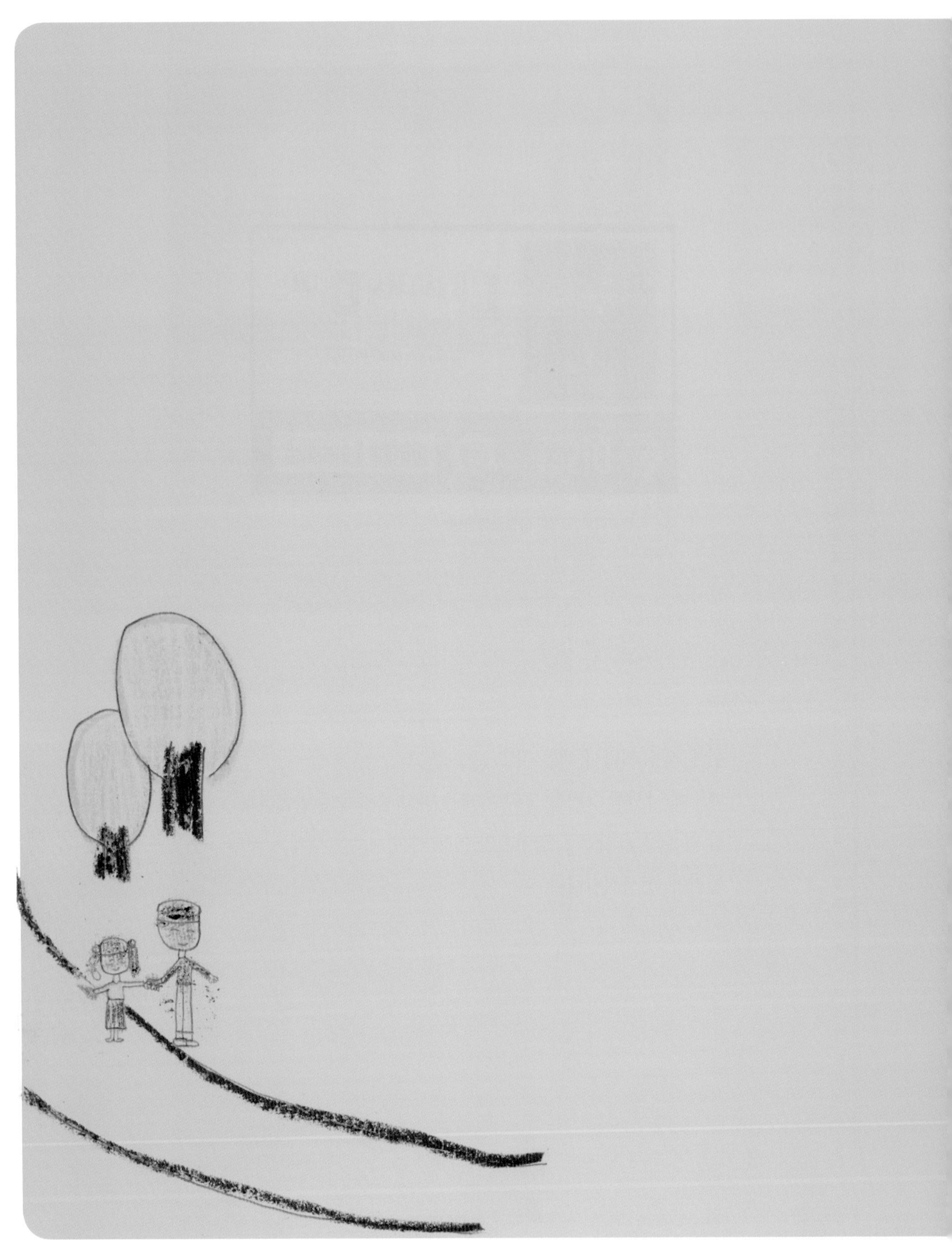

Part 4

My Creative Works

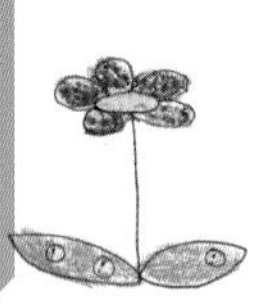

콘티 1 〈꽃들의 여행〉

어느 아침 해바라기, 국화, 장미, 무궁화가 여행을 갔어요. 첫 번째 꽃은 "난 일로" "난 일로" "난 알지?"

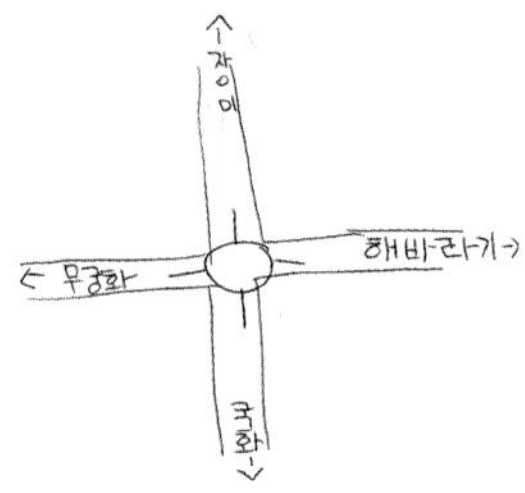

그런데 4송이는 한 덫에 걸렸어요!

하지만 장미에게 까시가 있어 덫을 풀었어요!

"장미만세!"

그리고 그날밤 장미에게 큰 잔치를 벌렸어요!

그리고 그들은 행복하게 살았고 아름다운 이야기는 끝이 납니다.

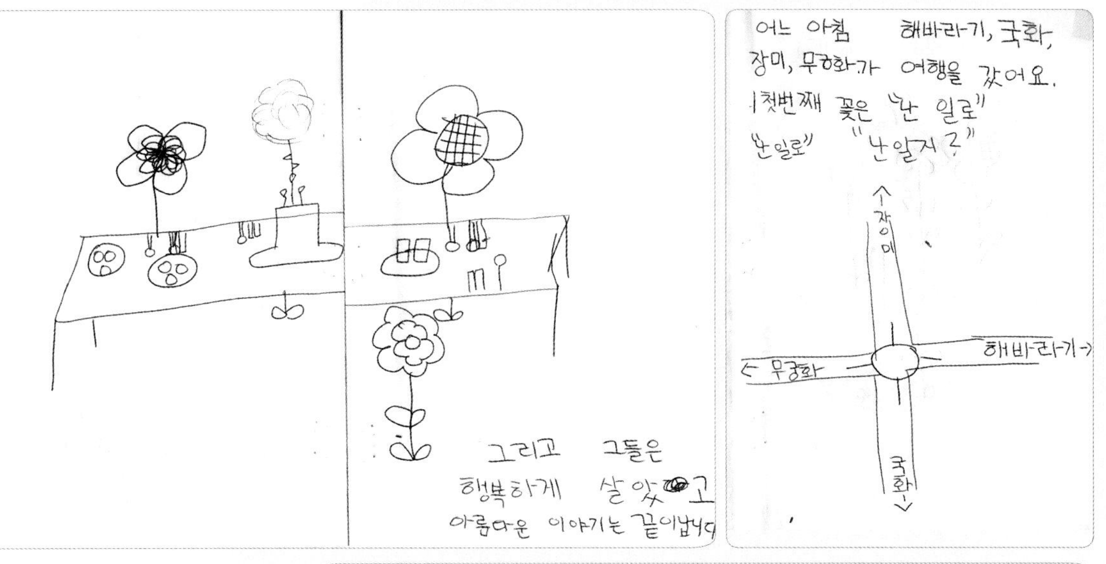
그리고 그들은
행복하게 살았고
아름다운 이야기는 끝이납니다
어느 아침 해바라기, 국화,
장미, 무궁화가 여행을 갔어요.
1첫번째 꽃은 "난 일로"
"난일로" "난일지?"
장미
해바라기
무궁화
국화

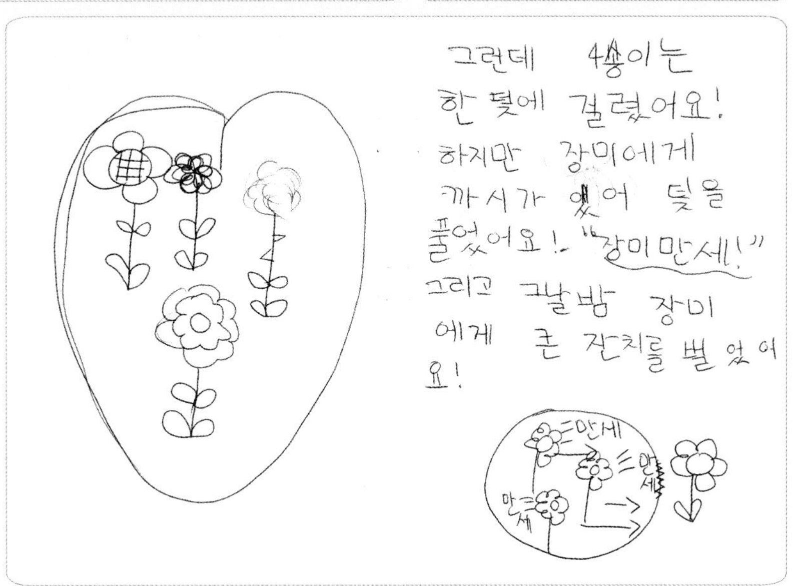
그런데 4송이는
한 덫에 걸렸어요!
하지만 장미에게
까시가 있어 덫을
풀었어요! "장미만세!"
그리고 그날밤 장미
에게 큰 잔치를 벌였어
요!
만세
만세
만세

꽃들의 여행 스토리를 콘티로 엮었습니다.

콘티 2 〈강아지와 고양이〉

옛날 어느 마음에 사는 게으른 농부가 천원을 주며 두부, 파, 계란, 초코릿을 사오라고 강아지에게 시켰어요.
똘이라는 이름을 가진 푸들 같은 강아지는 잽싸게 슈퍼로 갔어요.

가다가 우연히 고양이를 만났어요.
순해보였죠.
시간 가는 줄도 몰랐어요.
고양이 하고 놀다 나무 그늘에서 잠이 들었죠.
근데 고양이 손에 덫이……

강아지는 아이에게 도움을 청하자 집으로 데려가 정성껏 치료해 주었다.

겨울이 오자 고양이는 나았어요.
강아지가 자랑스러워서 자기도 모르게 강아지를 핥기 시작했어요. 꼭 귀염둥이처럼……

콘티 3 〈강아지와 고양이〉

이야기 주머니
옛날 어느 마을에 사는 게으른 농부가, 천원을 주며 두부, 파, 계란, 초코릿을 사오라고 강아지에게 시켰어요. 똘이라는 이름 가진 푸들 같은 강아지는 잽싸게 슈퍼로 갔어요.
슈퍼

이야기 주머니
가다가 우연히 고양이를 만났어요. 순해 보였죠 시간 가는 줄도 몰랐어요. 고양이 하고 놀다 나무 그늘에서 잠이 들었죠. 근데 고양이 손에 덫이.....

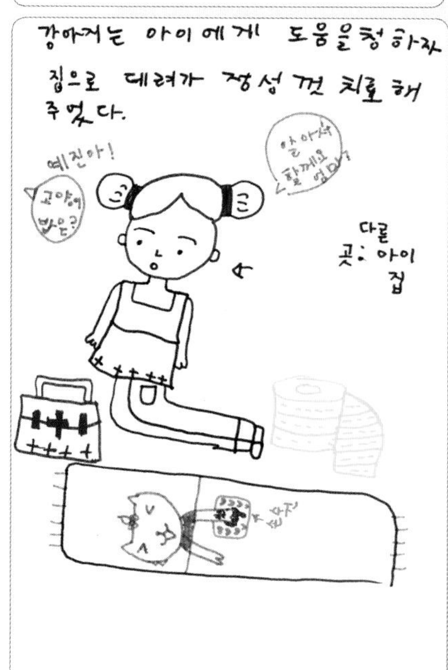
강아지는 아이에게 도움을 청하자 집으로 데려가 정성껏 치료해 주었다.
예진아!
다른 곳: 아이 집

겨울이 오자 고양이는 나았어요. 강아지가 자랑스러워서 자기도 모르게 강아지를
시작했어요. 꼭 귀염둥이
파란 구슬
5,9000
유아세트 동화
9,5000
2006 5.9 화요일

콘티 4 〈프랑스에서〉

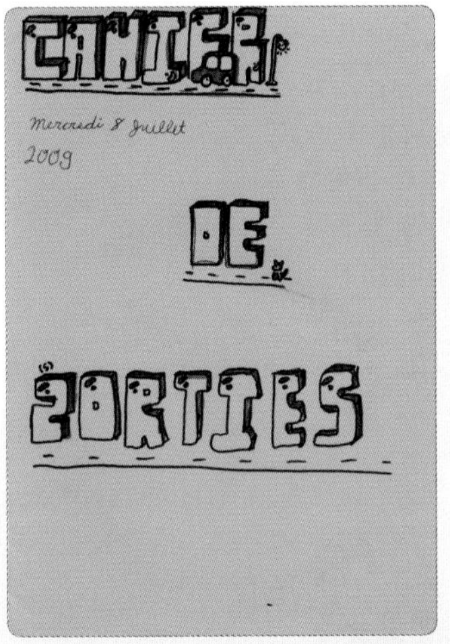

Le Mont Saint Michel -
→CAHIER DE SORTIES ←
visites

Je suis allé Le Mont Saint Michel.
St. Michel et tres froid.
J'ai aimée des glasse, et une statu dans le mont St. michel.
C'est prend boucout des bracelet et la oupes
St Michel c'est tres beau.

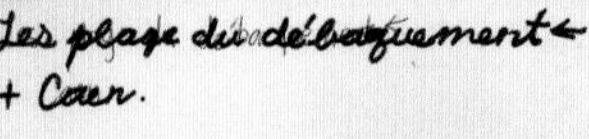
Les plage du débarquement ←
+ Caen.

Je suis allé `Les Plage du débarquement' hier. Et - Je suis allé `Le cemetary'. J'ai mangé la glace, Ju d'orange. J'ai acheté les bon bon dans le petite (town). Les Plage c'est tres beau. Il y a beaucoup de oiseau et le town il y a un mourrir oiseau!! J'ai aimé le town pas-que il y a beaucoup de vetement et bon bon. Et la glace c'est tres, tres delicious.

Deauville

Lundi, 13 juillet

Je suis allé Deauville. Dans le Deauville avec mon amis nous sommes alleés un plage. J'ai nagé et mangé. Le plage c'est tres beau. 5:30 Je suis allé shopping. J'ai ne pas acheté. Je suis partT 1:30 et Je suis arrivé 10/20.

→ Disney W/Land

Juillet, 14, 2009 Je suis allé le DisneyLand.
Dans le Disney J'ai acheté un crayon, un stylo, un mug, et la glaces. Je suis allé le Haunted House et J'ai eu ne pas peur! Apres je suis allé shopping! A le nuit j'ai un parade et le fireworks. C'est tres bon! Maintenant, Je suis tres fatigue!

Musée d'orsay

Juillet 16th

Je suis allé Musée d'orsay et le Notre Dame. Dans le Notre Dame Je suis vu le gorgols et statute C'est tres, tres beau!!
Dans le Musée je suis vu le Rodin et le painture de Monet, le painture de (other) artistes. J'aime le musée.

Asterix

Lundi, 20. Juillet. 2009

Hier

Nous sommes allés Asterix.
Dans le Asterix je suis allé le roler coaster x2, est le x3 ride de eau. est le violent chair.
C'est eu ne pas peur! C'est tres beau!
Apres J'ai tres tres fatigue!
Et Maintenant, Aussi jesuis fatigue!

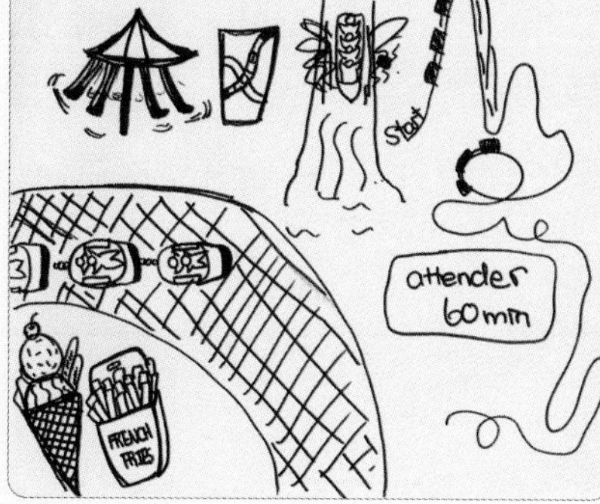

콘티 5 〈이슬 이야기〉

어느 날 벌이 훨훨 날아갔어요. 그런데 아이가 덧을 갔고 확~~ 쳤어요.

이상하네…

아직도 살아 있잖아!!

어느 날 아침 이슬이 뚝뚝 떨어졌어요.

마지막 날 밤 때 잘 잤습니다.

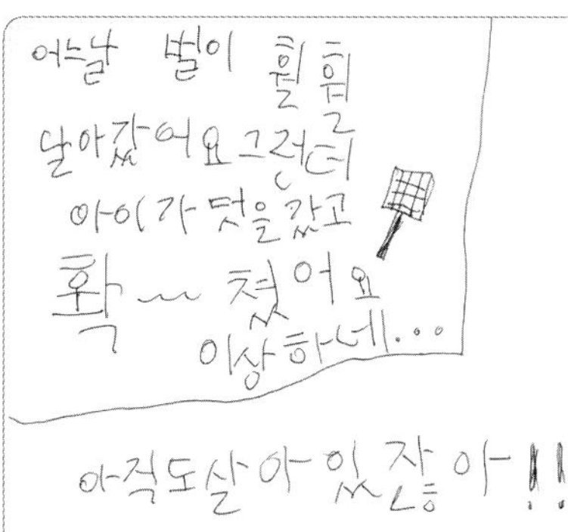
어느날 벌이 훨훨
날아갔어요 그런데
아이가 덧을갖고
확~ 쳤어요
이상하네...
아직도살아있잖아!!

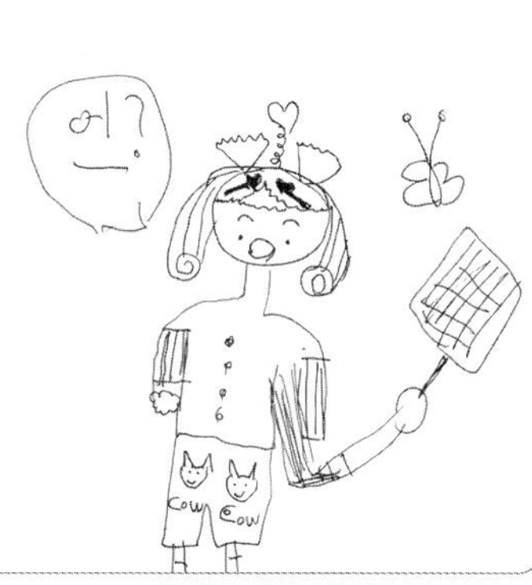
어?

어느날 아침 이슬이
뚝뚝 떨어졌어요.

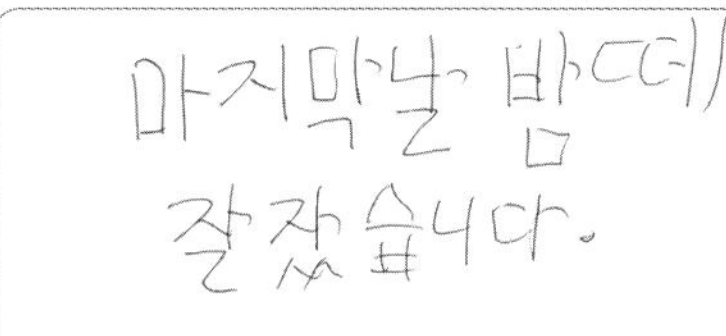
마지막날 밤떼
잘잤습니다.

콘티 6 〈장화를 좋아하는 고양이〉

장화가 없는 고양이가 가게에 가서 장화를 샀어요.

어느 날 밤 우르르쾅쾅 쏜살같이 비가 내립니다.

따르릉~

제가 어린 시절 이런 콘티(Continuity)를 만들면서
외국 유학 기간의 외로움을 잊어보았습니다.

2 A Moment of Pray

〈나를 위해 기도해요〉

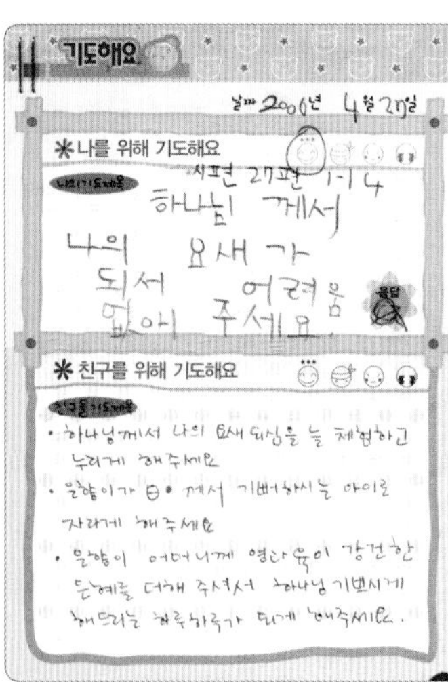

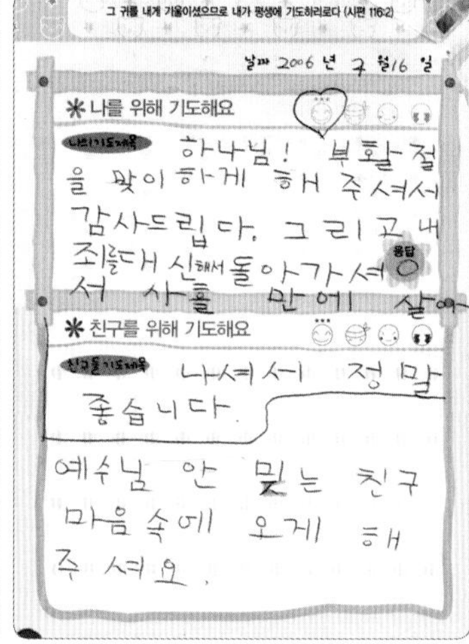

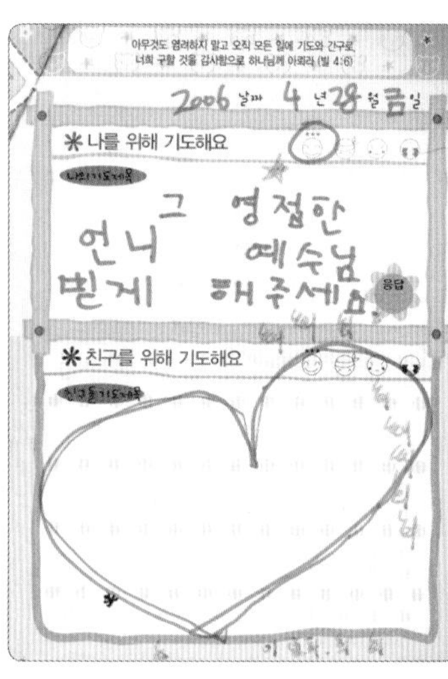

2006년 4월 27일

시편 27편 1-14

하나님께서 나의 요새가 돼서 어려움 없애 주세요.

April 27, 2006

Psalms Chapter 27 Verses 1-14

Lord, please be my fort and protect me from all trials.

2006년 4월 16일

하나님! 부활절을 맞이하게 해주셔서 감사드립니다. 그리고 내 죄를 대신해서 돌아가셔서 사흘 만에 살아나셔서 정말 좋습니다.

April 16, 2006

Lord! Thank you for Easter day. And I'm so happy you resurrected after three days dying for my sins.

2006년 4월 28일

그 영접한 언니 예수님 믿게 해주세요.

April 28, 2006

Please make the accepting girl believe in you, God.

2006년 5월 8일

신명기 5장 16절 말씀대로 부모님과 ϴ께 공경하여 오래 살 수 있게 해주세요. ♡
ϴ님 어머니 빨리 낫게 해주세요.

May 8, 2006

Just like how it was stated in Deuteronomy Chapter 5 Verse 16, please guide my parents to worship you and live a happy, healthy life. Lord, heal my mother.

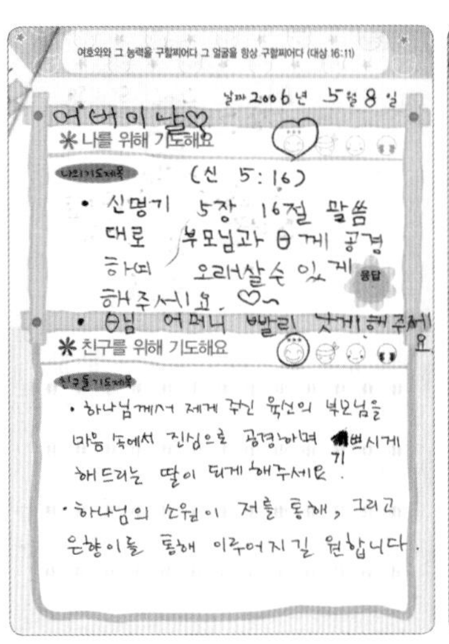

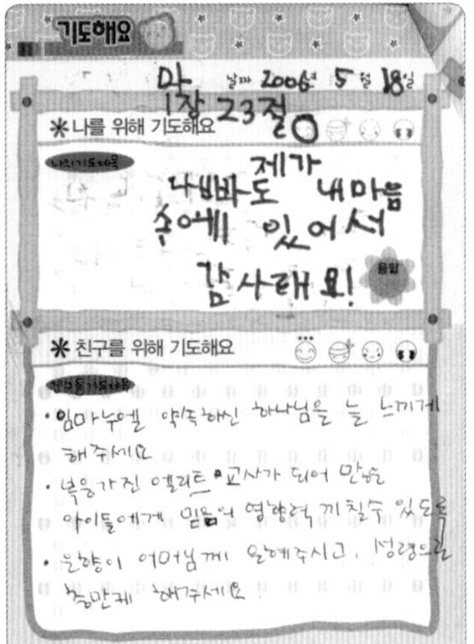

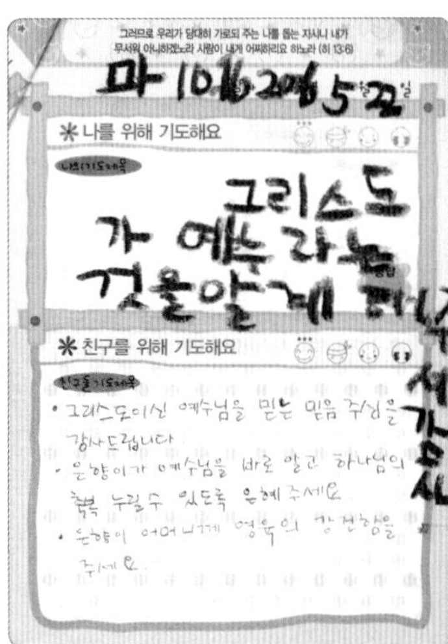

2006년 5월 18일

제가 나빠도 내 마음속에 있어서 감사해요!

May 18, 2006

Thank you for staying in my heart even when I am bad.

2006년 5월 22일

그리스도가 예수라는 것을 알게 해주셔서 감사합니다.

May 22, 2006

Thank you for letting me know that the Christ is Jesus Christ.

2006년 5월 25일

〈엄마〉 빨랑빨랑 낫게 해주세요! 제발! 제가 구원 받을 수 있도록 지혜주시고

May 25, 2006

<Mother> Help her heal faster! Please! Guide me to be forgiven.

2006년 5월 28일

하나님 만약에 계속 떡으로만 살게 되면 예수님 안에서 더 깊이 있게 해 주세요.

May 28, 2006

Lord, if I continue to live as bread, allow me to be inside you deeper.

2006년 5월 29일

하나님! 저한테서 벼룩 하나 모든 나쁜 게 없도록…

May 29, 2006

Lord, cleanse my sins and help me be sinless.

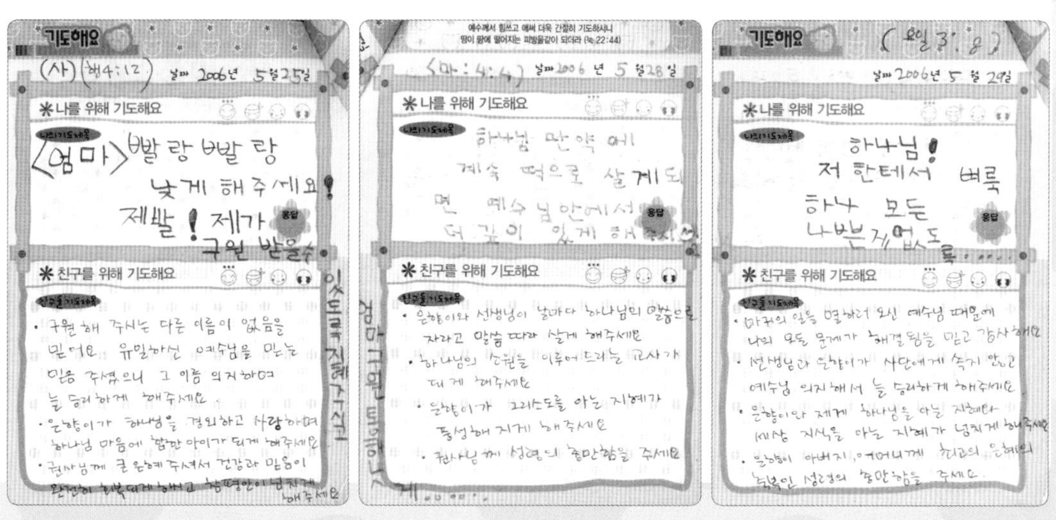

2006년 6월 25일

저도 어려움을 겪었을 때 하나님께 기도하는 것을 잊지 않도록 도와주세요!

June 25, 2006

Help me to not forget to pray to you, Lord, when I'm facing trials.

2006년 6월 27일

하나님! 제가 하나님 자녀되게 해줌에 감사드려요.

June 27, 2006

God! Thank you for accepting as your child.

2006년 7월 8일

하나님 제가 미국 잘 다녀오게 해주세요.

예수…… 기도 …… 다....

July 08, 2006

Lord! Please guide me towards a successful trip to America.

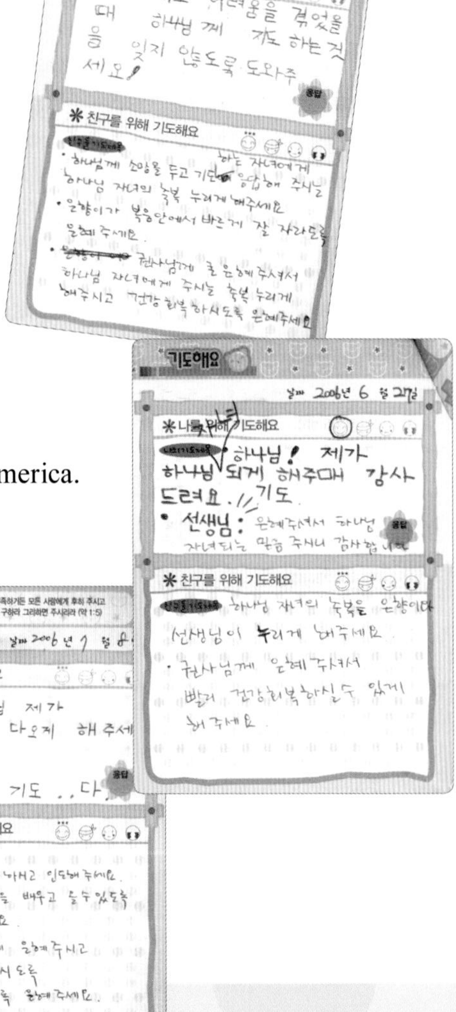

믿음 〈마태복음 17장 20절〉

할 수 있다!!

긍정적인 말을 더 많이 하자!!

작은 믿음만 있어도 해낸다.

Faith- Matthew Chapter 17 Verse 20

I can do it!

Say more positive things!

With just a little faith, anything is possible.

아버지 뜻대로 행하는 자 〈마태복음 7장 21절〉

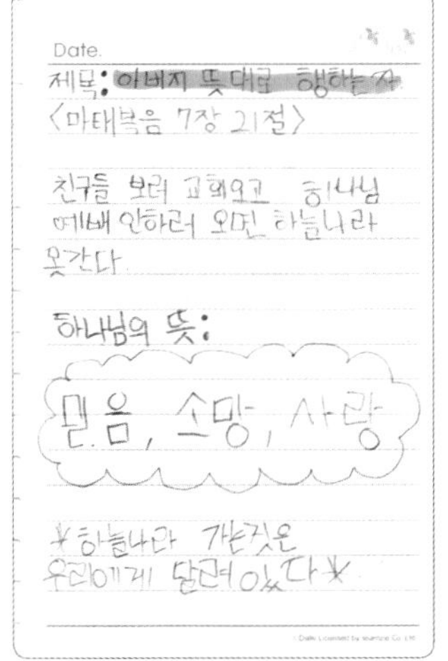

친구들 보러 교회 오고

하나님 예배 안 하러 오면 하늘나라 못간다.

하나님의 뜻: 믿음 소망 사랑

*하늘나라에 가는 것은 우리에게 달렸다.

它是由我们去天堂.

Title: The One Who Follows God <Matthew Chapter 7 Verse 21>

If you go to Church to see friends but not for God to pray, you cannot go to Heaven.

God’s Will: Faith, Hope and Love

*Going to Heaven depends on us.

8/10/08

무엇을 듣느냐가 중요하다. 〈요한복음 10장 1절~6절〉

하나님의 말씀을 들어라.

1. 하나님의 말
2. 다른 사람들의 말
3. 자기자신에게 하는 말

8/10/08

What you hear is important. John Chapter 10 verses 1-6

Listen to God's Words

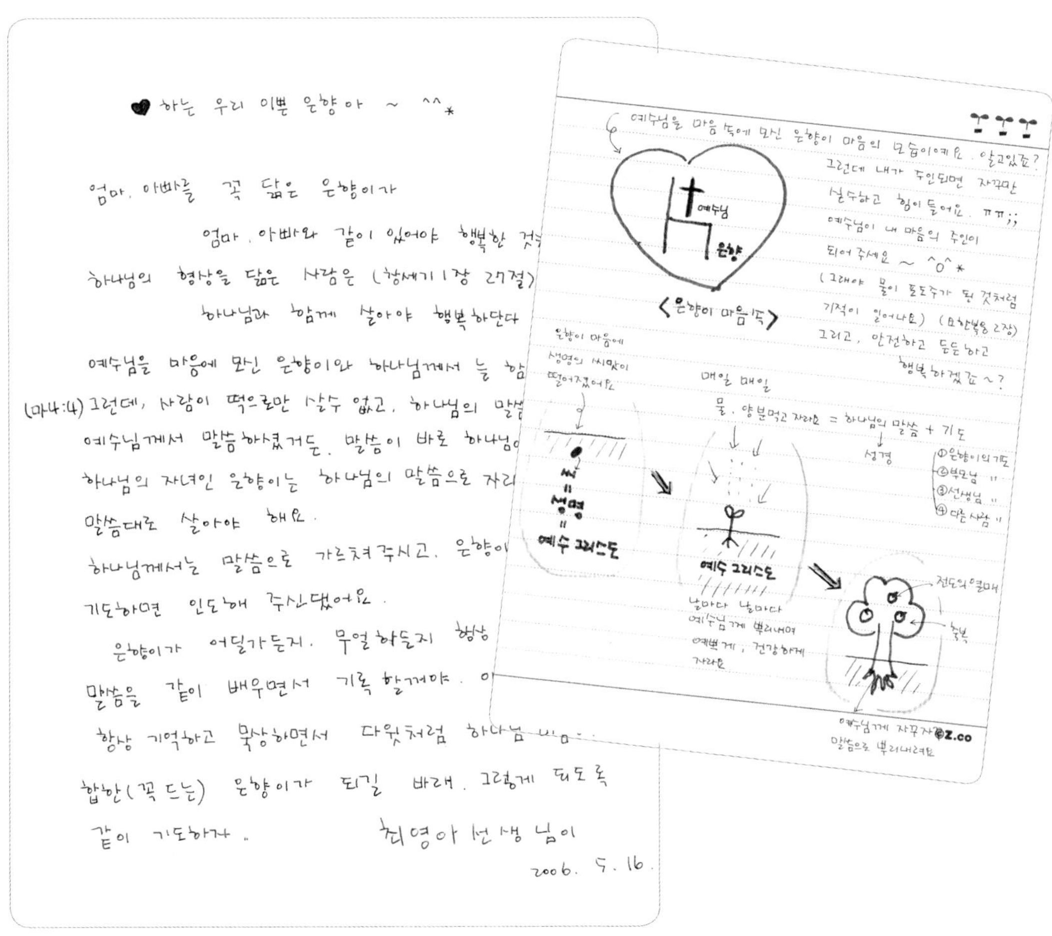

♥하는 우리 이쁜 은향아 ~ ^^*

엄마, 아빠를 꼭 닮은 은향이가
엄마, 아빠와 같이 있어야 행복한 것처
하나님의 형상을 닮은 사람은 (창세기 1장 27절)
하나님과 함께 살아야 행복하단다
예수님을 마음에 모신 은향이와 하나님께서 늘 함
(마4:4) 그런데, 사람이 떡으로만 살수 없고, 하나님의 말씀
예수님께서 말씀하셨거든. 말씀이 바로 하나님
하나님의 자녀인 은향이는 하나님의 말씀으로 자리
말씀대로 살아야 해요.
하나님께서는 말씀으로 가르쳐주시고, 은향이
기도하면 인도해 주신댔어요.
은향이가 어딜가든지, 무얼하든지 항상
말씀을 같이 배우면서 기록 할꺼야. 이
항상 기억하고 묵상하면서 다윗처럼 하나님 마음
합한(꼭 드는) 은향이가 되길 바래. 그렇게 되도록
같이 기도하자. 최영아 선생님이
2006. 5. 16.

예수님을 마음 속에 모신 은향이 마음의 모습이예요. 알고있죠?
그런데 내가 주인되면 자꾸만
실수하고 힘이 들어요. ㅠㅠ;;
예수님이 내 마음의 주인이
되어 주세요 ~ ^0^*
(그래야 물이 포도주가 된 것처럼
기적이 일어나요) (요한복음 2장)
그리고, 안전하고 든든하고
행복하겠죠~?

최영아 선생님이 미국으로 유학 가는 은향이에게 준 기도

항상 기억하고 묵상하면서 다윗처럼 하나님 마음에 꼭 드는 은향이가 되길 바래.

그렇게 되도록 함께 기도하자.

Always remember and meditate while I hope is a sure favorite EUN HANG the heart of God, like David. Let us pray together that way.

하나님의 말씀을 체계적으로 정리하였다.

God's Word was to organize.

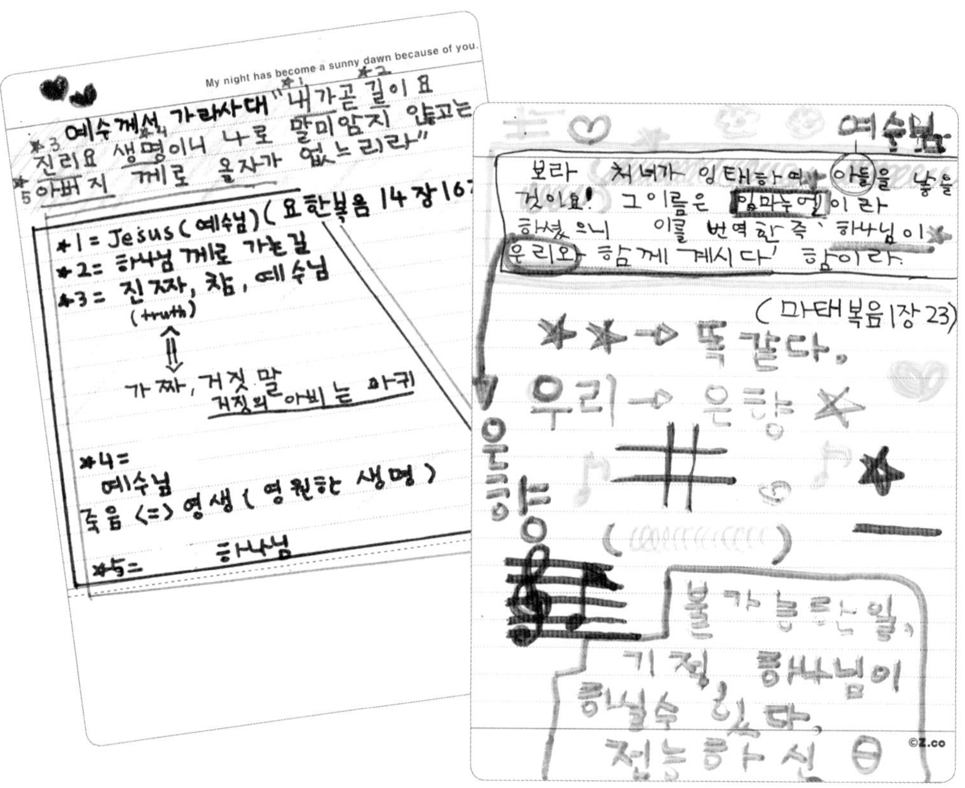

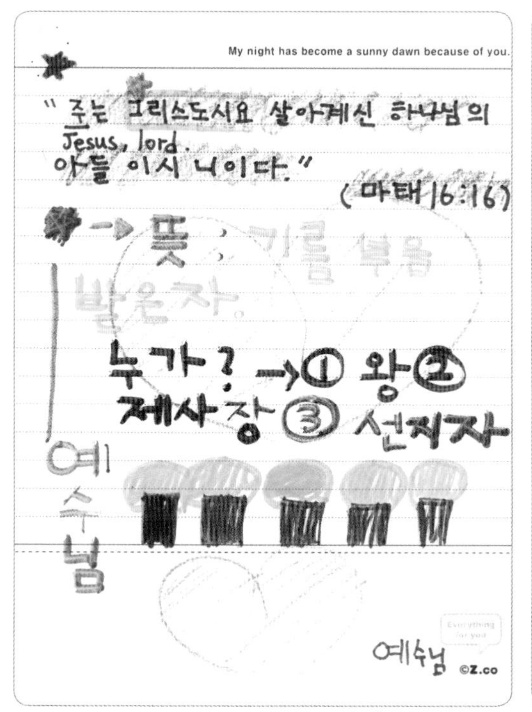

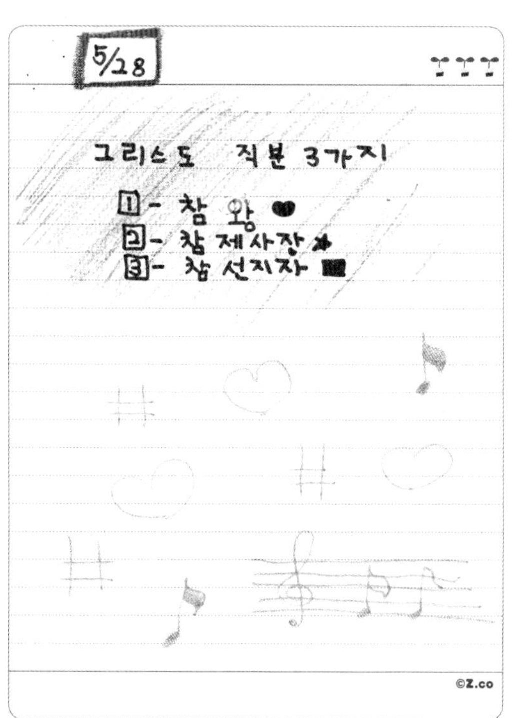

"내가 곧 길이요 진리요 생명이니
나로 말미암지 않고는 아버지께로 올 자가 없느니라."

성경공부를 이처럼 콘티(continuity)로 만들면 아주 재미 있고 쉽게 익힐 수 있어요.
Bible study thus creating a very interesting and CONTINUITY's easy to learn.

하나님의 아들이 나타나신 것은 마귀의 일을 멸하려 하심이니라. 〈히 4:14〉

The son of God appeared on this Earth to destroy evil. <Hebrews 4:14>

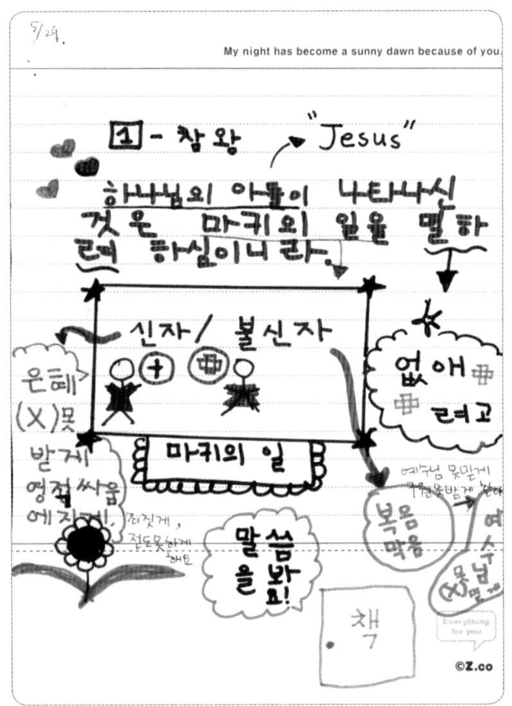

저는 하나님의 자녀가 되었어요.

I become a child of God.

영접하는 자 곧 그 이름을 믿는자들에게

하나님의 자녀가 되는 권세를 주셨으니 (요1:12)

하나님 말씀을 먹고 예쁘게 자라는 은향이

Mary growing up beautifully consuming God's Words.

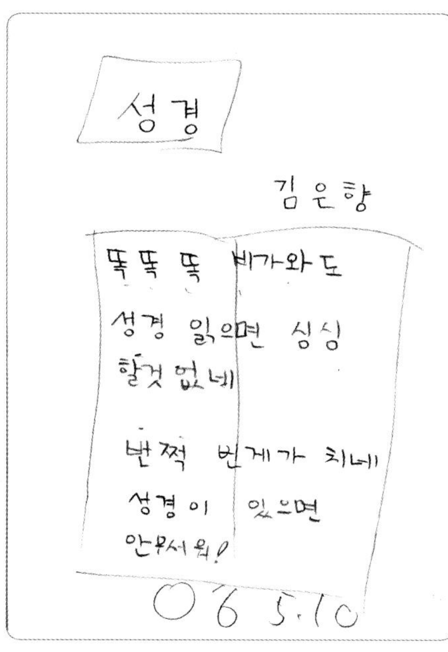

〈성경〉

똑똑똑 비가 와도
성경 읽으면 심심 할 것 없네

번쩍 번개가 치네
성경이 있으면
안 무서워!

<Bible>

Even on rainy days
Reading Bible brightens the gloomy days

The lightning strikes
With Bible
Nothing is scary!

〈하나님〉

사단 머리 깨뜨리라고
예수님을 보내신 하나님

죄 용서해 주라고 예수님을
보내신 하나님
천국 가는 길 만들기 위해
예수님을 보내신 하나님

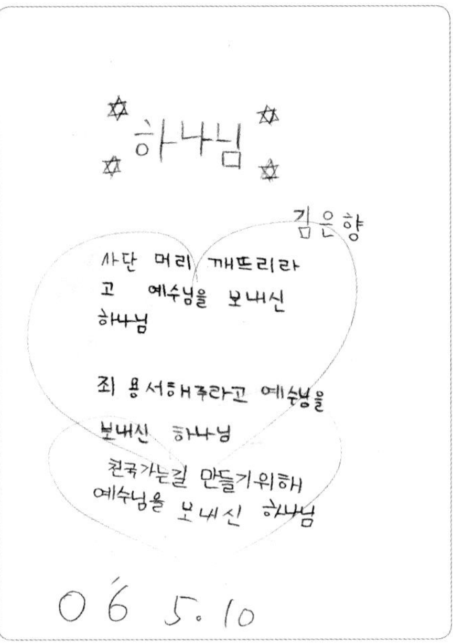

<God>

To destroy Satan
God sent Jesus

To forgive sins
God sent Jesus
To pave ways to Heaven
God sent Jesus.

내가 다니는 대구 북성교회

I attend church in Daegu bukseong.

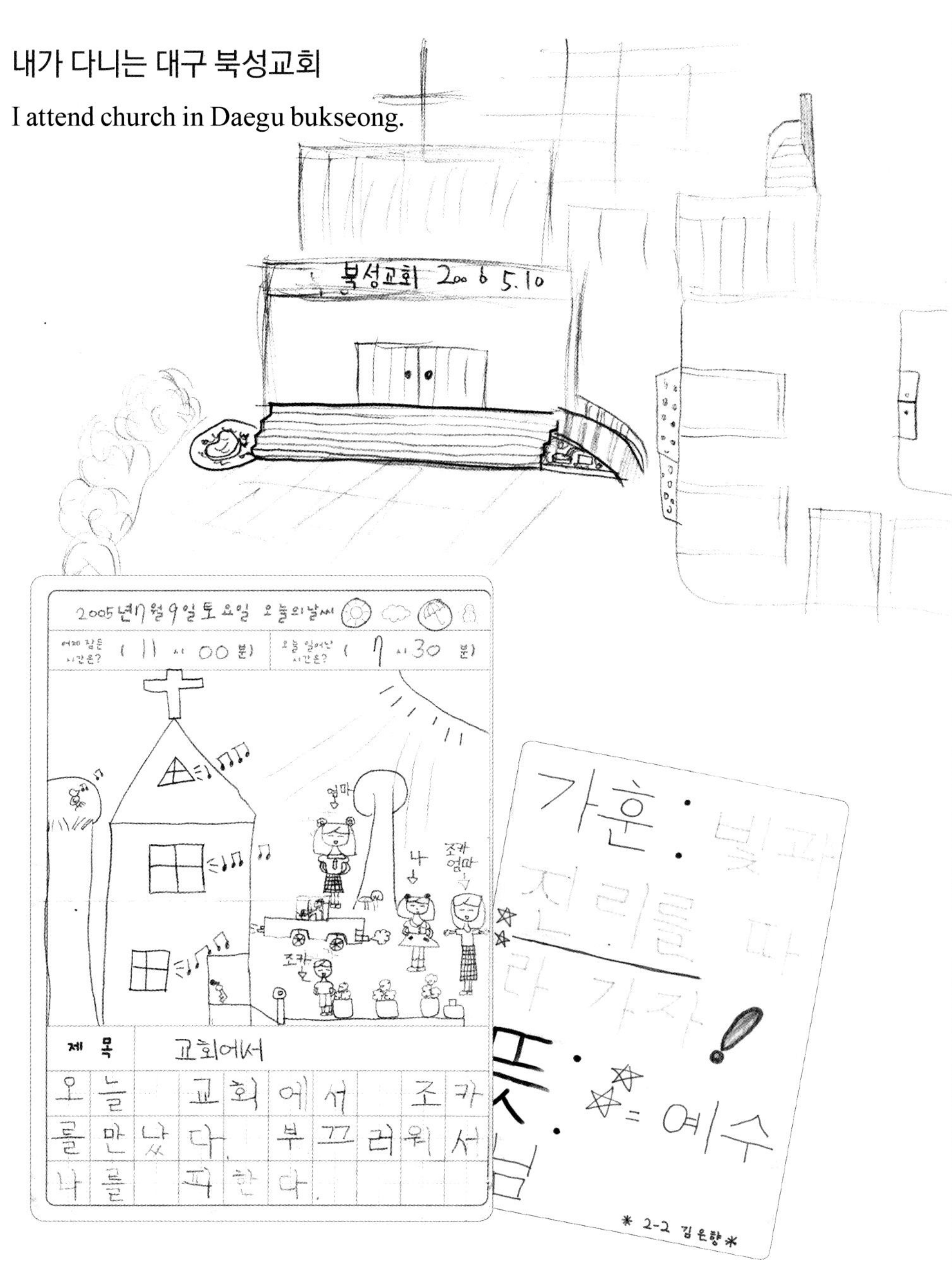

3 Children's Verse

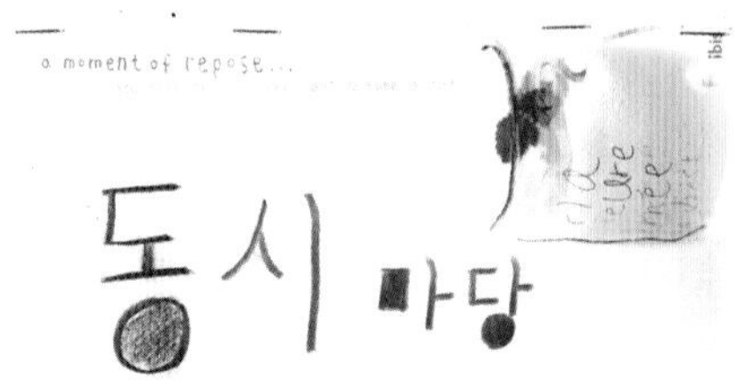

"미국 유학 시절에 쓴 동시(영문)"
어릴 때 쓴 글이라 틀린 곳이 여기 저기 보이네요.

<Many Color>

Red, Orange, Yellow, Green, Blue, dark Blue, Purple.
Very nice colors 7 Color.
This color makes beautiful rainbow
nice and good color.

many color

Red, Orange, Yellow,
Green, Blue, dark Blue,
purple.

Very nice colors
7 Color.

This color makes
beautiful rainbow

nice and good
color

<Pearl>

circle and
white
pretty
pearl
Why it is very beautiful?
Did pearl across the ocean?

<Music>

noisy!
noisy!
Whats that?!!
It's only music.
It's like movie(noisy, scary)
Why music is noisy?

<‘Yellow’ Color>

It’s light.
It’s pretty.
It’s colour like sunlight.
Can you guess?
Yes I do.
It’s ‘Yellow’
It’s easy.
Is your hair on T-shir.
It’s are yellow?

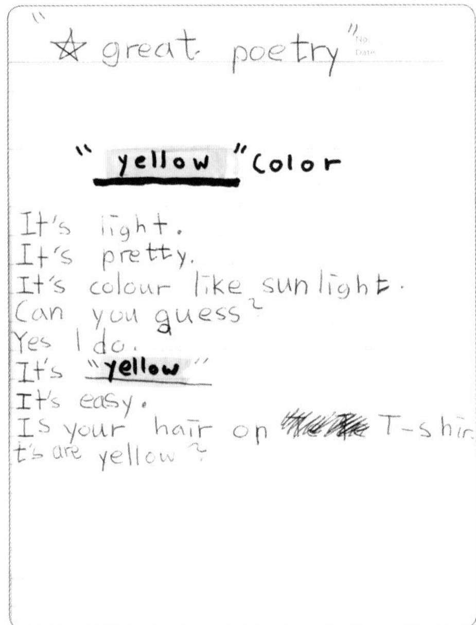
"☆ great poetry"

"yellow" Color

It's light.
It's pretty.
It's colour like sunlight.
Can you guess?
Yes I do.
It's "yellow"
It's easy.
Is your hair on T-shir
t's are yellow?

<Future>

future future.

My future is

"________"

I wish I had.

Teacher?

Doctor?

What I have to?

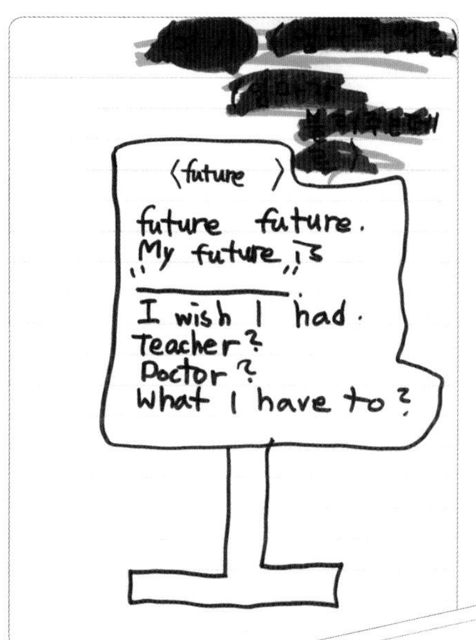

<Chair>

Thank you Chair.

because you make me comfortable.

You will sick.

I'm sorry.

Chair

Thank you chair.
because you make me comfortable.
You will Sick.
I'm sorry.

<To my grandfather>

granfa granfa
Now he is 93 year's old
I'm going to his house fun fun ………

<Mirror>

mirror who
is the best?
you gave me
the good face.
because I can
see you and
make up or
comb.
Thank you.

<Leave>

fly fly
fly fly
What is it?
It's green.
following that.
run run run.
I touch it.
It was leave.

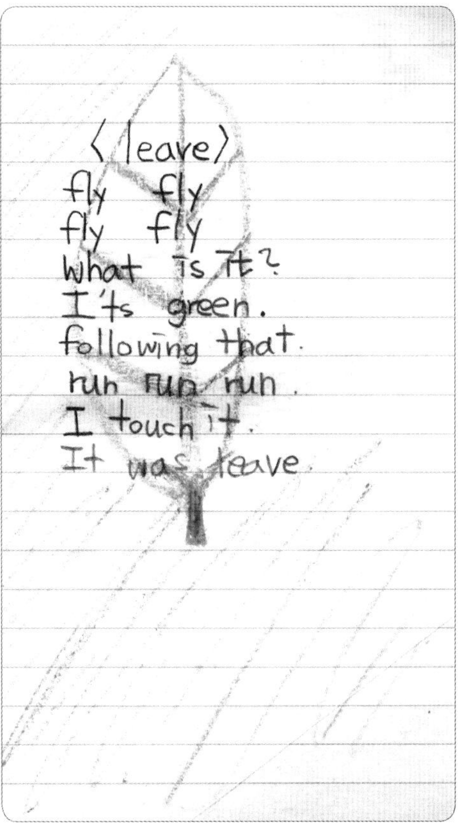

<Star>

twinkle twinkle

Sprinkle Sprinkle

What is it.

It is it.

It an star very beautiful.

How can it be such beautiful?

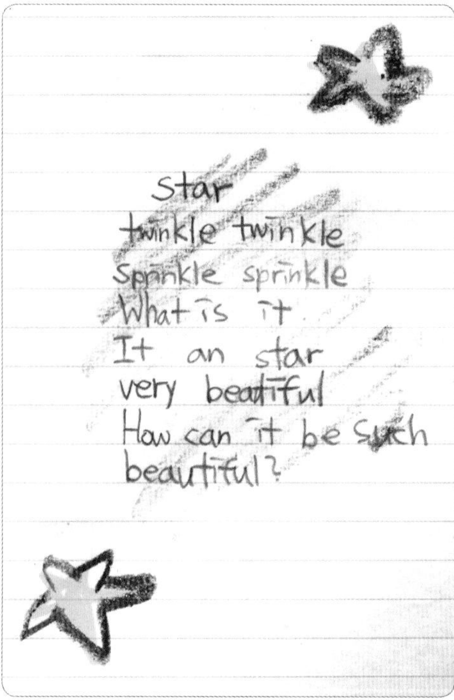

〈색연필〉

쓱싹쓱싹 색연필
가벼운 색연필
반짝이며 빛나는
아름다운 색연필
빨주노초파남보

우리의 소원을 들어줄까?
맞아. 색연필이 우리의
꿈을 그려줘
파란 삼촌 노란 아기
가족들이 색의 대로 색연필을
가지고 노는구나.

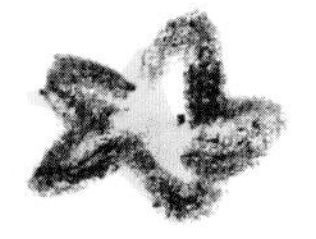

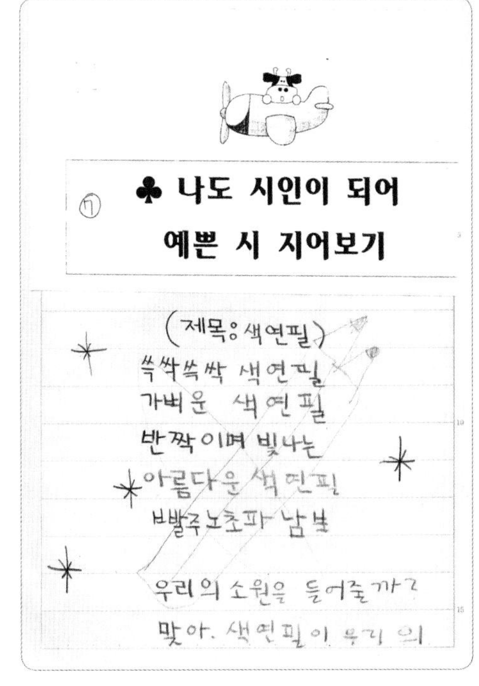

〈단풍〉

날아라 날아라
하늘높이 날아라
아이들이 가을을 좋아한다
하는데.....
그래서 그랬구나.
단풍은 예쁘지만
나비랑 같이 노는가보네
단풍으로 돛단배를
만들어볼까?
예쁘지만 개구쟁이 단풍으로

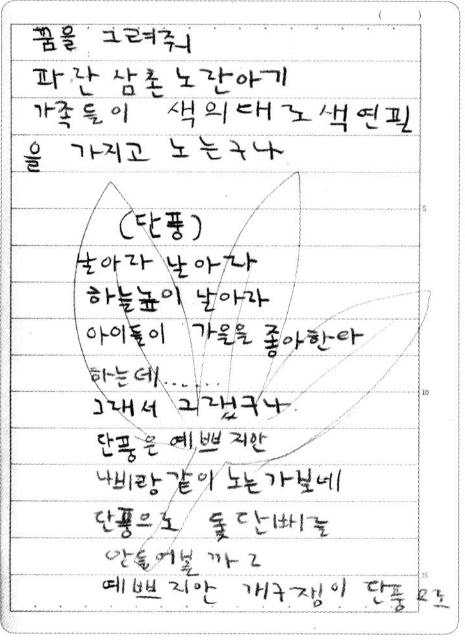

꿈을 그려줘
파란 삼촌 노란아기
가족들이 색의대로 색연필
을 가지고 노는구나

(단풍)
날아라 날아라
하늘높이 날아라
아이들이 가을을 좋아한다
하는데......
그래서 그랬구나.
단풍은 예쁘지만
나비랑같이 노는가보네
단풍으로 돛단배를
만들어볼까?
예쁘지만 개구쟁이 단풍으로

〈병아리 교실〉

선생님은 우리 보고
병아리래요
초롱초롱 맑은 눈이
참 예쁘대요

선생님은 우리 보고
병아리래요
삐악삐악 재잘재잘
참 시끄럽대요.

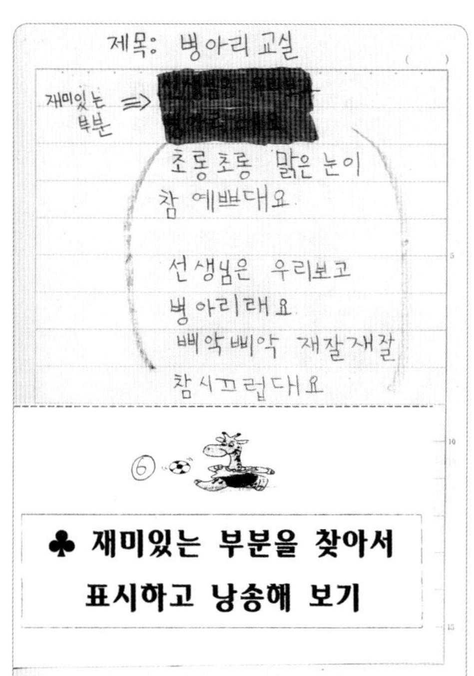

<The Class of Chicks>

Our teacher calls us
Chicks
She says our twinkling eyes are
Pretty

Our teacher calls us
Chicks
She says our chirping voices are
Loud.

〈낮과 밤〉

환한 낮이라도
두 눈만 감으면
캄캄 밤이 되지요
캄캄한 밤이라도
두 눈만 감으면
낮에 생긴 일이
환히 다 생각나지요

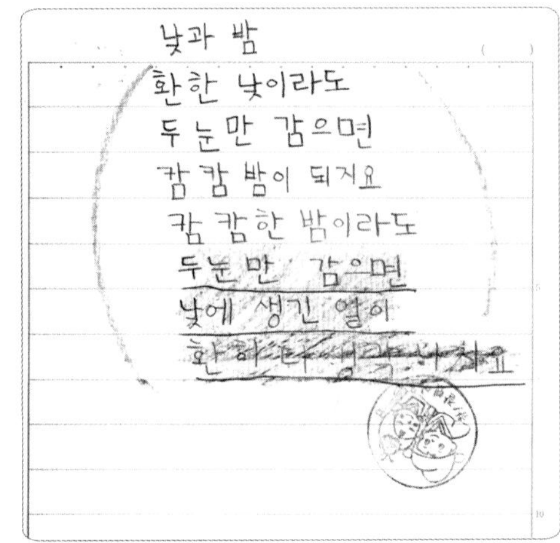
낮과 밤
환한 낮이라도
두 눈만 감으면
캄캄 밤이 되지요
캄캄한 밤이라도
두눈만 감으면
낮에 생긴 열이
[illegible]

<Day and Night>

Even in a bright day
When I close my two eyes
It becomes dark
Even in a dark night
When I close my two eyes
The things that happened in a day
Comes up to my mind brightly.

〈빗방울〉

톡톡 튀기다
파르르 떨다가
쪼르르 달리다
쭈르르 미끄럼
비오는날 차창문은
물방울 놀이터

<Rain Drops>

Pop Pop Pops
Run Run Runs
Slide Slide Slides
Car windows in rainy days
Are rain drops' playground.

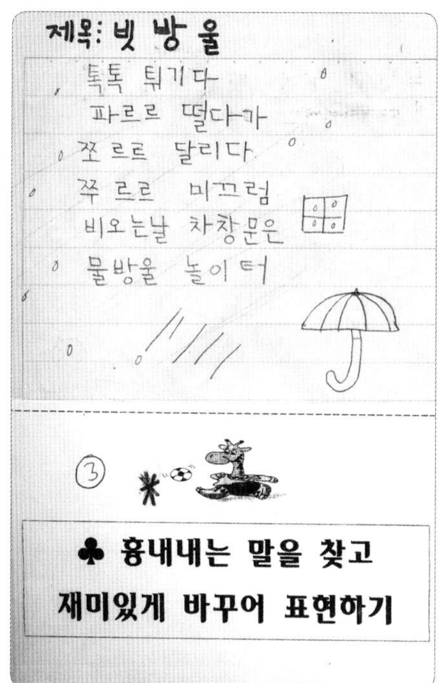

〈4월〉

춥지?
춥지?
벗은 가지에

찬바람의 감기며
자꾸 물어도

눈 꼭꼭
입 꼭꼭 말 없더니

대답대신 파랗게
싹이 돋았네

대답대신 예쁜 꽃이 피었네

<April>

Is it cold?
Is it cold?
With naked branches

Cold winds and cold flus
Even though I ask

Eyes Closed
Mouth closed with no response

Instead of a response
A green leaf blossomed

Instead of a response
A pretty flower blossomed.

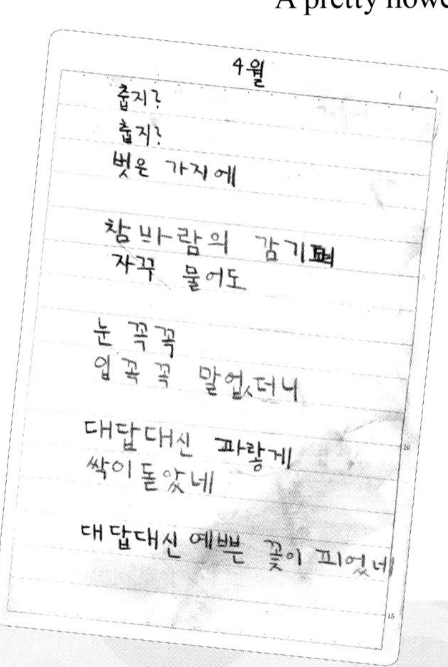

4월

춥지?
춥지?
벗은 가지에

찬 바람의 감기며
자꾸 물어도

눈 꼭꼭
입 꼭꼭 말없더니

대답대신 파랗게
싹이 돋았네

대답대신 예쁜 꽃이 피었네

〈우리는 하나〉

친구,
내 친구,
정다운 친구

선생님,
우리 선생님,
고마우신 선생님

학교,
우리 학교,
즐거운 학교

나,
친구, 선생님,
모두 모여
우리는 하나

<We are One>

Friend,
My friend,
A kind friend

Teacher,
Our teacher,
A thankful teacher

School,
Our school,
A fun school

Me,
Friends, teachers,
All gathered
We are one.

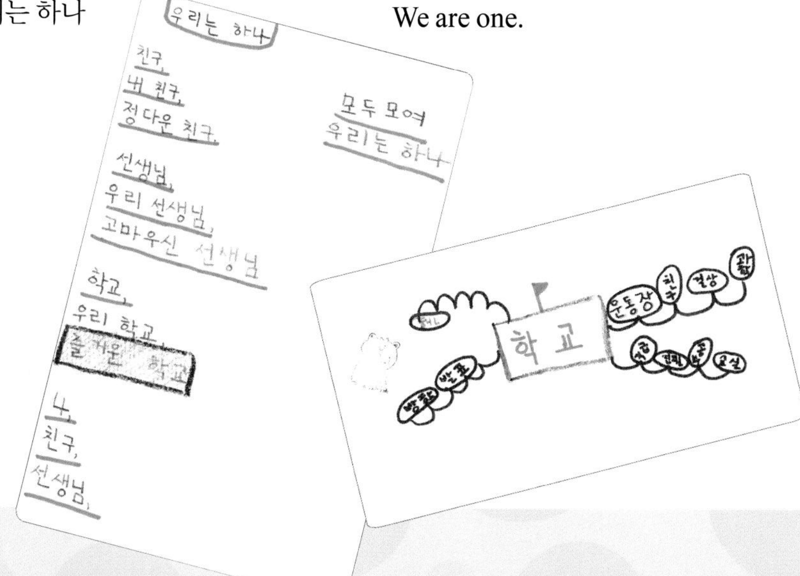

〈인사〉

만나면 서로서로
웃으며 인사
우리의 환한 얼굴
꽃이 되지요
한마디 주고 받은
상냥한 말에
우리의 밝은 마음
사랑이지요.

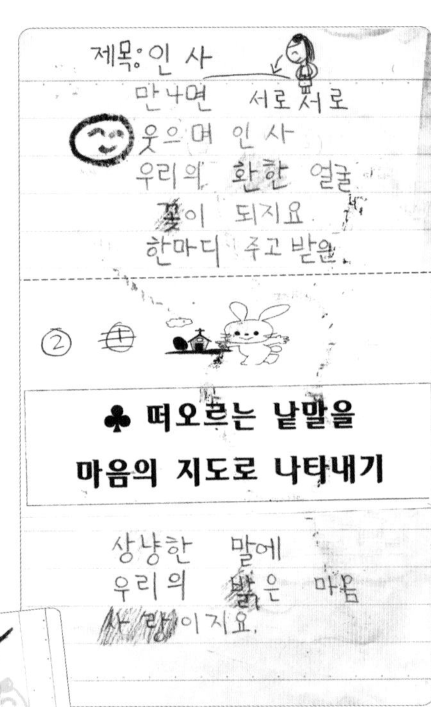

〈개구쟁이 낙서〉

개구쟁이 내동생
낙서를 한다
철로 없는 땅에
기차가 달리고
파아란 하늘엔
돛단배가 두둥실
개구쟁이 내동생
귀엽긴 하지만
줄어드는 도화지에
내 가슴은 콩닥콩닥

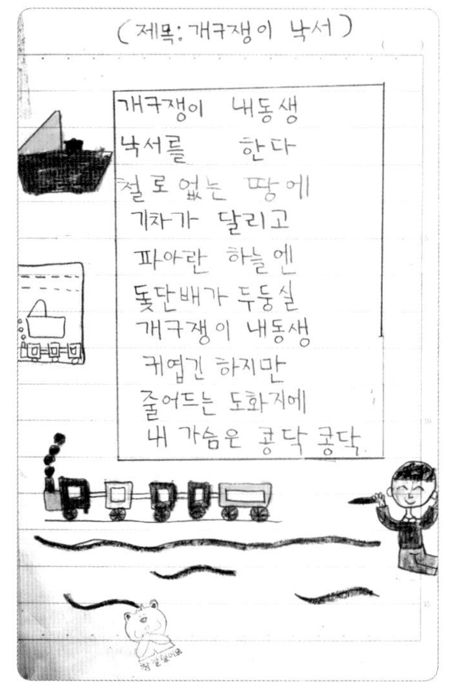

〈아빠의 손〉

아빠의 손을 잡고
길을 걸으면
아빠의 큰손에
내 손이 담기어
나도 키가 쑤욱
커진 것 같다

안 보아도 알아
안 만져봐도 알아
세상에서 제일
커다란 손
세상에서 제일
단단한 손
따뜻하고 고마운
우리 아빠손

<Dad's Hand>

Holding my dad's hand
And walking
Dad's big hand
Holds my hand
Feels like I grew
Taller like him.

I know without looking
I know without feeling
The biggest
Hand in the world
The hardest
Hand in the world
The warmest and greatest
Is my dad's hand.

〈좋겠다〉

꽃잎은 좋겠다
세수 안 해도
방울방울 이슬이
닦아주니까

나무는 좋겠다
목욕 안 해도
주룩주룩 소낙비
씻어주니까

<Lucky>

Lucky leaves
Even when you don’t wash your face
The dews
Wash your face for you.

Lucky trees
Even when you don’t shower
The rains
Wash you.

〈우리 대추나무〉

대추나무야 대추나무야
잘 자라라
우리 대추나무
작은 이파리도
무럭무럭 자라고
맛있는 대추도
주렁주렁 열려라

♣ 나의 경험을 떠올려서
④ 느낀 점 쓰기

제목: 우리 대추나무
대추나무야 대추나무야
잘 자라라
우리 대추나무
작은 이파리도
무럭무럭 자라고
맛있는 대추도
주렁주렁 열려라

〈낮과 밤〉

낮에는 햇님이 환하게 비추지요
우리들은 즐겁게 학교 가고요

밤에는 달님이 환하게 비추지요
우리들은 꿈나라로 여행 가고요

낮에는 까아만 그림자가
나를 따라다니지요

밤에는 온세상이 까맣게 변해서
그림자가 숨어버려요

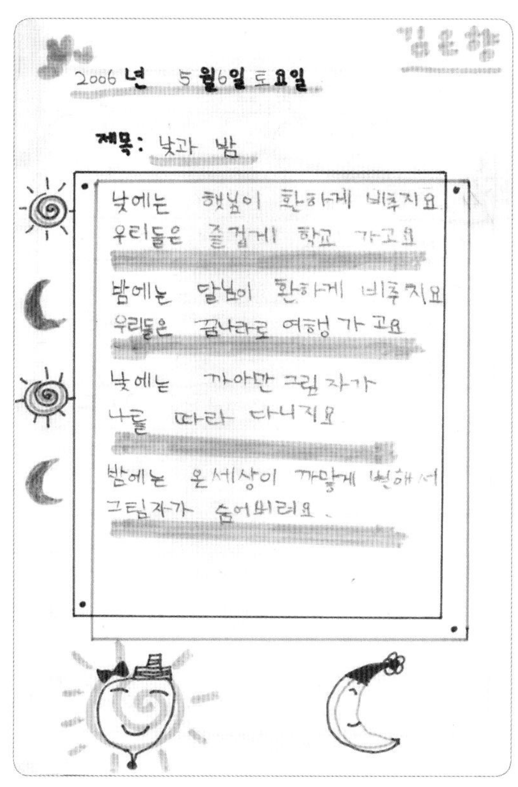
2006년 5월6일 토요일

제목: 낮과 밤

낮에는 햇님이 환하게 비추지요
우리들은 즐겁게 학교 가고요

밤에는 달님이 환하게 비추지요
우리들은 꿈나라로 여행 가고요

낮에는 까아만 그림자가
나를 따라 다니지요

밤에는 온세상이 까맣게 변해서
그림자가 숨어버려요.

〈쳇바퀴〉

다람쥐 3마리 쳇바퀴 돌리네
앞뒤로 신나게 쳇바퀴 돌리네

다람쥐 다섯 마리 쳇바퀴 돌리네
쉬지 않고 쳇바퀴 돌리네

다람쥐 다람쥐 오붓하게
사이좋게 살아가자

***나는 친구들과 사이좋게 지내고 공부도 신나게, 노는 것도 신나게 쉬지 않고 노력하겠다.

9월 2일 화요일

〈동시〉

〈쳇바퀴〉
다람쥐 3마리 쳇바퀴 돌리네
앞뒤로 신나게 쳇바퀴 돌리네

다람쥐 다섯마리 쳇바퀴 돌리네
쉬지않고 쳇바퀴 돌리네

다람쥐 다람쥐 오붓하게
사이좋게 살아가자

* 나는 친구들과 사이좋게지내고
공부도신나게, 노는것도 신나게 쉬지않고
노력하겠다.

오늘의 중요한 일 / 오늘의 착한일 / 오늘의 반성 / 내일의 할일

코니아~

〈마음의 상자〉

나의 마음을 들여다봅니다
상자 하나 있습니다
상자를 엽니다
상자가 나옵니다
상자를 또 엽니다
상자가 또 나옵니다

나의 생각을 들여다봅니다
꽃이 있습니다
꽃을 한잎 때봅니다
꽃잎이 나옵니다
꽃을 또 한잎 때봅니다
꽃잎이 또 나옵니다
마음은 하나이다
생각은 길러진다

<A Box of My Mind>

I look in to my mind
There is a box
I open the box
Another box comes out
I open the box
Another box comes out again

I look in to my mind
There is a flower
I pulled one leaf from a flower
The leaf comes out
I pulled one leaf again from a flower
The leaf comes out again
The mind is one
My thoughts grow.

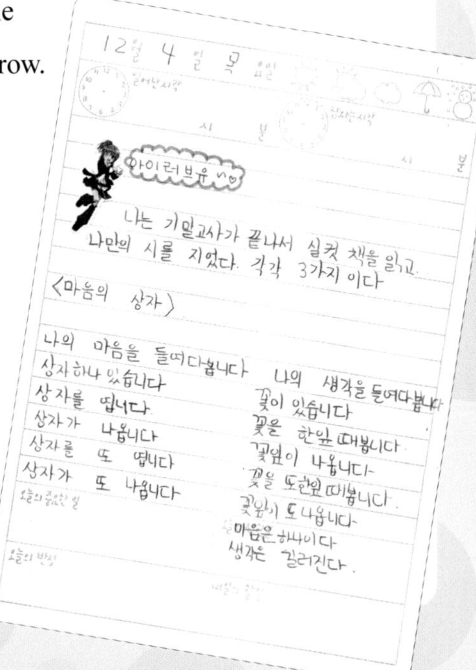

〈봄〉

봄이 옵니다. 봄이 옵니다.
벚꽃이 환영파티를 하네요.

짹짹짹. 짹짹짹.
새들이 새들이 환영 노래를
하네요.

와~ 아니 덥다.
아이들이 봄옷을
입고 봄을 맞이하러
나왔네요.

봄~ 아 봄~ 아
빨리와 혹시 비행기표라도
없어졌니?

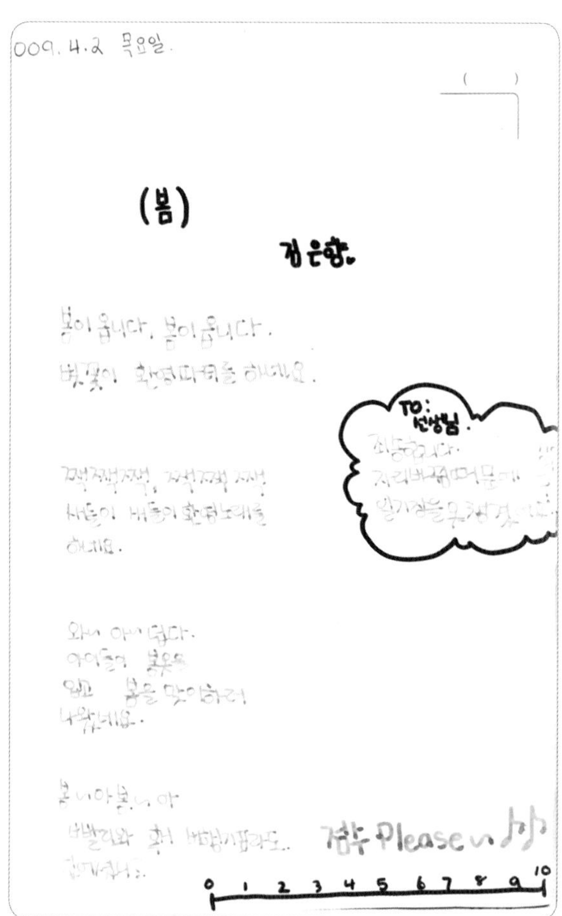

〈가정의 달〉

싱글벙글 어린이들의 웃음이
기다리고 있네
팔을 마중하러 나왔나보네....

〈꽃〉

꽃은 좋겠다
아침이면 이슬이
내려와 있어주니까

꽃은 좋겠다
사람들이
예뻐하니까

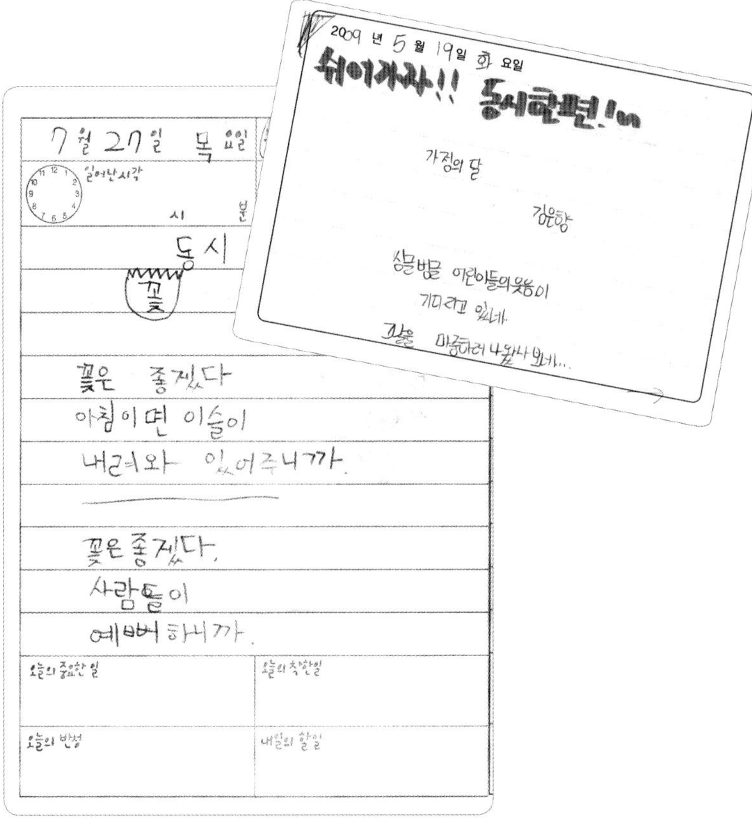

〈해와 달〉

해는 집의 엄마 같아요
왜? 깜깜할까 봐
비춰 주지요

달은 집의 아빠 같아요
밤에 무서울까 봐
비춰 주지요

8 월 1 일 화요일
일어난시각 시 분
잠자는시각 시 분
제목: 해와 달
해는 집의 엄마 같아요
왜? 깜깝 할까봐
비춰 주지요.
달은 집의 아빠같아요
밤에 무서울까봐 비춰
주지요
오늘의 중요한 일
오늘의 착한일
오늘의 반성
내일의 할일

<The Sun and The Moon>

The sun is like my mom
Why?
Because she shines the darkness for us to see.

The moon is like my dad
Why?
Because he shines the night for us to not be afraid.

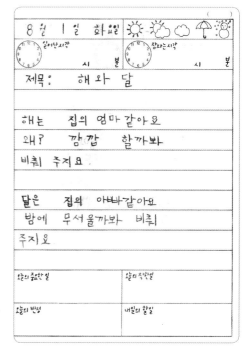

〈말〉

쫑알쫑알 말 정말
지겨워

재잘재잘 말 너무
귀찮아!

〈밭〉

풀 하면 밭

꽃 해도 밭
나는 밭이 좋아요!
풀도 꽃도 좋은가 봐!

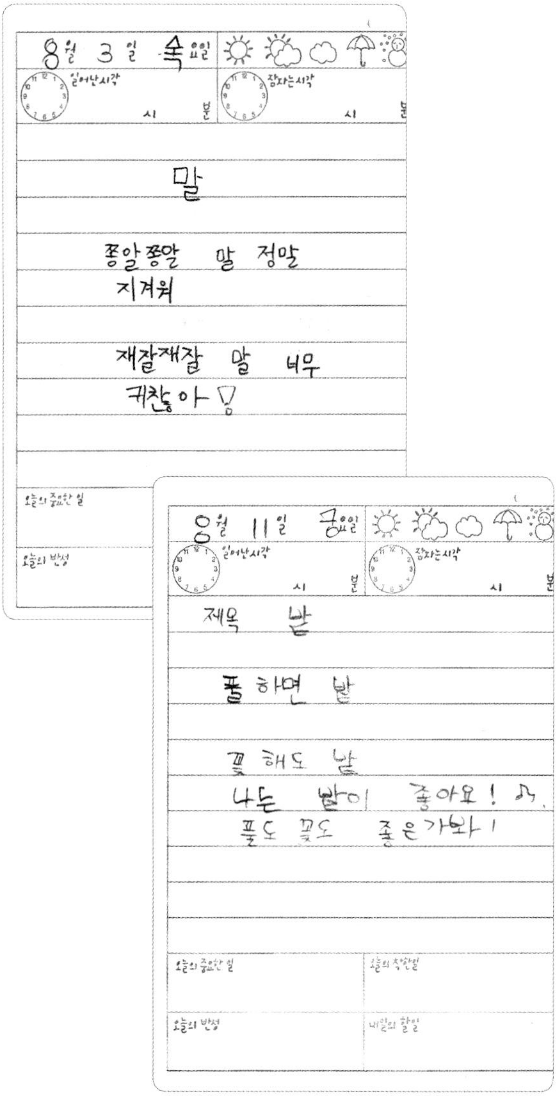

〈여름〉

아침 일찍 일어나면 이슬이 내 코에랑
푸른 잎에 맺히지요
보송보송 이슬방울이 내 코에 맺히면
친구들이랑 놀 때 이슬방울도 친구들을 데려오지요.

여름방학이 되면 매미소리에 갓난 애기도
잠에서 깨어나서 같이 노래 부르지요
매미도 여름방학이라고 덩달아 부르지요

나는 일어나서 창문 밖을 볼 때
온세상의 인생을 보는 것이 다 여름 덕분이지요
다 나를 낳아주신 엄마 덕분이지요.

10/ ← 여름

김은향

아침 일찍 일어나면 이슬이 내코에랑
푸른잎에 맺히지요
보송보송 이슬방울이 내코에 맺히면 친구들이랑
놀때 이슬방울도 친구들을데려오지요

여름방학이 되면 매미소리에 갓난애기도
잠에서 깨어나서 같이 노래부르지요. 매미도
여름방학이라고 덩달아 부르지요

나는 일어나서 창문 밖을 볼때 온세상의
인생을 보는것이 다 여름 덕분이지요 다 나를
낳아주신 엄마덕분이지요

<Summer>

When I wake up in the morning
The morning dews rest on top of my nose and green leaves
While the dews stay on my nose
The dews invite their friends when I am playing with my friends

In summer, the cicadas wake up sleeping babies
And harmonize
The cicadas sing along because it's summer.

Staring out the window after waking up
I thank summer for the entire world's lives
It's all because of my mother who gave birth to me.

〈어머니의 사랑〉

낳아 주신 우리 엄마
사랑해 주신 우리 엄마
안아 주신 우리 엄마
좋으신 우리 엄마

<Mom’s Love>

Mom who gave birth to me
Mom who loves me
Mom who hugs me
Mom is good.

◎어머니의 사랑◎
김은향

낳아 주신 우리 엄마
사랑해주신우리엄마
안아주신 우리엄마
좋으신 우리엄마

2006. 5.10

〈봄〉

나비가 날아요
봄이 외로운가 봐요

하늘이 푸르네요
봄의 기운이 좋은가 봐요

아이들이 숨바꼭질을 해요
봄도 숨었네요

사람들의 표정이 밝아요
봄이 진짜 왔나 봐요

지금의 계절을 느끼게 한 그 순간을 잘 떠올려 시에 담아 보세요 (다른 것을 글감으로 써도 괜찮습니다.).

〈봄, 여름, 가을, 겨울〉

아이의 머리는
따뜻해
아이의 어깨는 너무 더워

아이의 배는
썰렁 썰렁
아이의 발은
아이, 차가워

계절은 마술쇼에
가도 되겠다!

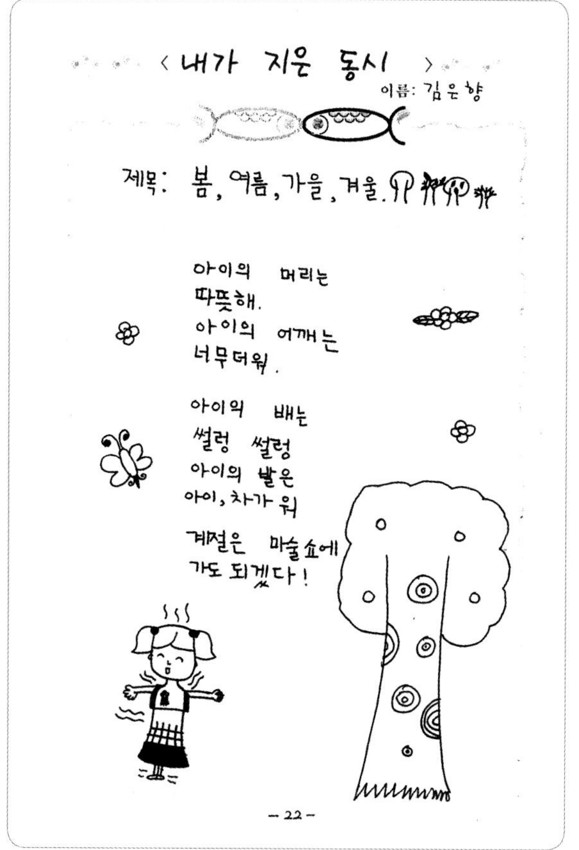

〈꽃씨〉

까만 꽃씨에서
파아란 싹이
나오고
파아란 싹이
자라
빨간꽃이
되고
빨간 꽃
안에서
까만 씨가
나오고

제가 왜 이 시를 좋아하냐면

사랑이라는 낱말이 들어가 있고 아름다운 시이고

저는 인사를 잘하고

언제나 환한 얼굴로 살려고 노력을 해서

이 시를 골랐습니다.

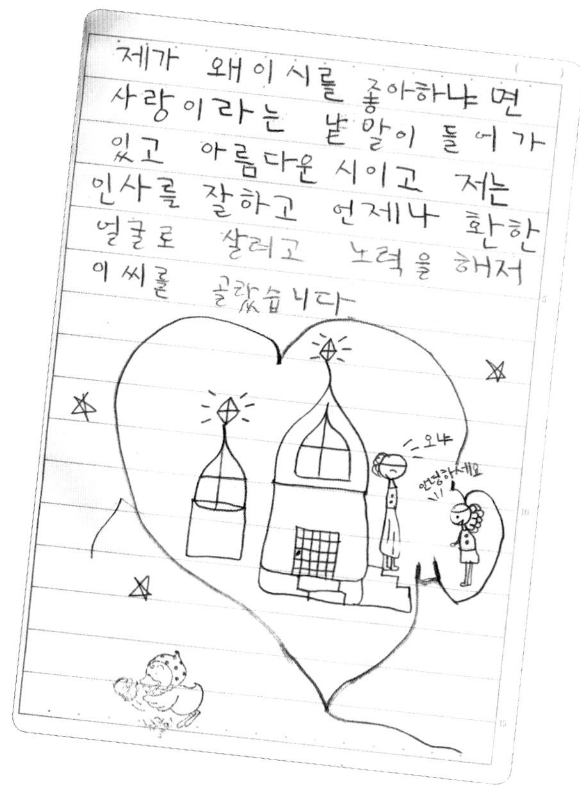

Happy
Birthday!
you
me
HAHA
JUST
KIDDING~
Lolita Lempicka
Beyoncé
RHYTHM PARADISE

Part 5

은향의 유학 스케치

1 미국 유학

2006년에서 2008년 사이에 미국 조지아주 아트란타에 있는 Mount Vernon Presbyterian School에서 2년간 유학을 하였다.

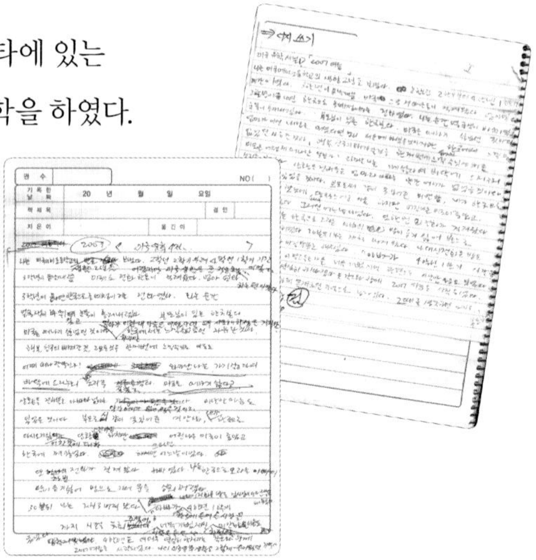

〈미국 유학 시절〉

미국 유학 시절, 「2007 여름」

나는 미국에서 초등학교의 생활 2년을 보냈다. 2학년 2학기부터 4학년 1학기 기간이였다. 3학년이 끝날 때쯤 미국으로 전화 한 통이 걸려왔다. 엄마였으나 3학년이 끝나면 한국으로 올 예정이라는 전화였다. 나는 순간 얼굴색이 바뀌였고, 눈물이 흘러내렸다. 부모님이 있는 한국보다 미국을 떠나기 싫었던 것이다. 엄마가 이런 내 맘을 아셨다면 꽤 서운해 하셨을 것이지만, 하지만 한국에서 느낄 수 없었던 자유란 것과, 행복, 친구의 배려란 것을 한꺼번에 느낄 수 있게 해준 미국을 어떻게 떠나란 말인가? 화가 난 나는 가기 싫다며 바닥에 드러누워 소리를 질렀다. 상황을 전해 들은 엄마와 아빠는 약간 어이가 없었을 것이다. 미안한 마음도 있었을 것이다. 부모로서 같이 못 있어 준 미안함, 내가 한국으로 다시 오기 싫어 한 것에 대한 당황스러운 마음. 하지만 어린 나는 미국이 좋았고, 한국에 가기 싫었다. 그러던 어느 날이었다. 또 한 번 전화가 걸려 왔다. 아빠였다. 나는 한국으로 오라는 아빠의 말이 듣기 싫어 방으로 가서 문을 잠궈 버렸다. 30분 뒤 나는 거실로 내려왔다. 나 대신 전화를 받은 집사님께서 이런 말씀을 해줬다. "아빠가 4학년 1학기 시간을 늦춰주셨어." 이 말을 들은 나는 너무 기뻤지만, 한편

으로는 미안한 마음도 있었다. 4학년은 더더욱 열심히 해야겠다는 각오와 함께 2007년 여름은 시작되었다. 나의 미국생활도 그렇게 즐거웠던 기억으로 남아 있다. 그때를 생각하면 아직도 살짝 미안한 맘이 있다.

<Studying Abroad In America, [2007 Summer]>

I attended an elementary school in the United States for two years: 2nd grade 2nd semester to 4th grade 1st semester. At the end of 3rd grade, I got a call from my mom saying that she and my dad had decided to bring me back to Korea after finishing 3rd grade. My face turned pale and tears rolled down my cheeks as soon as she said that. I wanted to stay in America rather than go back to my parents in Korea. I'm sure my mom would have been disappointed to hear that, but how could she expect for me to leave a place where freedom, happiness and kindness of friends could be felt all at once? With no intention of leaving this place, I began to cry my heart out while lying on the floor. Hearing about my strong disagreement, my parents couldn't understand and, on the other hand, felt guilty for not being able to be with me. At a young age, I grew fond of America and didn't want to go back to Korea. Then one day, I got another phone call; it was my dad. Not wanting to talk to him, I ran up to my room and locked the door. After 30 minutes, I went down to the living room. The dorm staff who answered the phone instead told me, "Your father postponed your leave to 4th grade 1st semester." I was so happy to hear that, but also felt sorry to my parents. With the motivation to study harder in my 4th grade year, the summer of 2007 began. My studies in America ended with a blissful memory. Whenever I reminisce these days, I feel sorry toward my parents just as I did back then.

사랑해
Kim.
Je T'aime
I LOVE YOU

영어로 쓴 그림일기

유학시절, 그리운 벗들과

선생님 영어로 쓸게요...

There once was a little pig named Sally.

She was so beautiful that even a beast wouldn't kill her.

She had a mom, dad, and a young brother.

It was her first day in school. And when she stepped in to her new classroom,

everyone was staring at her

They started whispering about her beauty. But especially the boys. A week passed and the school had a drawing contest to pick a each grade fine young artist to compete against other schools. That morning she woke unusually earlier than the other family members. She prepared her own lunch and breakfast and started practicing her drawing skills. When an hour passed she painted a drawing that she was proud of. First her mom woke up first like usual. But like other mothers would be surprised there was a fine beautiful, tasty looking french toast and egg fri and some milk, juice,

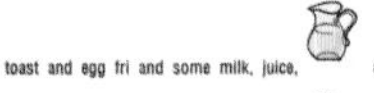

and coffee on the table. She there saw her daughter smiling at her. As if she was telling her to eat before it gets cold. So the whole family got together and was amazed by the great taste. Sally was really happy and realized she had to leave for school. She took all her stuff with her. When she arrived in her class they were just starting. Sally started painting a picture of her family and was the first person to turn it in. After school her mother prepared a hot bath for her. But who knew she would fall asleep in there......But she did. Her father carefully picked her up and put her to bed. In her dream she imagined she was a fine artist when she grew up. It was morning and when she went to school she was passing out valentines to her whole class but when her homeroom teacher announced the 1st grade fine young artist she didn't even wan' t to hear it. She saw the painting that her friend drew and was like real. But when she unplugged her ears she heard her name. Sally!!! She was so surprised that she almost fainted! SHE THOUGHT IT WAS A DREAM AND STARTED POKING HERSELF AND PINCHING HERSELF EVERYWHERE!!!!

but after school she found herself in the clinic because of what she did to check if it was real or not. But it was real!!!!

When she got home there family already knew and prepared a party for her!!!!!!! She was surprised and sorry that they prepared a party.

But they were a happy family that always cared and loved each other.

The End.

선생님께 보낸 편지

미국 한 반 친구들이랑 점심을 먹고

미국에서 동요를 많이 짓고 썼어요.

영어 초보 김은향의 흔적

I want
to be a
teacher.
Because I read
many Book

Mary

Mary is a friendly, cheerful, and intelligent young girl. She was always actively engaged in all camp activities and seemed to have a lot of fun here. Her English skills are also to be commended. She demonstrated excellent comprehension skills and was always able to follow along with ease. Her writing skills are developing well and will continue to grow and improve as her vocabulary expands. It was a pleasure having her at camp. Best of luck!

Marisa Cruickshank

창틈 사이로 쏟아져 내리는 햇살을

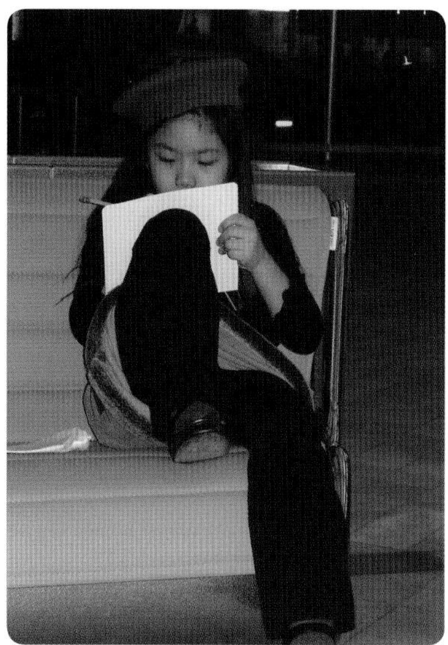

틈만 나면 메모나 그림을 그렸어요.

Dear Mom ♡ and Dad,

Hi~

I am having Sun at W.K.C ♡ International.

Kids camp! see you soon at the graduation ceremony.

♡ mary.

Mary

Mary's bright, energetic, and caring personality was immediately noticeable. Mary was always found in the company of many friends and always with a smile on her face. Also unlike other girls, she was athletic and brave when participating in golf and lacrosse. In fact, Mary's golf skills were exceptional! Inside the classroom, she was just as extraordinary as she was outside the classroom. With the same straightforward attitude, her English was always filled with confidence. Mary would always raise her hand with answers during class, and diligently complete any task that was assigned to her. It is without doubt that with continued education, Mary will achieve fluency in English and I wish her the best of luck in the pursuit of fluency and all her future endeavors.

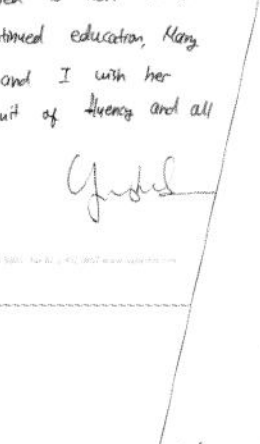

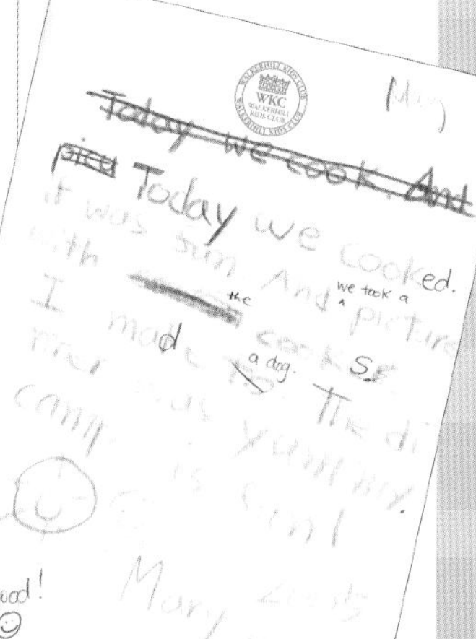

친구 Mary에게 생일축하카드

미국 유학 시절 생일파티

친구들과 함께하는 식사

It has been a delight teaching you.

I'll miss seeing you every day!! I hope your day is great.

♡

I your teacher, Ahannoh

Mount Vernon presbyterian School에서 학외활동

아련한 지난 추억

미국 유학, 친구들이랑

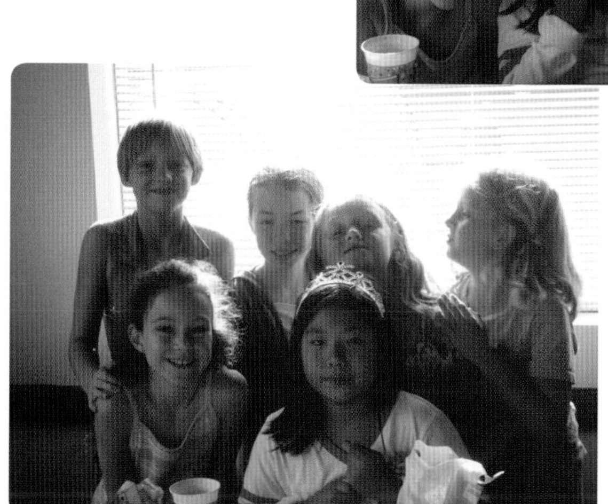

미국 유학시절 친구들

I can show you the world
Shining shimmering splendid
Tell me princess when was
your last time you let your
heart decide. I can open
your eyes. Take you wonder
by wonder. Over sideways
over wheeling on a Magic
Carpet ride! A whole new
world~ A new fantastic
point of view up when I'm
way up here it's crystal
clear cause now I'm in a
whole new world with you.

A WHOLE NEW WORLD

<A WHOLE NEW WORLD>

I can show you the world Shining shimmering splendid tell me princess when was your last rine you let your heart decide. I can open your eyes. Take you wonder by wonder. Over side ways over wheeling on a Magic carpet ride! A whole new world~ A new fantastic point of view up when I'm way up here it's crystal clear cause now I'm in a whole new world with you.

"Never Ends"

DATE

I still can't blow out that flee burning in me
You were the victim I thougt I could catch so easily,
It was a nice try
But it made me cry
You were the one, the one I depend on
But when I tried to reach your heart, I quickly abandoned
And now, I see you with her.
I'd love my heart to disappear
I'd love to live without that hurt
And when you're standing near
I still have that kind of fear
Cause it's just like a knife in my ears, when you call her "Dear".

by Masha Guess

미국에서 맞은 크리스마스

A Christmas greeting and good wishes to you who is thought about all the year through. Have a beautiful Christmas and a happy New Year!

TITE EXITÉE... ♡... ♡... ♡

Kim[berley]

♡ 사랑해

I ♥ U my Schlampe! ♪ ♫

bad girl !!

and what about A...?

don't forget life is a bith..!

by Masha Quest.

My dear Mary!

Thank you so much for everything! With you, I can be myself and feel comfortable. Thank you for sharing with me my laughter and my tears, good times and bad times. Nobody can replace you, in my heart, I will always keep a place for you. I love you so much! Don't forget those two CRAZY years!

We Rock!

Anna-Solia

My Dear Mary!

Thank you so much for everything! with you, T can be myself and feel comfortable. Thank you for sharing with me my laughter and my tears, good times and bad times. Nobody can replace you, in my heart, I will always keep a place for you. I love you so much! Don't forget those two crazy years!

We Rock! ♡

Anna-Solia

HAPPY BIRTHDAY MARY!!~

생일 축하해!

I hope you have a 대박 birthday today! ♡ Hehe I'm so Thankful I met you this year~

Thank you for welcoming me and taking care of me on the first day of school! "Hi…may I please sit here?"

LOL! It's been so much fun with you and Diana. Let's make more memories this year and definitely go downtown and eat Food! ♥

I hope you have a great chuseok break and eat a lot because you're Not fat or ugly at all!!

Jinjah why don't you believe me -_- haha so yeah! Have a wonderful birthday! Have fun and get FAT! Love you~

♡♡♡♡♡ -Kris

HAPPY BIRTHDAY MARY!!~
생일축하해! I hope you have a 대박 birthday today! ♥ Hehe I'm so thankful I met you this year~ Thank you for welcoming me and taking care of me on the first day of school! "Hi…may I please sit here?" LOL! It's been so much fun with you and Diana. Let's make more memories this year and definitely go downtown and eat FOOD! ♥ I hope you have a great chuseok break and eat a lot because you're NOT fat or ugly at all!! Jinjah why don't you believe me -_- haha so yeah! Have a wonderful birthday! Have fun and get FAT! Love you~
♡ ♡ ♡ ♡ ♡ - Kris

Happy Birthday!

you

me

HAHA JUST KIDDING~

2 중국 유학

2013 여름 중국 유학을 떠나기 전 중국어 공부를 하기 위해 만난

왕민(王民), 이건(李健), 왕옌(王燕) 선생님 고마워요.

2013년에서 2014년 1년간 중국 베이징 중국인민대학 부속중학교에 유학하였다.

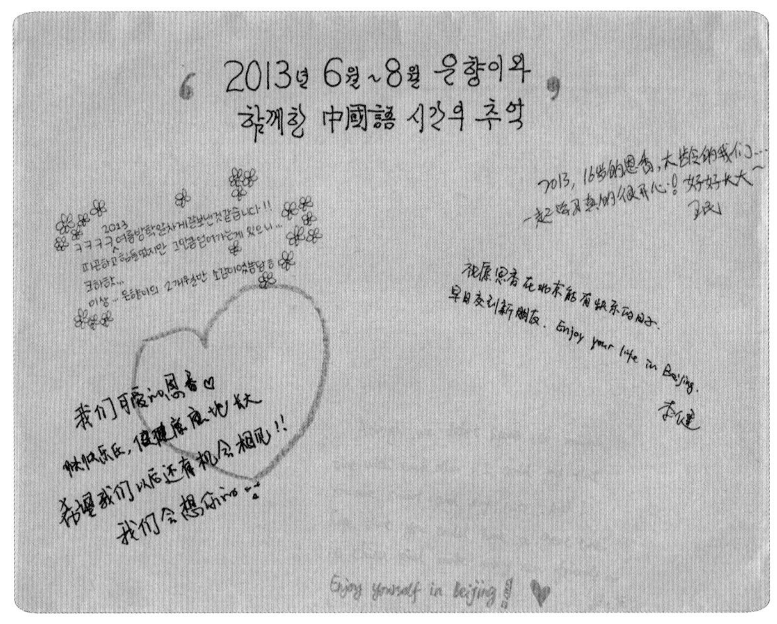

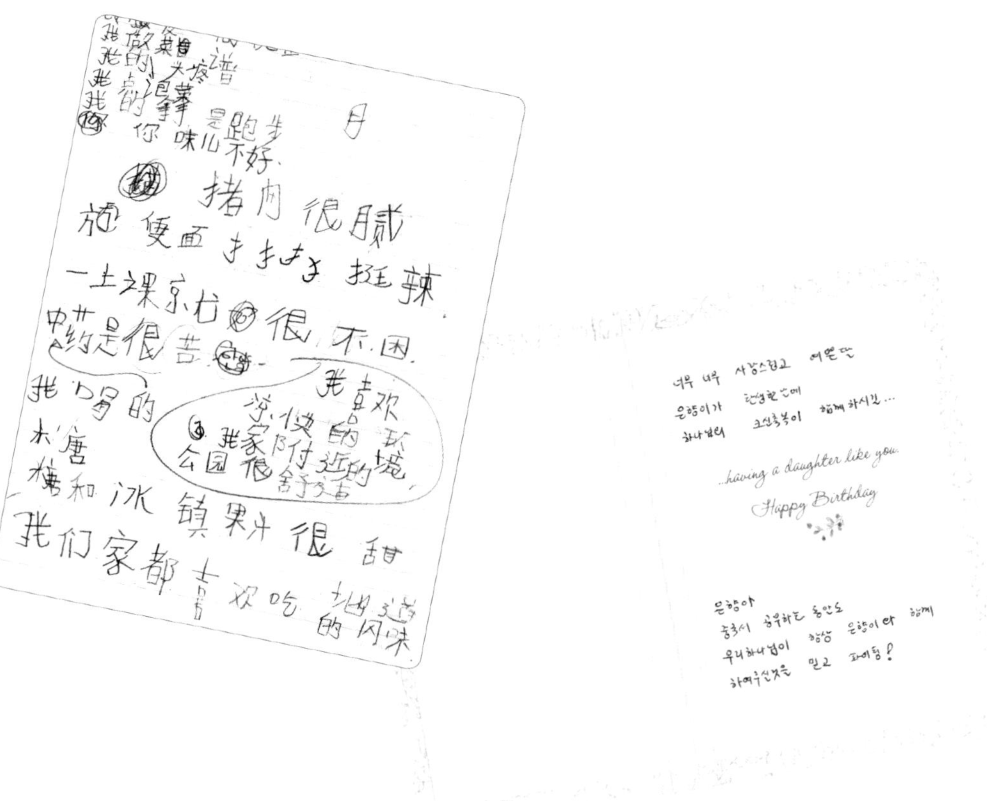

〈중국 유학기행〉

중국에서 그닥 오래 살지도 않았고 중국에 대해 많은 걸 알고 간 것도 아니다. 따지고 보면 중국말을 중국 사람이랑 끊김 없이 유창하게 할 수 있는 능력도 없었고 아직도 그만큼 잘 하지는 않는다. 그런데 단지 예전에 프랑스랑 미국에서 공부했을 때가 재미있었고 좋았기 때문에 중국에서의 경험 또한 그럴 거라 생각하고 중국을 가게 되었다. 처음에 중국 유학을 제안한 건 아빠였다. 앞으로 세계가 중국에 포커스를 둘 거라고 중국에 가보는 게 어떻겠냐고 물어보셨다. 처음엔 왠 뜬금없는 제안인가 싶었다. 그래서 일초의 망설임도 없

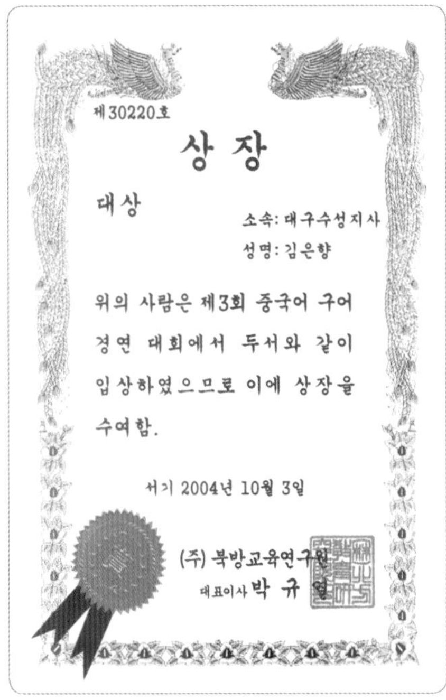

제30220호

상 장

대상

소속: 대구수성지사

성명: 김은향

위의 사람은 제3회 중국어 구어 경연 대회에서 두서와 같이 입상하였으므로 이에 상장을 수여함.

서기 2004년 10월 3일

(주) 북방교육연구원

대표이사 박 규 열

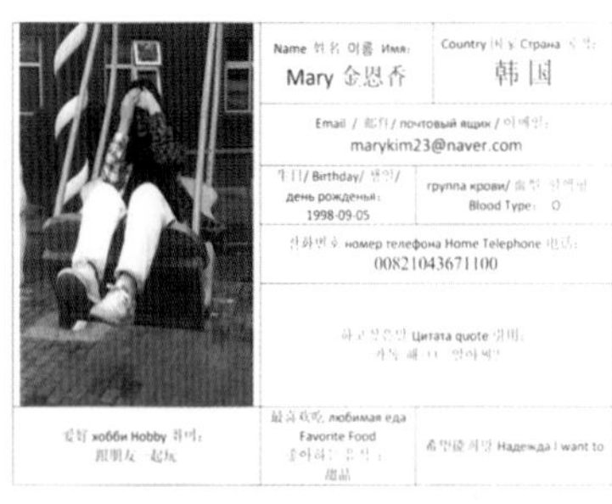

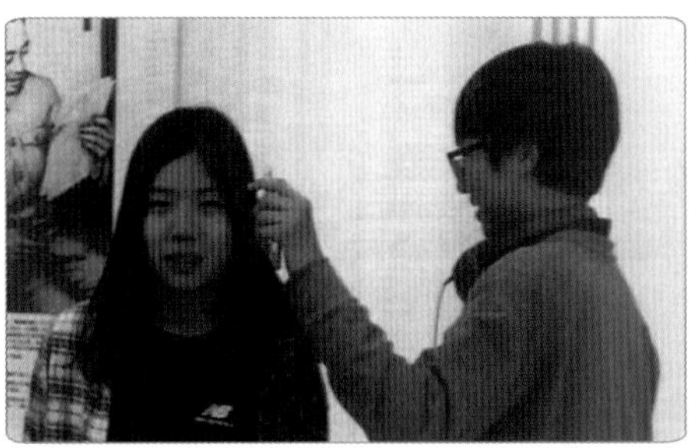

이 싫다고 중국을 왜 가야 하냐고 말했다. 그렇게 단숨에 거절하고 몇주 뒤에 무슨 바람이 불었는지 갑자기 중국 가보고 싶다고 했다. 거의 조르다시피 가겠다고 하는 내 모습이 신기하셨는지 알겠다고 알아보시겠다고 하셨다. 그러고부터 몇주 뒤에 9학년 마치자마자 가기로 했다. 나는 미국이랑 프랑스 가는 것처럼 즐거울 줄 알았다. 하지만 중국 가려면 어느 정도의 기본 실력은 있어야 했기에 여름방학 동안 중국어 공부를 죽어라 했다. 정확히 말하자면 몸은 매일 빠짐없이 수업을 하러 갔지만 어쩌면 정신은 이미 수업 끝나고 집에 와서 놀고 있을 생각을 하고 있었는지도 모른다. 솔직히 말하면 진짜 힘들었다. 황금 같은 여름방학인데 매일 수업을 6시간씩 하러 가야 했고 친구들을 만날 시간이 거의 없었다. 지루했던 몇달이 지나고 나서 드디어 중국을 갔다. 보통 기숙사 같으면 엄청나게 많은 걸 요구하지는 않는데, 내가 앞으로 지낼 기숙사에서는 요구하는 게 상당히 많았다. 이불부터 시작해서 베개, 서랍 등등 준

'제3회 전국 중국어 구어 경연대회에서 대상' 수상' 김은향

비해야 할 게 엄청 많았다. 그래서 이케아부터 시작해서 상점이란 상점은 다 찾아다닌 것 같다. 준비물을 사든 후에 기숙사 앞에 도착했을 때 설렘 반 걱정 반이었다. 과연 내가 아무것도 모르던 어렸을 때처럼 아무 생각없이 잘 적응할 수 있을까? 이런 생각밖에 안 했던 것 같다. 한 마디로 기분이 묘했다. 기숙사에 들어가고 대충 설명을 들은 뒤 엄마께서 먼지가 많이 껴 있다고 구석구석 닦아 주셨다. 짐정리를 끝낸 뒤 같은 방 쓸 나보다 한 살 많은 언니와 함께 저녁을 먹으러 갔다. 저녁을 먹고 난 뒤 방에 돌아와서 아무 생각없이 있었던 것 같다. 그러고 앉아 있는데 옆방 언니가 찾아왔다. 같은 방 쓰는 언니랑 되게 친한것 같았다. 둘이 자매 같았다. 괜히 내가 둘 사이를 방해하는 것이 아닌가 죄책감이 들었다. 그때 당시에는 의지할 게 폰밖에 없었던 것 같다. 친구들과 카톡을 주고 받으면서 첫 번째 밤이 지났다.

언니들이랑 조금 친해지고 며칠이 지난 후 주말에 시내를 가기로 했다. 시내를 간 게 터닝 포인트였던 것 같다. 그때는 나도 언니들이 너무 편하고 좋았다. 하지만 그 흔한 술 문화에 나는 낄 수 없었고 낄 자신도 없었다. 쿨한 척 해봤지만 속에서는 걱정이 가득했다. 시내를 다녀온 뒤 나는 울기만 한 것 같다. 언니들 앞에서 울기 싫어서 숨어서 울었지만 행여나 들킬까 봐 복도에서 울곤 했다. 괜찮냐고 물으면 가족이랑 친구들이 보고 싶다는 핑계로 울었다. 적응하기가 어렵고 힘들어서라고 그런 찌질한 이유를 대기는 싫었다. 결국에 나는 학교를 옮기게 되었다. 어쩌면 조금더 나은, 조금 더 아늑한 중국인민학교로 옮기게 되었다. 지켜야 하는 규정도 많았고 내가 이전에 몇주 있었던 학교와는 정말 달랐다. 가는곳마다 한국인이 있었지만 누가 봐도 정말 큰 학교였다. 아빠께서 이왕이면 좋은 학교에 보내려고 찾고 찾다가 좋은 분 만나서 인민대부중(人民大学附中学)에 입학하게 되었다. 중국어를 완벽하게 할 수 없었기 때문에 국제부에 들어가게 되었다. 내가 예상했던 거와 달리 국제반에는 한국인이 정말 없었다. 나 외에 두 명밖에 없었다. 나보다 한 살 많은 언니 한 명 그리고 나보다 두 살 어린 동생 한 명밖에 없었다. 나머지는 다 미국인, 중국인, 아니면 유럽 쪽에 학생들이었다. 그때 나는 다시 한 번 내가 영어를 할 수 있음에 감사하게 되었다. 다들 영어를 할 수 있었기 때문에 우리는 영어로 소통하였고 적응하는 데 전혀 문제가 없었다. 오히려 더 재밌었고 설레었던 것 같다. 지내면서 힘들었던 적이 진짜 많았다. 그럴 때마다 나랑 동갑인 친구들 한테 기대었던 것 같다. 그 중 내가 특히 정말 좋아했던 카자스탄에서 온 친구가 한 명 있었는데 러시아어를 쓰며 영어도 엄청 잘하는 친구였다. 처음에는 서로에게 선을 그었던 것 같은데 시간이 지날수록 정말 친해지고 제일 많이 같이 놀고 웃었던 친구 같다. 인민대부중은 국제부 기숙사랑 중국인 기숙사가 따로 있기 때문에 국제반이 아닌 중국어를 잘해서 보통반에 있는 한국인들이랑도 같이 살았다. 그래서 나는 같은 방 쓰는 동생의 언니랑 그 언니의 친구들이랑 되게 친하게 지냈다. 셋 다 동갑이었기 때문에 의지할 수 있었다. 내가 지금까지 한 기숙사 생활을 통틀어서 제일 재밌었고 기억에 남을 기숙사 생활이었던 것 같다. 힘들 때도 정말 많았지만 그만큼 새로운 경험들을 많이 하게 되었다. 친구들한테 의도치 않은 상처들도 많이 받았

고 싸우기도 많이 싸웠지만 그러면서 성장해 갔던 것 같다. 전혀 꾸미지 않은 모습으로 지내고 생활했던 일년이었던 것 같다. 가식도 필요없었고 특별히 꾸밀 필요도 없었다. 다들 힘든시기를 겪고 있었고 너무 순수했던 것 같다. 크리스찬으로서 다른 교회 다니는 친구들도 많이 만났다. 그게 가장 큰 위로였던 것 같다. 혼자서 공부하는 방법도 그때 배운 것 같다. 살려면, 살아 남을려면 공부를 해야 한다는 생각밖에 없었다. 기말고사나 중간고사 시기에는 새벽이 넘어갈 때까지도 종이를 붙들고 공부를 했다. 중간 중간에 슬럼프가 와서 다 놓고 아무 생각없이 지낸 적도 없지 않았지만 그래도 결과는 노력을 배신하지 않는다는 게 맞는 말인 것 같다. 한국인들끼리 서로 햇반이라 캔, 반찬 나눠 먹으면서 지냈던 시간은 아무나 경험할 수 있는 경험이 아닌 것 같다. 라면 하나가 웬만한 음식보다 맛있었고 학교 끝나고 과일 사러 슈퍼가는길도 즐거웠다. 귀찮은 빨래도 우리가 해야 했기 때문에 나중에는 빨래하러 가는 것조차 재밌었다.

1학기가 눈깜짝할 사이에 지나가고 2학기가 다가왔다. 2학기때 한국인이 제일 많았던 것같다. 한국인 남자애들 네 명이 단체로 들어오고 그 외에 두 명이 더 들어왔다. 따로 들어온 두 명은 나보다 나이가 한두 살 적었지만 단체로 들어온 남자애들 네 명은 나랑 동갑이었고 다들 어렸을때부터 친구였다. 처음에는 마냥 신기했다. 한국인이라서 반가웠고 동갑이라서 더 반가웠다. 2학기 때 학교생활이 제일 재밌었던 것 같다. 웃고 떠들며 잘 지냈던 것 같다. 몇 명은 최근에도 연락이 닿는다. 그 중 한 명은 여름에 서울에서부터 부산 찍고 여러 군데를 들렸다가 대구에 찾아왔다. 일 년 만에 보는 거라 진짜 반가웠다. 막창도 먹고 얘기도 엄청했는데 겨울에 오면 또 봐야겠지? 해가 끝나갈 때쯤 우울했던 건 사실이다. 일 년이었지만 같이 살 듯이 지냈기 때문에 헤어지려니 정말 아쉽고 슬펐다. 그래도 생각보다 안 울었던 것 같다. 다시 보리라 다짐했기 때문에 그랬던 것 같다. 아직도 연락되는 사람들이 많다. 그런 면에서는 페이스북이나 카톡이 진짜 좋은 것 같다.

중국에서 느낀 것이 참 많다. 정말 좋은 사람들도 만나고 좋은 경험들도 많이 했지만 제일 크게 느꼈던 건 중국의 발전이 아닌가 싶다. 나중에는 중국이 세계를 좌우할 거라는 말씀들을 어른들께서 많이 하시는데 이번에 내가 중국 가서 그게 사실임을 느꼈던 것 같다. 솔직히 말해서 나는 중국에서 계속 생활하라고 하면 못할 것 같다. 사람을 대하는 방식이나 모든 생활 습관들이 나랑 너무 안 맞다. 하지만 생활하면서 중국이 엄청나게 빠른 속도로 발전하고 있고 커져감을 느꼈다. 엄청나게 높고 럭셔리한 건물들 뒤에 숨겨진 중국의 다른 가난한 면이 없지 않아 문제가 아직 많이 있지만, 그래도 중국은 경제적인 면이나 기업적으로 빠른 성장을 해내가고 있는것은 확실한 것 같다. 중국의 부유한 집 아이들은 한국의 부유한 집 아이들과는 조금 달랐다. 학교 밖을 많이

안 나가서 잘은 모르겠지만, 한 가지 크게 와닿은 것은 중국 사람들은 자기 나라에 대한 애정이 큰 것 같다. 그만큼 자신감도 강한 것 같고 그만큼 가끔 기분 나쁠정도로 자랑을 한다. 하지만 그 자신감 때문에 더 빠른 속도로 앞으로 나아갈 것 같다. 다른 나라에서의 유학생활보다는 짧았지만 제일 의미 있고 파란만장 했던 일 년이 아니었나 싶다. 많은 것을 느끼고, 먹고, 배우고 돌아온 것 같다. 제일 나 다웠던 모습으로 꾸밈없이 지낸 일 년이었던 것 같다. 미국생활과 프랑스생활에 이은 세 번째 소중한 선물이다.

2014. 12. 30

〈中国留学记行〉

我在中国生活时间的不长，对中国了解也不多。如果真的要说具体点话就是，我虽然没有能与中国人流畅交流的能力，即使到现在也还是不能说的太好，但是因为之前在美国和法国的留学生活都很有意思，所以觉得在中国也会很有趣，就去了中国。一开始提出去中国留学的是爸爸。爸爸说，中国以后会成为世界的焦点，让我去中国看看。我当时就拒绝了，可是过了几周不知怎么的突然又想去中国了。爸爸也很吃惊，然后说咨询了一下，说过几周9年级毕业后就让我去。我以为会像美国和法国一样有趣，由于不知道去中国的话要具备怎样的语言能力，所以整个暑假都在学习中文，简直快要死掉了。准确的说是，身体每天都去上课，精神已经出窍想着回家玩儿了，真的很累。像金子一样贵重的暑期，每天却要学习6小时，几乎没有时间和朋友们见面。让人烦闷的几个月就这么过去了，终于去了中国。我一般对宿舍要求不多，可对于以后要生活的空间里要用的要求却很多。从宜家一直到商场，好像都找遍了。买了一些东西后，到了宿舍楼前，一半是激动一半是担心。真的能像小时候什么都不知道的我那样适应这里吗？总而言之，心情很奇妙。进了宿舍以后，大概听了一下关于宿舍的说明，妈妈说灰尘太多，角角落落都给我擦的很干净。整理好物品后，和将要跟我一起住的比我大一岁的姐姐一起出去吃了午饭。吃完晚饭回来后，脑子里空空的，好像什么都没有。都整理完之后，隔壁屋的姐姐过来玩儿了。她跟我同屋的姐姐好像很好，人像是姐妹一样。我会不会妨碍她们呢？有种负罪感。那时候能够依靠的好像除了手机没有别的了。在跟朋友用Kaka发着信息，第一个夜晚就这么过去了。

跟姐姐们变亲近几天后的一个周末我们一起去了市里。去市里像是一个转折点，那时候我觉得姐姐们非常随和非常好。但是那种到处都是的酒文化我无法接受，也没有融入的自信。很酷的尝试了一下，心里却充满了担心。从市里回来以后，我只想哭。不想在姐姐们面前哭，怕被听到，就跑去走廊里哭。被问及没关系吗，我借口说是想家和朋友了。“适应起来很困难”，不想说出这不堪的理由。于是我换了所学校。不管怎么说，稍微好一点的，到了稍微雅静点的地方。需要遵守的规章制度也很多，跟我之前上的学校完全不一样。虽然是所很大的学校，可是不管去哪儿却都有韩国人。爸爸说既然如此就去好的学校吧，就把我转学到了这个徐晓--人大附中。因为那时候我中文还不是太好，就进了国际

인민중학교 체육시간

部。和我想象中不一样，国际部里没怎么有韩国人，除了我之外只有两名。一个是比我大一岁的姐，一个是小我两岁的弟弟。除此之外都是美国人、中国人，要么就是欧洲来的学生。那时候再次感谢我自己能够说英语。因为大家都说英语，用英语沟通，所以适应起来一点问题都没有。像是有趣又像是激动。随着时间的流逝，觉得真的挺累的。每当这时候，好想依靠和我同龄的朋友们。其中一个特别好的是来自哈萨克斯坦的朋友，母语是俄语而英语超级好的朋友。刚开始的时候有点生疏，慢慢的我们关系越来越好，成了在一起玩儿的最多、笑的最多的朋友。人大附中的国际部宿舍和中国学生宿舍是分开的，我和另外两名不在国际部但是中文很好的普通班的两个韩国人在一个宿舍。所以，我和跟我同房间的妹妹的姐姐，以及那个姐姐的朋友们关系特别好。三个人都是同龄人，可以相互依靠。应该是到目前为止我住过的最有意思的宿舍了。虽然更多时候是累，但却学到了很多。有受到过朋友不经意的伤害，也有过吵架，但是却成长了。完全没有掩饰自我的一年。不需要伪装，不需要修饰。大家都经受着辛苦，都很单纯。我也认识了别的教会的朋友，算是最大的安慰了。那时候也学会了自学，想要生存的话，想要活下去的话，好想只有学习。期末或者期中考试期间，即使是凌晨了，还抓着张纸在学习。其间倦意袭来，即使是这样也知道自己努力了，觉得没有背叛自己的努力。韩国人之间分享罐头菜，这是任何经历都无法比拟的。比起其他食物，方面面更好吃，放学后去超市一起买水果也很开心。让人麻烦的洗衣服，以后回想起来定会很有趣。

第一学期很快就过去了，一眨眼到了第二学期。第二学期的韩国人好像最多，四个韩国男孩儿一起入学，还有两个韩国人分别单独入学。两个单独入学的韩国人比我小一两岁，一起入学的四个男孩儿跟我一样大，他们是从小一起长大的朋友。刚开始的时候还很新奇，因为是韩国人，又跟我一样大，能够认识都挺高兴的。第二学期笑着、闹着，感觉最有趣了，有几个人最近还有联系着。其中一个暑假放假从首尔到釜山，找到了大邱来。有一年没见，真的很亲。一起吃了烤猪肠，也聊了很多，寒假还会见吧？一年里的年末是忧伤的时候。虽然在一起只有一年，但是却像一起生活过一样，这么分开了，丝丝的悲伤。但是这次却没哭，相约下次再见。还保持联系的人很多，这样来看有脸书和卡卡真的很方便。

在中国感受很多，真的遇到了很多好的人，有了很多好的经历。但是印象最深的还是中国的发展速度。虽然常听大人们说，以后中国会左右世界的发展，这次去了中国才真切的明白这句话。坦白说，如果让我继续在中国继续生活下去，我没有这个自信。待人接物的方式、所有的生活习惯跟我都不一样。但是，真的会感觉到中国发展的速度很快。在高楼大厦背后虽然也隐藏着很多生活困难的人，但是中国经济性的一面、企业性的一面却是事实。中国富裕家庭的孩子和韩国富裕家庭的孩子也有点不一样。虽然没怎么去学校外面，却也知道中国人非常爱自己的国家，非常的自信、自豪。就是因为这种自信，才会有这么快的发展速度。这一年，虽然比在其他国家留学时间短，但却是最有意思和经历最丰富的一年。感受到了许多、也吃了很多好吃的、学了很多东西，是我最真实的一年，是继美国、法国生活之后的第三个珍贵的礼物。

2014. 12. 30

중국인민대학 부속중학교 친구들이 체육복에 해준 기념 사인

3 프랑스 유학

2009년에서 2011년 사이에 프랑스 노르만디 Ecole des Roches School에 유학하였다.

〈프랑스에서 공부하기〉

나는 2009~2011(12~14살)까지 프랑스 유학을 가 있었다.

처음에는 프랑스에 간다고 했을 때 나는 밤낮을 울면서 지냈다. 너무 가기 싫었었다. 주위 사람들의 기대치가 높아지고 내 스트레스는 쌓여갔던 시절 나는 무너지고 있었다. 프랑스어도 제대로 할 줄 모르던 나였다. 그런데 영어를 하는 러시아 친구를 만난 후부터 모든 것이 달라졌다. 그 아이는 나보다 언니였다. 이름은 Anna-Sofia Maksachava. 금발머리에 초록색 눈, 진짜 예쁜 아이였다. 그 아이와 같이 생활하면서 많은 것을 배우고 느꼈다. 공부할 때 옆에서 도와주고 친언니 같던 내 친구. 그래서인지 내 주위에 사람들이 항상 많았다. 한국인인 내가 신기했나 보다. 적응을 하게 되어 프랑스어 실력도 늘어갔다. 한국말하듯 발음도 좋아지고 말도 쭉쭉 나왔다. 공부를 하다가 피곤하면 자다가 혼나기도 했다. 기숙사 선생님, 친구들 모두 너무 좋은 사람들이었다. 싸울 때도 있었지만 한국애들보단 훨씬 어른스러웠다.

지금의 내가 프랑스에 있는 이유는 몇 년 간의 유학생활을 위한 거 같다. 집과 떨어져 있으면서 많이 배우고 느끼며 보았다. 프랑스 국제학교에 다니던 터라 많은 국적의 친구를 사귀었다. 중국, 러시아, 스페인, 멕시코, 말리, 아프리카, 가봉, 로마, 그리스, 아랍인, 모로코, 미국 등등. 내겐 신비롭고 재미난 시간이었다. 프랑스 문화도 배우며 프랑스의 역사도 알게 되는 소중한 시간. 역시 어떤 나라의 언어를 배울려면 직접 그 나라의 공기를 마셔봐야 한다.

<Mes études en France>

권 수	2009~2011 (12~14세 까지)	* 삶쓰기 프랑스 II	NO( )
기록한 날	20 년 월 일 요일		
책 제목		검 인	
지은이		옮긴이	

제목: 프랑스에서 공부하기.
처음에 프랑스 간다고 했을 때 나는 밤낮을 울면서 지냈다. 너무 가기 싫었었다.
주위 사람들의 기대치는 높아지고 내 스트레스는 쌓여가던 시절, 나는 무너지고 있었다.
프랑스어도 제대로 할 줄 모르던 나였다. 그런데 영어를 하는 러시아 친구를 만나고 부터
모든 것이 달라졌다. 그 아이는 나보다 언니였다. 이름은 Anna-Sofia Makvachava.
금발머리에 초록색 눈. 진짜 예쁜 아이였다. 그 아이와 같이 생활하면서 많은 것을 배우고
느꼈다. 공부할 때나 밖에서 도와주고 친언니 같았던 내 친구. 그래서인지 내 주위에
사람들이 항상 있었다. 한국인인 내가 신기했나 보다. 적응을 하게 되며 프랑스 실력도
늘어 갔다. 한국말 하듯 발음도 좋아지고 말도 술술 나왔다. 공부를 하다가
피곤하면 자다가 혼나기도 했다. 기숙사 선생님, 친구들 모두 너무 좋은 사람들이었다.
싸울 때도 많았지만 한국애들 보다 훨씬 어른스러웠다.
지금의 내가 있는 이유는 몇 년 간의 유학생활인 거 같다. 집과 떨어져 있으면서 많이
배우고 느꼈다. 프랑스 국제학교에 다니던 터라 많은 국적의 친구를 사귀었다.
중국, 러시아, 스웨덴, 멕시코, 일본, 아프리카 가봉, 모아, 그리스, 아랍인, 모로코, 미국,
등등. 내겐 신비롭고 재미난 시간이었다. 프랑스 문화도 배우며
프랑스의 역사도 알게 되는 소중한 시간. 역시 다른 나라의 언어를 배우려면
직접 그 나라의 공기를 마셔 봐야 한다. 4/29 검

Je suis restée de 2009 à 2011(à partir de 12 ans jusqu'à 14 ans) en France. Au début, quand j'ai entendu que je serai envoyée en France pour y apprendre, je pluerais jour et nuit parce que je n'ai pas tellement voulu y aller. En ce temps-là, je me suis très stressée et je tombais dans un plus profond désespoir contre tous les éspoirs des gens autour de moi. Je ne savais pas parler en français, mais dès la rencontre avec une fille russe qui a pu parler en anglais, tout a changé. Elle est plus vieille que moi et elle s'appelle Anna-Sofia Maksachava. Elle est une très belle fille qui a les cheveux blonds et les yeux verts. Avec elle, j'ai pu réussir dans mes études à l'étranger. Parce qu'elle était vraiment gentille pour moi et m'a beaucoup aidée pour mes études, il semblait qu'elle etait un membre de ma famille, c'est-à-dire, ma sœur.

J'ai eu beaucoup d'amis autour de moi en France, peut-être, parce que je suis coréenne(je ne le sais pas exactement). Je me suis adaptée et je suis devenue forte sur le français. J'ai eu une bonne prononciation du français et je n'ai pas eu ma langue française dans ma poche après l'adaptation comme je parle en coréen.

La surveillante au pensionnat m'a grondée quand j'étais moulue de fatigue après le long travail. Mais d'habitude, elle étais très gentille pour moi. Mes amis au pensionnat étaient aussi très gentils. De temps en temps, on s'est disputé mais ils sont plus raisonnables que les amis coréens.

Il semble que j'ai mûri pendant mon séjour à l'étranger. J'ai appris bien et j'ai expérimenté beaucoup en vivant en marge de ma famille. Parce que j'allais à l'école étrangère, j'ai eu beaucoup d'amis de toutes les parties du monde. Ils sont chinois, russes, espagnols, mexicains, maliens, africains, gabonais, italiens, greques, arabes, marocains, américains, etc. C'était un temps mystérieux et très amusant pour moi. Avec ce moment précieux, j'ai pu familiariser avec la culture française et aussi apprendre l'histoire de France. Je crois que pour apprendre une langue, c'est bien la raison qu'on devrait aller au pays où on parle cette langue.

프랑스 유학 시절, 주말 집에서 부모님 식사 초대

<Studying in France>

I went to France to study abroad from 2009 to 2011 (age 12~14)

When I first heard about my trip to France, I spent days in tears. I really didn't want to go. I was breaking down from stress over my parents' high expectations. Back then, my French was not yet fluent. When I stuck in these painful struggles, I met a Russian friend who spoke English and changed my life in France for the better. Her name was Anna-Sofia Maksachava, and she was older than me. Blonde hair and green eyes, she was beautiful. We became friends, and I learned a lot of valuable things from hanging out with her. She was like an older sister helping me with studies and taking care of me. Day by day, my French improved and I started adapting to the new environment. French no longer fumbled out from my mouth, but rather rolled off my tongue as smoothly as Korean did. I sometimes got in trouble from falling asleep during classes. The dorm teacher and friends I made were all kind to me. Although conflicts occasionally arose between me and my friends, I felt they were more mature than kids in Korea.

The times that I'd spent studying abroad made me who I am now. I've seen and learned many things during my time away from home. Because the school I attended was an International School, I encountered a diverse range of ethnicities. I made friends who came from China, Russia, Spain, Mexico, Mali, Africa, Gabon, Rome, Greece, Saudi Arabia, Morocco, and the United States. It was a mysterious and fun time for me. It was also important to learn about the culture and history of France. I realized the best way to learn a new language is to be a local of that language's country.

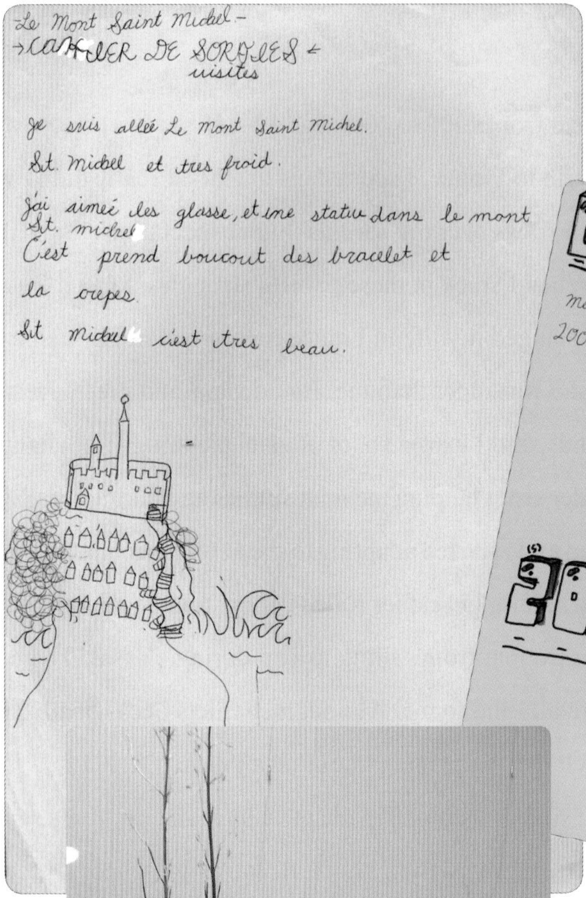

Le Mont Saint Michel –
→ CAHIER DE SORTIES ←
visites

Je suis allée Le Mont Saint Michel.
St. Michel et tres froid.
J'ai aimée les glasse, et une statu dans le mont St. michel.
C'est prend boucout des bracelet et
la crepes.
St michel c'est tres beau.

CAHIER
Mercredi 8 Juillet
2009
DE
SORTIES

나의 스트라우스와 꽃꽂이 수상

"프랑스는 역시 예술적 전통이 일상 생활 깊숙이 스며들어있는 아름다운 나라였습니다. 그만큼 사람들도 격조가 높은 신사의 나라라고 생각합니다."

Les plage du débarquement ←
+ Caen.

Je suis allé 'Les Plage du débarquement' hier. Et — Je suis allé 'Le cemetary'. J'ai mangé la glace, Ju d'orange. J'ai acheté les bon bon dans le petite (town). Les Plage c'est tres beau. Il y a beaucoup de oiseau et le town il y a un mourrir oiseau!! — — —. J'ai aimé le town pas-que il y a beaucoup de vetement et bon bon. Et la glace c'est tres, tres delicious.

Deauville

Lundi, 13 juillet

Je suis allé Deauville. Dans le Deauville avec mon amis ~~je~~ nous sommes alleés un plage. J'ai ~~nagée~~ nagé et mangé. Le plage c'est tres beau. 5:30 ~~J'ai sho~~ Je suis allé shopping. J'ai ne pas acheté. ~~Je~~ Je suis parti 7:30 et Je suis arrivé 10/20.

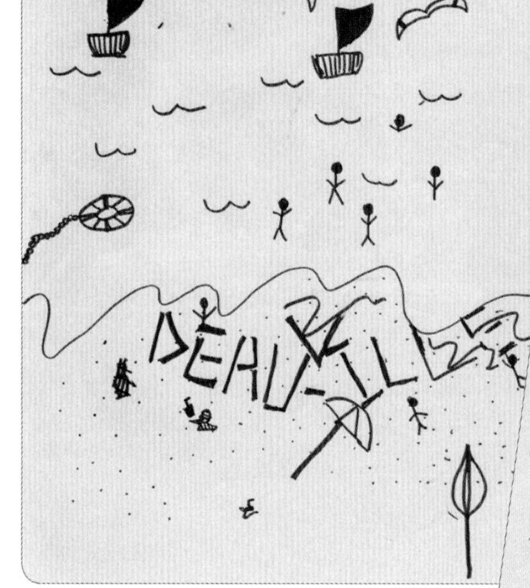

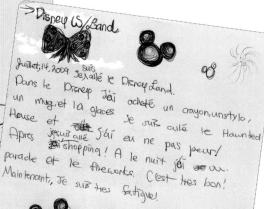

→Disney W/Land

Juillet, 14, 2009. Je suis allé le Disney Land. Dans le Disney J'ai acheté un crayon, un stylo, un mug, et la glaces. Je suis allé le Haunted House et ~~...~~ J'ai eu ne pas peur! Apres je suis allé ~~jai~~ shopping! A le nuit j'ai ~~vu~~ vu. parade et le fireworks. C'est tres bon! Maintenant, Je suis tres fatigue!

곳곳에 틀린 데가 눈에 띄네요.

Asterix

Wndi, 20, Juillet, 2009

Heir Nous sommes allés Asterix.

Dans le Asterix je suis allé le rder coaster×2, est le×3 ride de eau.

est le vident chair.

clest eu ne pas peur!

c'est tres beau!

Apres Jái trea tres fatigue!

Et Maintenant, Aussi jesuis fatigue!

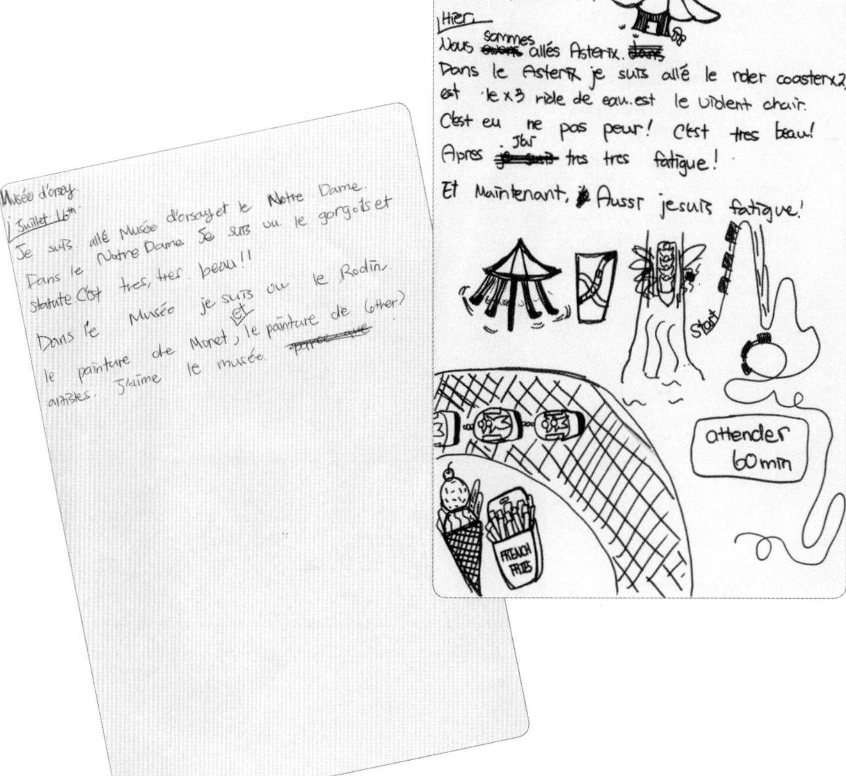
Musée d'orsay
Juillet 16th
Je suis allé Musée d'orsay et le Notre Dame.
Dans le Notre Dame Je suis vu le gorgots et statute. C'est tres, tres beau!!
Dans le Musée je suis vu le Rodin, le painture de Monet, et le painture de (other) artistes. J'aime le musée.

Asterix
Lundi, 20, Juillet, 2009
Hier,
Nous sommes allés Asterix.
Dans le Asterix je suis allé le rder coaster×2, est le×3 ride de eau. est le vident chair.
C'est eu ne pas peur! C'est tres beau!
Apres J'ai tres tres fatigue!
Et Maintenant, Aussi jesuis fatigue!

Désolé pour le drapeau
je sais pas le faire...
Bon courage et beaucoup
de bonheur et de
Réussite! ♡

M-H

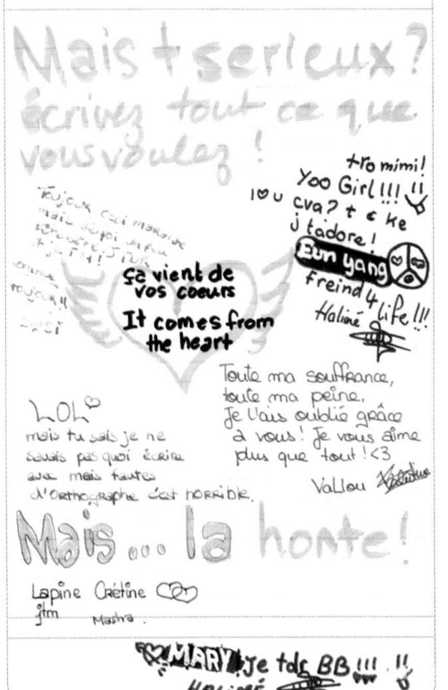

Ce pays qui ressemble à la tête d'une jument
Venue au grand galop de l'Asie lointaine
Pour se tremper dans la Méditerranée,
Ce pays est le nôtre.

Poignets en sang, dents serrées, pieds nus,
Une terre semblable à un tapis de soie,
Cet enfer, ce paradis est le nôtre

Que les portes se ferment qui sont celles des autre
Qu'elles se ferment à jamais,
Que les hommes cessent d'être les esclaves des homm
Cet appel est le nôtre.

Vivre comme un arbre, seul et libre,
Vivre en frères comme les arbres d'une forêt,
Cette attente est la nôtre.

Je t'aime

사랑해 Ich liebe dich Love

프랑스 친구가 건네준 쪽지

Marrante
Asiatique
Rocheuse
Intelligente 7+8×x
I love
Elève
Marie quand tu es venue tu ne
parler pas français mais tu a
su apprendre et ouvrir ton
eur au gens comme tu me l'a
fait tu es drôle intellige
et même quand tu tombe tes
gnone c'est de la magie
enne et maintenant on est pl
que des connaissance.
+M+C+L+

Lolita Lempicka
Beyoncé
Rhythm Paradise
et son temp
Jus d'Orange

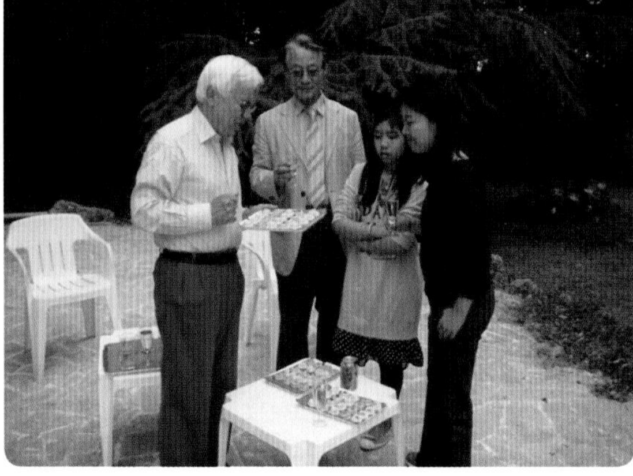

주말 집 파티

MA PETITE EXITÉE... ♡... ♡... ♡
Kim[berley]
♡ 사랑해
I ♥ U my Schlampe! ♪♫
don't forget and what about A...?
life is a bith...!
bad girl !!
by Masha Guest.

Si qqn t'♡ mais tu l'♡ pas.
dès que cette personne te quitte,
et tu te sens vide, c'est là que
tu réalise que quelque part tout au
~~tu l'avais~~ fond de ton coeur,
tu l'y avais.

Ma soeur adorée tu vas beaucoup
me manquer l'année prochaine!!
Je suis vraiment triste que tu ne seras
pas la à la fête de l'Ecole!
Et tu seras toujours ma
coréenne préférée!
Mais défois un peu exité.
사랑해 JTM! ♡

"어린 시절 프랑스에서 혼자 공부하기에는
힘에 겨웠지만 돌아다 보면 내가 성장하는데 큰 밑거름이 된 것 같아요."

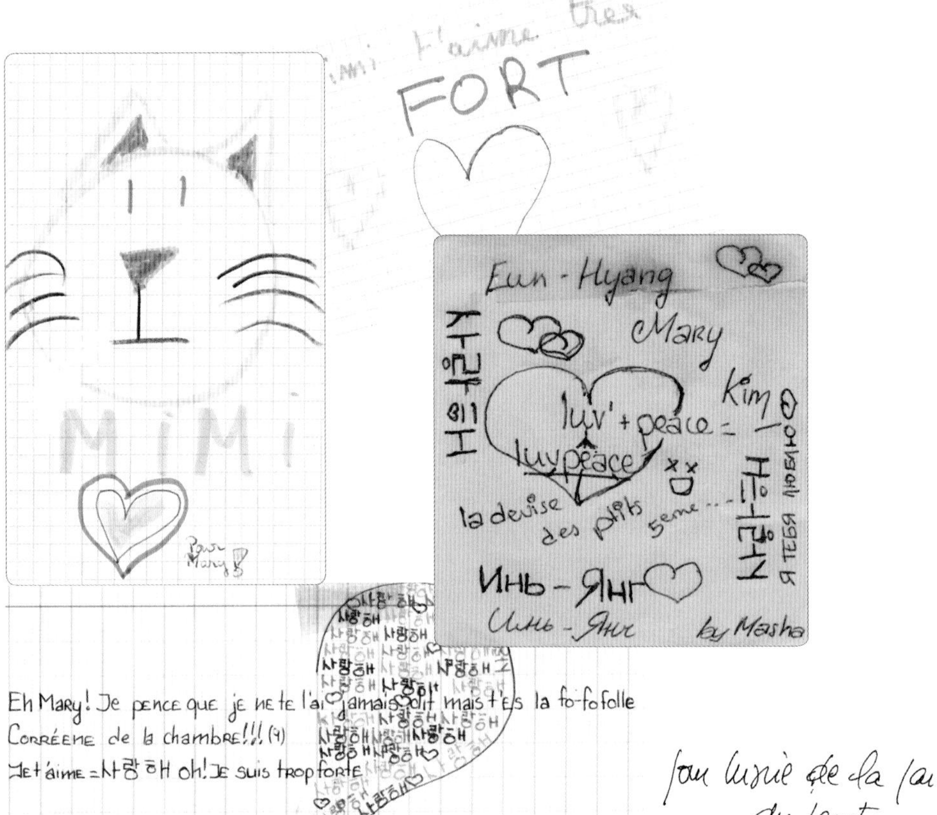
FORT
MiMi
Pour Mary
Eun-Hyang
Mary
Kim
luv' + peace =
luvpeace
la devise des plits 5eme...
Инь - Янг
by Masha
Eh Mary! Je pence que je ne te l'ai jamais dit mais t'es la fo-fofolle
Corréene de la chambre!!! (4)
Je t'aime = 사랑해 oh! Je suis trop forte
사랑해

자전거를 타면서

Eunn Hyang... Tu vas beaucoup me manquée, je pense que je ne vais pas passer une journée sans penser à toi: Le tennis SANS TOI, IMPOSSIBLE. En tout cas il faut que tu saches que même si au début de l'année à l'école on ne s'est pas très bien entendus, c'est du passé, car je ressend plus du tout la même chose. J'espère que tu vas passer un bon voyage avec KOREAN AIR, et j'aurais beaucoup aimer que tu viennes chez moi un weekend à saint Tropez. Voilà ma story. En tout cas avant d'aller au Rochs la première fille que j'ai vue à la télé, et bien c'est TOI. Je t'aime beaucoup et j'espère que tu vas faire de très bonnes études

corée.

Love... Love... Love... Love...

Made with love...

pour Eun Hyang

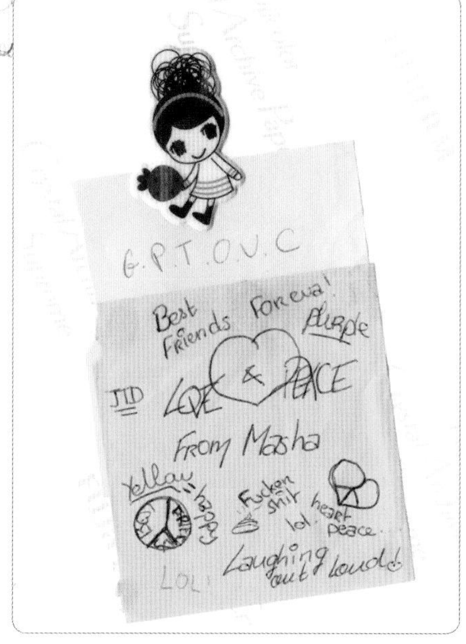

G.P.T.O.V.C
Best Friends Forever!
Purple
JTD
LOVE & PEACE
From Masha
Yellow
happy
Fucken shit
lol.
heart peace.
Laughing out loud!
LOL

Eun Hyang, tu vas vraiment me manquer. J'espère que je vais te revoir un jour. Je vais t'envoyer des lettres.

Je t'aime beaucoup. Je t'aime ♡

Je te met une photo de moi comme sa tu ne m'oublieras pas. ♡

Tu vas tous nous manquer

bisou de mes parents,

Najma

Bonne chance ... ton avenir

Bisou

TO: my PRETTY & THIN friend ♡

From: Walt Disney's great-great-granddaughter

눈이 엄청 온 프랑스
함계 사는 친구와~

ma petite Schlampe 사랑해 et tu vas beaucoup me manque. :(

봄이 오면 향기로운 꽃이 된 은향이

Mary

Je suis dans le Jura.
Je suis tombée de vélo, et j'ai eu 4 points de suture.
J'ai fait du canoë kayak sous la pluie. Sinon s'il fait beau je vais à la plage, s'il fait moche je vais à la piscine, faire du vélo, aux cascade du hérisson, à la ferme des bisons ou rien faire du shopping à Lons-le-saunier.
Gros bisous du Jura

Mimi

EDITIONS CELLARD · 13, rue de l'Economie 69500 BRON · Reproduction Interdite · CD 86

3 588780 010015

U 758228

FB 50301 M

Part 6

미지의 미래 여행

1 꿈

"제 꿈은 참 많았습니다.

화가, 디자이너, 기자에서 어느날 제가 병원에 수술하면서 의사가 되어 저처럼 아픈 사람들을 치료하며 봉사하는 사람이 되고 싶었습니다.

제가 국제학교를 다니며 미국, 프랑스, 중국 등 여러 나라를 다니며 공부하면서는 국제정치학, 사회복지학, 동양사학, 미학, 마술사 등 이것 저것 다 배우고 싶습니다.

저는 훌륭한 학자가 되어 주위의 이웃과 더불어 그들에게 헌신하는 길을 걷고 싶습니다."

I have a lot of dreams that I want to achieve. I wanted to be an artist, a designer, a reporter and a doctor who treats and heals injured people after a visit to the hospital for a surgery. While attending an international school in America, France, China and other countries, I want to study international politics, social work, Asian history, aesthetics and art history. My dream is to become a respectful scholar who helps the people in needs.

Dr. 김은향, 초딩 때의 꿈이었답니다.

2009년도 청와대 어린이 기자 지원서

성 명	김 은 향 (남 · 여)	생년월일	1998 년 9 월 5 일
학 교	대구 경동 초등학교	학년·반	4 학년 6 반
집주소	대구광역시 수성구 황금동 99-1 태왕아너스 102동 1001호		
e메일	marykim23@gmail.com	전 화	(053) 741 - 4747 부모님 핸드폰 011 - 509 0777

어린이 기자가 되고 싶은 이유는 무엇입니까?

안녕하십니까? 저는 어린이 기자단에 지원하는 김은향입니다. 저는 아주 어릴 적부터 신문을 많이 보시는 아버지를 보면서 '도대체 어떤 글들 때문에 저렇게 좋아하실까?' 라는 생각을 하다가 신문을 접하고 조금씩 읽게 되었습니다. 하지만 어린이들에게는 읽기 어려운 부분들이 있어 아쉬운 점이 많았습니다.

어린이 기자가 되고 싶은 가장 큰 이유는 제가 직접 쓴 기사가 실리는 신문을 볼 수 있게 된다는 것입니다. 전국에 있는 많은 친구들이 제 기사를 통해 현재 사회에서 일어나고 있는 일들을 쉽고 재미있게 읽게 되고, 생각 할 수 있다는 것이 가장 큰 매력이라고 생각합니다. 또 기자가 되면 평소 듣고, 보고 지나친 문제에 대해 더욱 세심하게 관찰하며 학생인 저에게 어린이 기자 생활이 좋은 경험이 될 수 있을 것 같습니다. 그리고 저는 사회의 전반적인 것에 관심이 많지만 특히 환경문제에 관심이 크기 때문에 환경오염의 실태를 살피고 개선 방향 등을 기사에 싣고, 어린이들에게 경각심을 심어 주고, 하나뿐인 소중한 지구를 조금이라도 살릴 수 있는 일에 기여할 수 있는 어린이 기자가 되고 싶습니다.

이번에 어린이 기자가 된다면 뜻깊은 초등학교 시절을 보내게 될 것이라고 확신합니다.

감사합니다.

※ 추천 인원은 초등학교별 1명을 원칙으로 하오니 교장선생님께서는 가급적 이점 유의하시어 추천하여 주시길 바랍니다.

추천사유 :

위 어린이는 성실하고 창의적이며 매사에 하고자 하는 의욕이 왕성하여 청와대 어린이 기자로 적극적으로 활동할 것이라 생각되어 추천합니다.

학교장

2009년도 「청와대 어린이 기자단」에 지원합니다.

2008. 9 . 22 .

지 원 자 김 은 향 김은향 ㊞ (또는 서명)

보 호 자 김 신 길 김신길 ㊞ (또는 서명)

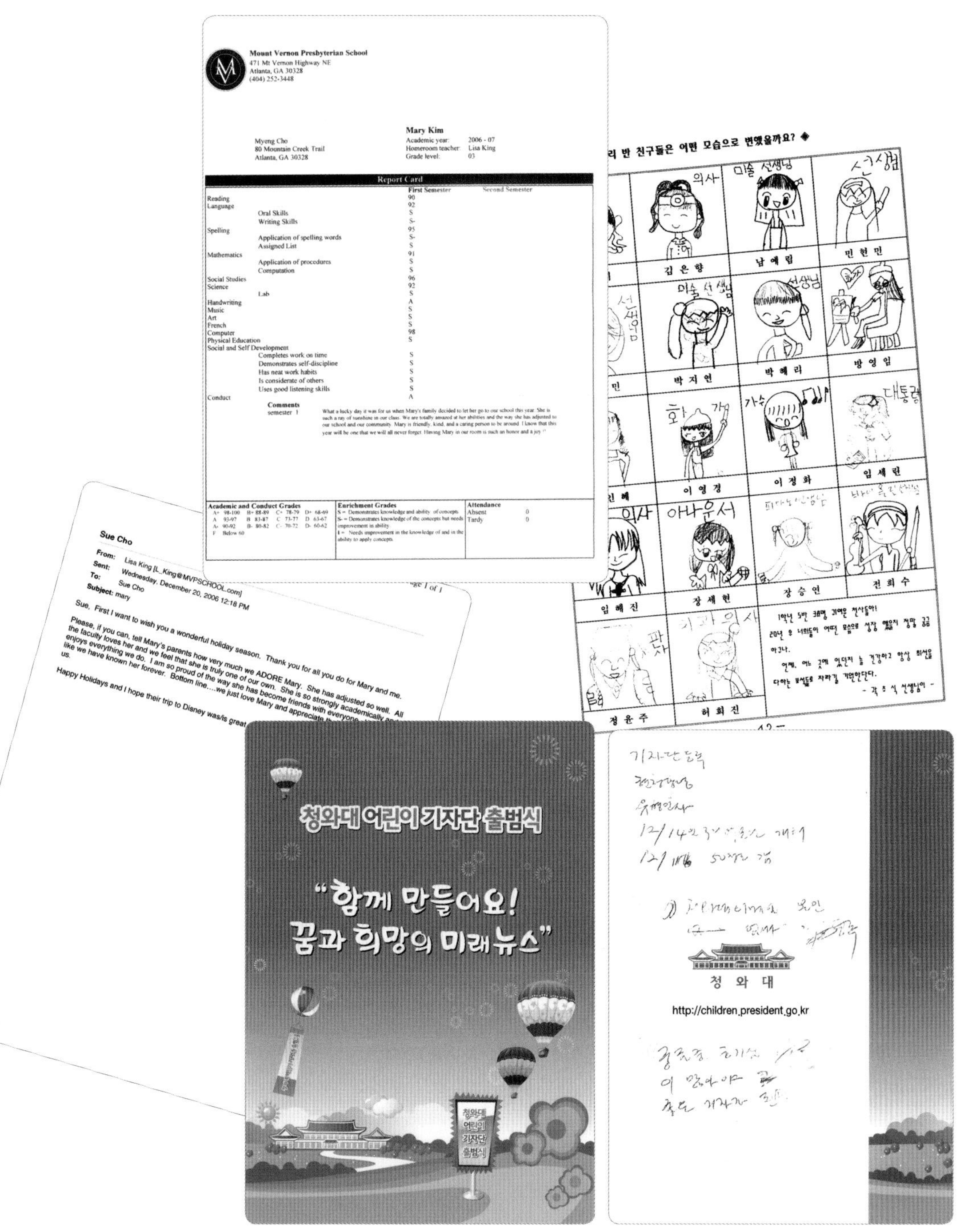

Mount Vernon Presbyterian School
471 Mt Vernon Highway NE
Atlanta, GA 30328
(404) 252-3448

Myeng Cho
80 Mountain Creek Trail
Atlanta, GA 30328

Mary Kim
Academic year: 2006 - 07
Homeroom teacher: Lisa King
Grade level: 03

Report Card

		First Semester	Second Semester
Reading		90	
Language		92	
	Oral Skills	S	
	Writing Skills	S-	
Spelling		95	
	Application of spelling words	S-	
	Assigned List	S	
Mathematics		91	
	Application of procedures	S	
	Computation	S	
Social Studies		96	
Science		92	
	Lab	S	
Handwriting		A	
Music		S	
Art		S	
French		S	
Computer		98	
Physical Education		S	
Social and Self Development			
	Completes work on time	S	
	Demonstrates self-discipline	S	
	Has neat work habits	S	
	Is considerate of others	S	
	Uses good listening skills	S	
Conduct		A	

Comments
semester 1

What a lucky day it was for us when Mary's family decided to let her go to our school this year. She is such a ray of sunshine in our class. We are totally amazed at her abilities and the way she has adjusted to our school and our community. Mary is friendly, kind, and a caring person to be around. I know that this year will be one that we will all never forget. Having Mary in our room is such an honor and a joy !!

Academic and Conduct Grades
A+ 98-100 B+ 88-89 C+ 78-79 D+ 68-69
A 93-97 B 83-87 C 73-77 D 63-67
A- 90-92 B- 80-82 C- 70-72 D- 60-62
F Below 60

Enrichment Grades
S = Demonstrates knowledge and ability of concepts
S- = Demonstrates knowledge of the concepts but needs improvement in ability
I = Needs improvement in the knowledge of and in the ability to apply concepts

Attendance
Absent 0
Tardy 0

Sue Cho

From: Lisa King [L_King@MVPSCHOOL.com]
Sent: Wednesday, December 20, 2006 12:18 PM
To: Sue Cho
Subject: mary

Sue, First I want to wish you a wonderful holiday season. Thank you for all you do for Mary and me.

Please, if you can, tell Mary's parents how very much we ADORE Mary. She has adjusted so well. All the faculty loves her and we feel that she is truly one of our own. She is so strongly academically and enjoys everything we do. I am so proud of the way she has become friends with everyone... like we have known her forever. Bottom line....we just love Mary and appreciate th... us.

Happy Holidays and I hope their trip to Disney was/is great...

Page 1 of 1

12/20/2006

청와대 어린이 기자단 활동(2009)

〈불어! 불어! 불어!〉

내가 프랑스어를 배우는 목적은 커서 언어를 유용하게 쓸 수 있기 때문이다.

가서 처음으로 친구와 어디서 왔는지 소개를 할 때 실수를 하면 어쩌나 하고 많이 떨렸다.

하고 싶은 말을 막상 못할 때에는 몸으로 표현하려고 애쓴 적이 있다.

공부를 할 때 발음과 읽는 것에는 자신감이 철철 넘쳐나와 단어나 이해하는 것에는 아직 험하고 험한 먼 길과 같다.

프랑스어를 배울 때 가장 어려운 점은 가끔 가다가 문법도 안 된다.

프랑스를 하기 싫을 때는 방학이다. 사람들이 한 문장 물어 보면 난 질색한다. 왜냐하면 귀찮고 황당하기 때문이다.

프랑스어, 영어, 중국어, 스페인어 중 좋아하는 순위는 1) 영어, 2) 프랑스어, 3) 스페인어, 4) 중국어.

영어는 내가 유일하게 잘하는 것이고, 프랑스어는 이제 될려고 하고, 스페인어는 재미있고, 중국어는 어렵기 때문에 이렇게 순위를 정하였다.

언어 한 가지 더를 배운다면 러시아 친구들이 많으니까 러시아어를 배우고 싶다.

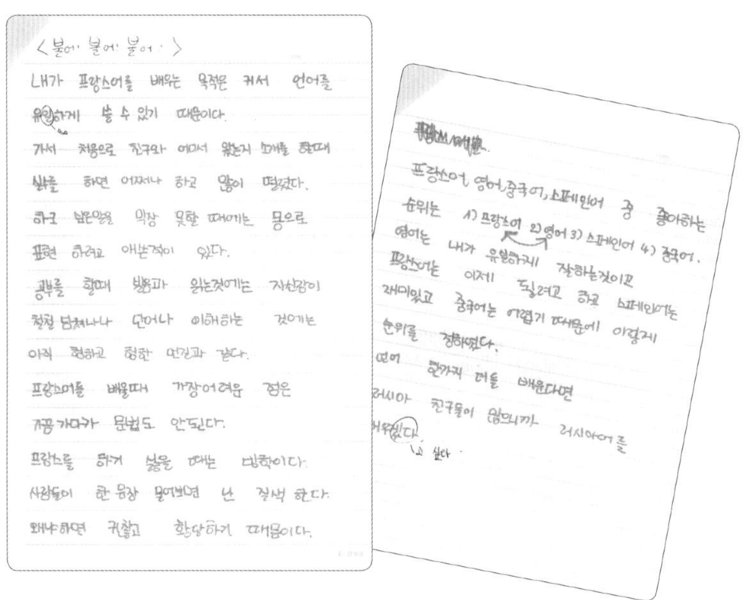

〈불어! 불어! 불어!〉
내가 프랑스어를 배우는 목적은 커서 언어를
유일하게 쓸 수 있기 때문이다.
가서 처음으로 친구와 어디서 왔는지 소개를 할때
실수를 하면 어쩌나 하고 많이 떨렸다.
하고 싶은말을 막상 못할 때에는 몸으로
표현 하려고 애쓴적이 있다.
공부를 할때 발음과 읽는것에는 자신감이
철철 넘쳐나나 단어나 이해하는 것에는
아직 험하고 험한 먼길과 같다.
프랑스어를 배울때 가장어려운 점은
가끔 가다가 문법도 안된다.
프랑스를 하기 싫을 때는 방학이다.
사람들이 한 문장 물어보면 난 질색 한다.
왜냐하면 귀찮고 황당하기 때문이다.

프랑스어, 영어, 중국어, 스페인어 중 좋아하는
순위는 1) 프랑스어 2) 영어 3) 스페인어 4) 중국어.
영어는 내가 유일하게 잘하는것이고
프랑스어는 이제 될려고 하고 스페인어는
재미있고 중국어는 어렵기 때문에 이렇게
순위를 정하였다.
언어 한가지 더를 배운다면
러시아 친구들이 많으니까 러시아어를
배우싶다.
고 싶다

<France, France, France>

I study French to speak the language fluently in the future.

When I first moved to France, introducing myself to my classmates was like a nightmare, always worrying about the mistakes I might make.

I frequently used body language to communicate when I faced language barriers.

I can confidently read and pronounce words, but when it comes to vocabulary and comprehending I still have a long way to go.

The hardest part in learning French is grammar.

Breaks are the time when I don't want to avoid studying French the most. I hate it when people ask me to translate a phrase in French because I get irritated and overwhelmed.

Let me rank the languages in order of favorite to least favorite: 1) English, 2) French, 3) Spanish, 4) Chinese.

I ranked like that because English is my only fluent language, French is almost fluent, Spanish is fun and Chinese is hard.

If I had to learn another language, I would choose Russian because I have many friends from Russia.

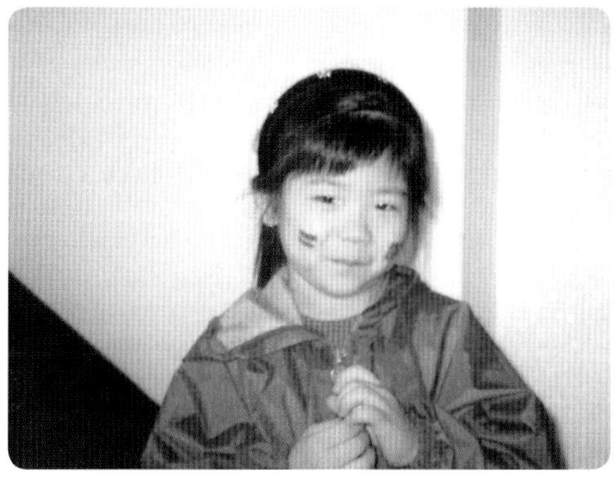

볼에 새겨진 프랑스 국기. I ♥ France

외모 목소리 성격 옷차림 행동 걸음걸이 ⇒ 은향이의 선생님에 대한 평가

〈호랑이 같은 나의 선생님〉

프랑스에 계시는 나의 기숙사 선생님은 호랑이 같으시다. 키가 아주 크시고 라면 같은 긴 꼬불한 빨간 머리카락에 안경을 쓰시고 잘 웃지 않는 'Madame Sorgues'은 첫 인상부터 아주 나빴다. 목소리는 가늘지도 굵지도 않은 컬컬한 목소리에 성격도 함께 아주 더럽다. 조금이라도 화장실을 숙제 시간에 가고 싶어 하면 소리를 지르며 '안돼', 찍소리만 내도 '하지만' 뛰어도 '안돼', 도대체 자기가 선생님일 뿐 누구길래 맘대로 하는지 우리는 도무지 이해가 안 간다.

매일 긴바지나 발목까지 오는 요란스러운 치마와 브래지어 끈이 보이는 단색의 티셔츠를 입고 인상을 쓰시는 우리 선생님.

말할 때 손이 올라가며 나 모르는 듯이 말씀하시고 우리가 딴짓할 때 소리내고 주의하라는 벨이나 알람 같은 팔찌를 끼신 선생님의 걸음걸이도 기분이 나쁘다.

주로 빨, 주, 파, 노의 색으로 구성된 옷들을 입으신다. 걸으실 때 또각또각 하이힐로 항상 키를 높이는 특이한 특기도 가지셨다.

그런 우리의 호랑이 선생님은 우리가 마냥 무섭고 신기하기만 하다.

<My Teacher Who Is Like a Tiger>

My dorm teacher in France reminds me of a tiger. 'Madame Sorgues' who is tall and has a red hair as curly as a noodle and wears glasses did not have a good first impression. Her voice is neither thin nor deep but hoarse and she has a bad temper. Going to the restroom during homework time, making a noise and running is not allowed to her, and she responses with a firm no all the time. All the students, including myself, wonder if she has the right to tell us what to do just for being our teacher.

Every day, Madame Sorgues wears long pants or skirts that come up to her ankle and monochrome shirts that shows her bra straps while making bitter impressions.

Her hands go up without her knowing when she talks, and she has a bell strapped on her wrist to warn us. Even the way she walks makes us feel uneasy.

She normally wears red, orange, blue or yellow colored clothes. When she walks in high heels, it makes noises and makes her look taller than she already is.

We find this tiger- like teacher scary but interesting.

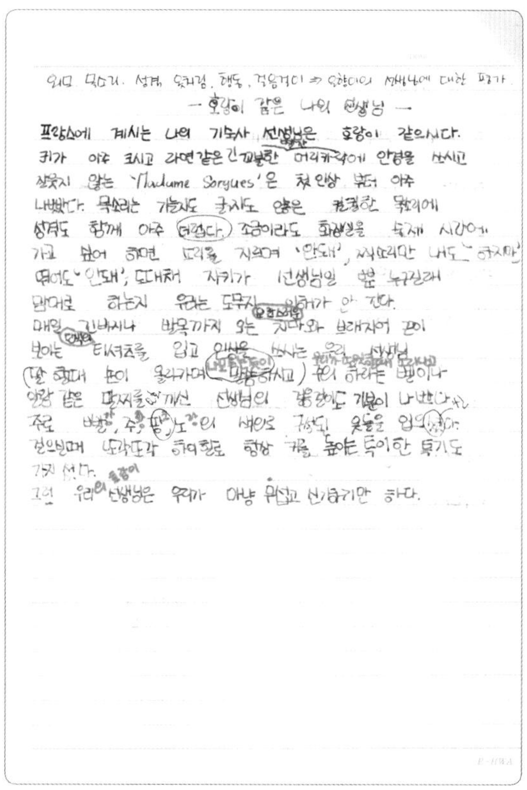
외모. 목소리. 성격. 옷차림. 행동. 걸음걸이 ⇒ 오향미의 선생님에 대한 평가

— 호랑이 같은 나의 선생님 —

프랑스에 계시는 나의 기독사 선생님은 호랑이 같으시다.
키가 아주 크시고 라면같은 긴 꼬불한 머리카락에 안경을 쓰시고
잘웃지 않는 'Madame Sorgues'은 첫 인상 부터 아주
나빴다. 목소리는 가늘지도 굵지도 않은 카랑한 목소리에
성격도 함께 아주 더럽다. 조금이라도 화장실을 숙제 시간에
가고 싶어 하면 소리를 지르며 '안돼', 찍소리만 내도 '하지만'
떼어도 '안돼'; 도대체 자기가 선생님일 뿐 누구길래
맘대로 하는지 우리는 도무지 이해가 안 간다.
매일 긴바지나 발목까지 오는 치마와 브래지어 끈이
보이는 (단색의) 티셔츠를 입고 인상을 쓰시는 우리 선생님
(말 할때 손이 올라가며 [illegible] 하시고) 우리 하라는 벨이나
팔찌 같은 팔찌를 끼신 선생님의 걸음걸이도 기분이 나빴다.
주로 빨강, 주황, 파랑, 노랑의 색으로 구성된 옷들을 입으신다.
걸으실때 또각또각 하이힐로 항상 키를 높이는 특이한 무기도
가지셨다.
그런 우리의 (호랑이) 선생님은 우리가 마냥 무섭고 신기하기만 하다.

〈Hyper 밤!〉

나는 할로윈 방학을 승마하면서 보낸 후 친구와 나는 밤을 샜다. 우리는 밤새도록 말하고, 먹고, 왔다갔다 거리며 어이 없게 보냈다. 우리방이 운 없게도 선생님 방 바로 옆방이라 찍소리만 내도 바로 달려오시는 예민한 선생님이시다.

라면같이 꼬불한 빨간색의 긴 머리카락, 까무잡잡한 피부에 안경을 끼시고 몸은 무지 마르신 우리 선생님께서는 한 번 화내시면 호랑이 같으시다. 만약 우리가 들켰다면 점수가 깎였을 것이다. 목소리는 가늘지도 굵지도 않는 컬컬한 기분 나쁜 목소리로 모두를 무섭게 한다.

우리는 잠이 그날따라 안 왔는지 왜 밤샘을 샌 것인지는 나도 우리도 모른다.

밤을 새고 난 그 다음 날, 우리는 아주 피곤했다. 햇살이 우리의 눈을 녹이며 살며시 자장가를 불러 주었다.

이 시간은 기억에 남는 이유는 흔하지만 끝까지 못 자는 사람들은 별로 없는데 선생님께 안 들키고 해낸 우리가 자신에게 감동 받았기 때문이다.

하지만 운이 좋게도 선생님에게는 팔찌가 있는데 벨처럼 소리가 나서 오는지 안 오는지 알 수가 있어 아주 유일하게 쓰인다.

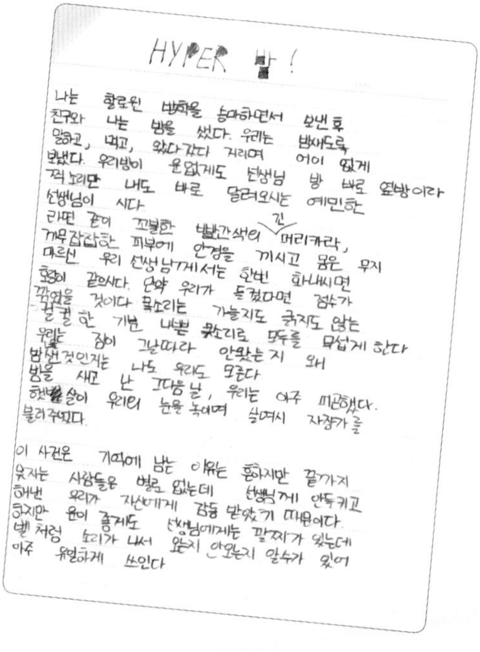
HYPER 밤!

나는 할로윈 방학을 승마하면서 보낸 후
친구와 나는 밤을 샜다. 우리는 밤새도록
말하고, 먹고, 왔다갔다 거리며 어이 없게
보냈다. 우리방이 운없게도 선생님 방 바로 옆방이라
찍 소리만 내도 바로 달려오시는 예민한
선생님이 시다
라면 같이 꼬불한 빨간색의 긴 머리카락,
까무잡잡한 피부에 안경을 끼시고 몸은 무지
마르신 우리 선생님께서는 한번 화내시면
호랑이 같으시다. 만약 우리가 들켰다면 점수가
깎였을 것이다 목소리는 가늘지도 굵지도 않는
컬컬 한 기분 나쁜 목소리로 모두를 무섭게 한다
우리는 잠이 그날따라 안왔는지 왜
밤샌것인지는 나도 우리도 모른다
밤을 새고 난 그다음 날, 우리는 아주 피곤했다.
햇살이 우리의 눈을 녹이며 살며시 자장가를
불러주었다.

이 사건은 기억에 남는 이유는 흔하지만 끝가지
못자는 사람들은 별로 없는데 선생님께 안들키고
해낸 우리가 자신에게 감동 받았기 때문이다
하지만 운이 좋게도 선생님에게는 팔찌가 있는데
벨 처럼 소리가 나서 오는지 안오는지 알수가 있어
아주 유일하게 쓰인다

〈내가 좋아하는 캐릭터〉

내가 좋아하는 캐릭터는 스폰지밥이다.

스폰지밥은 유치하지도 않고 아이들에게 웃음을 주는 캐릭터이다. 스폰지밥은 말 그대로 스폰지로 이루어진 바닷속 파인애플 속에 ≪Oarry≫라는 달팽이와 함께 사는 노란 캐릭터의 스폰지이다. 스폰지밥은 현재도 아이들의 인기를 독차지하고 있는 웃음거리 코미디언과 같다.

스폰지밥은 미국 캐릭터이다. ≪Datrick≫이라는 불가사리와 ≪징징이≫=Squidward 라는 오징어라는 친구들을 두고 있다. 징징이와는 항상 다투고 Datrick은 음식에 넘어가고 Mr.krab 햄버거 전문점 사장은 돈에 넘어가며 그 사이에서도 항상 쾌적한 생활을 하는 스폰지밥은 나의 캐릭터 친구와도 같다.

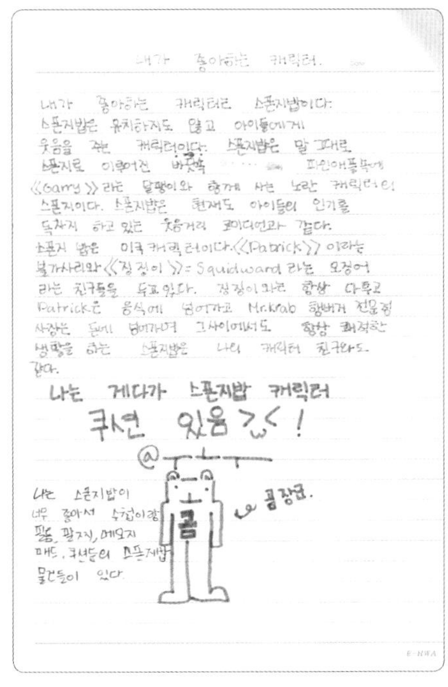

내가 좋아하는 캐릭터.

내가 좋아하는 캐릭터는 스폰지밥이다.
스폰지밥은 유치하지도 않고 아이들에게
웃음을 주는 캐릭터이다. 스폰지밥은 말 그대로
스폰지로 이루어진 바닷속 파인애플속에
≪Garry≫라는 달팽이와 함께 사는 노란 캐릭터의
스폰지이다. 스폰지밥은 현재도 아이들의 인기를
독차지 하고 있는 웃음거리 코미디언과 같다.
스폰지 밥은 미국 캐릭터이다.≪Patrick≫이라는
불가사리와≪징징이≫=Squidward 라는 오징어
라는 친구들을 두고 있다. 징징이와는 항상 다투고
Patrick은 음식에 넘어가고 Mr.krab 햄버거 전문점
사장은 돈에 넘어가며 그 사이에서도 항상 쾌적한
생활을 하는 스폰지밥은 나의 캐릭터 친구와도
같다.

나는 게다가 스폰지밥 캐릭터
쿠션 있음 >ω<!

나는 스폰지밥이
너무 좋아서 수집이랑
필통, 필기지, 메모지
패드, 쿠션들의 스폰지밥
물건들이 있다.

< 프랑스 >
프랑스 학교에서 기억에 남는일
가장 좋은 선생님
가장 무서운 선생님
학교가 좋나요, 프랑스 기숙사 생활
프랑스 음식 / 수업 과목 / [illegible]
프랑스어 생 / 한국인 밥 2009 / [illegible]
[illegible] / 제일 친한 프랑스 친구 ★"

< 가족 >
큰오빠의 연친, 엄마 보고 싶을때, 아빠의 직업,
아빠가 없다면 우린?, 엄마의 취미
작은 오빠의 [illegible] POD

좋아하는 취미 / 내가 자동차를 몰수 있다면
제일 무서운 동물

내가 좋아하는 스타일, 내가 좋아하는 스포츠
좋아하는 캐릭터, 하루 보이는
하루만 살자 나의 것, 제일 좋은 옷의
제일 좋은 색깔, 어느 공휴일이 " ?
비행장, 내 생일 파티 2009, 크리스마스
방학, 나의 교회 친구들, [illegible] 할꺼

< 만약 내가 [illegible]면 >
내가 나비라면, 내가 영화 주인공이라면, 내가 엄마라면
내가 날수 있다면, 내가 [illegible]라면,
내가 [illegible]라면,
내가 [illegible] 된다면 /
내가 디자이너라면, 드라마 [illegible]
[illegible] 있다면 / 내가 [illegible] 있다면
내가 미키라면, 또 다른 언어를 배울수 있다면, 내가 [illegible]이라면
시간을 되돌수 있다면
내가 작가라면 /
내가 [illegible]

< 기타 >
내가 태어났을때, 나의 꿈은
그림을 잘 그리려면, 한국에
가고 싶을때, 치아 교통, 제일
즐겨 먹는 음식, 독후감, 여행기,
시간여행을 할수 있다면, 내가 아는
해교미스테리, 강아지를 키울수
있다면, 존경하는 사람, 가장 가고
싶은 나라, 내 보물 1호, 슬펐을때,
국어 100% 받는 방법, 일기
제일 좋아하는 친구, 내가 동생이 생긴다면
내가 1살로 돌아간다면
2050 미래, 제일 좋아하는 음악
피아노 잘치는 법, 제일 [illegible]
[illegible]에서 살아남기, 제일 기억에 남는
여행, 어렸을적 [illegible]
제일 좋아하는 아이스크림, 사랑이
[illegible], 내가 갖고 싶은것
언어 잘 배우는 법 / 성격 & 인물

가장 어려웠었던 언어 공부, 내가 하고 싶은 하루 일기, 지금 숙제 하고 싶은것.
제일 좋아하는 꽃, 강아지의 키우고 싶은 동물. 내가 살고 싶은 집 design,
나의 이상형, 제일 좋은 과목 ★"

E-HWA

엄마, 아빠 먹구
[illegible] 잘 갔다오겠소~ 흠흠 왼간, 모르간, 오르간
[illegible] 조임 ~
아빠는 내가 아끼는 장난감이자 지갑이므로
수여합니다.
[illegible] 나의 구년이자 [illegible] 배게로 이 편지를 수여합니다
오빠 결혼식 기대 하겠소이다.
살빼고 엄마도 살빼고 나도 살빼기
하겠소이다 왼간, 모르간, 오르간?! ^^
잘 봤게 아빠. 지금 이편지를 두
[illegible] 수여하며 이상장을 드립니다
HAPPY NEW YEAR
새해 복 마이마이 받으소~~
코미디언 은향 올림
188 자

유소년 소녀 요리 경연 대회

〈수업 모습〉

나는 미국에서 수업을 듣는 아이들을 관찰하곤 했다. 왜냐하면 어떤 아이들은 예의가 없고 태도가 버릇이 없기 때문이다. 우리반에 여자애들보다 남자아이들이 더 잘 떠드는데 문제는 아이들도 그렇지만 선생님들이 더 문제라고 생각한다. 왜냐하면 아이들이 떠들어도 한국처럼 엄격하지 않기 때문이다. 선생님은 그냥 보고 수업진행을 하신다. 몇몇의 아이들은 가위로 장난치고 이야기를 하며 떠든다. 하지만 한국에서 그렇게 했다간 우리는 그 자리에서 깨꼬닥 죽는 것이다. 나는 어떨 땐 얘기를 하지만 거의 책을 보고 있다. 한국 같은 경우엔 아이들이 창난쳐도 그 아이들이 야단맞고 그래서 수업시간은 항상 조용하다. 하지만 5학년 우리 선생님은 너그러우시고 개구장이란 개구장이들은 우리반에 다 모였기 때문에 우리도 더 힘들다. 나는 한국이 더 엄격하다고 생각하는 반면에 아이들의 수가 훨씬 많아서 재미있고 분위기가 활기차서 좋다.

《《수업 모습》》

나는 미국에서 수업을 듣는 아이들을 관찰 하곤 했다.
왜냐하면 어떤 아이들은 예의가 없고 태도가 버릇이
없기 때문이다. 우리반에 여자애들보다 남자아이들이 더 잘
떠드는데 문제는 아이들도 그렇지만 선생님들이 더 문제라고
생각한다. 왜냐하면 아이들이 떠들어도 한국처럼
엄격하지 않기 때문이다. 선생님은 그냥 보고 수업진행을
하신다. 몇몇의 아이들은 가위로 장난치고 이야기를 하며
떠든다. 하지만 한국에서 그렇게 했다간 우리는
그자리에서 깨꼬닥 죽는것이다. 나는 어떨땐
얘기를 하지만 거의 책을보고있다. 한국 같은 경우엔
아이들이 장난쳐도 그 아이들이 야단맞고 그래서
수업시간은 항상 조용하다. 하지만 5학년 우리
선생님은 너그러우시고 개구장이란 개구장이들은
우리반에 다 모였기 때문에 우리도 더 힘들다.
나는 한국이 더 엄격하다고 생각하는 반면에
아이들의 수가 훨씬 많아서 재미있고 분위기가
활기차서 좋다.

"은향이는 호기심이 많아서
뭐든지 열심히 배우려고 했던 것 같아요."

"브레인 스토밍(Brainstorming)
단어 연쇄 연상 실험을 해보았습니다."

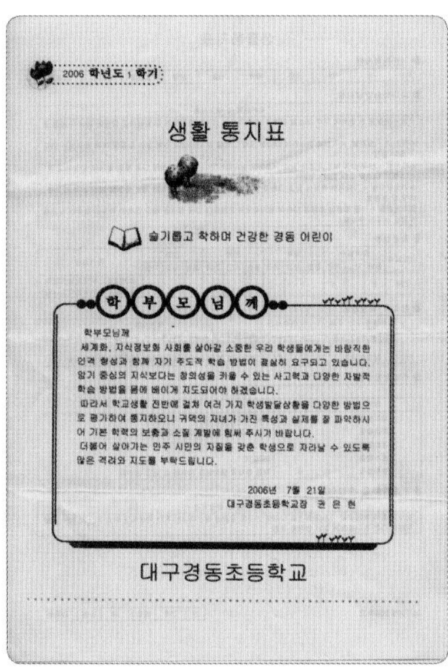

2006 학년도 1 학기

생활 통지표

슬기롭고 착하며 건강한 경동 어린이

학부모님께

학부모님께

세계화, 지식정보화 사회를 살아갈 소중한 우리 학생들에게는 바람직한 인격 형성과 함께 자기 주도적 학습 방법이 절실히 요구되고 있습니다. 암기 중심의 지식보다는 창의성을 키울 수 있는 사고력과 다양한 자발적 학습 방법을 몸에 배이게 지도되어야 하겠습니다.

따라서 학교생활 전반에 걸쳐 여러 가지 학생발달상황을 다양한 방법으로 평가하여 통지하오니 귀댁의 자녀가 가진 특성과 실제를 잘 파악하시어 기본 학력의 보충과 소질 계발에 힘써 주시기 바랍니다.

더불어 살아가는 민주 시민의 자질을 갖춘 학생으로 자라날 수 있도록 많은 격려와 지도를 부탁드립니다.

2006년 7월 21일

대구경동초등학교장 권 은 현

대구경동초등학교

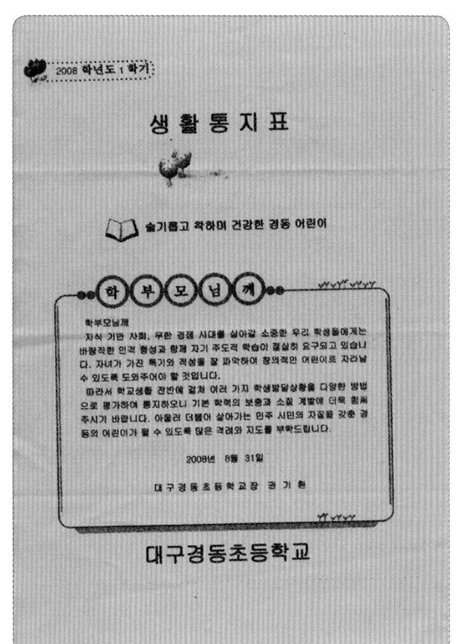

2008 학년도 1 학기

생 활 통 지 표

슬기롭고 착하며 건강한 경동 어린이

학부모님께

학부모님께

지식 기반 사회, 무한 경쟁 시대를 살아갈 소중한 우리 학생들에게는 바람직한 인격 형성과 함께 자기 주도적 학습이 절실히 요구되고 있습니다. 자녀가 가진 특기와 적성을 잘 파악하여 창의적인 어린이로 자라날 수 있도록 도와주어야 할 것입니다.

따라서 학교생활 전반에 걸쳐 여러 가지 학생발달상황을 다양한 방법으로 평가하여 통지하오니 기본 학력의 보충과 소질 계발에 더욱 힘써 주시기 바랍니다. 아울러 더불어 살아가는 민주 시민의 자질을 갖춘 경동의 어린이가 될 수 있도록 많은 격려와 지도를 부탁드립니다.

2008년 8월 31일

대 구 경 동 초 등 학 교 장 권 기 환

대구경동초등학교

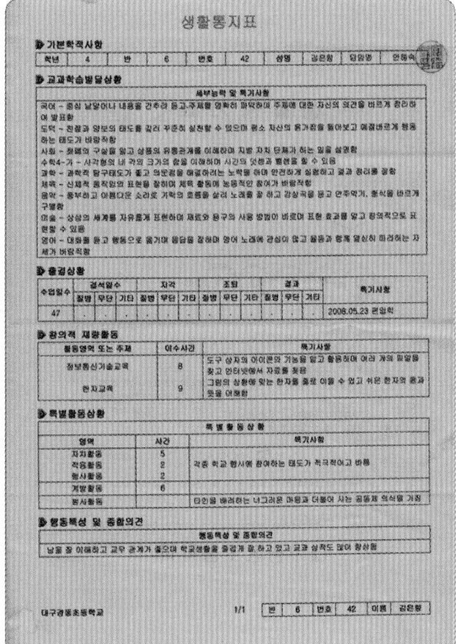

생활통지표

▶ 기본학적사항

학년	4	반	6	번호	42	성명	김은향	담임명	안해숙

▶ 교과학습발달상황

세부능력 및 특기사항
국어 - 중심 낱말이나 내용을 간추려 듣고 주제를 명확히 파악하며 주제에 대한 자신의 의견을 바르게 정리하여 발표함 도덕 - 친절과 양보의 태도를 길러 꾸준히 실천할 수 있으며 평소 자신의 용기점을 돌아보고 예절바르게 행동하는 태도가 바람직함 사회 - 촌락의 구실을 알고 상품의 유통관계를 이해하며 지방 자치 단체가 하는 일을 설명함 수학4-가 - 사각형의 네 각의 크기의 합을 이해하며 시간의 덧셈과 뺄셈을 할 수 있음 과학 - 과학적 탐구태도가 좋고 의문점을 해결하려는 노력을 하며 안전하게 실험하고 결과 정리를 잘함 체육 - 신체적 움직임의 표현을 잘하며 체육 활동에 능동적인 참여가 바람직함 음악 - 풍부하고 아름다운 소리로 가락의 흐름을 살려 노래를 잘 하고 감상곡을 듣고 연주악기, 형식을 바르게 구별함 미술 - 상상의 세계를 자유롭게 표현하며 재료와 용구의 사용 방법이 바르며 표현 효과를 알고 창의적으로 표현할 수 있음 영어 - 대화를 듣고 행동으로 옮기며 응답을 잘하며 영어 노래에 관심이 많고 율동과 함께 열심히 따라하는 자세가 바람직함

▶ 출결상황

수업일수	결석일수			지각			조퇴			결과			특기사항
	질병	무단	기타	질병	무단	기타	질병	무단	기타	질병	무단	기타	
47	.	.	.	.	.	.	.	.	.	.	.	.	2008.05.23 편입학

▶ 창의적 재량활동

활동영역 또는 주제	이수시간	특기사항
정보통신기술교육	8	도구 상자의 아이콘의 기능을 알고 활용하며 여러 개의 파일을 찾고 인터넷에서 자료를 찾음
한자교육	9	그림의 상황에 맞는 한자를 골라 이을 수 있고 쉬운 한자의 음과 뜻을 이해함

▶ 특별활동상황

특 별 활 동 상 황		
영역	시간	특기사항
자치활동	5	각종 학교 행사에 참여하는 태도가 적극적이고 바름
적응활동	2	
행사활동	2	
계발활동	6	
봉사활동		타인을 배려하는 너그러운 마음과 더불어 사는 공동체 의식을 가짐

▶ 행동특성 및 종합의견

행동특성 및 종합의견
남을 잘 이해하고 교우 관계가 좋으며 학교생활을 즐겁게 잘 하고 있고 교과 성적도 많이 향상됨

대구경동초등학교 1/1

반	6	번호	42	이름	김은향

자세히 보시면 안 돼요.

꽃꽂이와 플라워 아티스트가 된 은향이

2005 학년도 1 학기

학교생활통지표

슬기롭고 착하며 건강한 경동 어린이

학부모님께

세계화, 지식정보화 사회를 살아갈 소중한 우리 학생들에게는 바람직한 인격 형성과 함께 자기 주도적 학습 방법이 절실히 요구되고 있습니다. 암기 중심의 지식보다는 창의성을 키울 수 있는 사고력과 다양한 지발적 학습 방법을 몸에 배이게 지도되어야 하겠습니다.

따라서 학교 생활 전반에 걸쳐 여러 가지 학생발달상황을 다양한 방법으로 평가하여 통지하오니 귀댁의 자녀가 가진 특성과 실제를 잘 파악하시어 기본 학력의 보충과 소질 계발에 힘써 주시기 바랍니다.

더불어 살아가는 민주 시민의 자질을 갖춘 학생으로 자라날 수 있도록 많은 격려와 지도를 부탁드립니다.

2005년 7월 20일

대구경동초등학교장 권 은 현

대구경동초등학교

생활통지표

기본학적사항

학년	1	반	5반	번호	22	성명	김은향	담임명	곽추심

교과학습발달상황

세부능력 및 특기사항

국어 - 동시를 듣고 소리나 모양을 흉내내는 말을 잘 찾으며 불러주는 낱말이나 문장을 바른 자형으로 받아쓰기 잘함
수학1-가 - 구체물을 사용하여 여러 가지 모양을 잘 만들고 수 개념 형성이 바르며 연산 능력이 우수함
바른생활 - 학교에서 자신이 해야 할 일을 미루지 않고 잘하며 쓰레기의 분리수거를 바르게 함
슬기로운생활 - 하룻동안 시간이 지남에 따라 우리의 생활이 변한다는 것을 바르게 알며 여러 가지 교통 신호 만들기에 흥미를 가짐
즐거운생활 - 음색이 곱고 음정이 풍부하여 노래를 잘 부르고 여러 가지 재료를 사용하여 마을 꾸미기를 잘함
우리들은1학년 - 학교생활에 필요한 기초적인 방법과 지식을 익혀 자신감 있는 학교생활을 함

출결상황

수업일수	결석일수			지각			조퇴			결과			특기사항
	질병	사고	기타	질병	사고	기타	질병	사고	기타	질병	사고	기타	
111	.	.	.	.	.	.	.	.	.	.	.	.	

창의적 재량활동상황

활동영역 또는 주제	이수시간	특기사항
정보통신기술교육	15	컴퓨터 사용이 능숙하고 원하는 정보를 잘 선택함
창의성교육	14	끝말잇기를 잘 하고 그림의 지워진 부분을 상상하여 잘 그림

특별활동상황

영역	시간	특기사항
자치활동	3	
적응활동	6	명랑하고 적극적인 성격으로 원만한 교우 관계를 유지하고 있음
계발활동	3	자신의 소질을 계발하기 위하여 꾸준히 노력함
봉사활동		(2시간)
행사활동	3	

행동특성 및 종합의견

두뇌 명석하여 전교과 학업 성취도가 매우 높고 교우 관계도 원만하여 친구들의 신망이 두터움

대구경동초등학교 1/1 반 5반 번호 22 이름 김은향

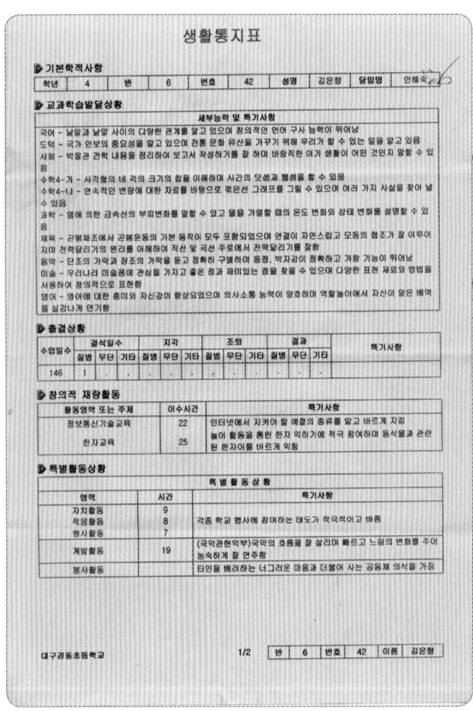

생활통지표

기본학적사항

학년	4	반	6	번호	42	성명	김은향	담임명	안해숙

교과학습발달상황

세부능력 및 특기사항

국어 - 낱말과 낱말 사이의 다양한 관계를 알고 있으며 창의적인 언어 구사 능력이 뛰어남
도덕 - 국가 안보의 중요성을 알고 있으며 전통 문화 유산을 가꾸기 위해 우리가 할 수 있는 일을 알고 있음
사회 - 박물관 견학 내용을 정리하여 보고서 작성하기를 잘 하며 바람직한 여가 생활이 어떤 것인지 말할 수 있음
수학4-가 - 사각형의 네 각의 크기의 합을 이해하며 시간의 덧셈과 뺄셈을 할 수 있음
수학4-나 - 연속적인 변량에 대한 자료를 바탕으로 꺾은선 그래프를 그릴 수 있으며 여러 가지 사실을 찾아 낼 수 있음
과학 - 열에 의한 금속선의 부피변화를 말할 수 있고 물을 가열할 때의 온도 변화와 상태 변화를 설명할 수 있음
체육 - 곤봉체조에서 곤봉운동의 기본 동작이 모두 포함되었으며 연결이 자연스럽고 모둠의 협조가 잘 이루어지며 전력달리기의 원리를 이해하여 직선 및 곡선 주로에서 전력달리기를 잘함
음악 - 단조의 가락과 장조의 가락을 듣고 정확히 구별하며 음정, 박자감이 정확하고 가창 기능이 뛰어남
미술 - 우리나라 미술품에 관심을 가지고 좋은 점과 재미있는 점을 찾을 수 있으며 다양한 표현 재료와 방법을 사용하여 창의적으로 표현함
영어 - 영어에 대한 흥미와 자신감이 향상되었으며 의사소통 능력이 향상하며 역할놀이에서 자신이 맡은 배역을 실감나게 연기함

출결상황

수업일수	결석일수			지각			조퇴			결과			특기사항
	질병	무단	기타	질병	무단	기타	질병	무단	기타	질병	무단	기타	
146	1	.	.	.	.	.	.	.	.	.	.	.	

창의적 재량활동

활동영역 또는 주제	이수시간	특기사항
정보통신기술교육	22	인터넷에서 지켜야 할 예절의 종류를 알고 바르게 지킴
한자교육	25	놀이 활동을 통한 한자 익히기에 적극 참여하여 동식물과 관련된 한자어를 바르게 익힘

특별활동상황

영역	시간	특기사항
자치활동	9	각종 학교 행사에 참여하는 태도가 적극적이고 바름
적응활동	8	
행사활동	7	
계발활동	19	(국악관현악부)국악의 흐름을 잘 살리며 빠르고 느림의 변화를 주어 능숙하게 잘 연주함
봉사활동		타인을 배려하는 너그러운 마음과 더불어 사는 공동체 의식을 가짐

대구경동초등학교 1/2 반 6 번호 42 이름 김은향

봉사활동상황

일자 또는 기간	장소 또는 주관기관명	활동내용	시간	시간누계
2008.06.09 - 2008.06.13	(교내)대구경동초등학교	환경정화활동 - 학교 주변 쓰레기 줍기	3	3
2008.07.01	(교내)대구경동초등학교	환경정화활동 - 학교 주변 쓰레기 줍기	1	4
2008.07.15	(교내)대구경동초등학교	환경정화활동 - 교실 청리 정돈하기	1	5
2008.09.16	(교내)대구경동초등학교	환경정화활동 - 교실 청리 정돈하기	1	6
2008.10.28	(교내)대구경동초등학교	환경정화활동 - 쓰레기 분리수거하기	1	7
2008.12.30	(교내)대구경동초등학교	환경정화활동 - 교실 청리 정돈하기	1	8

행동특성 및 종합의견

남을 잘 이해하고 교우 관계가 좋으며 학교생활을 즐겁게 잘 하고 있고 교과 성적도 많이 향상됨. 학급에서의 역할 분담 활동을 부지런히 수행하며 스스로 생각하여 일을 처리하는 능력이 뛰어남

2/2 반 6 번호 42 이름 김은향

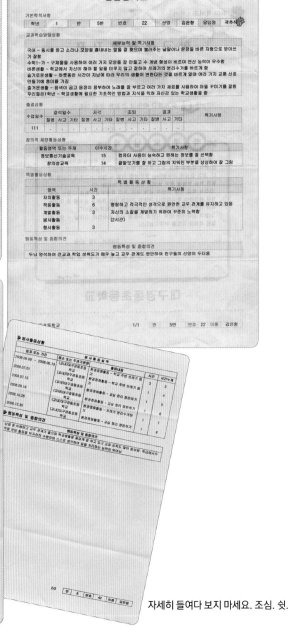

자세히 들여다 보지 마세요. 조심. 쉿.

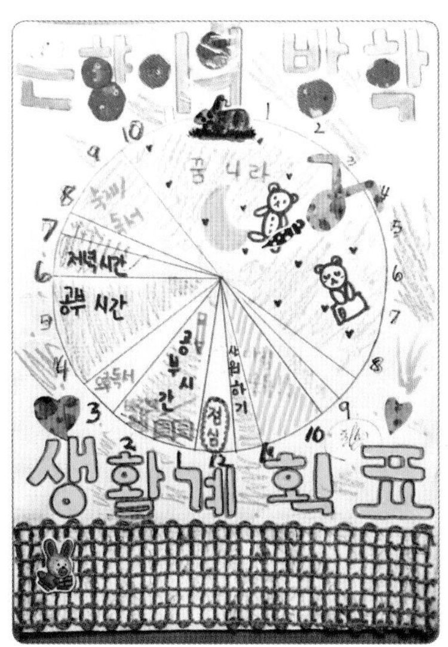
생활계획표
꿈나라
저녁시간
공부 시간

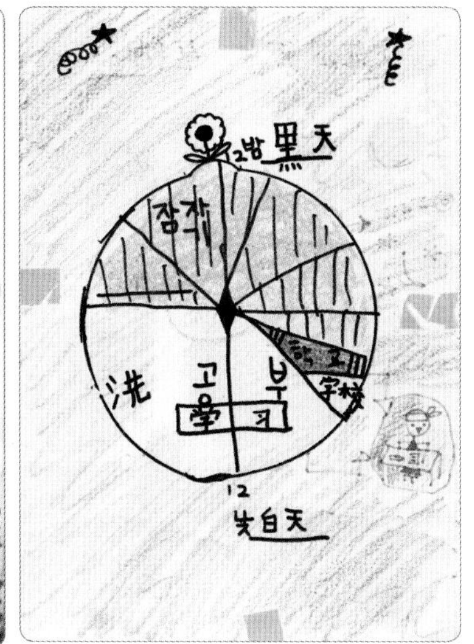
잠자기
黑天

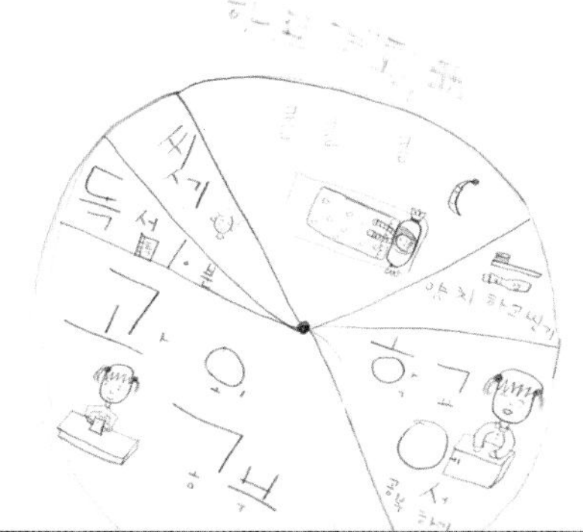

프로골퍼 김은향이예요?

dance
daisy
dog
door
daffodil
dinner
drink
daddy
drum
day
dress
doctor
draw
donkey
Sofa

2 상장

'사랑'
'헌신'
'봉사'

The Johns Hopkins University
Center for Talented Youth
certifies that
Eun Hyang Kim
has participated in
Writing And Imagination
YST Summer Program 2011
Chestertown, Maryland

Elizabeth Albert
Senior Director, Academic Programs
The Johns Hopkins University
Center for Talented Youth

Lea Ybarra, Ph.D.
Executive Director
The Johns Hopkins University
Center for Talented Youth

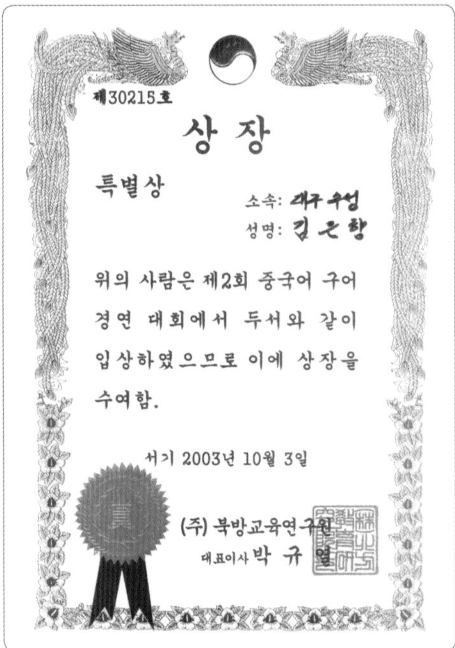
제30215호

상 장

특별상

소속: 대구 수성
성명: 김 은 향

위의 사람은 제2회 중국어 구어 경연 대회에서 두서와 같이 입상하였으므로 이에 상장을 수여함.

서기 2003년 10월 3일

(주) 북방교육연구원
대표이사 박 규 열

제2회 〈중국어구어경연대회 특별상〉(2003.10)

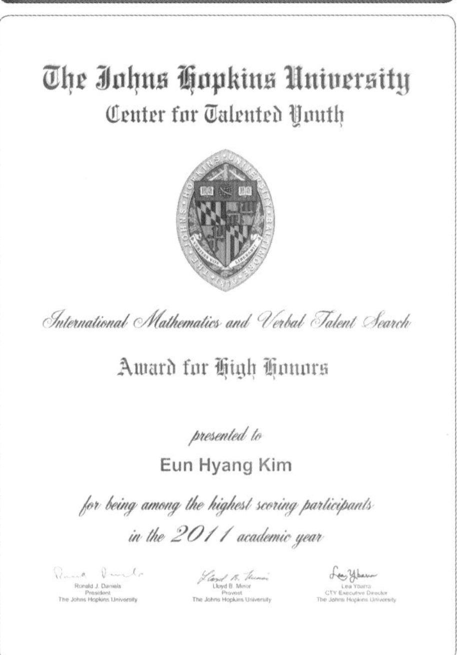
The Johns Hopkins University
Center for Talented Youth

International Mathematics and Verbal Talent Search

Award for High Honors

presented to
Eun Hyang Kim
for being among the highest scoring participants
in the 2011 academic year

Ronald J. Daniels
President
The Johns Hopkins University

Lloyd B. Minor
Provost
The Johns Hopkins University

Lea Ybarra
CTY Executive Director
The Johns Hopkins University

〈존 홉킨스대학교 재능 어린이센터 수료증〉(2011)

Westminster Summer Camp
proudly presents this certificate to
Mary Kim
in recognition of
Most Inquisitive
Group Leader
Director

〈웨스트민스트 여름 캠프 수료증〉

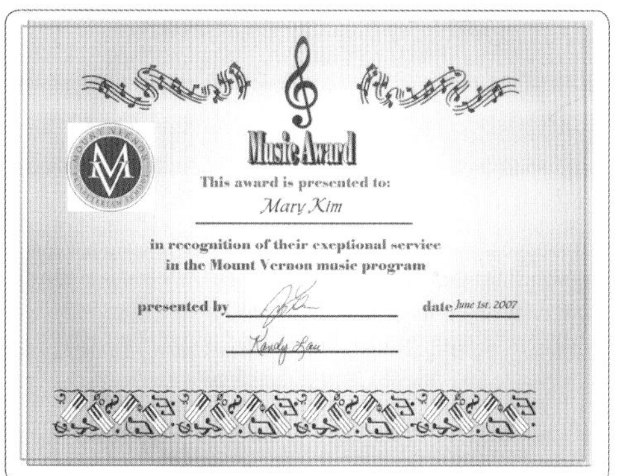

Music Award
This award is presented to:
Mary Kim
in recognition of their exeptional service
in the Mount Vernon music program
presented by
date June 1st, 2007

PREABYTERIAN SCHOOL, 〈마운트버몬 음악상〉(2007.6)

“대학에 진학해서 몇 가지 외국어를 더 배우고 싶습니다. 전세계를 뛰어다니며 사람들을 사랑하고 사람들을 위해 헌신하고 사람들과 함께 봉사하며 살아갈 것입니다.”

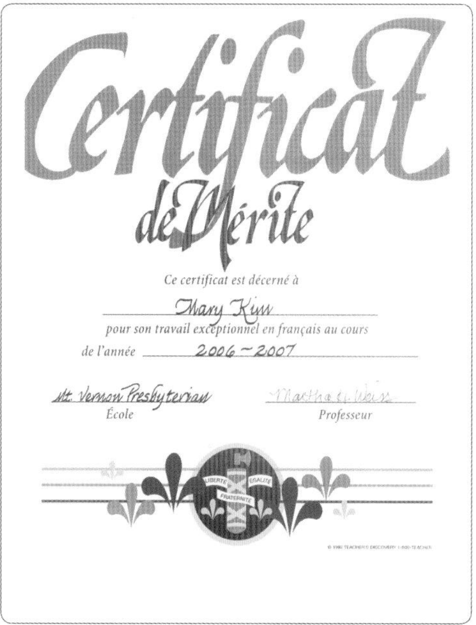

Certificat de Mérite
Ce certificat est décerné à
Mary Kim
pour son travail exceptionnel en français au cours
de l'année 2006~2007
Mt. Vernon Presbyterian
École
Professeur

〈Certificat de Mérite〉(2006~2007)

3 김은향의 프로필

〈일상의 은향이 모습〉

전 감정이 풍부하지만 냉정하기도 해요. 평범한 소녀.

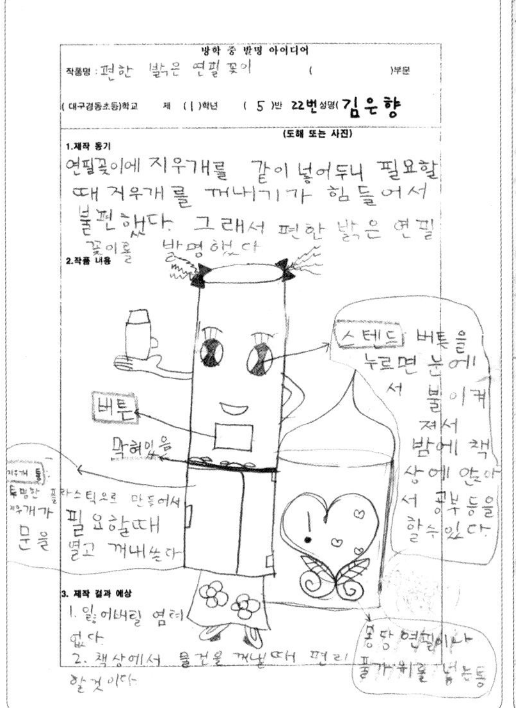

방학 중 발명 아이디어

작품명 : 편한 밝은 연필꽂이 ( )부문

(대구경동초등)학교 제 (1)학년 (5)반 22번 성명(김은향

(도해 또는 사진)

1.제작 동기

연필꽂이에 지우개를 같이 넣어두니 필요할 때 지우개를 꺼내기가 힘들어서 불편했다. 그래서 편한 밝은 연필꽂이를 발명했다

2.작품 내용

스텐드 버튼을 누르면 눈에서 불이켜져서 밤에 책상에 얹어서 공부등을 할수있다.

버튼

막혀있음

투명한 플라스틱으로 만들어서 지우개가 필요할때 문을 열고 꺼내쓴다

3. 제작 결과 예상

1. 잃어버릴 염려 없다

2. 책상에서 물건을 꺼낼때 편리할것이다

볼펜 연필이나 풀가위를 넣는통

Happy day 생활&건강
매일신문 2004년 11월 2일 화요일 13

가정에서 쉽게 할 수 있는 용도별 꽃장식

잠 잘 못들면 아이리스로 '꽃치료'

꽃의 기 받아 피로한 몸·마음 건강하게 회복

한가지 패션 트렌드 신물 미래 지향적 스타일 부상

가정에서 쉽게 할 수 있는 용도별 꽃장식

잠 잘 못들면 아이리스로 '꽃치료'

◇꽃의 기

꽃의 기 받아 피로한 몸·마음 건강하게 회복

언제나 햇살처럼 환하게 웃고 친구들에게 따뜻한 은향^^ 은향이는 언제나 열심히 자기 일을 하고 친구들도 감싸 줄 아는 참 예쁜 어린이란다. 수업 시간에도 자세를 바르게 하여 선생님을 바라보고 글씨도 정성스럽게 쓰는 은향이는 앞으로도 공부도 잘 하고 학교 생활도 잘 하는 그런 사람일거라고 선생님은 믿어. 가끔 선생님에게 애교스러운 편지도 써서 선생님을 기쁘게 해 주는 사랑하는 은향아~ 계속 즐겁고 밝게 그리고 행복하게 지내자♡ - 조성경 선생님이 -

謙讓恭敬

훌륭한 인재로 성장하길

예쁜 우리 은향이가 그린 것 2013년 7월 12일 이날 아침도 5숟갈도 못 먹고 미국에서 엄마 전화 받으며 울었다. 참 예쁘게, 마음은 울음이 많더니

이 상 규

대구국제오페라축제조직위원장에
김신길 아세아텍 ㈜대표이사

사단법인 대구국제오페라축제 조직위원회는 최근 제8차 정기총회를 열고 신임 조직위원장으로 김신길〈사진〉 ㈜아세아텍 대표이사를 선임했다고 28일 밝혔다.

김신길 신임 조직위원장은 ㈜아세아텍 대표이사, 대구경북기계공업협동조합 이사장, 대구상공회의소 부회장, 대신대 재단이사장, 국가조찬기도회 대구지역회장, 법무부 범죄예방 대구·경북지역협의회 운영부위원장으로 재임하면서 교육, 봉사, 경제 등 다방면에서 활발한 활동을 펼치고 있다. 한편 제9회 대구국제오페라축제는 9월 27일부터 10월 29일까지 대구오페라하우스를 중심으로 열린다.

박원수 기자

"은향이의 꿈의 열차, 미래를 향해 달려갑니다."

〈김은향의 프로필〉

Eun Hyang Kim

Educational Background

Letter and Sound Academy (Daegu, Korea)	Kindergarten	2003-2005
Kyung Dong Elementary School (Daegu, Korea)	1st & 2nd grade	2005-2006
Mount Vernon Presbyterian School (Atlanta, Georgia, USA)	3rd & 4th grade	2006-2008
Kyung Dong Elementary School (Daegu, Korea)	5th grade	2008-2009
Ecole des Roches School (Normandie, France)	6th grade	2009-2011
중국인민대학부속고등학교 (Beijing, China)		2013-2014
Daego International School, 12th Grade		2015

Certificates / Honors

- ▸ Won silver medal at Regional Rubby Match (Ecole des Roches School, France) 2010
- ▸ Won 2nd place at School Race (Ecole des Roches School, France) 2009
- ▸ Appointed as a Vise President of 5th grade (Kyung Dong Elementary) 2009
- ▸ Awarded as a 5th grade Academic Role Model (Kyung Dong Elementary) 2009
- ▸ Won 2nd place in Jump Rope Contest (Kyung Dong Elementary) 2008
- ▸ Won 2nd place in Book Illustration Contest (Kyung Dong Elementary) 2008
- ▸ Awarded the Certificate of Head of School (Mount Vernon Elementary, Atlanta, GA) 2007
- ▸ Awarded the Certificate of French Class (Mount Vernon Elementary, Atlanta, GA) 2007
- ▸ Won a Music Award (Mount Vernon Elementary, Atlanta, GA) 2007
- ▸ Awarded a 2nd grade Academic Role Model (Kyung Dong Elementary) 2006
- ▸ Won 1st place in Literary Essay Contest (Kyung Dong Elementary) 2005
- ▸ Won 2nd place in School Swimming Match 50m Freestyle (Kyung Dong Elementary) 2005
- ▸ Won 1st place in Korean Handwriting Contest (Kyung Dong Elementary) 2005
- ▸ Won 3rd place in Children Florist Contest (Kyung Dong Elementary) 2005
- ▸ Awarded the Curiosity Award (Letter and Sound Academy) 2005

- ▸ Won 1st place in Chinese Speaking Contest (Bookbang Education Group) 2004
- ▸ Won 3rd place in Children Florist Contest (National Florist Association) 2004
- ▸ Junior MBA Certificate (Citi Bank) 2004
- ▸ Won 3rd place in Chinese Speaking Contest (Bookbang Education Group) 2003

Extra Curricular Activities

- ▸ Junior Golf Member (Walkerhill Golf Club)
- ▸ Flower Arrangement / Florist
- ▸ UNSS Junior Tennis Player, Ecole des Roches School (Normandie, France)
- ▸ UNSS Sports Team, Ecole des Roches School (Normandie, France)

"몰디브에서, ♡ 저를 사랑해 주는
모든 이에게♥♥♥"

〈김은향의 프로필〉

김은향

학력

Letter and Sound Academy(대구, 한국)	유치원	2003-2005
경동 초등학교 (대구, 한국)	1학년, 2학년	2005-2006
Mount Vernon Presbyterian School (Atlanta, Georgia, USA)	3학년, 4학년	2006-2008
경동 초등학교 (대구, 한국)	5학년	2008-2009
Ecole des Roches School (Normandie, France)	6학년	2009-2011
중국인민대학부속고등학교 (Beijing, China)		2013-2014
대구국제중학교 12학년		2015

수상경력

▸지역학교 럭비 대항 은메달 수상 (Ecole des Roches School, France)	2010
▸교내 달리기 대회 은메달 수상 (Ecole des Roches School, France)	2009
▸학급 어린이회 부회장 임명 (대구경동초등학교)	2009
▸모범학생 표창장 (대구경동초등학교)	2009
▸교내 줄넘기 대회 우수상 수상 (대구경동초등학교)	2008
▸책표지 디자인 은상 수상 (대구경동초등학교)	2008
▸Head of School 표창장 수상 (Mount Vernon Elementary, Atlanta, GA)	2007
▸de Merite 프랑스어 표창장 수상 (Mount Vernon Elementary, Atlanta, GA)	2007
▸Music Award 수상 ((Mount Vernon Elementary, Atlanta, GA)	2007
▸모범학생 표창장 수상 (대구경동초등학교)	2006
▸독서편지쓰기 금상 수상 (대구경동초등학교)	2005
▸교내 수영대회 자유형 50m 부분 은상 수상 (대구경동초등학교)	2005
▸경동문화제 경필쓰기 부문 금상 수상 (대구경동초등학교)	2005
▸전국 꿈나무 꽃 예술 경연대회 동상 수상 (전국 꿈나무 꽃 예술)	2005
▸Curiosity Award (Letter and Sound Academy)	2005

▸중국어 구어 경연 대회 대상 입상 (북방교육연구원) 2004

▸전국 청소년 화훼장식 기능경기대회 특별상 수상 (사단법인 서라벌꽃예술협회) 2004

▸Junior MBA Certificate (Citi Bank) 2004

▸중국어 구어 경연 대회 특별상 입상 (북방교육연구원) 2003

과외활동

▸워커힐 쥬니어 골프 선수

▸화훼장식 활동

▸프랑스 UNSS 교내 테니스 선수 활동, Ecole des Roches School, France)

▸프랑스 UNSS 교내 스포츠 대표팀 활동, Ecole des Roches School, France)

몰디브에서 스쿠버다이빙

김은향

"에필로그는 내가 초등학교를 졸업하고 대구국제중학교에 지원하면서 영문으로 쓴 글이다. 눈 깜짝할 사이 대구국제중학교 12학년을 마치고 이젠 대학 진학을 앞두고 있다. 하고 싶은 공부는 너무너무 많다. 그리고 대학에 진학한 뒤에 외국어도 한두 가지 더 공부하고 싶다. 결론은 세상의 사람들과 더불어 소통하고 아끼고 아픔이 있으면 함께 나누며 살아가고 싶다. 그러기 위해서 대학에 진학하여 더 많은 시간을 미지의 배움에 투자하면서 달려갈 것이다."

나는 유치원 때부터 마라톤 선수의 신발을 신고 지금까지 트랙터 위를 달리고 있다.

나는 13살 된 소녀다. 내가 13년 동안 살아오면서 경험한 것이 참으로 많다. 사람은 살아가고 늙어 가면서 배우고 또는 토론할 것이 많다고 생각한다. 하지만 노력이 진짜로 무엇인가를 적응하면서 나의 마라톤 경주는 유치원 때부터 시작되었다.

내가 일곱 살이 되었을 때 국내 중국어 말하기 대회를 준비하기 시작했다. 그 대회는 대부분 1학년부터 6학년 학생들이 경쟁하는 걸 알면서도 지원했다. 관중들에게 읽을 중국어 책 한 권을 다 외우라고 일주일이 주어졌다. 유치원생에게는 너무나 힘에 겨운 큰 숙제였다. 그때 나의 생각은 두 갈래로 나누어졌다. 나는 이 마라톤을 계속 뛸 것인가? 아님 그만 둘 것인가? 심각하게 생각해 보았다. 하지만 엄마를 실망시키고 싶지 않아 계속 뛰었다. 수천 명의 사람들이 내 곁을 지나갔고 새로운 사람들이 달리기를 시작했다 그렇지만 나는 오직 나의 달리기에만 집중했다. 드디어 난 책 한 권을 다 외웠다. 나는 내가 무슨 꿈을 위해 달리고 있는지 모를 때 부모님은 내 꿈을 이루기 위해 더 달려야 한다고 응원하셨다. 부모님의 응원과 함께 나는 급수대까지 뛰고 또 뛰었다. 이 큰 대회에서 나는 최선을 다해야만 했다. 물을 마셨다. 그 물은 부모님의 사랑과 응원이었다. 나는 온힘을 다해 뛰었다. 나의 에너지가 100% 충전되어 멈추지 않았다. 나는 원래 승부욕이 강하지 않지만, 부모님 그리고 선생님을 위해 승부욕을 발휘했다. "나는 할 수 있다! 나는 할 수 있다!"를 머리 속으로 외쳤다. 나보다 5~6살 더 많은 언니 오빠들이랑 경쟁해서 1등하는 건 거의 불가능이었다. 하지만 나는 이 세상 어디에 이루어야 할 꿈을 위해 달리기를 계속 뛰었다. 멈추지 않았다. 트랙 위에 혹시나 돌이 있어 넘어지지 않도록 집중하며 뛰었다. 드디어 그 날이 왔었다. 수만은 눈들이 나를 지켜보는 가운데 나는 무대 위에서 긴장을 늦췄다. 내가 작게 느껴졌고 내 앞에 있는 마이크는 내 스스로 듣지도 못할 만큼 크게 울려 퍼졌다. 하지만 나는 뛰지 않고 걸었다. 왜냐하면 서두르다가 돌에 걸려 넘어질까 봐 나는 조심히 이야기를 들려주었다. 이야기가 다 끝나자 관객들의 박수가 비처럼 쏟아졌다. 다른 더 큰 꿈을 위해 트랙터 위를 건너면서 나는 내 자신이 정말 자랑스러웠다.

시간이 지나면서 나는 행복하게 트랙터 위를 조깅하고 있었다. 하지만 힘이 들었다. 그리고 초등학교 1학년 때 난 부모님이 하라는 대로 1학년 2학년 때 All A 성적표를 받았다. 나는 내가 미국으로 유학 가는지 몰랐다. 어느 날 갑자기 짐을 싸고 미국에 있는 보딩 스쿨에 가야 했다. 그때 나는 "부모님들이 나에게 싫증이 났구나"라고 생각했다. 미국에 도착했을 때 한국과는 다른 세상이었다. 하지만 내가 처음 미국에 도착했을 때보다는 놀라지 않았다. 나는 그 전에 이미 여름 방학이 되면 올란도 플로리다, 시카고, 오하이오를 여행을 다녀 온 경험이 있었다. 예상했던 대로 내가 지내는 보호자 집에는 아이들이 없었다. 마치 온세상이 나를 미워하는 것 같았다. 그때 나는 레이스에서 멈춰버리고 싶었다. 포기하고 싶은 마음에 다른 경쟁자들을 지나가게 했다. 하지만 친구들을 사귀고 난 뒤 나는 말했다. "별로 나쁘지 않군." 쓰러진 곳에서 다시 일어나 다시 뛰었다. 그 누구보다도 행복했다. 난 친구가 이렇게 큰 힘이 될 수 있는지 몰랐다. 때로는 넘어지고 슬픈 날이 있고 때로는 부모님이 보고 싶어 또 포기하고 싶었다. 하지만 그런 날들이 오면 옛 추억을 되새기곤 한다. 나는 내 자신에게 "너무 쉽게 포기해서 미안해, 은향아. 포기하기 전에 어떤 일들이 생길지 생각했어야 했는데. 힘내. 넌 할 수 있어!"라고 응원한다. 비록 내 입으로 내 자신에게 한 응원이지만 이 세상에 응원은 누가 하든 똑같은 응원이란 걸 깨달았다. 2년이 지나고 나의 꿈에 익숙해져 나는 내 꿈에 더 가까워졌다. 떨리지만 행복했다. 내가 또 다른 작은 꿈을 이뤘다는 게. 한국에는 이러한 속담

이 있다. "티끌모아 태산.' 내 생각에는 돈뿐만 아니라 노력에 관한 것일 수도 있다. 작은 꿈을 하나하나 이루다 보니 큰 꿈을 이루는 것이 더 가능해질 것이다. 그때부터 나는 노력하지 않고 포기하지 않겠다고 다짐했다.

얼마나 걸릴지 상관 안 하고 나는 뛰고 또 뛰었다. 2년이 지난 뒤 나는 프랑스에 있는 보딩스쿨을 다녔다. 슬픔에 가득 차 있는 나를 다행이 나의 새로운 친구들이 구해줬다. 친구들이 항상 내 옆에 있었기에 나는 계속 일어설 수 있었다. 다름 사람들이 넘어졌을 때 나는 우정 또는 돈으로 도움을 줬다. 나는 이 마라톤이 나의 작은 그림인 줄 생각했는데 알고 보니 이 레이스에는 많은 것이 있었다. 이 레이스를 통해 나는 노력 없이는 아무 것도 이뤄낼 수 없고, 꿈을 이루려면 실패는 따라오는 것이고, 그리고 이 세상에는 공짜가 없다는 것을 배웠다. 내가 무엇인가를 하고 싶으면 꼭 하나 정도는 걸림돌이 있을 것이다. 그러나 그 걸림돌을 뛰어넘어, 결승선을 향해 달리는, 나는 환호를 멀리서 들어본 적이 있다. 나도 그 환호와 열광을 느껴 보고 싶다. 이제 결승선이 1킬로미터 정도밖에 안 남았다. 환호를 받을 생각을 하니 너무 기쁘다. 나는 내가 대구국제중학교에 입학하는 꿈에 가깝다고 생각한다. 하지만 주변 사람들은 어렵다고 말한다. 내가 대구국제중학교에 입학하는 결승전에 간다면 모두에게 축하받고 싶다. 나는 활발하고 이룰 꿈이 있고, 그 꿈을 언젠간 날아서 이뤄낼 13살 아이다. 나는 절대로 포기하지 않는다는 말을 다시는 하지 않을 것이다. 나는 반드시 내 꿈을 이뤄내 결승전에서 환호를 받고 싶다. 저를 대구국제중학교에 고려해 주셔서 감사합니다.

2015. 11. 30

Eun-Hyang, Kim

I have put myself in the shoes of a marathon runner since kindergarten and I am still running on the track.

I am a 13 year old girl and I have experience a lot in these 13 years. I believe that in our lives, as we get older, there are many things to worry about and to discuss. However, the marathon race really started in kindergarten, when I started to get the hang of what working really was.

When I turned 7 years old I started preparing for the national Chinese speaking contest. I knew that I couldn't do it because it was normally for 1st graders to 6th graders, but I signed up. I had 1 week to memorize a book in Chinese to tell it to the audience. It was a lot of work for a kindergartener. That's when my thoughts split in half. I wondered whether I should keep on running this marathon or give up the race. However, I didn't want to disappoint my mom so I kept on running. Thousands of people passed by me, and new people were starting the race, but I concentrated only on the race. Finally, I've memorized the book. My parents encouraged me to run more and more as they wanted me to achieve my goal, even if I didn't know what kind of goal it was yet. With the encouragement of my parents, I started to run and run until I reached the water station. I had to do the best I could do for the big contest. I drank some water, which was the encouragement and the love of my parents. I ran with all my might. I didn't stop because now the power was 100% charged. I wasn't such a competitive person, but just for my parents and my teacher I had to be for the first time. 'I can do it! I can do it!' I kept on repeating the sentence over and over in my head. It was sort of impossible to get a first prize when all the other people are 5 or 6 years older than you. However, I kept on running just for the goal somewhere out there in the world waiting for me to achieve. I didn't stop running. I concentrated on the track to see if there aren't any rocks that I would trip over. It was the big day. I had to suddenly stop in the middle of the track to be calmed. I calmed myself down as I stepped my feet upon the stage with thousands of eyes wanting me to do something talented up here. I felt small and the microphone felt huge, too big for me to grab it. However, I started walking not running because I was worried that I would exaggerate and trip over a rock. I carefully announced the story. When I was done announcing the story, the applauses came out like pouring rain. I was really proud of myself as I skipped on the track to achieve the next goal on my way to the big goal.

Time had passed, I was jogging happily on the track but I was getting tired. Then I was in first grade, I did what my parents told me to do and I got A's in my report card for 1st and 2nd grade. I didn't know if I was going to go to a boarding school in America. One day I had to pack my things up and go to a boarding school. That's when I thought, 'My parents are tired of me!' When I went to America it was just a whole different world compared to Korea. However, I wasn't as surprised as the first time I was there. I already had an experience of a summer vacation in Orlando. Florida, Chicago and Ohio. I stayed at my guardians' house but, as I expected, there were no children. I felt like the whole world was against me and that's when I stopped running in the race. I let my competitors in the marathon race pass by, as I wanted to give it all up. However, I found some friends and I said, "Hey, this isn't so bad after all". I lifted my body up from the corner where I stopped and I started running as usual. I felt happier than anyone else. I didn't know that friends could be so helpful in these times. Sometimes I would fall down and feel sad and sometimes I would give up once again because I miss my parents so much. However, I thought of other times, When I was in that mood of failure and sadness. I cheered myself up saying, "I'm sorry, Eun Hyang, that I gave up easily. I should think about what will happen after before doing it. Cheer up, you can do this!" I learned that even though these sentences came out of my own mouth, I know that all encouragements are all the same encouragements no matter who says it in this world. 2 years passed and I was getting closer to the goal as I got the hang of what the goal will be. I was nervous but happy that I accomplished another small goal . In Korea, there is a Korean saying called ' Many drops make a shower', which I do not think represents only money but goals as well. As I achieved more and more goals it became more possible to achieve my big goal. That's when I decided from now on I will not give up easily on something without giving all my effort to it.

I ran and ran no matter how long it would take. 2 years have passed and I went to a boarding school in France. My mind, once filled with sadness, was fortunately saved by my new friends. My friends were always there for me. So I stood up again and kept on running. I have seen some people falling down, so I helped them out if I could by giving them some money or my friendship. I thought that this marathon race was just an image of me but there were a lot of things going on in the race. I learned through these experience, nothing is impossible once you try it, and the fact is that we always have to go through a certain time period of suffering to reach the actual goal, and that nothing is free in this world. If I want to do a certain kind of work, I always have to work at least one thing out. I have heard some applause for the people who had jumped over the finish line and I strive for that too. I am barely 1 kilometer away from the finish line, and I can't wait until everyone will clap for me. I feel like I am so close to be achieving my goal, although some people say that it is impossible to get in to the Daegu International School. However, getting into Daegu International School is my goal, and the finish line is close. I wish to cross the finish line to be able to be appreciated by everyone, and to achieve my personal goal. I am a 13 year old with a bright dream and a goal to achieve, and I plan to someday fly away and achieve the future of my dreams. I will never say again that I give up. I hope to reach the finish line – to achieve my goal – and to get applause by everyone. Thank you for considering me for the Daegu International School.

2015. 11. 30